THE BLACK JACKALS

By the same author

Four Days in June

Man of Honour
Rules of War
Brothers in Arms

Alamein

IAIN GALE

The Black Jackals

HarperCollins*Publishers*

HarperCollins*Publishers*
77–85 Fulham Palace Road,
Hammersmith, London W6 8JB

www.harpercollins.co.uk

Published by HarperCollins*Publishers* 2011
1

A catalogue record for this book
is available from the British Library

ISBN: 978 0 00 727864 0

This novel is entirely a work of fiction.
The incidents and some of the character's portrayed in it,
while based on real historical events and figures, are the work of the
author's imagination.

Map © John Gilkes

Set in Sabon by
Palimpsest Book Production Limited, Falkirk, Stirlingshire

Printed and bound in Great Britain by
Clays Ltd, St Ives plc

Mixed Sources
Product group from well-managed
forests and other controlled sources
www.fsc.org Cert no. SW-COC-001806
© 1996 Forest Stewardship Council
FSC

For Susie

GREAT BRITAIN

North Sea

NETHERLANDS

Dover

BELGIUM

Schelde

Dyle

Brussels

Wavre

Waterloo

English Channel

Essars

Aubigny • Arras

Crecy

Abbeville

Amiens *Somme*

St Valery-en-Caux • Arques-la-Bataille

Veules les-Roses

Le Havre

Rouen

FRANCE

Seine

Paris

N
W E
S

0   10   20   30   40   50 Miles
0   20   40   60   80 Kms

1

This had not been what was meant to happen. Not at all. But then he supposed that was what war was all about – the unexpected and the absurd always turning up just when you'd planned for something completely different.

Second Lieutenant Peter Lamb stared at the bridge and swore under his breath. This was not going according to plan. Certainly, the sappers had come and gone as directed. They had left their packages of high explosive, taped and tied to the bridge, out of sight of anyone who might attempt to cross it, and they had carefully concealed the wire in the long grass that grew up the riverbank, snaking it back as covertly as possible to Lamb's command trench, where it was connected to a simple plunger. Lamb gazed at the box and its T-shaped handle. When the time came, when the Germans began to show themselves, he would give the command and the little bridge which had presumably stood here at Gastuche for the last century would vanish.

That at least was the plan. But this was no training exercise. This was war, and the Germans had not come along the road obligingly in column like some friendly adversary to be mown down by his carefully prepared ambush and then blown to kingdom come with the bridge. In fact they had not come at all. Instead Lamb had been alarmed to see, some hours ago now, a procession of weary Belgian civilians advancing upon the bridge. He had told the men to hold their fire, but of course it had hardly been necessary. They were not about to open fire upon a herd of old men, women and children. At first he had watched them with bemusement as they had trickled across the bridge towards safety. But then the thought came to him. If this exodus did not stop then eventually the Germans would be caught up in it, and what would he do then? He did not suppose for one minute that his men would fire on civilians, but the enemy must not be allowed to take the bridge.

It was obvious to him that there was no choice. His orders were clear. Nothing for it now but to blow the bridge, and he wondered when he gave that command how many of them would have to die.

Peering over the brow of the shallow grassy slope behind which he and his men were sheltering, Lamb looked down towards the river and its little stone bridge and his eyes fixed on the desolate column of humanity moving slowly and sadly along the road towards them – an endless procession of men, women and children, driving, pushing and pulling carts and wagons of all shapes and sizes, laden with what few belongings they had managed to gather together before the Germans came.

The River Dyle was a good enough obstacle against tanks, and to allow the bridge to fall into enemy hands was out of the question. But it was also highly questionable that they would be able to hold it forever. The German advance through Belgium had been like a whirlwind and he wondered how many of the British, Belgian and French generals really believed that their armies and the tiny British Expeditionary Force would be able to hold back the Panzers. But they might be able to slow them down sufficiently for the French to be able to regroup and mount a counter-attack.

He had sent a runner back to Battalion at the first sight of the refugees but had received no other instruction than that it was had on good authority that anyone carrying a red blanket might be a fifth columnist. As far as Lamb could see, hundreds of these refugees had red blankets. He could not possibly have taken them all prisoner and so he had decided to ignore the instruction. It galled him that he was becoming used to ignoring orders. Only some of them, of course. This was typical of the sort of ridiculous rumours that had been circulating since they had arrived in France. He was surprised, though, at how readily people accepted them, officers and men alike, and it made him wonder whether he might have been wrong in placing so much faith in the army, and that new and unwelcome doubt filled him with dread. For it was not hard to see that their enemy had no such lack of confidence.

There was distant booming, somewhere quite far off, over to the east. Lamb raised his head again and, looking across the peaceful landscape in which a pale herd of cattle were grazing beside the arc of a river, scoured the horizon. But he could see nothing. They were still far away, then. But still close enough at that, he thought. And somewhere out there someone was taking a pounding, and ten to one it wasn't the Boche. There was a rustling noise behind him and Lamb turned to see his platoon sergeant, Jim Bennett, crouching above the trench.

'Beggin' yer pardon, Mr Lamb, sir. But the lads were wondering if they could stand down for a few minutes and get a brew on. And one for you too, sir?'

Lamb nodded. 'Yes, Sarnt. That should be fine.'

3

The booming noise came again.

'Did you hear that? Sounds as if the Belgians are getting it badly. Still holding them, though.'

'Reckon they'll manage it much longer, sir?'

Lamb smiled. He knew from the adjutant that the entire 3rd Division had been pulled back from the forward Belgian lines after some trivial dispute between their general and the Belgian commander who reckoned his men better trained than the British army. It was madness. But the Belgians would rather fight on their own than submit to foreign command. So now it was only a matter of time.

'Not really, Sarnt. Do you?'

Bennett grinned. 'They're brave enough, sir. Don't get me wrong. I'm not saying they're not. But you saw them come past here yesterday, sir. Couldn't get away fast enough. I give you that what's left up there must be better than that shower, but if you want my opinion, Mr Lamb, them Belgians couldn't hold back a platoon of Girl Guides, let alone Jerry.'

Lamb nodded. 'My thoughts too, Sarnt. We'd best stay alert. You'd better get that tea on or they'll all want some.'

As if to qualify his words, Lamb retrieved his tin helmet from where it had been lying on the parapet and placed it on his head, pushing the strap tight beneath his chin. Bennett nodded and ran crouching back to his trench.

Jim Bennett was the linchpin of Lamb's platoon. Had been since the start. While Lamb knew that the men would not question his word, he also knew that they would take a command more readily from Bennett, knowing that he was one of them. Lamb was an officer and as such came from another world. Another country. It was what the men expected but it made the sergeant's role absolutely vital.

In fact, Lamb mused, he was not perhaps as much of a 'gentleman' as his men might suspect. For the past hour he had been trying to compose a letter to his ex-wife, Julia. With little success. How did you write to someone to tell them that while you expected to be killed at any moment you had never stopped loving them, despite being unfaithful? He had embarked on the affair in the year that Hitler had come to power. His life with Kate was nothing like his marriage, where society ball had succeeded house party as his social life had jostled for position with his promising career as a London lawyer. He had met Julia at university, and they had married in haste. But Kate he had known since boyhood, and a chance encounter had led to a torrid affair which had put an end to his marriage. It was not sordid. Not in the way that Julia had made out in court. Of course he had not meant to betray his wife, but some uncontrollable urge had taken hold of him. Lamb prided himself on his ability to organise and control his feelings just as he did his men, and this uncharacteristic slip troubled him. He understood now that it must have been love. But now – now he just wanted to get home. To get back to some sort of normality and to the woman he wished he had never betrayed. He wondered when it would be over, whether they had any chance now of driving the Germans back across the Belgian border. The latest reports had not been good.

They had crossed from France two days ago, an expeditionary force of almost 250,000 British troops plus all their cumbersome logistical support, sent to help the French as they had in 1914 when Lamb's father had gone with them as a keen-eyed volunteer in the regiment to which he himself now belonged, the Royal North Kents. Number 1 platoon, B Company. Most of the army had been in France since last October. The 'phoney war', they had started to call it, and in truth it hadn't been bad.

The North Kents had remained in England, in camp close to Tonbridge, training to embark. He'd managed to get out of the camp on a few occasions, to take one or two of those fellow officers he counted as real friends – Freddie Long, Jimmy Bourne – to the haunts of his youth, good English pubs with friendly landlords and patrons more than ready to stand them a few drinks. That had been Lamb's phoney war. A few of the men had gone 'AWOL' and there had been the usual problems of the new men not knowing the ropes, but by the time they had crossed the channel in April he reckoned that Number 1 platoon was pretty sound. Which, although he wouldn't have admitted as much, made it something of an exception in the regiment. And that worried him.

They'd been brigaded with the Berkshires and the Durham Light Infantry in 2 Division, which in Lamb's mind affirmed the quality of his regiment. And now here they all were, the platoon, the regiment, the division and the entire BEF, strung out twenty miles along the river Dyle, in hastily dug trenches most of them, like Lamb's, on the steep slopes that ran down to the river. Waiting for the enemy. Lamb sensed their frustration.

The men had been filled with enthusiasm for their task. The 'phoney war' was finally over, the real war was on. The Belgian people had welcomed them with kisses and cheers, showers of flowers and cigarettes and chocolate. Lamb had believed, as they all had, that the Belgians might hold the line along the Albert canal. But that illusion had been shattered on their second day at what they now knew to be 'the front', when the sound of gunfire had cut through the early sunshine of Whitsunday morning, 14 May. His fears had been confirmed by the sight of hundreds of Belgian troops streaming back along the road across the river. A few of the lads had grinned at them as they had stumbled blindly past, but the more seasoned of them, Lamb included, had turned their heads away, chilled at the sight and not wanting to be touched by the Jonah of a retreating army.

Not long afterwards a runner had come up from Battalion to deliver the order he already had that they should do nothing but hold their ground and prevent the enemy from taking the bridge. But Corporal Briggs had quizzed him and found out that the word was that in the north the French too were retreating towards Antwerp, and Holland was lost. That had only been yesterday.

Lamb scanned the horizon again now for any sign of the enemy and strained his ears for the sound of engines that might have signalled the approach of trucks or tanks. Nothing. He glanced to the left and saw the men of his platoon sitting, hunched like him in their slit trenches, and wondered what thoughts were passing through their minds. Whether there was anything they too had left undone, left unsaid. It was not like him to leave loose ends. But then with Lamb his personal and professional lives had always been very different. He pressed down again with the pencil on a fresh sheet of his pocket book, and the thing snapped in two. Lamb swore. Like everything they had been given to take to this war, even the bloody pencils were third rate.

Lamb reached deep down into the breast pocket of his battledress tunic and fished out the spare he always carried. He was a natural soldier – organised, meticulous and particularly good at preparation. How then, he wondered, was it that he had allowed his private life to become such a damned mess? After the divorce he had fallen out of love with the law and returned to his first obsession. For the past seven years he had been the manager of a garage in Sevenoaks High Street. Motorbikes were his speciality, but he could turn his hand to anything mechanical. They said he had a magic touch. Wednesday evenings, though, he had devoted to the Territorials. The army suited him, even as a part-time soldier.

He needed to belong. At twenty-five he had been older than most of the recruits in his Territorial regiment, but when war had come at last the regular army had been only too glad to have him as an officer. Some of his fellow officers had been similarly recruited from the Territorial units although the core were professional soldiers. Two were fresh out of Sandhurst, straight from public school, and seemed to regard Lamb as they might a kindly uncle. He of course had merely converted from Territorial to regular officer and so had missed out on that venerable institution and its notorious training regime.

He loved the regiment and all that it stood for. The officers' mess at Tunbridge Wells was a darkly panelled haven of the old world, in which men who outside the army would never have enjoyed the luxury of servants took readily to a life where the stewards glided noiselessly between them bearing silver trays of whisky and champagne. The regimental history, portrayed so vividly in paintings around the walls of the mess, was as illustrious as any in the British army, and the colours that hung in the chapel bore honours including those of Tangier, Blenheim, Talavera, Waterloo, Sevastapol, South Africa, Ypres, the Somme and Arras. Officially the Royal North Kents, which had been raised during the Civil War, were known by a number of names, derived from their history: the 100th Foot; the Centurions; Boadicea's Bodyguard; the Tangier Tigers. One of his favourites was the Bordello Boys, which was derived from a famous episode at the Battle of Oudenarde in 1708 when the regiment had occupied a strategically placed brothel. But when he thought of the regiment it was always of the nickname derived in part from the animal on its cap badge, in part from the jet-black, cross-braided dress uniform worn by officers on mess nights. The North Kents would always be the 'Black Jackals' to him. Such things were important to Lamb. Heritage gave the men a sense of pride, a reason to fight and a reason to obey without question.

But he wondered what real use tradition might be against the enemy they now faced, an enemy expert in a new sort of warfare led by commanders who nursed bitter resentment over their nation's last humiliating defeat thirty years ago. The British army might be the best in the world in its heart and soul, but for years it had been starved of resources at the expense of the RAF and the Navy. That would be the way to win any future war, the experts had said. Well, he wondered where those 'experts' were now. Not sitting here, that was for sure. It occurred to him that his little band of thirty men, No 1 platoon, were equipped in almost exactly the same way that his father's platoon would have been when they had sat in almost exactly the same place twenty-five years ago. What had they learned? he wondered. Precious little. The Germans had cut a swathe through Europe with their Blitzkrieg tactics, and Lamb sensed that it was not just the Belgian soldiers who might be outmatched. His men would stand and fight and die if they were ordered to. But without the right weapons and equipment, he knew they would be quite powerless.

There was another succession of heavy thumps in the distance. They were more distinct now, and more clearly explosions. He turned and yelled towards the trench to his rear: 'Sarnt Bennett, to me. And where's that tea?'

The tall sergeant came doubling over carrying a tin mug of tea which slopped out over the sides onto the ground, 'Sorry, sir. Here you are. Lovely cup of char. They're getting closer.'

'Yes. And faster than I'd expected. Any word from Battalion?'

'Nothing from the Colonel, sir, but Major Cooke sent a runner with this.' He handed Lamb a note:

Enemy observed to be advancing steadily from the east, direction of Louvain. Hold and engage. Delay as long as you can, then blow bridge to your front and withdraw.

Lamb folded it and tucked it into his pocket. 'Well, that's us told, Sarnt.'

'Sir?'

'We're to sit here and give the Jerries a bloody nose before blowing that bridge down there and legging it.'

'Makes you think, sir, don't it? I mean, we come over here, the British army, best army in the world. And what happens? Bloody Belgians run away. The Frenchies can't make their minds up about where to fight. And we're left to do the donkey work. I don't think our top brass really knew what they were up against.'

Lamb smiled. 'Yes, Sarnt, I wonder whether they did. But it's not for us to question them. And now it's up to you and me and the rest of the lads to make the best we can of this mess. I want two-man fire teams all along that forward slope, well dug in before the Jerries get here. We're bound to be outnumbered and outgunned, so we've got to make the best use we can of what we have got, and that's surprise. Where's the anti-tank rifle?'

'Thompson's got it, sir. Over there in the trees.'

'Get Thompson to bring it up here. We don't know what's going to come at us down that road. But when it does, whatever it is, I want every shot to count. There's a platoon of sappers due here any minute to wire the bridge, but they're going to leave us the detonator. But before we blow it I'm going to take out as many Jerries as possible. We'll wait for them to get across the bridge and then open up, and then as their reinforcements come across we blow it. Got it?'

Bennett smiled. 'Got it, sir.'

The sergeant liked Lamb. He was a popular officer with the lads. Not perhaps what you'd call the classic 'officer and gentleman' like some of them were – toffs, if you like – but a damn sight better than those that had just come straight from school or university. Lamb was a proper officer, he reckoned. He cared for the men and you wouldn't get him ordering them to do something that he couldn't have done himself. But more than that, Lamb was an officer, and they respected him for that. He was from a different world and he had a natural authority. Some said that he had been married before, into the gentry or even grander. That was what some said. But that didn't matter to Bennett neither. What mattered was that Lamb spoke to him and to the other men as if they really mattered. That's what set their officer apart. Bennett came back to the present, then saluted and hobbled back towards where they'd left Private Thompson and his anti-tank rifle.

Still looking at the refugees swarming across the bridge, Lamb's eye began to fall naturally on individuals. He looked at a woman in a floral dress yelling at her son to come back from the edge of the road, another struggling to keep a curly-haired infant daughter perched on a cart amidst a pile of dark wooden furniture; a father carried his sleeping baby like a rag doll, his face a picture of worry. He tried to look away. He preferred to see these not as real people, but as a column, like any other column that might be advancing towards him. Not an enemy, of course, merely an obstacle to be negotiated. He began to calculate their numbers. One thousand, two? More? There seemed to be no end and no beginning. But all the time he kept seeing their little stories unfold. A woman seemed to have lost something, perhaps a pet. An old man could walk no more and was being helped to sit at the side of the road against the wall of the bridge by a pretty girl. And then he heard it.

The unmistakable rumble of approaching vehicles shook the road and sent the civilians into a panic. They quickened their pace. The old man got to his feet and started to walk. Belongings, which a moment ago had seemed so precious, tumbled from the carts and were forgotten in the new urgency to save themselves. Staring hard through his binoculars into the trees in the distance, Lamb began to make out the trucks and men on horses too, with slung rifles. And alongside them now he could see men on foot: men in grey, carrying their weapons at the trail.

He was sweating now, more than he would have normally done even on this hot summer's day. The grey soldiers were mingling with the civilians. He could see their helmets clearly as they moved determinedly forward, could see them pushing through the refugees, using their rifle butts and shouting commands as they hurried along the dusty road, heaving the carts and belongings into the roadside ditches to make a way for the trucks. Clearing a way towards the bridge, towards his position, advancing into battle. There was no time left. No choice. No option. Lamb heard his company commander's words, 'Whatever happens, Peter, blow that bloody bridge. It must not fall into enemy hands. I don't care who's on it. Mr Chamberlain himself. Just blow it.'

2

The lorries were driving forward, almost on the bridge, with the infantry running close alongside them. Lamb could see an open-topped staff car, and in the back seat two officers. They were laughing as they drove onto the bridge, and were almost at the centre now. Three lorries followed close behind, forcing the shuffling pedestrians aside. Then one of the men raised his hand and the car and the trucks stopped, although the refugees continued past them. The officer opened the door, got out and walked across to the parapet of the old bridge. He leaned against it and scanned the river and the opposite bank, forcing Lamb and his men to cower in their slit trenches, and then his eye alighted on something, something at the edge of the bridge. He gazed at it for an instant and then turned to the car and shouted something before starting to run back the way they had come.

Lamb muttered to the corporal at his side, 'Blast, he's twigged it.' Then, stifling his conscience, he swallowed dryly and gave a quick nod to the corporal. The man, a recent addition to the ranks, a volunteer named Valentine, looked at him and raised an eyebrow. Lamb nodded again. 'For Christ's sake man, let them have it!'.

Valentine shrugged and pushed down hard on the handle, and almost simultaneously it seemed the bridge went up with a deafening explosion, sending fragments of brick and stone flying high in the air along with what remained of the officers and their driver, parts of two of the trucks and their occupants, and the civilians who had been pushing past them towards salvation.

Lamb shielded his eyes and yelled down the line to the platoon, 'Take cover. Get down, all of you. Watch your heads.'

As he spoke small pieces of masonry, wood and nameless debris began to fall among them, clattering off their tin hats. Luckily the larger pieces were confined to the vicinity of the bridge, and most fell into the river. As the smoke began to clear Lamb peered down the grassy bank to survey their handiwork.

He could see the span of the bridge, and there in the middle of it a large hole, as if some giant had taken a bite through the side of the wall. Beyond it lay a yawning void. Good, he thought. That should hold them for a while at least. But then as the smoke dispersed he saw around the bridge, across the road and in the river below, dozens of bodies and parts of bodies and burnt and shattered fragments of what had been possessions. Lamb stared as his heart filled with guilt and pity, and he tried again not to look at people, merely objects. But there was the woman in the floral dress, and over there the man and his daughter. What was left of them. He knew that he had timed it as well as he could, had allowed two German lorries onto the bridge before blowing it. Now he noticed among the civilian corpses a number in field grey, and he felt the better for it. But the feeling did not last for long, for amid the patter of the falling fragments, another sound arose − a low moaning, punctuated with terrible screams. He shook his head, and Valentine looked at him with pitying eyes.

Lamb spoke. 'Well done, Corporal. That'll slow up the Boche.'

The man looked at him and Lamb noticed, not for the first time, the irritating smirk that seemed to lie permanently around his thin lips and his curiously educated accent. 'Please don't thank me, sir. Not for doing that.'

'I had no choice, man. You saw. The enemy . . .'

'I saw, sir. And I promise that I shan't tell anyone what it was that you just did. Why should I want to do that, sir? They might get the wrong end of the stick.'

Lamb stared at him and was just about to challenge his remark when a voice from his rear shattered the opportunity.

'Sir, look. Over there. In the trees.'

Lamb raised his field glasses and looked through them across the river towards a spinney of poplars by the edge of the road. At first he thought the shapes he could see were more refugees, but then he saw the flash of steel and knew at once that they were the enemy.

'All right, here they come. No one fire until I give the command. Parry, set up the mortar over there. Zero in on the centre of the bridge. They might try and use the wreckage to get across.'

He had hardly spoken when there was a burst of machine-gun fire from the opposite bank. 'Take cover.'

Lamb pulled his revolver from the canvas holster on the left side of his webbing belt and yelled, 'Sarnt Bennett, Corporal Briggs. Get that Bren working. Thompson, you and Massey get on the anti-tank rifle. Save it till you see any tanks. The rest of you save your ammunition until you see a good target, then let them have it.'

He felt anger now. Anger at what he had just been compelled to do, an act that sickened him and went so much against everything that he believed in. Killing helpless civilians. And here now was the chance to assuage

15

that anger, against the men who had caused it. He heard the Bren rattle into action and saw the flash from the muzzles of the German rifles as the enemy responded. There were shouts from across the river.

Lamb yelled at the section closest to him, 'Perkins, Dawlish, all of you, keep your heads down and your guns trained on the road. See the first flash of field grey that comes into range and you open fire. Smart, get on the blower back to Company HQ. Tell them we have contact. Enemy tanks, estimate zero six, infantry four zero plus.'

As his batman spoke into the handset of the .38 radio, the enemy machine gun crackled again and turned over a few sods of earth on the lower part of the riverbank. Smart turned to him. 'Can't raise them, sir. Line's dead. Not a thing.'

'Keep trying.'

Lamb opened the chamber of his revolver, checked that it was full and snapped it shut again. His fellow officers agreed: the Enfield pistol was a sad excuse for a sidearm. They said the enemy had automatics that never jammed and fired like a dream. He couldn't wait to get his hands on one. But that of course would mean either taking one off a dead German or winning one himself in hand-to-hand fighting. Perhaps, he thought, in the next few minutes he would have a chance to do both. But his keenness quickly turned to disappointment.

Bennett was at his side. 'Pull back, sir. CO's orders. We're to pull out.'

Lamb shook his head. 'What?'

'We're pulling out, sir. From the CO.'

Lamb shook his head again and laughed. 'No, Sarnt Bennett. This is no time for one of your pranks. There's hundreds of Jerries over there and it's our business to deal with them and see they don't get across this damned river.'

'Sorry, sir. It came direct from Battalion, it did. Our orders are to withdraw. Clear as day, sir.'

Lamb frowned. This was no joke. 'You must have got it wrong. We can't be pulling out, Bennett. We've just blown the bloody bridge and we've got the enemy pinned down. And what about those poor bloody civilians down there dead in the river? I'm telling you, man, the Jerries won't get across here for hours, and then we'll be waiting for them. You can see that. What we need is reinforcements.' He turned to his batman. The poor man was still trying to contact company HQ. 'Anything?'

Smart shook his head.

'Right. Is that runner still here, Sarnt?

'Sir.'

'Then get him to take this message back to Company HQ: "Need reinforcements soonest. Your order not understood. Please send help. Enemy now in range preparing to engage."'

The sergeant pursed his lips and nodded. 'I'm sorry, Mister Lamb, sir. That runner is straight from the CO. It was quite clear, sir. Pull everyone out, he said. Everyone, sir. And that means us. I'm sorry.'

Lamb stared at him. This was madness. First they tell him to stand his ground and to blow a bridge, killing dozens of innocent people, and then they tell him to abandon the position.

Lamb shook his head. 'I'm sorry too, Sarnt.' He paused. 'I'm sorry because I just can't do that. Not until we've killed a few more of them, at least. Then perhaps we'll come along. Eh? Why don't you tell the Major that we're . . . I know. Just tell a runner to tell him we're caught up in a firefight and trying to disengage. Tell him that we'll be with him presently. Just as soon as we can retire without the risk of taking any further casualties.' He was damned if he was going to pull back now.

The sergeant looked at him and smiled. He had somehow sensed that Lamb wasn't going to take an order like that without some sort of protest. 'Very good, sir. If that's your orders, that's your orders.'

'That is an order, Sarnt Bennett. Send one of the men back to the CO. Thank you.'

The sergeant turned and was about to go when he looked back. 'There was one other thing, sir. Runner said that he'd heard on the wireless at Battalion HQ that Mr Chamberlain's been given the heave-ho. Winston Churchill's the new PM. Fat lot of good that'll do us though, sir, eh?'

'Thank you, Sarnt.'

Lamb smiled and, as his sergeant turned and trotted off at a running crouch to send word to Battalion HQ that they would not be obeying the new orders, he turned back to his front. It was strangely quiet again now, save for the occasional groan from one of the wounded. So Chamberlain, the great appeaser, had finally gone and Churchill was in. He wondered what his father would have made of that. He had never had a good word to say for Churchill after the Dardanelles. Lamb frowned. The man was damned old, too. Didn't the country need new blood now? A young man at the helm? The news did nothing to raise his downcast spirits. He peered across the river and began to make out small grey-clad figures darting through the trees. They were moving up in some strength. Within minutes he knew they would be dug in. Focusing his field glasses, he froze as he noticed that at the edge of the road across the bridge, where the charge had blown a hole, a party of men were climbing down into a section that remained above the river bed, passing down planking and metal sheets. A bridging party.

Without thinking he shouted to Valentine, who was in the neighbouring trench, 'Corporal, how many grenades do you have in that hole?'

18

'Dunno, sir. I've still got mine, and White has the same. Then there's Perkins and Butterworth.'

'Right. Get them all over here to me and yell across to Mays to do the same with his lot. Double quick. And bring a sandbag.'

'A sandbag, sir?'

'You heard me. A sandbag. Empty.'

He was staring intently now as the Germans began to dig themselves into holes around the places where the debris of the bridge had already raked the earth into shallow holes.

Mays came running up to the trench, clutching four hand grenades against his tunic. 'Here you are, sir. Corporal Valentine's on his way.'

'Thank you, Mays. Get back and keep up a steady sniping fire against those men. Tell Sarnt Bennett to get the Bren firing at them too. Long range, I know. Just try to stop them digging in.'

Mays went off and Lamb watched him go. He admired his lanky stride and remembered a cricket match back at the depot at Tonbridge, officers versus men, when Mays's spin bowling had caught them all on the wrong foot. He was a mild-mannered man, a farmer's boy who wrote letters home at any lull in the fighting, and, though he would never admit to it, had been going out with the same childhood sweetheart since he was 16. Lamb hoped that he would make it through to see her again when this lot was over.

As he was thinking, Valentine slipped into the slit trench next to Smart and Lamb. 'Grenades, sir. As many as we could find.'

'How many?'

'I've got four, sir. And a sandbag.' He lingered over the word as if to emphasise its apparent absurdity, and held out the limp piece of canvas sacking.

19

'Right, with Smart's that makes nine. Thank you, Corporal. Pile them on the floor. There.'

Valentine placed the grenades gingerly in a roughly geometric pile with those that Mays had left and stood back to admire his handiwork.

Lamb, who had been staring at the Germans through his field glasses, now saw him. 'Right. Now get back and help Mays to keep those Jerries' heads down.'

He opened the sack and gave it to Smart. 'Right. You hold it, I'll fill.'

Taking the grenades from the pile on the floor of the trench one by one, he placed each of them carefully inside the sandbag, conscious all the while that time was running out. 'Right, Smart. Well, man, aren't you going to wish me luck?'

Smart stared at him but before his batman could say anything Lamb was up and over the top of the trench and running hell for leather down the grassy embankment towards the German lines, the heavy bag of grenades clutched tightly to his chest.

He slipped and slithered down the muddy slope, praying with every step that he wouldn't fall and hearing his heart pounding in his chest, all the while keeping his eye on the Germans ahead of him. Over to his right he was aware of a flash and then the deep rattle of a machine gun. The earth around his running feet began to fly in all directions as bullets tore into the grass and mud. From his rear he heard the familiar answering cough of the Bren, and the enemy machine gun stopped. But then as soon as their own had paused to reload and change barrels, the Germans opened up again.

As he ran further to the left, away from the gun, he was aware that it must now be traversing, following him, but always just a fraction behind. He had reached the river now and almost stopped as he felt a bullet whistle past his face. Rifle fire now, from the opposite parapet. The Bren was in action again and he could hear the intermittent crack of the bolt-action Enfield rifles. Bennett, Mays and Valentine were doing well. Lamb kept on running, jumped the headless bodies of two civilians and saw dead ahead of him the helmeted heads and field-grey torsos of the Germans digging into the earth to the right of the bridge, preparing a fire pit for mortars and machine guns. That was his first objective, and then he'd find the bridging unit. Suddenly nothing else mattered but to reach them and to do what he had set out to do. Any other thoughts of home were now gone from his mind. Nothing there now but the urge to do whatever it took to make sure that the men digging those holes and spanning that chasm would never finish their job.

He was within thirty-five yards of them now, and still the air around him seemed to be thick with bullets, as if he were standing in a swarm of bees. He did not think that he had been hit, but then in the past few minutes he had really ceased to care and had begun to feel almost invulnerable. A sudden sense of euphoria swept over him. In the lee of the upper span of the ruined bridge he stopped and used the remains of a civilian cart and its dead horse for cover. German bullets thwacked into the horse's cadaver, sending sprays of blood in all directions. Lamb kept his head down and, taking two grenades from the bag, primed both. Then, holding one in each hand he released the levers, counted to four, half raised himself for a moment and, judging his target, threw them quickly, one after the other, conscious that his left arm would not be as strong or as able as his right. Ducking down, he watched them arc and saw them land. Then he covered his head. The blast rocked the bridge for an instant and was followed by screams.

Lamb took two more bombs from the bag and pulled

their pins, careful to hold the levers down. He lifted his thumbs, counted and then rose again and threw them in swift succession. Two more explosions and a rattle of machine-gun fire told him that they had done their job. There was shouting in the German lines now, along with the screaming of the wounded. One of the bombs had burst off target, against the side of the bridge, sending a welcome column of brick dust into the air and obscuring Lamb from the enemy gunners. But as he prepared the next two grenades there was a burst of automatic fire and bullets smacked into the horse; one of them, bursting through its withers, touched him on the arm and tore open his tunic. He looked down and saw blood but was aware that it had merely grazed him. He stood now, hoping to get a better aim, ignoring the fact that he was more visible, and after releasing the levers and counting, hurled the two bombs towards the Germans. From behind him a welcome salvo told him that his men were still giving covering fire. Three grenades left. He was unsure what effect he had had thus far, but judging from the commotion he had connected with something. His heart was beating faster now, the sweat pouring off him. Half blinded by the dust, he primed two more grenades. The blood from his arm had trickled down his sleeve and was slimy in his fingers, almost making him drop one of the Mills bombs. Through the smoke he saw the figure of a tall German officer signalling to two men carrying a machine gun and pointing directly to him. Not hesitating, Lamb took his thumb off the lever of one grenade, let the seconds tick by and then threw it at the group. He did the same with the other bomb before turning and slinging it towards the half-dug-in gunners. He knew that he had hit them and that the immediate threat had gone, but they would lose no time now in pouring all their fire on to him and there was only one way back.

He pulled the last grenade from the bag and drew the pin, still holding the lever down. Then, turning, he began to run. After five paces he turned and found himself looking at the levelled rifles of a score of the enemy. Praying that they would miss, he counted to four, threw the grenade as the rounds began to whistle in and, not waiting to see the result, spun round and ran. Uphill now. Harder, but he knew that the explosion would cover him for a moment. Again the grass flew high as the bullets struck home. He felt a sharp pain in his heel and presumed he had been hit, but kept running. Now was not the time to stop and look at any damage. He was aware too of a growing ache in his arm where the bullet had grazed it and hoped that that was all that it was. He was nearing the trenches now and the German rifle fire had lessened, although the machine gun on his left was still firing. Where the devil was the Bren? Reaching the last few yards before his trench, he could hear the men cheering him on and then he was home, slithering down the side and thumping on the muddy floor. He could hear his breathing, almost as if it were another man's, and a steady thumping which he realised was his heart.

Fred Smart just stared at him. 'Bloody hell, sir. That was fuckin' incredible – if you'll pardon my French, sir. Sorry, sir.'

Lamb grinned, happy and surprised to be alive and, wiping the sweat from his eyes with his bloody right hand, gasped for breath. 'Thank you, Smart. How did I do?'

'Pretty well, sir, I'll say. You blew that lot in the bridge to blazes and that machine gun that was setting up with them an' all.'

'Did I stop them digging?'

'You stopped them, sir. They won't be doing any more digging where they've gone.'

He looked out over the top of the trench and surveyed his handiwork. In the centre of the bridge lay the bridging party, six of them, all dead. Beyond, where the Germans had been entrenching positions, were more dead, and he could see wounded being carried back by enemy medics. Across to the right a crew lay about its mangled machine gun. He had killed perhaps twenty men, all told. More importantly, though, he had stopped the enemy digging in positions and crossing the river. For the present.

Smart looked at him. 'Hadn't you better get that wound dressed, Mister Lamb? Get Thompson to have a look at it, sir.'

Private Thompson, aside from being in charge of the anti-tank rifle, was also the platoon medic, and while every man carried a field dressing he had charge of the medical supplies.

'No, Smart. It's nothing. Just a graze.' However, he wasn't so sure. He felt the twinge in his foot and looked down to see that the back of his boot had been shot off. Fearing the worst, he quickly bent to see what damage had been done and was relieved to see that although covered in blood his heel had only been nicked. Looking back at his arm, though, he could see that what he had thought a mere graze might well be something worse.

He unbuttoned the cuff of his tunic and rolled up the sleeve, then did the same for his shirt. In his forearm just below the elbow was a neat gash where the bullet had torn through the cloth and into the flesh and muscle. It had not gone deep, but enough to cause him discomfort and to restrict his use of the muscles.

'Damn.'

Smart held back the tunic and began to swab at the wound with some gauze. 'Looks clean enough, sir. I'll get Thompson, though, and we'll get you fixed up back at Company.'

Lamb shook his head. 'I have no plans to move to the rear just yet, Smart. We've got unfinished business here.'

Smart stopped swabbing and listened: 'They've ceased firing, sir.'

Lamb listened. It was true. Since he had regained the position the Germans had ceased fire. He wondered why. He saw Bennett running across to him, careful to crouch down as he did so.

Valentine came close behind him. 'My God, sir. That was the most heroic thing I think I've ever seen. Well done, sir.'

Lamb smiled. 'Well done you, Bennett, with that covering fire. And you, Valentine. All of you. Where's Corporal Mays?'

'Bren's jammed, sir. He's trying to fix it now. Perhaps you should 'ave a look, sir.'

The men were well aware that in civilian life Lamb had been in charge of a motor garage and respected his expertise with engines, which on more than one occasion had proved useful in camp.

'Yes, perhaps I should.'

He started as Smart's final swabbing touched a particularly sensitive area of the wound in his arm. Bennett saw it. 'You're hit, sir. Not bad, is it?'

'No, Sarnt. Not that bad. I'll live.'

Valentine, who was squatting at the edge of the trench, looking with interest at Smart's handiwork, spoke. 'Have you noticed they've stopped firing, sir?'

'Yes, and we were wondering why.'

Valentine smiled. 'Perhaps they're just frightened in case we're all as mad as our Lieutenant.'

Bennett glared at him but said nothing.

Smart, winding a bandage around Lamb's arm, piped up, 'That's it. I reckon you've terrified them good and proper, sir. They didn't know what they were up against.

Perhaps they're packing up now to go back to Germany like good little Huns, sir.'

They laughed. But Lamb did not smile. He was looking back down towards the bridge. 'No. I think they're just waiting.'

So they waited. For two hours they sat in the afternoon sunshine, drinking strong, sweet tea thick with powdered milk. Lamb listened to them chatting. The conversations ranged over football, their girls and some film with George Formby that had them laughing in the aisles, and it seemed almost as if for them the war had ended here. Some of them, he rightly guessed, would be praying that by some miracle it had. One of them, Butterworth, the platoon wit, even suggested that Mr Churchill had been on the telephone to Herr Hitler and told him that he might as well go home to Berlin because their Mister Lamb wasn't going to give up his bridge.

Lamb laughed with them at that.

They had grown closer during the course of the last few months and he had come to know their individual characters and idiosyncrasies.

Aside from Bennett and Mays, there was Smart, his batman: ever-loyal Fred Smart, still living at home with his parents in their little cottage in Godstone; Butterworth, a giant of a man with hands that looked clumsy but were able to strip down a Bren gun faster than any other man in the platoon; Tapley, the runner, short and slight, with a weasel's face and deep brown eyes, Tapley the lady's man who could charm a pint of milk or a bottle of wine from any French girl. Perkins was the dedicated soldier of the group, gritty and uncompromising and more convinced than any of them of the urgency of crushing Hitler. Hughes was the great thinker, always mulling over some problem or other that the rest of them might have missed.

His solutions tended to be right, and Lamb had him marked down as a possible future corporal. Short and stocky, George Stubbs the mortar man was always singing or humming to himself – the old favourites, mostly, songs that helped to calm his shaky nerves: 'Pack up Your Troubles', 'It's a Long Way to Tipperary', 'The Siegfried Line'. But lately he had begun to favour some of the more recent popular songs, George Formby in particular. 'Imagine Me on the Maginot Line'. That always got them all laughing. Wilknson mostly, always keen for a joke. Most of them practical.

And then there was Valentine. Lamb smiled and shook his head. He closed his eyes, and was even beginning to think that he might take some rest, when he heard it – a low rumble which quickly grew in intensity until the ground seemed to shake. Christ. They were bringing up their tanks.

Instantly he shouted down along the line and back towards the woods, 'Sarnt Bennett. Enemy tanks to our front. Bring up the anti-tank rifle.'

He thought they would try a crossing now, while they had surprise on their side and they think we're shaken. But if we can stand our ground we might just hold off the first wave. We can't really destroy tanks. No hope of that with what we've got to hand. But if we can take out as many of the infantry as we can before we pull back, then at least we'll have done something to atone for the deaths of those poor blighters in the river.

He yelled towards the rear and saw the Boys anti-tank rifle gunner and his mate sitting in a nearby slit trench lining up the slim-barrelled weapon on a make-believe target on the opposite bank. 'Thompson, hold your fire with the Boys until you can get a clear shot. 500 yards. No more.'

There was an answering 'Sir'. Lamb cast a pitying look

at Thompson. The recoil from the anti-tank rifle was well known. He took out his binoculars from their canvas case on the right of his belt and scanned the road again and the trees on either side. Then he saw them. There were two in the lead. Panzer Mark IVs, by the look of them, with small triangular pennons flying and the squat angular turret and short-barrelled cannon that he recognised from the silhouettes on the recognition charts at the officer training school. His stomach felt suddenly hollow, and he could feel himself sweating. More tanks were following on behind. A whole squadron, perhaps more. And he knew that save for the single anti-tank weapon, the less than reliable Boys anti-tank rifle, they were powerless against such armour. Certainly, when it had first been introduced four years ago, it had been able to penetrate the armour of any tank, but tanks had come a long way in four years, and Lamb knew that against the machines facing them, the best the Reich could muster, it would be almost useless. Even their grenades, the egg-shaped Mills bombs developed in the last war, would merely bounce off the hulls. All they would be able to do would be to rake the ground around the advancing vehicles with small-arms fire as the infantry crept forward in the lee of the tanks and try to keep their heads down as the shells crashed in.

He yelled again, 'Wait for it, lads. It's the infantry we're after. Wait for the . . .' He had not finished his sentence when there was a whoosh from the opposite bank and a shell flew towards them, hitting the bank just to their front, its explosion sending up a cloud of earth and foliage. 'Keep down. Keep your eyes on the road.'

Another shell flew in, closer now, and there was a yell as a shard of shrapnel hit one of the platoon. Lamb kept looking at the road. The tanks had pulled up now and were just sitting there, lobbing their shells across the bank. Of course, he thought, there's no need for them to move forward. They think they can just blast us out, and they probably can. They must know we don't have any heavy weapons.

Two more shells came crashing into the position, and one hit home. Lamb looked at where it had landed and was aware of a jumble of bloody bodies and the noise of men in agony. He wondered whether he had been foolish to stay here. Perhaps they should have pulled back as Battalion had ordered. Perhaps the colonel knew best after all. Lamb began to doubt himself, and then banished the thought. Something inside him said that they had to make this count. They had to take out some of the enemy to atone for killing the civilians, except now he had been responsible for the death of his men. Perhaps, he thought, it's too late. They have us pinned down. How can we retire now? If only their infantry would come forward.

As the thought crossed his mind he saw the small grey figures moving in the wake of the tanks, which began to rumble forward towards the river bank. He put his field glasses to his eyes and picked up the figure of an officer in a peaked cap, shouting at the infantrymen, urging them on with his hand. Against all probability they were advancing to attack. Lamb smiled. Someone somewhere in the enemy higher command had obviously decreed that this crossing had to be taken, and taken by a certain time. That was the German way, and nothing in the field manual could stop that order. Lamb knew that it would be the death warrant for some of the men out there behind the tanks. As many as he could kill, he thought. 'Sarnt Bennett. Here they come.'

He turned to the men in his immediate vicinity. 'Open fire. Make them all count.'

At once the slit trenches became a frenzy of action as

29

the men fired at their chosen targets, loosing off round after round against the German infantry. Lamb could see figures falling now as the men in grey tried to tuck themselves in behind the tanks. But still some were left exposed to be picked off by the keen-eyed British riflemen. And even as the infantry fell the German tanks continued to fire as they advanced, and the shells crashed in. Now their machine guns had opened up from the tanks and there was sub-machine gun fire too coming in from a handful of infantry that had found some cover on the opposite bank.

Corporal Mays came running at a crouch up to Lamb's slit trench, enemy bullets raking the ground around his feet, and threw himself flat on the earth. 'Sir, Austin's copped it. Jerry machine gun, sir. We've got to get out of here, Mister Lamb.'

Lamb nodded. Yes, that was enough, he thought. Enough for the poor devils who had died on the bridge. Now they could go. 'Yes, Corporal. Find Sarnt Bennett. Tell the men to pull back. Keep as low as possible, don't look back and run as fast as you can to the woods. We'll form up on the other side of them, behind cover, and get back to Battalion.'

'Sir.'

The man took off, and Lamb turned back to the enemy. The lead tanks had lined themselves up and were pouring shellfire into their positions. There was a cry from along the line and Lamb was aware of a man tossed into the air like a puppet amid a cloud of earth and debris. He saw Bennett to his left.

The sergeant shouted over the noise, 'Runner from Company, sir. Battalion says to disengage and get back. There's a barrage coming down to cover our withdrawal, and CO says that unless we want to be under it we'd better move. We've to fall back through the Guards, sir.'

30

Lamb managed a smile. He knew that he had done all that he could.

He waved the men back out of the trenches and saw them follow Bennett into the woods. Then he took a last look at the great grey monsters as they loosed off another barrage, and then at last turned towards the rear. The shells were crashing around him now, hitting trees and ripping off their branches. Lamb began to lengthen his pace, but he had not gone two yards before something hit him hard on the back like a hammer blow, knocking the breath from him, and he was briefly aware of being shoved forward, face down in the mud. And then his world went black.

3

The first thing that Lamb saw as his vision returned was a man's face. His mouth felt horribly dry and he tried to ignore the cracking headache that was pounding inside his skull and to focus on the face. The man had a moustache, slicked-back hair and was wearing a monocle. Lamb had never seen the man before. For one awful moment his mind was filled with images of German villains from the pictures: Conrad Veidt or Raymond Lovell. He presumed that he had been captured and that this must be a German officer.

But then the man spoke and instantly he knew that he was safe. 'I say, old chap, well done. We thought for a moment you might be a gonner.'

He turned away and towards the door flap of the small tent in which Lamb could now see he was lying. 'Sarnt-Major, fetch that brandy in here, will you. The Lieutenant wants a drink.'

An RSM entered and filled the tent with his huge presence. Lamb was aware of his peaked cap, the cheese-cutter peak pressed flat against his nose. The next moment a gentle hand was lifting Lamb's throbbing head from the camp bed on which he was lying and then another hand placed a tin cup to his mouth, tilting it so that he could drink. He sipped and felt the raw liquid burn its way down his throat. He coughed, almost retched and shook his head. The pain swelled, and he stopped. The man laughed. 'That's it. Good man. Knew you'd be better for a sharp'ner. Bit of a narrow squeak you had, eh? Thank you, Sarnt-Major.'

Lamb was aware of the big man executing a perfect about turn and, as his vision became clearer, was able to look more closely at his saviour. The officer was a thin man with a hawk-like nose and, when combined with these features, what seemed an unlikely cheery smile. As Lamb managed to sit up he extended his hand.

'Fortescue, Captain, Second Coldstream. Detached from 1 Div HQ.' He paused. 'And you are?'

Lamb had spotted the three crowns on his shoulder. 'Peter Lamb, sir. North Kents. Thank you, sir. I mean, I presume you saved my life.'

The captain smiled and shrugged. 'Nothing at all, old man, no trouble. Absolute pleasure. Couldn't leave you there, could we? Jerry would have put you in the bag. Glad to have you aboard. You're damned lucky. It's not every man gets hit hard in the back with half a tree and lives to tell the tale. That last shell burst was damned close too. Seems to have hit you on the arm and the leg.'

'No, sir. Actually those are from earlier.'

'Well, you have been knocked about a bit, haven't you? Have another sip of the old brown stuff.'

Lamb sat up and drank a little more of the brandy. The pain in his head was slightly less but now the throbbing in his arm where he had been hit was beginning to nag again. 'My platoon, sir. Where are they?'

'I think my Sarnt-Major's found most of them. Few of them knocked about a bit. That last salvo did for a couple, I'm afraid. Lucky we were there, to your rear.'

'Sorry, sir?'

'We came in from the woods. Managed to hold off Jerry long enough to get you chaps out. Though what the devil you were doing there in the first place Gawd only knows. We were told you'd pulled out. We're the rearguard, you see.'

'Rearguard?'

'Absolutely. That's us. Rearguard. Last in, last out. Incidentally, why were you there? We were told you'd all pulled back.'

Lamb considered his answer carefully before giving it. 'Think I must have misread the order, sir. I was quite certain that it said "hold until relieved".'

The captain smiled and paused. 'You're either very brave, Lieutenant, or very stupid. I'd prefer to believe that it might be the former. In normal circumstances I should probably write this down and inform your CO. But these are hardly normal circumstances, are they?'

'No, sir.'

'We are a rearguard, Lieutenant. We are retreating *per se*, and as far as I'm aware the entire British Expeditionary Force might be coming with us.'

Lamb looked at him askance. 'Sir?'

'We've been told to cover a retreat. As far as the river Lescaut. But if you want my opinion we might have to fall back a little further.'

'How far, sir?'

'That's anyone's guess, I'm afraid. Gawd knows. I most certainly don't. All I know is that we're the Johnnies with the unenviable task of seeing that the rest of you Territorials make it out alive and to the next defensive line. Or as many of you as we can find.'

Lamb recoiled for a moment. This was not what he had expected. He had come out here to drive back Hitler. Had presumed that the BEF would at least put up a fight

34

for a good deal longer than this. And there it was again, the dig heard so often in the mess. For all his bravery, he was still a Territorial, at least in the eyes of men like Captain Fortescue, regular soldiers. He was determined, though, that by the end of this business he would be treated with the same respect as them. But the man was not spiteful, merely a stickler for protocol. All that you would expect from the Guards, he thought. And, what was more, for all Lamb knew he had saved his life.

He looked about himself and took in his surroundings. He was sitting in some sort of command post, with a wireless set, discarded packs and various miscellaneous pieces of equipment, on the edge of a copse looking out across an open field. He pondered the captain's words again. Covering a retreat. Surely it would not happen that quickly.

There was a pause in which the Coldstream officer stared disconsolately at the ground and twiddled a stick in the earth floor of his command post in an attempt at the regimental insignia.

Lamb broke the silence. 'Excuse me, sir. My men?'

'Ah yes, of course, right ho. Let's find your mob and then you can get on your way, eh?' He turned to bark an order in a voice that Lamb thought would have been well suited to the King's Birthday Parade at Horse Guards: 'Sarnt-Major, find the North Kents, if you will. I'm pleased that we managed to get most of you out. You number three corporals, one sergeant and seventeen men, if my Sarnt-Major's right, and he's never been known to be wrong.'

'I don't remember much of what happened.'

'Hardly surprising when a bloody great tank shell goes off ten yards behind you. You're lucky to be alive, Lieutenant.'

'Are many wounded?'

'Yes. I do remember one man in a pretty bad state.

Lost his foot. And a couple of other minor casualties. One of the NCOs too.'

'My sergeant?'

'No. Not him. He's sound. One of your corporals, though. Wound to the face. Nothing much really. Deal of blood. But he seemed damned put out about it. Funny sort of cove. Quite unlike your usual ranker. Educated, if you get my drift, and far too lippy by half.'

'Valentine.'

'Was that his name? Funny sort of name too. Take my advice, Lieutenant, and pack him off on an officer training course the first chance you get. That sort are never anything but trouble. Far too willing to express an opinion. Men aren't intended to have opinions. They can think what they damn well like, of course, but they should never express opinions. Yes, make him an officer. I should.'

Lamb smiled. 'He seems disinclined towards promotion, sir.'

'Disinclined? Just sign the form man and the army will do the rest. Disinclined, my Aunt Fanny. He'll be an officer and bloody well like it. Disinclined indeed.'

Lamb had no desire to continue the conversation and so quickly changed the subject. 'Did the Jerries get across the river, sir?'

'They've stopped pushing forward for the present but, yes, you might say it is in their hands. They've taken a fair pummelling, though. Our big guns gave them a bloody nose. Saw one of their tanks go right up. Bit of a Horlicks down there all round, though, isn't it?'

'Yes, bit of a Horlicks, sir.'

'Dozens of dead Jerries, of course, but women and children too. Seems that someone must have pressed the button and blew the bridge sky high when it was packed with civilians. Bloody shame. Poor devils. I wonder who gave the order.'

Lamb said nothing but groaned inwardly and heard

Valentine's words again. Surely it's what anyone in his place would have done, wasn't it? They were his orders.

The captain was speaking again. 'I expect there'll be a Board of Enquiry. Generally is. Don't know if anyone can be bothered, though, at the moment, with all this going on. Your Divisional General won't be pleased. Montgomery. Known him all my life. Family friend. Half hoped that I might bump into him down here. And he takes no prisoners, I'll tell you that. But he can't abide waste of life. A soldiers' soldier, d'you see. No problem at all with killing armed men. All for it, in fact. Killing the enemy. But he won't have civilians hurt at all. Quite right too, of course. Who would? Something to do with something or other he saw in the last bash. Feel sorry for the poor bugger who gave the order to blow the bridge. Wasn't you, I suppose?'

Lamb looked away. 'Er, no, sir. I can safely say I didn't push anything.'

'That's lucky then. I should get yourself back to your battalion if you can find it. Last I heard they were heading for Tournai. But you never can tell in this sort of scrap where they'll pitch up. Things seem to change all the time at the moment, don't they?' He pointed to Lamb's arm. 'I'd get that properly seen to, if I were you. Our MO's had a look at it, but you never know. Funny things, arms.'

There was a commotion outside. 'Anyway, that'll be your men now. Good to have met you, Lieutenant. Remember me to your general, if you see him.'

'I shall, sir. Thank you.'

'Here's your soldier servant. Cheero.'

Captain Fortescue left the tent and Smart saluted him and entered. 'Soldier servant? That me then, sir?'

'Yes, Smart, that's you, except we call you a batman. You're only a servant to the Guards.'

Lamb managed to get to his feet and, helped by a gentle arm from Smart, left the tent. Outside the men had been drawn up by Sergeant Bennett, and they made a welcome sight. Lamb counted three lines of seven including the mortar team. He saw Thomson standing to the right with his anti-tank rifle. Six casualties. It looked as if Mays's section had suffered worst.

'Well done, Sarnt. Who've we lost?'

'Austin, Joyncey and McCarthy all bought it, sir. Hale and Smith are wounded. Corporal Valentine's got a scratch on his face, sir, and Peters is wounded bad, sir. Don't think he'll make it through the night.'

'Thank you, Sarnt. I'll see him in a moment.' He turned to the men. 'Gather round.'

As the men drew closer he continued: 'Seems that we're in a bit of a fix. Company HQ seems to have fallen back to Tournai, so we're going to follow them.'

There was a voice from the second rank. Wilkinson. 'Are we retreating, sir?'

'No, Wilkinson. We're not retreating, just pulling back to regroup so that we can counter-attack.' He looked at his watch. It was nearing 2 p.m. 'Right, we'll march till 1800 hours, then make camp. If we get a step on we might even catch up with Company HQ.'

'Or Brigade, sir.'

'Or Brigade, Tapley. Thank you. All right, Sarnt Bennett. Take me to the wounded.'

They had lain the men beneath the shade of some trees close to the company transport. A number of guardsmen were standing about the vehicles talking and clicked smartly to attention, saluting as Lamb appeared. The three men were lying on blankets. Hale was sitting up puffing on a Woodbine. Smith was staring at the sky. Peters, though, was lying with his head on one side and as Lamb approached he noticed that his eyes, though wide open, were staring vacantly into the middle distance. His skin was drained of colour. Death could not be far off. He went to the less badly wounded first. 'Hale. You look well enough to be up and about. Where did they get you?'

'Leg, sir. Went clean through the ankle, sir. Can't walk, sir.'

Lamb nodded. 'Don't worry. They'll get you out all right. You'll be back in Blighty before us. What about you, Smith?'

Smith looked up at Lamb and smiled. 'Shoulder, sir. Bloody great bit of shrapnel. Hurts a bit.'

'I bet it does. You'll be home soon.'

He walked across to Peters. Bennett whispered to him. 'Stomach wound, sir. MO's had a look. It's not good, sir. Got his liver too.'

Lamb knelt down by the boy's head. 'Peters. I know you can hear me. They think you'll be fine, old chap. Is there anyone you'd like me to write to to tell them you're on your way back home?'

Peters moved his lips and tried to turn his head, but Lamb noticed the grimace of pain that passed across his ashen face. 'Don't try to move, old chap. Just tell me or the sergeant here. Just a name.'

The boy's mouth moved again and Lamb bent close so that his ear was close to Peters's mouth. He heard a word. 'Mother.'

'All right, old chap. I got that. You rest now.'

Getting to his feet Lamb turned to Bennett. 'He hasn't got long, Sarnt. Make sure that the Guards give him a decent burial and mark the grave. I'm sure they will.'

He walked back across the camp and noticed as he did how neatly it had been set up in the short time the Guards had been there. That was one thing you could always say of the British army: they knew how to lay out a camp. Latrines in the right place, tent lines and vehicle park, command post set back from the front, trenches well dug in and supported. It was exemplary. He reached the men, who were standing at ease and shuffled to attention as he arrived.

'As you were. All right. Corporal Mays, Briggs, Valentine. Let's get going.'

Observed closely by the Coldstreamers, they left the camp, in as orderly and Guardsman-like a file as they could manage. The Guards saluted as they passed and were acknowledged. Behind them the noise of gunfire spoke of the speed of the German advance.

They had not gone far when they crossed a railway line and found themselves on the edge of a wood. There was a noise of engines, and without further warning a carrier roared towards them through the undergrowth to their right and then following it around the flank of the wood came three light tanks with British markings.

From the front seat of the carrier a man in a black beret addressed them, 'Hallo. You chaps falling back? We must be covering you. 2nd RDG. Who are you?'

Lamb spoke. 'North Kents, sir.'

'Really? North Kents? Your mob have been through here already. Quite a while ago. Badly shot up, some of them. You'll need to hurry to catch them, though. Any wounded?'

'Yes, three, as a matter of fact. One bad. We left them with the Guards.'

'We're under orders to carry them back if we can. See what we can do, old man. Pip pip.'

With that he waved his hand and the carrier and its three tanks rumbled past them towards the front. Lamb couldn't help thinking that to the officer it still seemed like some big game. And the man seemed to be enjoying it.

He turned to Bennett. 'Looks as if we'll have to hurry if we want to catch up.'

They moved around the edge of the wood and as they hit the road on the other side found a long column of

British infantry moving in the same direction, towards the rear. The men's expressions said it all. Many of them had bandaged heads and limbs and the few trucks which drove with them were packed with wounded. Lamb stopped. They all did. But it was Corporal Mays who spoke for them all. 'Oh, my good God.'

Lamb stared. It seemed as if for an instant the entire British army was on the road, 'pulling back'.

Bennett could see his face. 'It's not good, sir, is it?'

'No, Sarnt. It's not good at all. But I don't think we'll join their party. I think we'll go south west. Just as quick to Tournai that way.'

'And a much prettier road, I'd guess, sir. Without that lot's long faces.'

'You'll never see a happy retreating army, Sarnt. Come on. If we're lucky we'll be there by tomorrow. Or in Brussels. You never know.'

The sergeant laughed. But Lamb knew that there was no real mirth in it.

4

The high sun beat down on the dusty road and, even where the tall poplars that lined its sides offered shade, sent shafts of light across the surface in bright white lines. The land lay flat about them, with a distant low horizon punctuated here and there with the steeples of village churches. On either side the crops crew tall in the fields and cattle stood in the meadows. On the grassy banks of the road the cornflowers bloomed. They had passed close to the north of the town of Wavre, and Lamb, consulting the motoring map of northern France he had had the foresight to purchase in London on embarkation leave, had thought it best, in view of the large numbers of refugees and soldiers on the other road, to stay on their own and hug the edge of the woods to the west of the town. But now they were back out in the open and, he thought, horribly vulnerable to air attack. They had trained for it, of course. This was the future of warfare, after all. But none of them had ever experienced the reality. For all he knew there might be German planes heading towards them at that very moment, ready to rain down bombs and strafe them with machine-gun fire as they walked along through the bucolic scene, just as they had done in Poland and Holland. And he had no idea as to where the RAF might be. But he was not prepared to trust that they would be directly above his head whenever the German dive-bombers struck.

'Keep your ears open for enemy bombers, all of you. Listen out. You'll hear them before you see them.'

Even though it was coming on to 3.30 in the afternoon it was, supposed Lamb, a hot day even for this time of year in northern France. They had spent the night in an empty barn and he could not get the stench of stored manure out of his nostrils. The men too were aware of the smell, which, although they had not had any direct contact with the muck, seemed to have permeated their clothes. He knew too that, after five hours of marching, the men would be sweating uncomfortably in their thick battledress, just as he was. But at least it wasn't raining. To be retreating was bad enough, but a soldier retreating through the pouring rain was never the happiest man in the world. He wondered where the other platoons in his company might be, and for that matter Company HQ. And what of Bourne and Long? He wondered whether they too were as lost as he, and attempting to rejoin the battalion. What a bloody mess. Suddenly weary, he spoke. 'Sarnt Bennett, let's give them a rest.'

'All right, you lot. Fall out and take a rest.'

The men moved to the side of the road, removed their packs and sat on them, most of them flipping open breast pockets to take out a packet of Woodbines or Gold Flake. Others lay back in the sunshine, feeling its warmth now as welcome rather than oppressive. They were hungry and thirsty and they all needed a shave, but at least they were safe. Lamb opened a pocket and pulled out a silver cigarette case packed with Craven As – a wedding present from Julia, engraved on the lid with both of their initials. He took one out, tapped it twice on the tin and lit up, enjoying the bitter taste as the smoke circulated through mouth and nose.

He turned to Bennett, who was lighting his own cigarette. 'How are we off for rations, Sarnt?'

'We're all right, sir. Down to about two days' worth a man, I should say. That's bully and biscuit mainly.'

'Well, that should do us. I dare say we'll find the Company soon. Or even the Battalion. They can't be more than a day's march ahead of us.'

'Hope so, sir. The men are feeling a bit adrift.'

'Well, Captain Fortescue assured me that they withdrew along this road. So the best we can do is follow them. 'Fraid you've only got me for now.'

Bennett smiled. 'That'll do us, sir.'

He finished his cigarette and threw the butt to the ground, grinding it out with the sole of his boot before opening the map case that hung at his side and drawing out the precious road map. He opened it up and peered at a square. Bennett joined him. 'We're here, by my reckoning, just south of Brussels. Seems that the order is to regroup at Tournai, which is here. About thirty miles away.' Giving one edge of the map to the sergeant, Lamb pointed at the square. 'There's a village up ahead. Looks like Rixensart. Reckon we might even find the Company there, Sarnt. They can't have gone too far.'

'Looks hopeful, sir.'

'Right then. Let's get them up.' He folded the map and replaced it in the case.

Bennett yelled, 'Come on, lads. On yer feet. Let's keep going.'

There were a few groans and one comment of 'slave driver' and 'don't he know there's a war on' from unknown grumblers that earned a shout from Corporal Mays. But without much trouble the platoon got back on the road.

The town that lay ahead of them was nothing remarkable.

The countryside quickly gave way to a street lined with small terraced houses typical of the region. There was a church to the right and on the left a large open area of parkland that at one point he thought might have belonged to a château.

Lamb scanned the street and saw no one. No civilians, and certainly no sign of any military personnel. He turned to Smart, who was behind him with the RT. 'Bit strange, Smart, don't you think?'

They entered in textbook formation with Corporal Mays and No. 1 section up front, then twenty-five yards behind Lamb's HQ group, including Valentine and Briggs. Then came Sergeant Bennett with the mortar crew, and finally the two other sections each led by a lance corporal, one either side of the road, Valentine's bringing up the rear.

Lamb slowed the pace and they walked into the town. Still there was no sign of the inhabitants.

Smart spoke. 'Looks like they've upped sticks and gone, sir. Perhaps they knew we was coming.'

It certainly looked as if the population had left in a hurry. A few bags had been forgotten and stood forlorn outside a house whose door swung on its hinges.

Papers blew across the street and a cat crossed his path. He looked up and saw that most of the houses had been shuttered, although what use that might have been, had it been the Germans and not his platoon who had arrived, he could not think.

Bennett came up. 'They've gone, sir. Everyone. Cleared out. Not long ago, neither. Coffee's still hot in the pots.'

'Yes, Sarnt. So it would seem. Smart, any joy with the RT?'

'Nothing, sir. Dead as a doornail.'

'I suppose there's nothing to be done but to carry on, Sarnt. Our chaps must have come through here in a hell of a hurry.'

'Perhaps that's why the civvies all cleared out, sir, if they saw the British army running away like that, sir. Well, stands to reason they'd want to leg it too.'

Lamb knew that he was right. 'Tournai is due west. We'll take a left turn here, Sarnt.'

Bennett barked the order as if he were on the parade ground at Tunbridge Wells, and his words echoed through the silent streets. The men wheeled down the road past the park and were soon clear of the houses and in open countryside once again.

On they marched, crossing a major road packed with civilians heading north west towards Brussels. They reminded Lamb of the people on the bridge, of the little girl with the doll and the pretty young woman in the red skirt, and again he felt the shame boiling inside him. As they waited for a gap in the column, the men stared at the refugees and Lamb realised that the sight would have an irreversible effect on their morale.

He turned to Bennett. 'Can we get a song together? Might gee up the men as they march.'

'Think we can manage it, sir. Stubbs is our best singer. What shall we have?'

'Oh I don't know. Something from the last war, perhaps? "Tipperary" or "Pack up Your Troubles"?'

'What about "The Siegfried Line", sir? That's a good 'un. The lads like that.'

'All right, Sarnt. Make it that one then.'

Bennett went over to Stubbs, who was carrying the 2-inch mortar on his shoulder, and had a quiet word in his ear. Within seconds, as they at last began to cross the main road, edging with care through the civilians, he had begun to sing:

'We're going to hang out the washing on the
    Siegfried Line.

Have you any dirty washing, Mother dear?
We're going to hang out the washing on the
    Siegfried Line,
Cos the washing day is here . . .'

Without prompting the men joined in, all of them familiar
with the words of the song which had filled the cinema
screens on their last leave. Lamb, though, felt its full irony.
Nevertheless he joined in, singing as loudly as he could so
that the men would hear him. When the song was over
Thompson started up another, 'Run Rabbit Run', a real
crowd-pleaser. In the chorus Smart yelled 'bang' at the
appropriate place and raised a smile. They were in better
spirits now, he thought, and it made the distance seem less.

Looking ahead, through the lines of grey refugees, Lamb
thought that he saw a figure in a helmet. Then another.
He could see rifles now and shouted to Bennett, 'Soldiers.
Up ahead. Can you see? What are they?'

Both men looked hard through the milling throng of
civilians and past the horses, carts and vehicles. It was
true. There were soldiers, and the first thing he saw was
the colour of their uniforms. Khaki. Lamb smiled with
relief and recognised their helmets as British. 'It's all right,
Sarnt. They're ours.'

The men were dawdling along in front of them, moving
even slower than the refugees, and Lamb and his men
were able to catch up with them quickly. He accosted the
last of them, a corporal: 'Corporal.'

The man spun round and, recognising an officer, saluted
before yelling out to his mates, 'Oi, get the Sergeant.
There's an officer here.' The other men came running.

There were six of them, but it became instantly apparent
that they were not from the same unit. As the sergeant
made his way back, Lamb spoke to the corporal. 'Who
are you?'

'Stanton, sir. Lancashire Fusiliers. We're all sorts really. Lost our units.'

'Right, Corporal Stanton. Well, we're adrift too. You'd best fall in with us for the time being.'

The sergeant, a Scot, had arrived by now and saluted Lamb. 'Sergeant McKracken, sir, 1st Royal Scots. Got knocked out up near Limal by a shellburst, sir, and when I came to the platoon had gone. You've met Corporal Stanton, sir, and then there's another from his mob, Driscoll. Then there's two from the North Staffs, Blake and Mitchell, and there's Archer. He's a gunner. Gone a bit deaf – from the shelling, sir.'

'Has he? Well, we're pretty much in the same boat, Sergeant. We're North Kents. My name's Lamb. Lost our people at Wavre. We're heading south west. Same as you, judging from your choice of route. Can I meet your men?'

McKracken nodded. 'Of course, sir.'

They walked across to where the five men were standing. As Lamb approached, three of them, Stanton, Driscoll and Blake, stood to attention. Lamb noticed that the other two did not – Archer, clearly on account of his deafness. The other man looked up and with a sullen, ash-grey face stared at Lamb, who put on a smile and spoke. 'Good morning. Seems as if you men are in the same boat as us. Gone adrift. Well, I intend to find our unit, and the best thing would be for you to fall in with us. Sarnt McKracken here agrees. Who are you? Corporal Stanton, I know you already.'

One by one the others introduced themselves with name, rank and serial number: 'Driscoll, Private, sir. Lancashire Fusiliers. Me and the Corporal here got lost when Jerry attacked on the Dyle. Had to keep low and when it blew over we couldn't find the unit.'

'Blake, sir, Private, North Staffs. Same with us, sir, really. Our RSM told us to stick to the Bren in our trench, and we did just that. Shot up a few Jerries. Didn't we, Taff?

48

But they just kept coming, sir. We was about to pull out when an officer comes over and tells us to hang on. Says reinforcements is coming up the line. So we hung, on, didn't we, Taff?' He turned to the ashen-faced man, who looked at him blankly. 'But no one came. Not a soul. Officer must have got it wrong.'

The other man spat suddenly and looked up at Lamb. 'Mitchell, sir, North Staffs. Like Blake says, an officer told us that we'd be relieved, but we never were. Ran out of ammo, and then we scarpered. Passed all our mates, killed. No reinforcements. Nothing.' The man stared again at the ground. Lamb turned to the last man, the gunner: 'And you, you must be Archer.'

The man looked up and frowned. 'Sorry, sir. Can't hear a blind thing. Gone deaf, see? On account of the shelling. Can't hear a thing, sir.'

Lamb nodded his head. 'Yes, I see.' He patted the man on the shoulder. 'Not to worry. Stick with us. You'll be all right.'

He turned to McKracken. 'Well done for getting them together, Sarnt. They seem in good spirits. All save one.' He gestured to Mitchell.

'Yes, sir. I'll keep my eye on him.'

'Jolly good. You'd better see my sergeant.' He turned. 'Sarnt Bennett!'

Bennett arrived. Lamb spoke quietly to him. 'Six odds and sods to join us, Sarnt Bennett. They're either hopelessly lost or they're deserters. But I'll give them the benefit of the doubt. They don't look like bad sorts and they seem keen to go on, in any case. But keep your eye on them.'

Bennett smiled: 'Very good sir. I'll treat them just as if they were my own.'

With their newly acquired 'odds and sods' in tow, they pushed on across the fields, on roads that at times seemed no more than dust tracks. Another small town appeared, La Hulpe, but it too was deserted. They were climbing steadily now along a natural ridge and by Lamb's compass were moving west by south west. He felt the pain in his heel with each step but said nothing. Smart, though, could see him wince. The pain in his back where he had been hit by the tree was also proving a hindrance to marching, and he hoped it did not presage anything serious. He knew too that he must keep up the pace for the men if they were to make any ground before nightfall. He was taking them west and then had thought it best to head north towards Brussels.

He saw a signpost pointing to the left off the road and for a reason he couldn't fathom the names it bore struck him as curiously familiar: Lasne, Plancenoit.

Then as he looked, he was transported back to officer training classes in Tonbridge, to a young man seated at a desk studying long-distant British victories. Plancenoit. That was it. Wasn't that the name of the village on the left flank of another British army? The village through which the Prussians had advanced to save the day and grant them victory over another tyrant. His men were marching onto the field of Waterloo. Smiling, he signalled to Bennett to come up. The man was nonplussed as to his grin.

'Yes, sir?'

'Sarnt Bennett, do you have any idea where we are? Where exactly we're going, I mean?'

'On the road to Tournai, sir?'

'Yes, of course we are, but here. Right here. Do you realise where we are right now?'

'Can't say as I do, sir.'

'Waterloo, man. We're on the battlefield of Waterloo.'

The sergeant smiled. 'Are we, sir? Well, I'll be . . . Shall I tell the men, sir? It might buck them up.'

'Yes, go ahead, Sarnt. Why don't you tell them?

Anything to keep their spirits up, and we'll need to stop soon enough anyway.'

They were in Plancenoit now and walking past the little church with its walled graveyard before turning right down a hedge-lined avenue. After a few minutes, and after a steady climb uphill beneath a canopy of branches, they emerged onto a plain. Away to the west the sun was sinking on the horizon, sending a glow across fields high with green corn and barley. To their left the landscape opened out before them and he could see the centre of what had been Wellington's line. The men, although they had been informed by Sergeant Bennett as to where they were, seemed largely oblivious to the significance of the place and carried on marching along the crest of the ridge.

Valentine, however, approached Lamb wearing his usual, irritating grin. 'Quite a coincidence, sir, isn't it? Us being here.'

'Yes, Corporal. I can't say that I'd been expecting it.'

'To tell the truth, sir, I think we are a little off course.'

'You do?'

'A little too far south, sir. In fact I suspect that we're actually in the French sector.'

Lamb cursed. Might he have allowed the romantic idea of being in this place to divert him from their purpose? Worse than that, he seemed to have been caught out by Valentine.

They were nearing a crossroads now. It occurred to Lamb that it must surely be Wellington's crossroads – his command post, at the centre of the ridge where the British infantry had stood against Napoleon. Up ahead he could see a lorry, and around it a group of soldiers.

Lamb counted six of them and whispered, 'All right, Corporal, get ready.'

As the shadowy figures ahead noticed them, Lamb's men froze and readied their weapons. He drew his revolver

51

and waved the platoon forward as they began to edge away into a loose battle formation. He was trying to look more closely now at the men by the lorry in the half light, to make out the shape of their helmets, the easiest give-away to their nationality. And then he saw to his relief that they were the distinctive bowl-shaped helmets of the French 'poilus'. 'All right, men, they're French. Seems you must be right, Valentine.'

He moved to the front of the column and walked on. The French soldiers looked round and, seeing the shallow helmet of the British Tommy, did not bother even to pick up their guns, which lay piled against the side of the vehicle. One of them walked towards Lamb, and as they got closer to one another he opened a cigarette case. 'Cigarette?'

Lamb noticed that he wore the insignia of an officer. A lieutenant of infantry. He reached out and took one of the precious cigarettes. Filterless, Turkish. 'Thank you, Lieutenant.'

The man spoke in good English. 'Etienne de Noyon, 116th Infantry. We did not expect to see you English down here. You are lost?'

'Yes, I suspect that we are. Sorry, Peter Lamb, North Kents. We've become detached from our unit. I don't suppose they've come this way?'

The Frenchman shrugged. 'I don't think so. But then we've been here ourselves for barely two hours and we've seen a few Tommies.' He laughed and lit their cigarettes. 'What d'you think? We're supposed to be a road block, but how can we do that with one truck and six men?'

Lamb raised an eyebrow. 'That's bad news. In that case we are lost.' The sun was sinking faster now. 'Is there somewhere near here we can bunk down for the night? A barn?'

'There's the farmhouse, of course. It's all shut up, though.'

He laughed and took a long drag of the cigarette before speaking. 'It's the farm that you British held out against us for so long back then. You know where we are?'

Lamb nodded. 'Yes, of course. Funny, isn't it?'

The Frenchman laughed. 'Yes. Even funnier for me because then the Boche were on your side.'

Lamb smiled at him. 'I don't think we'd get much sleep there anyway. Too many ghosts. Anywhere else?'

'There is another house up there past the crossroads. Opposite the big farm. To the north. But I think another British officer is staying there already. Curious that two of you should come here on the same day. Perhaps you know him. He came with a driver in a car.'

Lamb looked puzzled. What on earth was a staff officer doing so far south? And without an escort? 'Thank you. We'll take that road and try our luck. At least it's in the right direction.'

The French man clicked his heels and bobbed his head. Lamb returned the compliment. '*Bonne chance*. Wish us luck with our road block.'

They turned right at the crossroads and continued for a short way between steep banks to either side. Then, as the road evened out, they saw on the right the walls of a farm and, opposite, a small group of houses, two cottages and what looked like a barn. In one of the houses a light was burning at the window against the blackout. It was as good as any a place to stop, and they were with friends.

Lamb turned to Bennett before walking on alone towards the door. 'All right, Sarnt. We'll bivouac here.'

'You heard the officer. Off the road. Unsling yer packs. We're making camp.'

'What's up, Sergeant?' It was Stubbs.

'We're stopping here for the night, lad. Mister Lamb's orders.'

'Funny place to stop, innit? Like an old shack. We sleeping 'ere? Don't feel good.'

'Officer knows best, Stubbs. Less of your lip. This is a historic place anyway. Waterloo.'

'I thought that was a railway station.' Johnson now.

Massey answered him. 'You're just pig ignorant, you are.'

'You shut it, Massey, or I'll give you bloody ignorant.'

Bennett stepped in. 'Right, you two. Stow it, both of you, or you'll be on a charge. Stubbs, get a brew on. Johnson, you get some stew going. Massey, find some kindling.'

Lamb could hear them as he made his way up the road. He stopped before the door and knocked three times. There was a commotion within and he heard the click of a rifle bolt. His pistol was still drawn and he kept it at the ready.

There was a shout: 'Who's there?'

Lamb, feeling rather foolish, could think of nothing better to do than answer: 'Lieutenant Lamb. North Kents.'

The door opened and he found himself looking down the barrel of a rifle. To his intense relief, though, he also saw that it was held by a British soldier. A sergeant. Seeing his face and uniform the man smiled and lowered his gun. 'Sorry, sir. Can't be too careful these days, can you.' The man saluted.

Lamb shook his head and returned the salute. 'No, Sergeant. You can't. Incidentally, though, what would you have done if I'd said I was a German?'

'Shot you, sir. Through the door, sir. Then scarpered.'

'Lucky me.'

There was a shout from behind the sergeant. 'Dawes, who is it? That French fella again? We could do with a drop more of that brandy he found us before.'

The sergeant half-turned. 'No, sir, it's not the French officer, sir. It's a British officer, sir.'

The room was poorly lit, by the light of just two candles which burned in the necks of two empty wine bottles. It was a humble farmhouse, sparsely furnished and with little in the way of decoration save a single framed engraving and a small black wooden cross which hung above the fireplace in which the miserable remains of an attempt at a fire burned. Moving aside, the sergeant revealed a dining table laid for dinner for one, on the opposite side of which was seated a British officer. Judging from the three pips and a crown at his shoulder, he was a brigadier.

He smiled at Lamb. 'I say, hello. You're one of us. Who are you?'

Before replying, Lamb took in the sight before him. Even in his youth as a subaltern on the Somme and in Paschendaele, Brigadier Julian Meadows, 'Dewy Meadows' to his chums, had never been what one might have called a small man, and what Lamb had presumed might be the universal hardships of soldiering over the past few weeks appeared to have had little effect upon a figure happily formed by years of lunches with similarly clubable fellows and which still swelled the fabric of his cleverly tailored Savile Row service dress. His corpulent form was topped off by an almost bald head, save for a circlet of bright white hair at the temples and a similarly white moustache which splayed out from his top lip. The brigadier burped but managed to suppress the noise and dabbed at his moustache.

'Lieutenant Peter Lamb, sir, North Kents. 6th Brigade. We're trying to get back to our unit.'

The man looked at him in surprise. 'You're adrift, then?'

'Sir.'

'Same here, my boy. My driver took a wrong turn and we've ended up in this midden of a place. Still, the fodder's not at all bad. My driver managed all this.' He waved his hand expansively over the table which, Lamb now noticed, was laid with ham, cooked meat, wine, brandy and half a roast chicken. 'Bloody good cook. Bloody rotten driver. I suppose you realise where we are?'

'Yes, sir.'

'Funny really. Particularly with the Frogs here too. Like the old days, eh?'

'Yes, sir. It must be. I wonder if you'd have any idea, sir, where the rest of my brigade might have got to?'

The man looked at him. 'What? No, can't say that I have. You'd be best to keep going north. Probably catch up with them somewhere.'

'Catch up with them?'

'Yes, generally the entire army's heading north. New plan. Don't suppose you've heard. Frogs seem to be about to throw in the towel. Never did have any staying power. Not after the last lot.'

He looked closely at Lamb. 'Too young for that, I suppose. Weren't you?'

'Yes, sir. But my father served. In the Dardanelles.'

'Dardanelles. That wasn't a war, man. Bloody holiday compared to the Western Front. This is where we fought in hell. Right here. In Belgium. Mud and blood, my boy. Mud and blood.'

Stifling his anger, Lamb replied, 'Yes, sir, I believe it was hell here.'

The brigadier nodded sagaciously, pleased that the young man appeared to agree with his assertion.

'Yes. Quite awful. I'm heading west myself. Pressing engagement. In fact I wonder whether you couldn't be of some use to me. I've a message here from my opposite number on the French staff which simply must get to GHQ soonest. You couldn't oblige and ensure it gets there? Just give it to the senior officer of whichever regiment or brigade HQ you next encounter. He'll do the rest, I'm sure. That's how it works, you see.'

Lamb was dumbstruck. A prior engagement? The man was talking as if he were late for a regimental dinner. 'Wouldn't it be better if you were to take it yourself, sir?'

'Nonsense, man. I'm a Brigadier. Better things to do than deliver messages.'

'But it was given into your hand by the French, sir.'

The officer suddenly grew very serious. 'Precisely. And now I'm giving it into your hand, Lieutenant. Now you get it to GHQ by whatever means you find necessary. That's an order.'

'Sir.'

'Any more of that claret?'

'Right away, sir.'

The brigadier smiled at Lamb. 'Care for a drink?'

'Don't think I should, sir. Do you?'

'Nonsense. Course you should. All officers should drink, what? Should all be able to drink and to get drunk. But not violent. D'you see? That's for the men. Have a drink, Lamb.'

And so Lamb sat down at the table and had a drink with the brigadier and made small talk. They spoke of home and of cricket and the brigadier talked of hunting in Somerset and racing at Newmarket and of his London club in St James's which had ruined its windows with ghastly blackout blinds and he told Lamb how hard it was now to get really good Cognac, and at length after his second glass of wine Lamb managed to persuade the brigadier that his presence really was needed with the platoon and after an interminable goodbye left the house and pulled the door closed behind him.

Lamb stood and breathed in deeply. After the fug of the room the night air was cool and sweet and he felt suddenly alive. He began to walk south, back towards the battlefield.

At the crossroads the French lieutenant and his men

were chatting and laughing. One of them had cranked up a gramophone and a recent popular song by Jean Sablon cut through the night:

J'attendrai, le jour et la nuit, j'attendrai toujours ton
    retour.
J'attendrai, car l'oiseau qui s'enfuit vient chercher
    l'oubli, dans son nid,
Le temps passe et court en battant tristement dans
    mon coeur si lourd
Et pourtant, j'attendrai ton retour.

Walking to a bank of the sunken road, Lamb saw in the moonlight the silhouette of a British tin hat and recognised at once the angular profile beneath it. 'Evening, Tapley.'

The man who was standing sentry swiftly extinguished his cigarette. 'And a fine one, sir. Have you seen the stars?'

Lamb looked up. It was cloudless and the stars twinkled in their heaven as they always had. He spotted the Plough and Orion's Belt and felt comforted – a boy once again by his father's side, a boy in pyjamas, beneath the night sky in Kent, staring in wonder and pride as his father named the constellations.

'Yes, I can see them. Not long till you're relieved, is it? Then I should try and get some sleep, Tapley. We've a long march tomorrow, and who knows where the enemy are.'

The man nodded and smiled at him and it occurred to him that part of his role was that of a father, looking after his family of men, adrift in France, looking to him for leadership and inspiration.

They were like Wellington's men the night before Waterloo, he had decided, retreating up this dirt road. Then on the very next day the great general had turned the tables on his arch enemy with a famous victory. But Lamb suspected that there would be no such chance for his men, or for his army. There would be no second Waterloo. He had been surprised by the attitude of the French officer to the fate of his country and wondered whether it was widespread. How, he wondered, could a nation that had fought with such bravery in the Great War now just give in against the old foe? And this time, Lamb knew, their enemy was not just the old foe, but a new and ghastly one that had risen from the ashes of a country ground down by reparations imposed by the French. Hitler had taken the bones of a broken Germany and fashioned them into a new creature – a nameless horror that must be stopped, whatever it took to do so.

He reached the crossroads and stopped, then turned to look into the starry night down the road along which they had come, back towards the east, and wondered how long it would take the Germans who lay that way to reach the spot on which he now stood. Soon some German officer would be here, gloating over the fact that they had taken the site of Wellington's victory. He lit a cigarette and took a long drag. Then he heard the village clock across the valley strike eight, and after a few last puffs, he threw it down and ground out the light before heading back towards his men, filled with thoughts of home.

5

Lamb and his men arrived on the outskirts of Tournai just as the church clocks were striking the hour and joined a column of British infantry making its slow progress along the cobbled street. Three o'clock, thought Lamb. Good, that would give the men good time to rest before the next day's march. He wondered where their battalion was now – presumably regrouping with the brigade. Two days was a long time to be adrift from your unit. Obviously the first priority was to deliver the brigadier's message. That done, they would set off in earnest in search of the battalion. He decided that he would take the note from the brigadier to the highest-ranking officer in the town and take his cue from him. His own instinct was to go north.

Smart turned to him. 'Blimey, sir. It's like Piccadilly Circus here.'

It looked to Lamb as if every regiment in the British army must be converging on the town, and by every means available. There were Matilda tanks, staff cars, Bedford trucks, Bren carriers and civilian cars and lorries containing troops. Some were even travelling in open hay wagons drawn by horses. Most of the infantry, though, were on foot. As they advanced further into the town it became clear that the German bombers had paid more than a passing a visit here, very recently. Smoking ruins stood on every street. In some cases entire terraces had been reduced to rubble.

Bennett whistled. 'Blimey, sir. This place ain't half taken a pounding. Poor sods. I hope they got out before it happened.'

They passed firemen and civilians working together still trying to extinguish the flames, which continued to burn, mostly from open gas mains. Everywhere there was evidence of the human loss. Clothes and possessions littered the rubble. Lamb saw a woman to his left, half naked, sitting on a pile of bricks. She was sobbing uncontrollably and Lamb wondered what nameless horror had fuelled her grief. As he looked a huge explosion split the air. The men turned to look and to their left saw the façade of several shops tumble to the street. A controlled blast, by the look of it, he thought, trying to stem the fires, and then, sure enough, he saw British engineers laying charges.

They rounded a bend in the street and entered the city centre, or what was left of it. The bombers had known their target, Lamb presumed. This had not been a specific military raid or an attack on factories but simply an attempt to destroy the ancient city and terrorise its population into subjugation. And from what he could see it had almost succeeded. The scene was of utter desolation. Buildings that he presumed had been until hours ago major historic landmarks were now no more than smoking shells. Yet still above them all stood the cathedral with its distinctive towers. And through it all, across roads still being cleared of debris, thousands of British soldiers were making their way.

Bennett spoke. 'Crikey, Mister Lamb, the whole blinkin' army's 'ere. Reckon we might even find our mob in this lot.'

'I doubt it, Sarnt. They've probably headed further north. That would be logical.'

That at least would be what his major, the affable Denis Cooke, would have done. The logical thing. But was there any logic in this war? Any war? Particularly in the sort of war with which he now found himself confronted.

They crossed the river by the main bridge, which, incredibly, was still standing. At a crossroads, standing on an artfully arranged pile of rubble, he found a red-capped British military policeman attempting to direct the traffic and not having much success.

Leaving the men with Bennett, Lamb dodged across the columns. 'I need to find the GOC. I have a vital message for him. Do you know where he might be?'

The man looked blank and did not stop waving his arms. He shook his head. 'Can't say, sir. Sorry. Last time I heard he was in the town hall, but that copped it in the last raid. He'll have moved on by now, sir. Things are very fluid at present.'

Lamb smiled. 'Very fluid.' The classic army euphemism for shambolic. Nonetheless, he decided it would after all be best to make for what was left of the town hall.

'Thank you, Sarnt. You couldn't, I suppose, point us in the direction of the town hall?'

'Just carry on the way you're going, sir. Can't miss it. Great big barrack of a place, it is. Good luck, sir.'

They continued into the town and within minutes were standing in a small park in the centre of which, as the MP had predicted, stood his 'great barrack of a place', a seventeenth-century château lumped onto part of a medieval monastery. At the moment, though, it looked rather less than imposing. Bombs had rained down here, and the grass was pock-marked with craters. But where the carefully manicured gardens had not been touched the flowers still bloomed. It was a grotesque sight, made all the more so by the row upon row of corpses which were being laid out on the grass, their legs sticking out grotesquely from beneath the blankets and sheets in which they had been wrapped to preserve something of their dignity in death. He saw a few legs in battledress but they were civilians mostly. Children too. Lamb didn't bother to count. The town hall was a mess, with its roof caved in, rafters sticking up like teeth and two walls gone. It seemed to him unlikely that it was still functioning as the British HQ. On the right, though, a smaller, similarly elegant building was still standing. Outside two British soldiers stood sentry.

Lamb turned to Bennett. 'I'm going in there, Sarnt. Looks more promising. Get the men away from here, will you? Don't want them looking at any more dead bodies more than they have to, particularly civilians.'

As Bennett led the platoon away across the park, Lamb crossed the grass to the door of the building and to his delight managed to talk his way past the sentries by mention that he had a message from Brigadier Meadows. Once inside he was met with a scene of some confusion. Men were walking and running across his path and no one seemed to be aware of him. He tried to accost a passing captain but was ignored. Directly ahead of him was a passageway lined with nineteenth-century portraits of black-clad council officials, and more from instinct than anything else he walked down it. No one stopped him. At the end was a door; Lamb turned the brass handle and entered. He found himself in a large library, lined on all sides with well-stocked mahogany shelves.

At the far end of the room, beneath a low-hung chandelier, a tall, lean man, a colonel from his insignia and red tabs, was pouring over several maps spread out over a table with another staff officer, a major. As Lamb entered they both looked up.

The major spoke. 'Yes? What is it now? We're very busy in here. If it's that bloody mayor again, tell him that his surrender to the Jerries will have to wait. We're not planning to go anywhere just yet.'

He turned back to the map.

Lamb coughed and saluted. 'No, sir. Lieutenant Lamb, sir. North Kents.'

The colonel looked up this time, returned a casual salute and raised an eyebrow. 'Yes?'

'I have a vitally important message from Brigadier Meadows, sir, from 1 Corps. He ordered me to get it to GHQ by whatever means possible.'

The major and colonel looked at each other, then the colonel spoke, smiling. 'And I suppose I'm the nearest thing that you can find to GHQ?'

'Yes, sir. I suppose so, sir.'

'Yes, you're very probably right. I think I am.' He turned to the major. 'I am, aren't I, Simpson?'

'Yes, sir. I'm very much afraid you are. At least here in Tournai at present.'

The colonel frowned. 'A signal from Dewy Meadows? A vital message? That hardly sounds likely. Not from Dewy.'

Lamb cringed. He had of course thought all along that the brigadier seemed an unlikely source of vital information, if not actually bogus. But nothing surprised him now in the army.

The colonel continued, puzzled, 'Where did you find him?'

Lamb knew as he said it that his answer would sound absurd. 'At Waterloo, sir. On the battlefield, that is. He was bivouacked there.'

The colonel laughed out loud. 'Waterloo, eh? Trust Dewy. What the devil was he doing there?' He looked down at the map. 'Isn't that in the French sector anyway? Simpson?'

The major nodded. 'French Second Corps, sir. Though we think they've been overrun by now.'

'Poor old Dewy's probably in the bag by now then. That'll teach him to get lost.' He turned back to Lamb. 'He was lost?'

'Yes, sir.'

'And you got through to here with the message? How the devil did you manage that?'

'I just followed the map, sir, and stayed off the main roads. There were air attacks, dozens of them, sir, and refugees. Thousands. But we just read the map. It wasn't that difficult.'

The colonel nodded. 'We? How many men are you?'

'My platoon, sir. That is, less casualties. Twenty-six at present.'

'You brought twenty-six men with a message from Dewy Meadows, cross-country to here, presumably through enemy lines, and then you found me. You did well. You're quite a man, Mister . . . what did you say your name was again?'

'Lamb, sir. Peter Lamb.'

The colonel paused for a moment, then looked at the major. 'Lamb? Wasn't that last dispatch about a chap called Lamb?'

The major nodded. 'Yes, sir. Report came down from the Coldstreams. Apparently he held up a German division at the Dyle. Took out a bridging party single handed with grenades. They thought he might be mentioned in dispatches.'

'Was that you?'

Lamb nodded. 'Yes, sir. I suppose it was.'

The colonel thought for a moment and then looked at the major. 'Do you think?'

'Well, sir. If he is who he says he is, then he's the best we've seen here. It's worth a go, sir.'

The colonel looked back at Lamb and seemed as if he was about to say something. But then he stopped and stared hard at Lamb. 'Hold on. Who won the cup last year?'

Lamb frowned. 'Sorry, sir?'

'Who won the cup, man? The cup. The football league. Who won it?'

Lamb racked his brain. Names tumbled out – Everton, Liverpool, Chelsea. Football had never been his game. Rugby and cricket, yes, from school. He had been in the first XV, full back. But football? He had of course mugged up enough to be able to talk to the men about it. A fellow officer had once told him that was one of the smartest things a subaltern could do. He tried desperately to remember. The colonel was looking worried. He turned to the major who, Lamb noticed, had flipped open the flap of the holster at his belt.

Then suddenly Lamb had it. 'No one won it, sir. There was no league last year. It was abandoned after war was declared. Everton won the first division . . . and Portsmouth won the FA Cup.'

The colonel gave a sigh of relief and smiled. 'Good God, man. That was close. Didn't think you'd get it. Thought we'd have to shoot you. Well done, Lamb. Sorry. Can't be too careful. Fifth columnists. Now where's this vital note?'

Lamb walked forward and handed over the paper to the colonel, who carefully unfolded it and read.

Lamb was astonished. Here he was surrounded by chaos and yet somehow the news of his exploit had reached the staff. Some things, he thought, still worked in the British army. And then he wondered whether, if they knew about that, they had also heard of his blowing up the civilians on the bridge. He hoped that Fortescue had been discreet.

The colonel looked at him and smiled. 'So you managed to give Jerry a bit of a bloody nose, didn't you?'

'Well, we did manage to cut up a column pretty badly, sir. Three days ago.'

The colonel looked at him, narrowing his eyes. 'Well done, Lamb. Good work. You might even get a gong.'

The colonel was still smiling but Lamb worried that he might know about the civilian deaths. He wondered whether he should explain it, but did not know what he could say. He froze, waiting for the inevitable 'but'. Instead the colonel beamed at him. 'Yes, damn good work, eh, Simpson?'

'Yes, sir. Damn good.'

The colonel turned back to the note before handing it to the major, who handed it back. After a while the colonel folded it up and laid it on the desk. He stared at it for a while and then looked at Lamb, fixing him with deep brown eyes. 'Have you read this?'

'No, sir. Of course not. Absolutely not.'

'No. You wouldn't, would you? Silly of me. But I think you'd better have a look now as you're here, before I give it to the General whenever I find him, seeing as you went to the trouble of getting it here.' He handed the piece of paper to Lamb. 'Go on then, man.'

Lamb took it and looked. It was headed in French: 'Headquarters 1st Army' and bore the insignia of the French military. It was dated 16 May. It read:

'No information. Communications cut. All liaison unworkable. Rear areas blocked with convoys and wrecked columns. Petrol trains ablaze. Utter chaos.'

Lamb looked up from the paper at the colonel. 'The Brigadier told me it was urgent. I thought it must be information about the enemy.'

67

'It was urgent. Two days ago. Not any more, though. Meadows hasn't a clue. It just tells us what we already know. The German First Panzer Division under Guderian have broken through at Amiens and cut off the French 1st and 9th Armies. To put it bluntly, we're surrounded.'

The major walked away from the table and stared out of the window at a desolation which mirrored the destitution in his soul.

Lamb gazed at the colonel: 'Christ. I'm sorry, sir. But I mean . . . God help us.'

'Yes, God help us, Lamb. Although I doubt whether even he can now.'

The colonel pointed to the map. 'In four days we've been pushed back sixty miles. And that's only in the north. At least here we're making a stand. It's taken Guderian's Panzers less than three days to reach Amiens. Another two and he'll be at the sea. 7th Panzer Division are closing on Arras with the 5th, and the 6th and 8th are pushing through the centre. As far as we can tell. But, to be perfectly frank, they could be anywhere.'

Lamb looked down at the map as the colonel's hands swept across it, and instantly saw the extent of the disaster.

The colonel went on, 'The Germans have been training for this for years. They're fighting fit and they damn well know it. And what have we been doing, Lamb? We've been sitting on our fat backsides doing sweet Fanny Adams.' There was real bitterness in his voice. 'Britain is a great country, Lamb. The greatest in the world, with a strong, resolute people and a powerful Empire. But look at the men you brought out here. Look at the British army. Our soldiers.'

Lamb frowned and began to speak, 'My sergeant, sir . . .'

'Yes, I dare say your sergeant's a good man, and a few others besides him. But what of the rest? Think about it.'

'They're a good bunch, sir. Loyal as they come.'

'I've no doubt as to that, Lieutenant. But just how fit are they?'

Lamb bristled. 'They can march, sir. And they can fight.'

'But can they march and fight one after the other, laddie? Hitler's Nazis can do that. That's why they've come sweeping through Belgium. That's why we're sitting here fifty miles back, trying to work out what we can do and waiting for their damned tanks to roll into town.'

It was hard to argue against the colonel's logic. It backed up everything Lamb had seen so far.

'Lamb, your men, our men, this army. The good few aside. You must see, they're gutter scrapings, the victims of the depression. It's not just the army that's been starved of resources. The entire country's been living on subsistence rations. Save for a privileged few. Me and Meadows included, if you want. And where are most of those fat cats now? On the General Staff.'

Lamb knew he was right. Many in his regiment were men laid off before the General Strike, or their sons – men who had been brought up on thin porridge and meat just once a week, men who had been offered the promise of a future they never saw, and little else. They were underfed and ill-educated. He was leading the legacy of the last twenty years. He thought of the brigadier with his roast chicken and brandy.

The colonel continued: 'I tell you, Lamb, something's got to be done. And fast. D'you know one of our major problems? Our tanks' guns can't penetrate their tanks' hull armour. Not even the new Matildas have a real chance, and most of the others only have machine guns. And have you seen what these new 88-millimetre guns of theirs can do to one of our tanks? They were designed as anti-aircraft guns, for Christ's sake, and the Jerries have started using them against our armour. We haven't

69

a chance. We're the worst-trained, worst-equipped army ever to be sent by Britain to fight on foreign soil. And that's saying something for the nation that fought in the Crimea and the Afghan wars.'

Lamb was taking it all in. He looked closely at the map. Saw the blue pencil lines marking the British and French corps and divisions. It was true. They were cut off and being pushed closer and closer towards the French coast.

'Won't the French be able to break through and cut the German lines? What about their tanks?'

The colonel sighed. 'It would be good to think so, and in the last lot they might have done just that. But this French army is very different to the one I fought alongside in '17. They're sick of war. The French have all but thrown in the towel, and Churchill knows it.'

Lamb wondered how the colonel was able to know what the Prime Minister thought and began to realise that he might be something more than a mere colonel.

The colonel looked over the piles on his desk and found another piece of paper. He handed it to Lamb. 'Here, read that now. Then tell me your thoughts.'

Lamb read. On writing paper headed 'British Broadcasting Corporation' it was dated 18.30 hours, 14 May. That was three days ago.

For immediate broadcast to the nation: All small boat owners are requested to present themselves with their vessels as quickly as possible to a representative of the Admiralty.

He frowned, 'I'm sorry, what does it mean, sir?'

'What do you think it means?'

'It sounds as if we might be trying to get together a sort of people's navy. All the boats we can get.'

'Yes, that's about it.'

'But why would we do that? Unless . . . But that's ridiculous.'

'Yes. I think you've got it now. We're preparing to evacuate the entire army, or whatever there might be left of it. We want to take them off the beaches back to England.'

'The entire army, sir?'

'That's right. As many as we can. Frogs, too, if we can.'

'Can it be done?

He took a long pause. 'No one's ever tried. There are two schools of thought. Gort's behind it. Think the PM is too. The Frenchies aren't keen, though. As you might have guessed.'

'Where can we manage it?'

'The Channel ports. We had thought of Calais alone but it would seem that we need Boulogne and Dunkirk too. If we can get the small craft onto the beaches we might be able to ferry the men out to the Navy.'

'So we are running away then.'

'If we are going to be able to continue to fight this war then we have to save what's left of the BEF. The French are sunk. I have that on the highest authority. And I do mean the highest. There is no way that we can hope now to meet and repulse a German attack in the north. We can only retreat to victory.'

'So are you telling me that I should make my way to the Channel ports, sir?'

The colonel shook his head. 'No, I shouldn't do that if I were you. You seem a very able soldier and I am going to give you what may well be the best piece of advice you'll get in this war. Get yourself and your men away to the west. There's no point in going any further north. Jerry's already cut our communications and you'll never get through, but he's still chasing our tails to the west. Besides, up there you'll be one among tens, hundreds of thousands scrabbling for a place on those boats at Dunkirk. No, laddie, the west is your best bet. If I were you I'd duck down to Arras and then head for the Somme. You'll still find Jerries, but there may not be quite so many of them.'

'The Somme, sir?'

'Not the old battlefield. Further downstream, towards the coast. I know it seems unlikely, but we've a division heading down there now. Pulled away from the Saar yesterday. 51st Highland, General Fortune. The original plan was that if this situation arose and the French could be rallied then it would be the nucleus of a fresh BEF. But to be perfectly frank it looks increasingly unlikely that the French will stand at all. So it's likely that we'll have to get the Scots off as well. Just ten thousand of them. Should be easier there than with the half million up at Calais and Dunkirk.' He paused and stared at Lamb. 'Actually, I've an idea. Lamb, I want you to do something for me. And this really is vitally important. Not like Meadows's nonsense. Communications are shot to pieces or near as dammit with General Fortune's HQ, and we have no way of letting him know the situation. I want you to take him a message, from me.'

He looked across at the major. 'Simpson, write this down please, will you?'

He looked back at Lamb and paused, then said, 'Tell him that the Jerries have cut us off at Amiens and the French look as if they're about to give in. Or pretty damn soon. If that happens tell him we're going to get them all away. All of his division. The plan is to get them off from Le Havre. Tell him that they should hold out on the Somme until further notice and bear in mind that Le Havre needs to be kept accessible. The French might order

72

him south – he's under their command – but if he has to fall back he should make for Le Havre. Tell him that whatever else he might hear, from whatever source, even Churchill himself, ships are on their way. Tell them at all costs that they should not surrender without further orders. No surrender. Got it? They hang on until the ships arrive.'

Lamb looked at him. 'Are you sure it's me you want to do this, sir? Perhaps a dispatch rider would be quicker. Or a team of them. Surely that sort of order should come from someone on the staff? Shouldn't I try and rejoin my unit, sir?'

The colonel shook his head. 'No use, Lamb. Isn't that right, Simpson? Dispatch riders are no go. Being picked off all the time by Jerry snipers. And you can forget your unit for the time being, Lamb. Very soon they'll just be one of hundreds trying to get home any way they can. It's up to you to do the same. Besides, I can't spare anyone on the staff, laddie. Even if I knew where they all were any more. No, you'll do. And that's an order. You'll have to do. In fact I think you're just the man for the job. If you can hold up an entire Jerry regiment with a few grenades, Lamb, seems to me you've a far better chance of getting through than any staff Johnny. And I think a few more heroics might be of use to you in future.'

'Yes, sir. I see.'

'That's it then. Well done.'

He looked to the major, who gave him the piece of paper on which he had been writing, and a pen. The colonel read it over briefly and then signed it. He gave the note to Lamb and returned the pen to Simpson. 'And now you'd better get a move on. I'm afraid you can't show that note to anyone but the General or someone on his staff. Oh, and one other vital thing. Of course, almost forgot. To make sure that you get to General Fortune and that he believes you, tell him that Colonel "R" sent you. Just that, Colonel "R". He'll know exactly who and what you mean. He'll believe you. Got it? Colonel "R". That's all you need to know.'

'Yes, sir.'

The colonel smiled at him. 'Good. Well, good luck, Lieutenant. Perhaps we'll meet again. I'd like to think so.'

6

It took Lamb a little time to digest what had just happened. He had walked in thinking that he was at the end of a mission to deliver a message, and had left charged with another much greater task. How, he wondered, had that been managed? How had he got himself into this mess? Now, rather than heading north to find his regiment and try to get back home, he had been ordered to take his men west by a colonel whom he knew only as 'R' to find a general commanding a Scottish division cut off from the main force and to tell that general that his men were to fight to the death.

He shook his head and spoke out loud to himself as he walked from the corridor into the buzzing atrium of the mayoral building: 'You stupid bugger.' No one heard him.

It wasn't, he thought, as if he would ever avoid such tasks. He was only too keen to prove himself and would have volunteered for anything that might help his country. But this really did seem a ludicrous errand, and for all he knew as hair-brained as the last. Why, he wondered, should he really trust the colonel – Colonel 'R' or whatever his name was – any more than the brigadier?

Certainly the man had seemed more *compos mentis* than Dewy Meadows, but he wondered if he had lost the ability to tell any more. Everyone seemed as mad as each other in this strange kind of warfare.

But, he reasoned, what alternative did he have? To go against what had effectively been a direct order and not to deliver the message to General Fortune and head north to find the regiment? Who knew where that might land him? Fortune might never know to fight on. He might try to withdraw south, deeper into France. Then they would risk losing an entire division if France fell. This was not what Lamb had really expected his war to be like. He had seen himself at the head of a platoon, leading from the front, as he had done with the German column, not on an errand to find some brass hat and tell him to retreat. But if that was to be his role, then so be it. They all of them had some part to play in overthrowing the Nazis, however small and apparently insignificant or crazy it might seem.

He found the platoon on the far side of the park, away from the area being used as a temporary morgue for the victims of the air raids. They were sitting on the grass, smoking and chatting. Bennett saw Lamb approaching and stood up. 'Officer present. Put those fags out. Snap to it.'

The men grumbled and stood up, grinding their cigarette butts into the grass. Lamb reached them. 'Stand easy. We've been given new orders. We're heading west.'

The men stared at him. Corporal Mays spoke. 'Sorry, sir, but I thought we was trying to find the battalion. Haven't they gone north?'

Bennett stared at him. 'Mays.'

'It's all right, Sarnt. Yes, Mays, you're quite right, they have, and yes, we were – heading north that is. But all that's changed, I'm afraid. We've just been given an important job to do. Fresh orders from on high. In any case I doubt very much whether we'd find the battalion now. From what I've just been told the situation is really very fluid at the moment.'

Bennett smiled at the expression.

Lamb went on. 'So let's get to it, shall we? We need to make for Arras. That's about thirty-five miles away. We'll see how we do and try to find a billet on the way.'

But Valentine hadn't finished. 'May I ask, sir, what the nature might be of this "important job" we have to do?'

Lamb detected the sarcasm in his tone, but didn't show his annoyance. 'No, I'm sorry, Corporal. I'm afraid that I can't tell you that. At least not yet. Suffice it to say that it is important and we should feel honoured to have been given it.'

Valentine smirked in that way that irked Lamb so intensely. He ignored it and turned to Bennett. 'All right, Sarnt, let's get on. We don't want to be caught in any more air raids here.'

Unsure of his bearings, Lamb retraced their steps through the ruined town amid the sound of more explosions as more streets were torn down by the Royal Engineers, and they found themselves back at the crossroads. The MP sergeant had gone, to be replaced by another whose efforts, to judge by the jam of trucks and staff cars on all sides, were meeting with a similar lack of success. Leaving the chaos behind, Lamb wheeled them to the left, through the sad, dusty streets, into the Rue St Martin, past broken houses and the smashed possessions of their absent occupants lying across the cobbles. Ahead of them a long line of refugees stretched away far down the road. For a change, though, there were none of the usual accompanying files of British soldiers, and they seemed to be the only unit heading south west. Lamb was hardly surprised. If the British were to use this road it would be to fall back on

Arras, and according to the major they were not planning to go anywhere at the moment.

They marched at a steady pace, in single file, with each section or weapons group of the platoon travelling on alternate sides of the road, passing the slow-moving civilians, who hardly gave them a glance, so caught up were they in their own private miseries. No one spoke and there was no sound save for the steady tramp of the men's boots and the clattering and jangling of the pots and pans hanging from the civilian carts. As they reached the outskirts of the town and the shattered buildings began to give way to open fields and trees, Lamb fell back to his usual position on the march in the 'O' group, with Smart and with Valentine and Briggs, the commanders of number two and three sections, close behind with the two runners.

They had gone no more than a mile down the road when they heard it. From directly behind them a series of explosions tore through the afternoon. They turned and saw the skies behind them above Tournai filled with a swarm of black aeroplanes and watched the bombs falling like evil confetti from their open bellies. As they hit the ground the earth shook, flames leapt up and great columns of black smoke rose high above the city.

Smart summed up all their thoughts. 'Christ. Poor devils.'

The refugees had seen it too, and a terrible wailing now began to come from them. Their homes were being torn apart, and friends and family they had left behind were dying with the British under the black rain.

Lamb turned back to the front. 'Come on. Nothing we can do about it now.'

He wondered if the colonel and the major had found shelter, and the frustrated MPs. The town would be even more chaotic after that lot, he thought, and for an instant the idea came to him again of abandoning the colonel's madcap mission. Perhaps the man had been killed. Who then would know about his order? But the idea passed as quickly as it came, with a feeling of guilt at having even considered it. He had been given an order and it was vital that he should transmit the colonel's message to General Fortune, though yet again he wondered at why a mere colonel should be giving a message to a general. And what on earth was all that Colonel 'R' business about, he wondered. It was like something out of a novel by Childers or Buchan. For a moment Lamb wondered whether he might be being drawn into something more complex than merely delivering a message. But then he thought the better of it and dismissed it as fantasy.

Behind them the bombs continued to fall on Tournai. Lamb turned to see yet another wave of the large, twin-engined bombers hovering in the sky, bigger than the Stukas they had encountered, planes with the capacity to obliterate entire towns rather than just kill troops and destroy tanks on the ground.

Bennett was beside him. 'Lucky we left when we did, sir. You were right. Poor devils.'

'Yes, the Jerries seem intent on flattening the place. That's one lesson we can take away from this campaign. Once they've started something they tend to finish the job.'

They left the weeping refugees to watch the destruction of their homes and hurried past the column. Soon, Lamb knew, this road would be filled with British troops, pulling back from Tournai as was inevitable, and he wanted to make sure that he had a good head start before that happened.

The country had opened out now and even the shelter of the trees had gone. It was incredibly flat, with a low horizon that he guessed must stretch for ten miles on either side before it hit poplars or buildings. He felt horribly exposed. There were ditches on either side of the road, and those he supposed would have to do as cover should they be attacked from above.

The pace seemed desperately slow to Lamb and there were no songs now. He almost suggested one, but thought better of it. There was a time for such things, and too much had happened. They all knew it. At length they found themselves among more buildings, a few red brick houses and on the left a huge factory. Closed, by the look of it. A sign told them they were entering the village of Orchies and Lamb realised that while his mind had been wandering they had in fact been travelling at a good pace.

He called to Bennett. 'Sarnt, we'll halt for the night at Douai. It's about another ten miles. We'll make it by sunset, easily.'

There was a groan from some of the men. Bennett answered it. 'All right, you can still walk, can't you? You'll be thankful of it tomorrow when we've got less of a way to go to Arras.'

Valentine spoke from the rear of the 'O' Group. 'Sergeant, don't you think it would be better to go all the way to Arras now?'

Bennett heard him. 'Not your place to argue, Corporal Valentine. Mister Lamb has given an order. You're here to obey it.'

They carried on, and while he kept his eyes on the countryside around them Lamb's thoughts drifted away from the immediate scene. He wondered what they would make of this at home, if they ever found out. How could he possibly ever tell his mother about what he had done at the bridge? How could he tell them of what he had seen? Of the death and the ghastly wounds. Of what weapons can do to a body. Could he, he wondered even tell them about the mission he was now on? He wondered what their fate would be, and then his mind filled with the secret terror that haunted every soldier and which you had to brush aside as soon as it came on: the question of whether he would live. He had not noticed that Valentine had changed position and was walking directly behind him now, and for once he was glad when he heard the man's voice.

'Sir. We're nearly at Douai, aren't we? I don't mean to be disrespectful, sir, or to challenge your authority, but don't you think it would be a better idea to go straight on to Arras?'

'No, Valentine, I don't. The men need to rest, and we need to scrounge some rations. Douai is the obvious choice. It probably hasn't been bombed yet either.'

Lamb chided himself for having to justify his decision to a corporal. What was it about Valentine? He was determined now to get rid of him at the earliest opportunity. This, he presumed, would not be until they made it back to England. If they ever did. But he thought that he might take the opportunity to sow the seeds of a potential move:

'What I can't understand, Valentine, is, if you have so many bright ideas, why you're still a corporal. I mean, a chap like you with a sound education, an obviously clever brain, you should be on an officer training plan. Have you ever thought about it?'

Valentine smiled and, as always when he did, Lamb felt a sense of distaste. 'I didn't want the responsibility, sir, you see. Don't really think that I'd make an officer. Prefer to take orders.'

'When we make it back to the battalion, Valentine, and I'm quite sure we will eventually, I'm putting you up for a commission.'

Valentine continued to smile. 'I don't think that would be an awfully good idea, sir.'

81

'You don't?'

'No, sir.'

'Why exactly?'

'I told you, sir. Can't be doing with the responsibility. Like what happened to you on the bridge, sir. I couldn't very well live with that on my conscience, you see, sir. Must be very hard for you, sir.'

Lamb tried to stifle his rage. 'That be damned, Valentine. You'll be an officer and like it.'

'Sir.'

Their conversation at an end, Valentine returned to his place in the line. Lamb cursed himself. He had been goaded by Valentine and unwittingly had shown his hand. Worse than that, he was not sure how the man had managed it. There was just something about him that made Lamb drop his guard. Yes. He was decided. Corporal Valentine had to go, and the sooner the better.

7

It was close to 1 o'clock in the afternoon on the 21st when they finally reached the suburbs of Arras. The town had suffered badly from shelling and air attack, and many of the roadside buildings had been hit. Some were still smoking, others had had their walls ripped off to reveal domestic interiors that looked like stage sets, thought Lamb, with everything perfectly in place, except the floor. Even pictures and clocks remained hanging on the wall-papered walls. In one half-demolished house a wrought-iron bedstead and mattress hung suspended on a jagged section of wooden flooring, its sheets flung back as if the owner had just leapt from his bed.

They marched into Arras, attempting as usual to look as soldierly as possible despite their appearance. But the atmosphere was very different here to that of Tournai. As they filtered into the town Lamb saw a column of British infantry on a road to the left advancing to converge with them. As they grew closer he caught sight of their eyes and saw in them utter despair similar to what he had seen in the faces of the refugees. He walked across to an officer, a young lieutenant of roughly his own age, who still had something of the

83

military about him. 'I say. Who are you? Where have you come from?'

The young man smiled. 'Where we've come from is not somewhere you want to go. We're Royal Sussex. They caught us up at Albert. Bloody Panzers. Went through us like a knife through butter. Christ, it was bloody murder. What I want to know is where were our tanks and our artillery? We had nothing. Nothing. And where were the bloody French? And the Raff. They just tore us to pieces. We didn't have a chance.'

Lamb could see that the man was about to burst into tears, and he steadied him with a hand on his arm. 'All right, old chap. You're safe now. This is Arras.'

From the ranks came an awful yell: 'No, no. Oh God, no. Not that.'

The officer turned in alarm as a sergeant comforted the man, and then he looked back to Lamb. 'One of my men. Saw his best mate run over by a tank, poor bugger. Crushed everything below his chest and pushed his brains out through his head. That's what they do if they hit you.'

Lamb recoiled in horror. 'Good God. Poor sod.'

'Nearly drove him mad. Then he got shot in the face himself. Blinded. Now he keeps seeing his mate.'

They had fallen into step with the Sussex now and were walking together into the centre of the town, into the old square that in the Great War had been used as a casualty clearing station. Lamb recognised it from his father's post-cards and saw that it had been put to the same use again now as men lay on stretchers and on blankets across its cobbles. In the far corner Lamb noticed a group of officers who appeared to be giving directions.

Lamb turned to Bennett. 'Halt the men here, Sarnt. They can stand easy and take a break. Find some char if you can. There's bound to be a wagon somewhere.'

He said goodbye to the Sussex officer and pointed

towards the command group: 'I'm off over there. Looks like someone's trying to make order out of this chaos.'

As Bennett gave the order to rest, Lamb strode across the Grand Place, taking care to make his way around the wounded, whose number seemed to be growing by the minute. He approached one of the officers, who had walked away from the central group and was writing notes in a pad – a captain in battledress wearing the insignia of the Northumbrian Fusiliers. He saluted. 'Excuse me, sir. Lieutenant Lamb, North Kents.' The officer acknowledged him and Lamb continued: 'The thing is, I'm trying to find my unit.'

The man looked at him with weary eyes and smiled, shaking his head. 'Isn't everyone? 'Fraid it's no use, old chap. You're all adrift, more or less. Where have you come from? Sorry – Clarke, motorcycle platoon, Northumbrian Fusiliers.'

'We've just marched here from Tournai, sir, but we lost contact with the battalion back at Wavre.'

The man nodded. 'Then likely as not they'll be further north. You're miles off track. Useless to try and find them. Not now at least. Anyway, I'm sure that we can use you here. We're going to attack.'

'Attack?' He looked around at the scene of desolation, and the hundreds of wounded men, some it seemed close to death. 'Might I ask with what, sir?'

The captain smiled. 'Well you may. Two battalions of infantry, apparently, and seventy-five tanks. Oh, and a few armoured cars and anti-tank guns and us lot. We're going in two columns.'

'Is that it?'

The officer ignored his lack of etiquette. ''Fraid it is. We were supposed to be two divisions, but something got a bit muddled and we're all there is. Still, got to try something, haven't we?'

Lamb pointed across to the staff officers who were conferring over a map. 'Can I ask who that is, sir?'

'General Martel, and that's General Franklyn. That's why the attacking force is called Frankforce. I'm attached to him directly, which explains why I know so much. I should attach whatever men you've got to that unit over there, if I were you. 8th Durham Light Infantry. They're attached to the right column. They'll find a use for you. We need every man who can fire a rifle.'

Lamb paused for a moment, unsure as to whether he should argue that he was already on a mission under orders from the colonel. It did not take him too long however, to realise that this was neither the time nor the place for such action. He would have to accept the captain's orders and join in the attack. He smiled.

'What exactly are we attacking, sir?'

'Well, no one's quite sure. Certainly not the generals there. We know that there's a Panzer division out there, and as likely as not there's an SS unit behind them. That's how they operated in Poland. But we'll need to take some prisoners to find out who they are.'

Lamb stared at him, incredulous. 'Sorry, sir. Do I understand that we're attacking two divisions with barely a brigade? That's suicide.'

'Perhaps. But those our our orders, Lieutenant. Gort's promised the French that we would mount an offensive and I'm very much afraid that we're it. We're all there is to spare. H Hour is 1400. Good luck.'

Lamb returned to his men who, as predicted, with the ever-present resourcefulness of the British Tommy to sniff out a brew, had managed to find themselves some tea.

Bennett handed Lamb a tin mug. 'Tea, sir?'

'Thank you, Sarnt.'

Lamb took a welcome swig and spoke. 'Well, we're moving off.'

'Sir?'

'We're going to attack.'

Bennett looked at him. 'Attack, sir? Just us, sir?'

'No, Sarnt. We're attaching to the Durham Light Infantry. Going in behind a tank attack. Could be a bit messy.'

'I see, sir. Shall I tell the lads.'

'No, Sarnt. I think perhaps I'd better do that.'

He turned to the men, who had separated into smaller groups, his three sections and the odds and sods by themselves. As usual Valentine was standing alone, smoking his Turkish cigarette with an air of detachment.

Lamb addressed the little group. 'Now, we've been given new orders, men. We're going into an attack with the Durham Light Infantry. There's little hope, I'm afraid, of trying to find the battalion now. Seems they're probably much further north. So I've decided it's best to stick with our friends here. We'll go in behind a tank attack on the German lines to the south, and with any luck we might push them back and give everyone a bit of breathing space. Then I'll decide what we should do next. The DLI can use every man they can get.' He turned to the odds and sods. 'That applies to you too. But if you want to try and find your own units I quite understand. That's your duty. But as far as I'm concerned you'd be more than welcome to come with us and I'd love to have you.'

There was some murmuring and nodding among the men. Lamb saw Mitchell shake his head and then Stanton and Blake turn on him aggressively and mutter something inaudible. Eventually Mitchell shrugged and McKracken nodded and smiled. A few of them lit fresh cigarettes as the Scots sergeant turned to Lamb.

'We're with you, sir. Proud to be.'

Lamb turned to Bennett. 'Right, Sarnt, we'd better be ready to move. Check weapons and ammo. I dare say you'll be able to draw fresh rounds from the DLI if you need them. H Hour is 1400. Best not be late for the party.'

For all their readiness, though, it was shortly after 3 o'clock by Lamb's watch that the assault began. The two columns approached the enemy from Neuville and Vimy, at a distance of about a kilometre from one another. The left column was led by the Matilda tanks of the 4th Royal Tank Regiment and the right by the 7th Royal Tank Regiment, while the infantry moved in their wake, using a tactic that had been devised during the Great War by generals who had learned their craft as cavalrymen. Lamb had been across to talk to the CO of a company of the DLI who had eagerly accepted the extra hands. His platoon had attached itself to the company, moving up with the right column, and were able to operate again as a platoon. He was pleased too that the odds and sods had chosen to stay with him, apparently having built up a respect for their new temporary officer.

They pushed on now through the outskirts of the town and over the open ground of wide farmland, an additional fourth platoon in the extreme left-hand company of the DLI, and Lamb noticed that the Matildas had crushed everything in their path – trees, carts, cars and of course men. He marvelled at the sheer power of the machines but was horribly aware that the German armour was stronger and could if given the chance do much worse damage.

It seemed to him that everywhere the ground was littered with German corpses and smashed anti-tank guns, and he could see the men taking heart from it. He turned to Smart: 'Now they're paying for it. We've broken through, Smart. This is it.'

To their right he saw a column of Germans, weaponless and with their hands on their heads, being led back by men of the DLI. The platoon and the rest of the company cheered.

Mays spoke. 'They're on the run, sir.'

'Looks like it, Corporal. Let's hope we keep it up.'

They were moving faster now in the wake of the tanks. They entered a village and continued south west. Lamb looked at a signpost. 'Warlus 5 km'. That was about three miles, he reckoned. They had moved off the major roads now and were crossing open fields along a single-lane track.

Corporal Mays was close by. 'Blimey, sir. They've upped sticks and scarpered.'

It was true. He realised that they hadn't been fired on by a German since the advance had begun. Shells had come in to their right and left but there was no evidence of infantry resistance.

Moving on, they began to pass the corpses of men in different uniforms. The green flashes of the Wehrmacht were replaced by black facings with a white skull and crossbones and two lightning flashes. Lamb knew who the dead men were. SS. The elite of Hitler's army. Ruthless Nazis, better trained and equipped than any other. But even they had been broken by the new British tanks, thought Lamb. Perhaps they did have a chance after all.

He turned to Valentine, who had appeared at his side. 'Look, Corporal. We're even beating the SS, Hitler's elite troops.'

Valentine smiled and nodded. 'Very good, sir, that is good. We do seem to be doing rather well.' There was something in the tone of his words, however, almost a sense of sarcasm, that told Lamb that they were not really meant.

Bennett was with him. 'Look, sir. These blokes in black. They're like the Guards, aren't they, sir? I mean, if we're killing them we can't be doing bad.'

'No, Sarnt, you're right. I don't think we're doing so badly at all. They seem to be breaking.'

Lamb and his men had moved into open formation,

spread out across the track and into the fields on either side, in line with number 2 platoon of the DLI. He looked closely at the village ahead, watching for any sign of movement, the slightest glint of light on steel, which would give away the position of an enemy sniper.

They walked forward steadily through fields dappled with sunshine. The crops grew high, and it was an effort pushing one's boots through the tightly packed stalks. Lamb noticed the large numbers of bright red poppies. There were other flowers too, vivid blue cornflowers among them, and while there were no birds Lamb saw a rabbit run from him away through the waving wheat, towards the village.

They continued, waiting for the first shot from the enemy position. Brigade intelligence had reported that while many of the German troops had fallen back, at least one company, if not more, had remained here in Warlus. The tanks had done their job. Now it was the infantry's turn. Clear the village, they had been told. And that meant street by street, house by house. A bloody business, thought Lamb. It seemed that the population had gone. At least he could detect no sign of civilian life, save for the debris that littered the streets.

From their rear the 3-inch mortars of the DLI company began to throw shells over their heads and into the houses and yards ahead. Lamb and his men could hear nothing but the whine of the incoming rounds, the explosions and the more distant rumble of heavier shells as the tanks and guns that had detached to their flanks continued to fire. They were within two hundred yards of the first buildings now. Lamb could see the houses quite clearly, red pantiled, brick and lime-washed walls, muddied with the dirt of two centuries. The village was dominated by a tall church tower and he knew that if the Germans were still here that would be where they would have positioned their observers and any heavy weapons they might have. He turned to Bennett. 'Watch that tower, Sarnt. It's perfect for a machine-gun post.'

He had hardly spoken when there was a flash from the belfry, and instants later bullets ploughed up the earth to their left and right. One of them hit Potter square in the chest, killing him instantly; another took three fingers of the left hand of one of the runners, and he fell to the ground, moaning.

'Christ. They're in there. Get down.'

The platoon hit the ground as more rounds zinged past them and thudded into the clay. Rifle fire began to open up now. There was a shout as one of the men, Lamb couldn't see whether it was one of his, was hit and died. And then another. Clark. They were pinned down. Sitting targets. There was only one thing to be done.

Lamb scrambled to his feet, the bullets striking the field around him. 'Come on. Anyone who stays out here is a dead man. Follow me and you've got a chance.' He began to run as quickly as he could. He was an able athlete, but his feet felt like lead. He was aware of other men rising from the ground around him, some of them being hit and falling over. Others, though, were running with him now. They were ten yards from the outlying buildings. Five. More small arms opened up on them from the windows. Other men began to fall.

'Grenades,' yelled Lamb and drew one from his belt, pulling the pin as he ran forward. Reaching the wall, he stood on his toes and dropped a grenade through the open window before dropping down to crouch, hands over his ears. It exploded inside the house with a brick-shaking thud, followed by screams.

'Right. Get in there.' Two of the men, Johnson and Bayfield, nipped round the corner of the house and vaulted a five-bar gate into the yard. The machine gun in the tower opened up, and both men fell to the ground. They did not move. Watching the blood seep from their bodies, Lamb cursed to himself and yelled back to Bennett, who was crouching with the others in the cover offered by the lee of the house.

'This is useless. We don't stand a chance. We'll have to get round the flank without them seeing us. Smart, run and get Parry and Stubbs up here with the mortar. Sarnt Bennett, you stay here with Corporal Mays's section, what's left of them, and Briggs's men too. I'll take Valentine's and the odds and sods. Get Stubbs to lay down his mortar fire over the top of this house. The rest of you keep up a steady covering fire on that bloody bell tower. And use the Bren. I don't think we need worry about tanks here.'

Leaving Bennett with the remaining four men of Briggs's section and Mays's five, along with the mortar team, Lamb began to move off, keeping tight against the wall which ran to the right of the bombed house, conscious all the time that he might be spotted by the machine gunners in the tower. From behind them he heard the reassuring sound of the Bren opening up and the thud of their mortar. Directly behind him came Valentine with his four remaining men, and then the six odds and sods. They moved fast and ran across the gaps between the single-storey village houses. They were out of sight of the church tower now but could still hear the covering fire from behind. There was a small green on the right and ahead of them a cross-roads, with the left fork leading down to the church. Lamb approached it and cautiously peered around the corner of a green shuttered house to their left. He ducked his head back in. Two German soldiers had positioned themselves some fifty yards down the road with a heavy machine gun covering the crossroads. Lamb signalled to the men behind him and whispered.

'There's a machine gun up there. We'll go in through this house and try and flank it.'

He moved to the front door and waited. From the rear came the crump of a mortar round and Bren fire. Lamb put his shoulder to the door and splintered the lintel to open it. They filed quietly inside, guns at the ready, but it was clearly empty. As silently as possible Lamb moved across the room and then through the house until they reached the garden door. He tried it and then found a key in the lock and turned it. The garden, as he had thought, was walled to a height of six feet and they moved into it easily, screened by trees from the surrounding houses. They moved through an outbuilding and found themselves in another yard. They moved cautiously through a stable and into a garden where they were still behind cover of a wall. Lamb realised that they must now be directly opposite the machine gun and motioned to the others to keep silent. They could hear the two Germans chatting quietly. Lamb raised his hand and signalled that they should go forward. They moved quietly and quickly through another iron-roofed shed and rounded the corner into the street before the church. One more short move and they were out of the group of buildings and behind a wall facing the church. They could hear more German voices now. Lamb guessed that they must have made the church their strong-point, perhaps their HQ. He turned and made a sign, holding up four fingers, and waved them forward, then pointed to his pistol and a grenade. Valentine, White, Perkins and Butterworth each took a grenade from their belt and on Lamb's command pulled the pins, holding down the trigger. He did the same, mouthing to them, 'One, two, three'.

Together they emerged from behind the wall and ran towards the sound of the German voices. There were five of them, as far as he could see, two behind a low wall on the right, two behind a wall and railings on the left and one behind a pillar close to the door of the church. Three were armed with rifles, two with Schmeisser machine pistols. All, he noted, were wearing the black uniform of the SS. In an instant Lamb and his men had thrown the grenades and began to open fire. The five bombs found their targets easily and the Germans screamed as the fragments tore into them. What the grenades did not kill the bullets did. There was a brief hiatus and then all hell broke loose as the machine gun above them in the tower opened up. Bullets ricocheted off the tarmac road and one hit White in the shoulder. He fell with a moan.

Lamb shouted, 'Get in. Stay close to the tower. They can't hit us there.'

The men moved close to the tower and found that the gun could not reach them.

Lamb realised that beside the church were gates to a park. A château, he guessed. It seemed logical that any commander would make such a place his base, a final citadel. He turned to Valentine. 'You stay here with your three. I'm taking the others in there.'

'Do you think that wise, sir?'

Lamb looked at him. 'What?'

'I only wondered whether it was wise. They still have a gun in the tower and we don't know where else they are. They're sure to come running after that firing.'

Lamb stared at him. 'When I want your opinion, Corporal, I'll ask for it. Stay here.' He shouted across to the odds and sods behind the wall, 'You men follow me and be quick on your feet. Valentine, cover the tower.'

While Perkins and Butterworth fired directly past the bell tower, Valentine helped the wounded White into the lee of the church and the others ran across the road. There was no sign of any Germans, but Lamb knew that any there were would come running to the sound of the guns. They moved through the entrance gates and walked along the edge of the drive. After about fifty yards they saw through the trees a modest seventeenth-century château. Lamb reasoned that six men would be more conspicuous than two and motioned to one of the hangers-on, a man from the Norfolks named Hunt, to follow him and to the other four to remain in the woods as back-up. He motioned to his watch and made five fingers. Then the two of them ran across the grass and round the side of the house towards the front.

Inside the small château of Warlus, Adolf Kurtz watched and waited for the British to enter, as he had been doing ever since the firefight had begun. He was biding his time, waiting for them, ready to fight to the last. Kurtz brushed a speck of dirt from his sleeve just as the first British soldier appeared, framed in the doorway, and fired. The bullet hit the man between the eyes and he fell backwards, stone dead. Instants later Kurtz saw another Tommy take cover at the side of the door and realised that his pistol was pointed directly at him.

The doorway did not hide the British officer and, without thinking, Kurtz squeezed the trigger gently and fired the Mauser at Lamb. A click. Nothing happened. He looked at the British officer with disbelief. Lamb stared, wide-eyed. He had thought that his last moment had come, had looked down the barrel of a gun and cheated death. He quickly extended his arm so that the muzzle of his pistol was resting on Kurtz's tunic, just below the silver breast button. Kurtz dropped his gun to his side.

It had taken Lamb all of his self-control not to shoot, but now he realised whom he had captured: a captain in the SS. He managed to speak. 'I believe you are my prisoner, Herr Captain. Please drop your weapon.'

Kurtz shrugged and dropped the gun to the floor. 'I am not obliged under the rules of the Geneva Convention to tell you anything, Lieutenant, apart from my name, rank and serial number. Is that not right? And please remember I am your superior officer.'

Lamb smiled. 'You're no superior of mine, chum.'

'My name is Adolf Kurtz. Hauptsturmführer, SS.' He smiled to gauge Lamb's reaction and scowled when there was none. 'My serial number you do not need.'

'And your unit?'

'I told you, Lieutenant. I am not obliged . . .'

Lamb cut him short. 'And I'm not bloody well obliged to take you alive. But I will. We both know that's what I need to know. Your unit. And I think you're going to tell me, Herr Kurtz.'

Kurtz bristled at the lack of military etiquette. 'I don't think so.'

There were more men in the house now, drawn in by the sound of gunfire: Briggs, Mitchell and two others, with Bennett and Valentine.

Lamb turned to Bennett. 'Sarnt Bennett. This is Mister Kurtz. We're taking him in. He hasn't told me his unit yet but if you or any of the men should happen to catch anything he might say in passing, as it were, make sure you get it down. Sort of thing a man might say if he were to slip and take a fall. If you know what I mean.'

Bennett nodded. 'Sir.'

Lamb went on, 'I presume they've cleared off. This one was waiting to do the job on his own?'

'Yes, sir, we chased 'em down the street. Shot two and captured one other.'

'All right. We'll leave number 3 section here on the bridge to wait for our lads. Corporal Briggs's men, and the Bren and a mortar. If the Jerries attack in force, tell them to fall back due north, towards Aubigny.'

96

He looked again at Kurtz. A captain in the SS. That was a good catch. Heaven knew what information he might have. He would get him to whatever senior command there might be in Arras and see what they made of him. He gazed at Kurtz and wondered what made a man like that.

'Sarnt, we'll have to keep a close watch on that one.'

'I'll do it myself, sir. Me and Farrell.'

'Good. I don't want to lose him. Looks like the attack might have been a success. Let's go and find out how far we've pushed them back, shall we.'

8

Lamb made his way up the road, trying to preserve some sort of order among his men as they milled through the stragglers and the wounded. They had come far in the last few hours and had skirted Arras, moving to the north west in their attempt to find an officer of some seniority to whom Lamb might deliver his prisoner, but all they had seen were isolated units, at the most of company strength. They entered a small village named Mont St Eloi. British troops were moving in both directions on the road and it was hard to gauge which were moving forward to the front. Still, though, Lamb felt heartened. Clearly the offensive had met with at least some degree of success. He wished now that he could have stayed with the Durhams and shared in part of the victory. That would have felt good after what seemed like weeks of pulling back.

Sergeant Bennett drew level with him. 'What shall we do with the prisoner, sir?'

'We'll have to keep him with us until we find a senior officer. They might have a use for him back at HQ.' Lamb spotted a captain of the DLI on the opposite side of the road, at the head of his men, and turned to Bennett. 'Come on, here's our chance.'

Motioning Kurtz across the road, Lamb approached the captain. 'Sir, German prisoner. He's SS. An officer. I thought that Brigade might be able to use him.'

The captain stopped and looked at them as his men passed by. 'Yes, I can see that. 'Fraid I can't really help you, though, old boy. Thing is, I can't really take charge of him. We've just been told to pull back. Awfully sorry. You'll have to hang on to him.'

Lamb stared at him, unable to believe that he was hearing correctly. 'I'm sorry, sir. Pull back? But we routed them, didn't we? The SS. Their best men. They ran away from us.'

'Yes, well, be that as it may, Lieutenant. It seems that now they're coming back. Jerry turned his big guns on the new Matildas and shot up the regiment badly. Without that tank support we're lost.' He went on, 'The DLI are moving back to Vimy Ridge. I should go with them, if I were you, otherwise you'll get caught up with the tanks. The French are meant to be covering our western flank with their tanks. We know from prisoners that we're up against the SS Totenkopf motorized division and a regiment from the 7th Panzer Division. We blocked them for a while but they won't give up. Tanks everywhere. The French are a bit peeved too. Seems that some of our anti-tank boys got their Somuas confused with Jerry Panzers and opened up. Made a bit of a mess.'

'Any idea as to our losses?'

'It's not looking good. Latest report was that we'd lost fifty tanks. But I can't believe it. That's two thirds of what went in.'

'What about the infantry?'

'Almost as bad. Fifty per cent casualties. But we took three hundred prisoners. If we've managed to keep them, that is. Sorry, must go.' And with that the captain was gone.

Bennett looked at Lamb. 'D'you believe him, sir? Fifty per cent casualties and all them tanks. That can't be right. Perhaps he was fifth column.'

Lamb shook his head. 'No, Sarnt, he was the real thing. And I don't think he was exaggerating. Look at this lot.'

He pointed to the column of infantry advancing down the road towards them: a tattered band of bandaged and wounded men, some hobbling on makeshift crutches, others huddled together in an open farm wagon. For a moment Lamb was sunk in despair. He had seen the fighting spirit of the German army out there, and it frightened him.

A dispatch rider came roaring up the side of the column. Lamb waved him down. 'Is this right? Are we pulling back?'

The man nodded and raised his goggles. 'Too true, sir, I'm afraid. I've just seen ten of our tanks blown up. Burnt to a cinder. They've got their heavy artillery down there. 88s. Shells screaming in everywhere. Bloody murder. You'd better scarper, sir, before you're all picked up.' He spotted Kurtz. 'Don't know where you're going to put him.' The man roared off, and as he did a shell came crashing in over their heads to explode thirty yards to the rear with a deafening crash.

Lamb yelled, 'Right. We're packing up. Quick as you can.'

But the dispatch rider had been right. Where were they to go? The colonel had advised heading west towards the Somme and what seemed to be a second line of defence, but now it was evident that the Germans were outpacing them.

As they got back on the road, Lamb wondered how it could possibly have happened so quickly. Two hours ago they had been triumphant. Now they were abandoning Arras.

A Durhams officer passed him with a handful of men.

'Is it true? That you're falling back on Vimy?'

'Yes. Doesn't seem right, does it? We won the bloody battle and now we're running away.'

'Where were you?'

'Near a place called Aubigny. We wouldn't have got out if it hadn't been for some French tanks.'

Lamb grimaced. Aubigny. That was the village he'd told Briggs's section to fall back on. He realised that Kurtz was standing right beside him.

'You look troubled, Lieutenant.'

'No, not at all, Captain.'

Kurtz smiled. 'I know why you are troubled. It is because you know that we will win. We must. We are the superior race.'

'That's nonsense and you know it. It's all bluster. You're no better a man than I am.'

'But you are better than a Jew, aren't you? Or a Russian peasant. You are English. Anglo-Saxon. Aryan like me. But you have been perverted by alien blood. That is why we will win. You can still join us.'

Lamb stared at him. 'What makes you think I'd ever join you after what I've seen in this campaign? Killing women and children.'

Kurtz shrugged. 'It's war, Captain.'

Lamb said nothing but thought of the civilians he had ordered blown to pieces on the bridge and felt desperately ashamed that he might have something in common with this man. 'It may be war, Captain, but it's war by no rules that I recognise.'

Kurtz laughed and shook his head. 'Rules? There are no universal rules in this war, Lieutenant. Didn't you know that? We have made new rules. For the entire world.'

Lamb turned his head. 'Sarnt Bennett, double the guard on this man.'

It was useless trying to reason. Kurtz was a slave to Nazi doctrine, and Lamb realised that there must be hundreds, thousands of German officers out there who shared the same mindset. And if that was the case, then this was going to be a very long war.

Valentine noticed it first. The noise in the air. 'Planes, sir. Best take cover.'

The noise was clear now: a steady drone of engines. Lamb and Bennett yelled at the men: 'Get down. Get in the ditches. Enemy aircraft. Take cover.'

The men ran to the roadside and threw themselves down into the mud-filled drainage ditches at either side, covering their heads with their hands and trying to inch ever further into the grass-covered earth. Kurtz, dragged by Lamb into the nearest culvert, did the same, although he tried to push away Lamb's grasping hand.

Bennett was beside them and placed his hand on the German's shoulder. 'Now, now, sir. Be a good German officer and don't try and get away. Wouldn't want to have to shoot you, sir, would we?'

Kurtz turned on him. 'Lieutenant, tell your sergeant not to be so insolent.'

Lamb looked puzzled. 'Oh, was he being rude? Sarnt Bennett, do be polite to the officer. He is in the SS, after all.'

Bennett looked at him and smiled. 'Oh yes, sir. Polite, sir. I forgot.' Lamb looked away and Bennett swung his huge fist and smashed it into Kurtz's lower abdomen. The German doubled over with surprise and pain, spluttering. 'That better, sir? Sorry to have forgotten my manners.'

Kurtz rose to respond but found himself looking straight down the barrel of Bennett's rifle, and as he did so the planes began to come in. They were Stukas, six of them, and their sirens wailed like banshees as they went into their attack dive.

Kurtz looked up and, still holding his stomach, smiled and said nothing.

The lead plane was above them now and they watched as its single bomb whistled down towards the road. The long columns of troops and refugees had split and scattered at the first sound of the planes, and most had found some safety in the ditches, but others had not and were running up the road as fast as they could towards the relative cover of the village. It was too late for them. The first of the bombs smacked into the road and blew ten men to eternity and, as it came out of its dive, the Stuka rattled off its machine guns and did for another two. Then the bombs were falling all about them. Lamb ducked his head far down and prayed for deliverance.

The second and third bombs crashed in dangerously close. The fourth was closer still, and fragments from its casing came spinning through the air towards them. Lamb yelled out to stay low and heard a gurgle from his left. Turning, he saw Farrell staring wildly and then noticed the foot-long piece of bomb protruding from his upper torso. Within seconds the man was dead, but Lamb's attention had been diverted by then from his own man, for a grey form was slipping up and over the lip of the ditch and had begun to run now, away from the road.

Lamb instinctively stood up and yelled: 'He's getting away. Stop him.' But his words were drowned by the explosion of two more bombs and he was flung to the ground by the force.

Bennett looked up. He was cradling Farrell's body in his hands. 'He's gone, sir. And the Jerry too. Sorry, sir.'

'Not your fault, Sarnt.'

He looked through the smoke towards the trees and fancied that he could see Kurtz's field-grey form slipping into them.

*   *   *

103

Kurtz could feel the wet warmth on his head, and putting his hand up he found that he had been cut. A piece of shrapnel from that last bomb, he guessed. He felt it again, probing and not minding the pain. It seemed about three inches long but mercifully not too deep. He took out a handkerchief and clasped it to the wound and then sat up to take in his surroundings. He was about two hundred yards from the road and he could see the British still crouching in the cover of the ditches. The Stukas had come in for a second run and their machine guns were strafing the road, bringing havoc and death. The road was a mess, peppered with bomb craters and dead bodies. The wounded moaned and shrieked and the place smelt of death and spent explosive and the sickly sweetness of burnt flesh.

Kurtz moved quickly from his position near the road and ran into open country beyond for as far as he could in a single sprint, making it into a thicket of trees. Pausing to catch his breath, he tried to get his bearings. This was where his rural childhood really paid off. He had grown up in a farm in Bavaria, and the hard life had made him fit and resourceful and had given him a keen sense of orientation. He knew that the British had been taking him towards Arras, but had then diverged and gone north west along the Calais road, he guessed, so now, after going directly west, he must be somewhere around fifteen kilometres north of Warlus and perhaps the same distance west of Arras.

If the British offensive had been as successful as it had seemed then he would be well behind enemy lines. But part of him had a hunch that things had not gone as smoothly for the enemy as had seemed. Those Tommies on the road back there had been mostly wounded and they were pouring back from the direction of the fighting. There was no time to lose. Kurtz moved out through the back of the copse and struck out across the open fields.

On his left he began to pass small villages and hamlets. After about five or six kilometres, by his reckoning, he stopped and caught his breath. Lying in the hedgerow alongside a farm track, he could see up ahead a cluster of buildings and the edge of a village. There was no sign of any military presence, but Kurtz was sure that it must be held by the British. Still, his only hope of survival now was to somehow find exactly where he was and navigate his way back to his own lines. And here was as good a place to start as any. He began to run, crouching, along the hedgerow and after a few hundred yards stopped and looked again at the village. He could hear voices now, and to his astonishment they were talking in German. Kurtz stuck his head over the top of the hedge and saw, not fifty yards away, two German soldiers standing in the middle of the road, smoking cigarettes. He moved out of the hedge and shouted to them, 'Don't shoot. I'm SS.'

Then he saw the death's head markings on their uniforms and not for the first time that day Kurtz couldn't believe his luck. 'Gradl, Bohrman. Put those cigarettes out.'

They turned together and dropped the cigarettes, half in astonishment. 'Hauptsturmführer.' They snapped to attention.

Kurtz smiled at them. 'Boys, you'll never know how good it is to see you. Who's in charge?'

'Oberschaführer Kuchenlein, sir.'

'Then let's go and find him.'

Kuchenlein was as amazed as Kurtz on seeing his captain. 'We thought we'd lost you, sir.'

'You very nearly did, Kuchenlein. I was taken prisoner. But I escaped, as you can see. No one keeps me captive. Where are the officers? Where's Zech?'

'Lieutenant Zech rallied the men, sir. He said to follow you, but by then we'd lost you.'

'Where is he?'

'He's dead, sir.'

'Dead? How?'

'We've had a real rough time of it, sir.'

'Then you're promoted, Kuchenlein.'

He tousled Kuchenlein's hair and clapped him on the shoulder. 'You knew I wouldn't abandon my comrades. Now fill me in. What's happened here.'

'After you went we managed to get away from the village and back to the battalion. Then we had orders to advance again. It seems that General Rommel had managed to destroy a number of their tanks. On his own, sir.'

Kurtz frowned. Rommel. Why was it always the Wehrmacht who saved the day, and the nation's golden boy, General Erwin Rommel?

'Yes, go on.'

'So we went back and found that the British had abandoned Warlus and we just carried on. There was no resistance, sir. None at all. Our Stukas had done a good job though. We must have seen hundreds of dead Tommies and burnt-out tanks and lorries. And so we came to this place. It's called Aubigny. Bit of a dump. We managed to storm the town, sir. There were only five Tommies holding it, but they had a barricade on the bridge. Reckon they were helped by the villagers. They shot down some good men, sir. Richter, Bunzl and Lieutenant Zech.'

Kurtz shook his head. 'You did well, Kuchenlein. And the British? Where are they now?'

'One of them was killed, and we took the other three prisoner. It's OK, we beat them up a bit. For the Lieutenant.'

Kurtz wiped the blood from the cut on his forehead. 'Kill them.'

'Yes, sir. Right now?'

'Yes. Now in the town square. Hang them from lamp-posts. Then report back to me. No, wait there. I'll come and watch.'

9

Lamb looked across at the lifeless body of Private Farrell and cursed. No doubt Kurtz would rejoin his unit. It would not be hard to find, unlike theirs. How could he have let this happen? He stood up and shouted, 'Sarnt Bennett, Mays, Valentine. Is anyone hit?'

He looked around and at once saw carnage. The length of the road was strewn with the bodies of the dead and wounded. Someone was shouting for a stretcher-bearer. A man close by who had been hit by a bomb fragment and lost an arm and half his face was calling for his mother. Lamb stared and then snapped out of his trance: 'Christ almighty. Sarnt Bennett, who's left?'

Bennett was standing at the roadside, beside the smoking wreck of a cart and its dead dray horse. 'There's Smart, sir, Corporal Mays, Wilkinson, Tapley, that's all from number 1 section. Stubbs and Parry, sir. Valentine, of course. Perkins, Butterworth and Hughes. And then there's the odds and sods. Four of them.'

'I make that twelve of us plus four hangers-on. Good God. We've lost half our strength.'

Lamb walked over to Bennett and looked him in the eyes.

'I promised all of them I'd bring them through. All of them. I've failed.'

Bennett shook his head and managed a smile. 'No, you haven't, sir. You've saved half of us. And don't forget, some are wounded.'

'But the others. Perhaps I expect too much.'

'We'd have done it anyway, sir. Even without your orders. It's not you, Mister Lamb. It's the war. And don't forget Corporal Briggs's section. Back at Warlus, sir.'

'Yes, of course. You're right. We'll head back to the town. Although it's possible that they've fallen back further north in all this mess. We had better make sure. It's entirely in the wrong direction of course, but the only thing to do is to make for Aubigny and then work our way back down towards Warlus from there. And we should bury Farrell, Sarnt. Can't leave him like that.'

'Very good, sir.' He turned to the men who had crawled out of their ditches and were brushing the mud from their battledress. 'Come on you lot. Wilkinson, Tapley. We'll bury Farrell here. Then we're off to find Corporal Briggs's section.'

Valentine said nothing but Lamb could tell from his expression that there was something about the plan of which he did not approve.

The shallow grave dug, four of the men helped to heave Farrell's body into the mud and then covered it with soil. They pushed his rifle, minus the firing pin, deep into the mud at its head and hung his tin hat on the butt. Lamb bowed his head and the others followed suit. He felt a hollowness in his stomach. He had known that this moment would come, that he would be obliged to conduct a field burial service for one of his platoon, but that knowledge made none of it any easier. He began, 'Lord God, who givest and takest away, look down upon this thy servant and grant him everlasting peace.'

He turned away from the grave and wondered whether he had said enough. Enough to honour the final moments and precious memories of a man. He was haunted again by the men he had lost, saw their faces and heard their voices in his head. They were good men, whatever the colonel had said, men who believed in what they were fighting for, however well trained and fit they might be. He looked at those who were left: Bennett, his trusted cockney sergeant, Smart, loyal to the end, Parry and Stubbs, Frank Mays, Wilkinson and Tapley, Perkins, Butterworth and Hughes, and of course the enigmatic Valentine.

They shuffled away from Farrell's grave. Lamb heard a few muttered goodbyes. Some of them touched the tin hat for luck. He looked at Bennett and nodded. The sergeant spoke. 'Right lads. Let's get on.'

They turned and moved into column, moving off quickly down the road, and Lamb prayed that he would be in time, that Briggs's section would not have been overrun.

He took out his map and, seeing that there was a turning off the road to the left, led the men into the hamlet of Ecoivres. They skirted the place to the north and passed through three other settlements which, unlike those on the main road, were not deserted. Why, he wondered, were the people still here? Why did they not join the stream of refugees? Some were fleeing, certainly. A dozen or so laden horse carts passed by, moving in the direction of Arras. But for the most part the French watched from their windows as Lamb and his handful of men passed through their villages.

Lamb wondered whether Briggs and his men had fallen back. Perhaps they might even be in Aubigny at the projected rendezvous point. The thought of adding them to the depleted platoon cheered him, and he rounded the

109

bend in the road with an unusually buoyant feeling. It was then that he heard the firing: a machine gun, some distance up ahead. Lamb crouched and signalled to the men to do the same. There was an embankment to their right and he motioned to Bennett to come with him and peer over the top. The two men climbed slowly and raised their heads above the crest.

It took all of Lamb's self-control to remain silent at the sight that met his eyes. Bennett stared, wide eyed. Across the field before them, perhaps 300 yards away and down a shallow slope in what looked like a chalk quarry, a German officer was walking past some lifeless bodies. From their clothes they seemed clearly to be civilians. To the right, beside the quarry, stood two half-tracks with more Germans milling around their open doors. Lamb watched as the officer drew his pistol and emptied the chamber into one of the bodies. It jerked, then the man climbed from the pit and rejoined the machine-gun teams, and as he turned Lamb caught sight of his face and recognised him as their former prisoner, Kurtz. For a moment his hand went to his pistol and he looked at Bennett who was also instinctively moving his rifle. But Lamb placed a hand on the barrel and shook his head. The range was not a problem, but he knew that the consequence might be disastrous, whatever their sense of outrage.

Lamb knew at once that it was more than likely Briggs and the others were among the dead, and he cursed himself again for having allowed Kurtz to escape.

He shook his head, tapped Bennett on the shoulder and together they slithered silently down to the men.

Lamb spoke quietly. 'It's no good. The Jerries have taken the town. They must have captured Briggs and the others.' He paused. 'I think you know what that means.'

They said nothing.

Lamb went on, 'We need to get out of here pretty sharpish before they spot us. Follow me.'

Running at a crouch, they moved quickly back across the fields the way they had come. Lamb's only hope was that, his thirst for blood temporarily slaked, Kurtz would stay in the village. They could move on by night, he thought, try to skirt the German front line. He guessed that Kurtz's unit must be one of the furthermost advanced of the Germans in this area. In any case it was the only hope he had. To go directly west was madness now, but perhaps they could head north and then cut across and outpace the advancing Germans to the Somme. Paramount in his mind now was to deliver the message to General Fortune. It was clear to him, after witnessing the débâcle at Arras, that the Germans were winning, and winning fast. The British might have the power to mount a good, quick attack, but the sheer weight of numbers and firepower in the advancing German army was overwhelming.

The colonel had told him that once they took Arras the Germans would surely head due north to cut off the BEF in an ever-tightening pocket. By heading north east and then south west rather than directly into the advancing Germans, Lamb reasoned, he and his men stood a fighting chance of just missing the Panzers and jumping out of the deadly noose.

After they had gone perhaps two miles from the town, Lamb held up his hand. They stopped for a moment and he listened for the sound of pursuit, but heard nothing. To their left he saw a building – a barn. He waved to Bennett and indicated that they should make for it. It would keep them under cover from enemy planes and motorcycle riders until dark, and then they would start off again.

They ran low and closed in on the barn. Lamb wasn't taking any chances. They had to be sure it was not occupied. He looked at Bennett and made a signal, pointing at himself and then at Smart and Tapley who were tucked in close behind, indicating that the three of them would edge to the door and open it. Bennett and the others stopped and knelt low in the wheat while Lamb and the two men moved forward. The door was shut but not locked, a bolt hanging open, and it was quite possible that someone was inside. Lamb moved to the door and with the other men on either side quickly pushed it open and pointed his pistol into the dark. Nothing. The two privates closed in, and together they entered. It was dark inside save for the light from three or four slits in the roof where the tiles and rafters had fallen in.

Lamb turned to Tapley. 'There's no one here. Get the others.' And then, 'No, wait.' He could hear something. A human or animal sound. Sobbing.

He paused in the silence and identified the direction from which it was coming. In the far corner, on a pile of hay, was a dark shape. At first he thought it might be a wounded soldier, of either side, and kept his pistol ready. But then the shape sat up and in the shafts of light breaking through the rafters of the barn Lamb saw at once that it was a girl. She was in her early twenties, he guessed, and her face, which would have been beautiful at any other time, was a white mask of terror. Lamb moved closer and for a moment he wondered whether she might lash out at him. She pulled back further into the shadows and began to whimper more loudly.

He stopped and looked at her in the semi-darkness. She had a gash on her head and her green floral dress had been torn at the front. She edged away from him again and began to mutter in French.

Lamb held up his hands in mock surrender and spoke softly. 'Don't worry. We're British. Anglais. Amis.'

The girl's gaze changed slowly from horror to a smile

and she began to cry, almost hysterically, wiping at her face and pushing back her hair. Lamb reached forward and knelt down beside her in the straw. She wiped at her eyes with the back of her hands, smudging her make-up, smiled up at him and then, realising that her dress was wide open, pulled it together as best she could.

Lamb realised that, apart from gazing into her eyes, he had also without realising it been staring at her exposed skin, seduced by its pale softness, and felt suddenly embarrassed that he should be having such thoughts when she was clearly in great distress. He covered his shame with another smile. 'Please, go on. Tell me what happened. The Germans?'

She nodded. 'I . . . I ran out of the back door when they came.' Her English was good, he thought, better certainly than his French. 'The Germans came to take us. They took my father and my brother. But when I got out I just ran into another German.' She was stifling the sobs now. 'He grabbed me. He grabbed my arm and held it tight. It hurt. Then he tore at my clothes and . . . touched me.' She stopped, sobbing again. Lamb turned away but she went on: 'I scratched his face. Right in his eye. There was blood and he shouted and let go. So I ran. I ran and ran. They fired after me. One of the bullets hit my leg. It knocked me over but it only hit the skin. And then they gave up and I came here. I thought you were Germans.'

Lamb shook his head. 'No, mademoiselle. Anglais. But the Germans are still in your town. There's been some shooting.' He did not think this was the time to tell her about the executions, but something in her face told him that she had probably guessed.

'I heard it. Where can I go?'

'You'd best come with us. We're heading north.' He had decided now that they would head up to Bethune and then directly west to Etaples. Then they would have to

113

use the coast to try to get down to Fortune's division on the Somme. He just prayed that the Germans would not beat them to it. 'You'd better come with us. For a while at least. Do you have anyone you can stay with?'

'I have a cousin in Montreuil. It's near Etaples. I could stay there. My mother's neice.' She paused, looking alarmed. 'Oh God, my mother, my father, my brother. What will they do? The Germans . . .'

'Don't worry about them now, miss. You stay with us. Here, have some of this.'

He reached into his tunic and brought out a hip flask. It was something he kept only for the direst of emergencies. He unscrewed the cap and held it out to her. She sniffed at it.

'It's brandy. Cognac.'

The girl took a swig and coughed. 'It's quite good. Much better than I thought you would have.' She flashed a smile at him and again Lamb felt conscious of the moment.

'I'd get some rest now, miss, if I were you. You're safe now.'

She smiled again. 'Please call me Madeleine. Madeleine Dujolle.'

Lamb smiled back at her. 'Thank you. I'm Peter Lamb. Lieutenant. North Kents. These are what's left of my men. Corporal Valentine here will lend you his blanket roll.' He turned to Bennett. 'We'll stay here till nightfall, Sarnt. Post a man on each side of the barn, inside if you can. I want to know the slightest movement out there. See if you can rustle up some food. Whatever you've got. But no fires. We don't want to burn the place down. The rest of you get some kip, and that means you too, Sarnt. Better make the most of it. I reckon we're all going to need it over the next few days.'

* * *

Some twenty miles to the south, Panzer Major Manfred Kessler tapped a cigarette on his case three times. He flicked at his lighter and lit it and then looked again at the map which his second-in-command Hauptman Fender had spread out on one of the track-guards of his command tank. He poked a finger at the map, at a place marked 'Cuinchy'.

'If we are here, Fender, then the enemy must be over there. And we've got them on the run.'

'Yes, sir. It would seem so.'

'And you say we've received an order to halt?'

'Yes, sir. The radio operator just picked it up. In code. From High Command: 'You are to deny the canal line to the enemy but on no account to cross it.'

'What the hell do they think we're going to do then? Sit here and drink wine? We're winning, aren't we? Why don't we attack?'

Fender shook his head. 'I don't know, sir. It seems crazy to me too.'

'You see, Fender, our strategic orders are to strike out into France, not back up here.' He dragged his finger across the map. 'Here. The master plan. I think we should obey those orders, don't you.'

'Yes, of course, sir. But perhaps we shouldn't leave the rest of the division, the battalion.'

Kessler shrugged. 'All right, my friend, I'll wait two days here. We'll refit and rearm. Maybe we'll even kill a few Englishmen. But if we haven't got orders to move west by then I will not be answerable for my actions. I'll tell you something, Fender. I intend to be the first officer in this battle group to reach the Seine or the coast, which-ever comes first, and no one, not even Herr General Rommel himself, is going to beat me. Besides I've got a bet on it with Major Freidrich. Five hundred Reichsmarks that I get there first. If we win I'll buy every officer in the company a bottle of champagne. The finest in Paris.'

Kessler laughed. 'I'm having a good war, Fender. First Poland, now France. The Führer has fulfilled his promise.' They had worked hard to achieve it, and Rommel had accomplished miracles. The Wehrmacht had never been stronger – an army risen from the ashes of disaster and economic ruin in 1918. He was a proud soldier, from a military family. Fighting was in his blood, and with it the ancient code of honour by which the Prussian army had lived for two hundred years and more. He admired Hitler for not having tried to interfere with that. Oh, he had his own private army, his SS, but Kessler knew that it was the regular army, the Wehrmacht-Heer, that was the backbone of Germany's fight.

His own company had done particularly well. Of the fifteen tanks at the start of the campaign, in Number 2 Company, 2nd Battalion, 25th Panzer Regiment in Hoth's 7th Division under Rommel, there were twelve still service-able, although only six had not been hit at all.

'Look here. D'you see how we're strangling them? If we carry on like this we could be by the sea in a day. They're finished.' He made a circle with his hands. 'Then we just tighten the noose and the whole British and French armies are ours. There has never been a more brilliant campaign. Not even Frederick the Great himself could have done it. What a time! What an hour to be German! The world is ours, Fender. God is with us, the Führer is with us and no one can stop us.'

10

All day they had been moving across the fields, and for a day before that. They had left the barn at nightfall on the 23rd, as he had planned, and moved steadily back towards the road, picking it up slightly further north. The girl was surprisingly fit and hardly held them back, and they had started out at a good pace. Their journey had not been without trouble. Twice they had encountered, moving in the opposite direction, small columns of straggling British and French troops, with and without officers, who seemed without purpose. Lamb had moved on quickly past them, remembering from his officer training lectures how easily loss of morale in one unit could infect another. On two other occasions the whine of engines in the skies above them had prompted a scramble for the roadside ditch and they had watched from cover as dive bombers zeroed in on some unlucky target to right or left. Now, though, the difficulty was moving through the pitch black while remaining on constant alert, and it had taken its toll. He could see that they were flagging.

It had been Lamb's original plan only to move at night. But it had occurred to him that time was of the absolute essence if they were to beat the Panzers to the Somme, and so as day broke he had spoken to Bennett, and they had carried on. Actually they were hardly marching now, more walking or loping along. It was close to four in the afternoon and he could feel the men's tiredness as they reached a sign reading Béthune. Going through the outskirts, they decided to skirt the town to the east. Finally, Lamb called a halt. They were on a long straight road, lined with trees, barns and small houses, most of them boarded up. A column of French tanks, with a few infantry stragglers, was moving slowly but steadily ahead of them in the same direction, which Lamb guessed was north east.

'We'll halt here for ten minutes, Sarnt. Where are we?'

'The sign says Essars, sir. Wherever that is.'

Lamb took out his map and looked at the area around Béthune. Essars was on the north-east side. 'There should be a canal and a bridge. We've gone too far east. We need to get back on the road.'

But before they could retrace their steps Lamb saw two figures approaching them – an officer and a sergeant, both of them wearing British battledress.

Lamb said, 'Let me talk to them, Sarnt. They look right enough but you can never be too careful. Jerries get up to all sort of tricks.'

Lamb walked towards them, hand close to his holster, and saw that both of theirs were still buttoned. The sergeant was a thin man with a moustache, the officer short and wearing a peaked service cap.

As he got closer the officer stepped forward with an extraordinary nonchalance. 'Hello. Lieutenant Petrie, Royal Berwicks. We hold the crossing back there. Old bridge. Got it mined for detonation. Who are you?'

'Lamb. North Kents.'

'Pleased to have you.' He looked at Lamb's men: 'Bit of a hotchpotch, aren't you?' Then he noticed the girl: 'I say, you've got a civvie in tow. A woman.'

How observant of you, thought Lamb, but said nothing except: 'Yes. Her village was attacked by the SS. I think they shot her family. She's pretty shaken up.'

Petrie grimaced. 'Yes. We've been getting all sorts of reports in about them. Rumours flying everywhere. Apparently they're shooting our men in cold blood if they surrender. Do the same if I catch them.'

Would you? Lamb wondered. And would he, now? Probably, after the scene he had witnessed at Aubigny. Lamb knew the Berwicks by reputation – a hard-bitten, old-fashioned regular regiment without the luxury of a Territorial battalion. Petrie, by the look of him, was typical of their officers: a dedicated lifetime soldier, most probably with a poor opinion of the 'part-time' additions to the army's officer class. So far, though, he seemed happy enough to accept Lamb.

Petrie went on, 'As I said, you're more than welcome, old chap. We need all the hands we can get. Expecting Jerry to turn up any day. Can't really understand why he hasn't yet, but we're ready for him when he does. We've dug in well and burnt every barge we could find. Go over the bridge and past the sentries. My command post's in the old village hall in the *centre ville*. Can't miss it. Got a tricolour outside. That should be a good enough place for your young lady to get some rest. You really do all look quite done in.'

Lamb smiled and thanked him, and together they made their way up the road and crossed the bridge into the little town. Part of Lamb's mind told him that they should continue to make their way to Etaples and then towards General Fortune, but Petrie's words had cut into him. They did all look done in, and he owed it to the men to rest them, even if it meant the possibility of getting caught up in another battle, defending another bridge. That was what this campaign seemed to be all about to him: holding bridges before blowing them sky-high. They were the tactics of despair, and they all knew it.

They found the Hôtel de Ville with little trouble, and after Bennett's brief negotiation with an Irish orderly sergeant Lamb managed to get them a small back office to themselves. The men collapsed to the floor with exhaustion. Lamb took care to offer the only seat in the place to Madeleine, and then he too lay down. He stared at the ceiling for a moment before turning his head to the left and by chance finding her face. She was remarkably beautiful, he thought, and even as he did so he felt instantly ashamed. She was smiling at him now, and he smiled back before turning his face away and staring into space – wondering about his feelings and desperately hoping that he wasn't falling in love with this French girl. They would have to lose her soon. It could not be far to her cousin's house near Etaples. If they could get away from here tomorrow they might even make it by nightfall. He wanted rid of her. She had no part in their war anyway and was a hindrance, despite her physical fitness. No one wanted a woman with them in a fight. Did they? One more day with her – that was all they would have. That, he thought, was all he could take to stop himself feeling anything more. And he so desperately wanted not to feel anything for her.

Evening came and Lamb's men began to stir. He felt rested and saw that Madeleine had fallen asleep in the chair. A battledress top was hanging apparently unwanted on a hook, and Lamb got up and draped it around her shoulders. Then he roused the slumbering Bennett and left the room as the men began to rise with the usual chorus of farts and snorts. Outside the air was cool and they could hear the water of the canal as it splashed against the concrete sides of the embankment.

Madeleine came out through the door and had joined him before he realised it. 'Have you got a cigarette?'

'Of course.'

Lamb felt inside and took out the case, opening it for her. She shivered. 'Would you be kind and light it for me? I'm a little cold. I really don't want to take my hands out of these pockets.'

He picked the cigarette from the case and placed it between his lips, then took out his lighter and flicked the spark until the end was glowing. Then, very carefully and trying very hard not to make anything out of a situation already charged with latent sexuality, he placed it between her lips, and knew at once that he had failed. The sooner they got her to her cousin's house, he thought, the better.

She took a hand from her pocket and removed the cigarette before speaking. 'Thank you for helping me. I don't know what I would have done.'

He smiled. 'Lucky for you we came along. But we'd better get you to your cousin soon. You shouldn't be here, in the front line.'

'I like it here. It feels right – to be with the men who are fighting to save my country. Give me a gun and I'll kill some of the Boche bastards too. I could, you know.'

Lamb laughed. Yes, he thought, I do believe you could.

A man came running up the road from the direction of the canal. 'Mister Lamb, sir. Mister Petrie says can you please come and see him on the other side of the canal, sir.'

Madeleine took the cigarette from her lips and dropped it to the ground before standing on it. 'You must go to your friend. You are needed.' She turned and walked back into the town hall.

Lamb watched her go. Watched the moonlight on the backs of her legs and the way that her thin dress clung to the contours of her body. His head was buzzing with his

121

sudden desire for her, and all sorts of unanswered questions. The Somme seemed a very long way off, but the Germans were not going to come this night. And so they would leave tomorrow. He would square it with Petrie: explain about the colonel and the message for General Fortune. The lieutenant seemed reasonable. But for tonight he would face the task in hand as best he could. He turned to the runner. 'Thank you. Tell the lieutenant I'll be with him presently.'

Lamb stared out over the canal and shouted to Bennett, who was standing with a group of NCOs from Petrie's men:

'Sarnt Bennett, have one last look, will you. Get our lot into shape and get them to dig in along the canal as best they can. I want everything used as barricades. Everything. Anything you can find.'

He walked away from the town hall towards the canal and reached the bridge. Looking south, he saw that Petrie and his company sergeant-major were on the far side, discussing arcs of fire. He walked onto the bridge and had just reached Petrie when a dispatch rider came roaring up the road from the south. He stopped his bike by the three men and, dismounting, to Lamb's astonishment ignored Petrie, lifted his goggles and handed Lamb a note: 'You in command here, sir?'

'Not exactly, no.'

'Oh, sorry, sir. My mistake. Anyway. Message from Brigade. General Gort's given the word for the rest of us to fall back to the canal from Arras. Seems the Jerries are coming up from the south. Right behind us. That's it, sir.' And then the man was gone.

Petrie spoke. 'Extraordinary man. Well, that's it then. They've driven a bloody great wedge between us and the rest of the French and our chaps to the south. What d'you think?'

'It looks that way. They've cut the whole force in two. I suppose that now we've really got to hold this place, at least until we know all the Arras lot are safe.' Damn, he thought, seeing his chances of slipping off the following morning ebbing away.

'Yes. Looks like it. Your lot dug in?'

'They're about it right now. My Sarnt's seeing to that. I wonder how long they'll be.'

'Who? The Arras mob?'

'No, the Jerries. I'll bet they get here first. Nothing to stop them. This is the front line now. Think I'll get back. My Sarnt's promised me a mug of some sort of stew he's put together with our French friend. Beans and tomatoes liberated from someone's garden.'

'Sounds good. Let me know if you've any to spare.'

'Incidentally, why did you call me over?'

'Well, it's the most extraordinary thing really. Probably nothing. But everything was deathly quiet. Then we heard a dog barking, didn't we, Sarnt Major? Quite far away. S'pose it must have been that dispatch rider just now upset them.' As he spoke there was another noise, a bark. 'Listen. There you are. There it is again. Closer now, wouldn't you say, Sarnt Major?'

'Yes, sir. Definitely closer, sir.'

There were more dogs barking now, and by the sound of it they were getting closer. Then Lamb heard the noise change. It was not barking any more but more like a growling, getting alternately louder and softer. He turned to Petrie and looked puzzled, and then it dawned on him. It was the sound of soldiers marching on a tarmac road. He said, 'Christ. They're Jerries.'

Petrie, more from instinct than anything else, fired the Very pistol he was holding into the night sky and a white flare shot up, revealing two lines of German soldiers moving steadily up the long road to their south. 'God. Run.'

As one, Petrie, Lamb and the CSM turned and sprinted

back across the bridge, expecting at any moment to feel a bullet in their backs. But no shot came. Instead they heard shouts and splashes and as they reached the far end and turned back to look they saw that the Germans had not followed them at all but jumped into the canal, fearful of their own lives.

The three men continued to run. Lamb saw Bennett. 'They're here. The Jerries. Get the Brens set up. And the mortar.'

Bennett snapped into action. 'Valentine, Mays, get your men in the dugouts. Perkins, get ready with the mortar. The rest of you, hold your fire till I say so.'

Lamb saw Petrie standing close to the edge of the canal. He seemed to be doing something to the Very pistol. Lamb realised he was trying to eject the spent cartridge and remembered that the signal for blowing the bridge was a white flare followed by a red. It seemed, though, that the white one had stuck. He could see the Germans now, climbing back up out of the water and the embankment and beginning to regain the far end of the bridge. He shouted at Petrie: 'Quick man. They're coming over.'

Petrie pushed and pulled at the weapon to no avail, and then in desperation he bashed it hard against his thigh. There was a click and the spent cartridge tumbled out of the pistol. Fumbling in his haste, Petrie loaded the red one and raised the gun again towards the sky. The trigger slid back and a red flare shot up above the town. Petrie ran, as did Lamb, and both men threw themselves with the others into the shelter of a sandbagged dugout just as a huge explosion tore open the night.

The bridge flew up into the air, sending massive concrete boulders bouncing like bales of hay around what had been the road.

Lamb turned to Petrie. 'I think that's what they call "the nick of time".'

'Thank God.'

'I shouldn't breathe too soon. They're bound to try again. They don't give up, you know.' Even as he spoke they heard the sound of small-arms fire coming from the far side of the bridge. Lamb turned to Bennett. 'Sarnt-Major, give them the mortar, but be sparing with the ammo. Just give them a taste of it.'

Within a few minutes it was clear that the Germans were as determined as Lamb had thought. The small-arms fire grew in intensity, and while most of the platoon and Petrie's men crouched down in their dugouts, Perkins's mortar and those from the Fusiliers sent round after round crashing over the canal to explode on the other bank, lighting up the darkness with white flashes. Lamb wished he could run back to the town hall and see how Madeleine was, but he knew that was impossible. His place was here, with his men.

There was a shout. Petrie's sergeant-major: 'They're coming, sir. They're trying to cross.'

Lamb peered over the sandbags and saw that while some of the enemy were trying to use the huge stone blocks as giant stepping stones, others were dragging small rubber dinghies down to the water's edge. He yelled: 'Right, everyone. Let them have it.'

Together Lamb's men and the Berwicks opened up with their rifles. Lamb himself had found an abandoned Enfield and, having checked its mechanism, was using it rather than his unreliable side arm. By the occasional light of mortar bombs and grenades he managed to zero in on one of the Germans who was trying to get a boat into the water. He took aim at his upper body and fired. The bullet hit the man's chest and sent him flying backwards to fall against the opposite bank. Lamb paused momentarily, both pleased and surprised by the accuracy of his shot. Then he did the same with another man, and another. The bullets were flying over his head now, hitting the sandbags and ricocheting in all directions. He heard the Bren guns rattle off and the answering chug of the MG34s on the opposite bank. Everywhere, it seemed, grey-clad figures were tumbling to the ground and into the water, but as soon as one fell another would appear to take his place. Christ, he thought, how many of the buggers can there be?

Petrie came up at a running crouch. 'I'm sending a runner back to Brigade to request artillery support, if there's any to be had. Determined buggers, aren't they.'

An enemy mortar bomb came screaming in over their heads and crashed into a house close behind, destroying a wall and sending splinters in all directions. A man screamed as one took off his foot.

Petrie shouted: 'Stretcher-bearer! It's getting a little hot, isn't it? Where's your girl?'

'In the town hall. I hope she's all right.'

'She'll be fine, old man. Bit scared, I should imagine. Just as long as we can keep the Jerries back on their side of the canal.'

Both men looked out again at the water and saw in the moonlight that some of the rubber boats had now actually made it into the water.

Lamb shouted back, 'Parry, can you hit one of those boats?'

'Sorry, sir. Didn't see them from back here, sir.'

There was a thump behind them and a mortar shell flew up and hit the water about four yards to the right of the lead dinghy. 'No. More to your left, about five degrees. Try that.'

Another bomb went over their heads and this time Parry was on target. It burst directly in the centre of the boat, killing the six Germans bunched together and sending their torn bodies outwards into the canal while the craft itself disintegrated.

'Well done, Parry.'

The second dinghy steered round the body parts and kept on coming while more were lowered into the water. Lamb shouted to Bennett, 'Sarnt Bennett, they need to keep their fire going. Where's the bloody Bren?'

'Jammed again, sir.'

There was nothing for it. Lamb turned and sprinted across the road through a hail of German bullets to the Bren gun position.

Private Butterworth was sitting behind the sandbags, his hands at the gun, trying to free the clip. 'Sorry, sir. Thing just jammed, sir. I've tried to adjust the regulator but it doesn't want to budge.'

Lamb saw that he had a tear in his battledress and fresh blood on his arm. 'You're hit. Get yourself back to the MO. Lieutenant Petrie will show you where. Get that patched up.'

He took the gun from Butterworth and, being careful not to burn himself on the hot barrel, began to unlock it and slide it forward. Then he began to turn the regulator and heard the hiss as more gas seeped in. He had always liked engineering and felt at home with machines, but he had never thought that his skill might be of use in saving his life under fire. He took out his revolver and gave the mechanism a few sharp taps. There, finally, a use for the thing! He pointed the Bren gun across the river and pressed the trigger; there was a clear click and then a stream of bullets sputtered from the muzzle. Lamb carried on firing, sending fire into a clump of trees on the far bank where the flashes told him there was a high concentration of the enemy.

He was aware of someone standing behind him. It was Valentine. 'Shall I take over, sir? You'll have better things to do, being an officer.'

Lamb thanked him, but wondered how the man was

able to twist even an offer of help into a barbed comment. Even under fire. The Germans were advancing across the ruins of the bridge now.

'Direct your fire to the centre. Stop them coming over those rocks.' Valentine swung the gun, and as Lamb watched he shot down every man on the stones. 'Good shooting, Corporal. Perhaps we'll make you a marksman.'

Valentine frowned and Lamb left the dugout as he began to fire again; another group of the enemy tried the same tactic and met the same fate.

Petrie found him: 'I think they're tiring. They seem to be pulling back into the trees.'

'Let's hope that's not because they've called up their bombers.'

The two men watched through the darkness as the Germans hauled and carried their wounded into the shelter of the woods. Still the rifles cracked.

Petrie shouted: 'Cease firing.'

Silence. The two men listened, dreading the hum that would herald an air attack. But none came.

Lamb marvelled at the suicidal bravery of the German troops as he surveyed the scene before him. The bodies of over forty German soldiers lay scattered across the terrain in front of him.

An officer approached him from the left – a captain. The newcomer was a short man with a lean build and a hawk-like nose and when he spoke it was with the faintest hint of an Irish accent.

'You Lamb? Well done. Thank you for helping the Lieutenant here. We made quite a mess of them, didn't we? Sorry, Captain Campbell. My Company HQ's a mile away to the left. Had a bit of bother there too, but nothing like this. Have you seen who they are? SS.'

Lamb looked at the dead lying in the water and saw the familiar death's head on their collar. Kurtz's men.

Campbell went on: 'I dare say they'll try it on again, so we'll have to be ready for anything. Imagine your Territorial chaps haven't seen anything like this lot before. Don't worry: my chaps are trained to handle them. I suppose you've seen quite a lot that you didn't expect to. Still, we'll hold them off. Won't we, Petrie?'

He shot a glance at the lieutenant, who was looking a little embarrassed at his captain's arrogance. Campbell went on. 'You might like to know that the Jerries have taken the coast from Etaples all the way up to Calais. Seem to be holding them there, though. But it's bad news for our lot. All down to us now. Just as well the Regulars are in it now, but well done to you for holding it for us.'

He turned and walked away with Petrie. Lamb was seething with rage at the man's speech. 'Holding it for them . . . the Regulars will take over now!' It was the mess at Tonbridge all over again – the 'friendly' banter and ribbing between 1st and 2nd Battalion of his own regiment in which, despite all the tradition and camaraderie that he loved, he was made to feel that he could never be one of them. It was almost as if he had been made up from the ranks. Well now, whether they liked it or not, they were all united against a common enemy. They would see who was the better soldier. He looked down again at the dead SS men and across to the opposite bank. How did you manage it? he asked himself. By what strange throw of the dice did you come to be opposite us again? It occurred to him how fickle fate was in war and how he and his men, all of them, were mere pawns in a lunatic game. With Kurtz out there too he knew that, although all was quiet now, the Germans would try something soon and that when they did he was not sure how long the Berwicks would be able to hold out.

But he knew too that he and his men had achieved everything he could here. What he had to do went against all his principles, in particular that no soldier should ever abandon a position or one of his comrades, but Lamb had been given a mission to complete: to deliver an order whose knowledge might mean life or death not to a company but to thousands of men, and he was determined to do that, whatever it took. The canal, he knew, would fall eventually, and something told him that that too was now France's destiny. The British would never stop the Nazis here. That would have to wait for another day, another place. A new dawn. They would leave tomorrow, at daybreak.

He turned to Bennett, who was nursing a slight wound to his cheek, and spoke as quietly as he could manage. 'We're leaving here tomorrow, Sarnt. Pass the word to the lads and tell them to keep it quiet. Petrie doesn't know, and neither does Captain Campbell. Could be a bit tricky.'

Lamb thought for a moment but it was not a hard decision to take Bennett into his confidence. The man was as close to him now as any officer; more so than most.

'This order I've been given, Bennett. It's absolutely vital that it gets through to the general.'

'Sir?'

'To General Fortune, Sarnt. CO of 51st Division, on the Somme. So whatever happens, whatever, just remember that. This order is more important than anything else. Any man and any officer. Got it?'

'Yes, sir. I see. What about the girl, sir? Will she be coming along with us?'

Lamb thought for a moment. 'No, she'll have to stay here now.' He paused for a moment and shook his head. 'We can't leave her to fall into enemy hands. She'll need to move east. According to that captain the Jerries have taken the coast, so when we do break out of here and head west we'll be behind enemy lines.'

It hadn't really occurred to him that Madeleine should not come with them, and it hurt him to think that they would be losing her. But there was no alternative. It would be hard enough for the sixteen of them as trained soldiers.

He walked over to the town hall and went inside. Part of the building had been used as a dressing station and it reeked of morphine and blood. He found her, not as he had supposed he would, in the back office, but in the makeshift ward. To his astonishment, she was busily binding a bandage around a stomach wound, whispering to the wounded man as she did so. Lamb came up behind her and coughed and she turned to him and smiled, sending his head into confusion. Lamb looked at the wounded man and reckoned that he would not hear much of what he was about to say. Then, mastering his feelings, he spoke as she turned back to her job. 'Madeleine, I've been thinking and I'm afraid that I don't think you should come with us. The Germans have taken Abbeville and marched up the coast. They're almost at Calais. And that means that anything west of the canal is behind enemy lines. That's no place for a girl. Better to make your way to the east, inside our lines. Don't you know anyone out that way?'

She stopped bandaging, shook her head and stared at the floor, then cut the bandage with scissors and pinned the ends together. 'No. I don't think so. I think I will come with you.' She began washing her hands in a basin of warm water which, as she did so, turned steadily more red.

'Look, it's simply not practical. It's far too dangerous for a girl like you.'

She looked up at him and he saw the fury in her eyes. 'A girl like me? A girl who can change dressings on bloody wounds? A girl who's just shoved half a man's intestines back into his belly? A girl who can keep up with you men across country on the run? Is that the sort of girl you can't take with you, Lieutenant?'

Lamb said nothing, then, 'Where did you learn to do that?'

'Before the war I was a vet. Well, learning to be a vet. It's the same thing. Wounded cow, wounded man. You learn. Besides, I live on a farm. Sorry, lived on a farm.'

'It's still too dangerous. And if you're caught, God knows . . .'

'Yes, if I'm caught I'll be killed. Eventually. Well, what does it matter to me? Half my village is dead, and my parents and brother too, I'm sure. What's my life now? Besides, perhaps I can be of some use to you.'

She had moved on now and was unwinding the bandage from the head of one of Petrie's men. He was moaning. Carefully she peeled away the fabric from the congealed blood and revealed a jagged shrapnel wound, through which the brain could be seen. She gasped quietly and began to dab very carefully at the wound, cleaning with calm precision.

Well, thought Lamb, watching her hands at work, perhaps you really could be useful to us, although he knew full well now what he had suspected for some time. Something inside him was telling him he needed no persuasion to let her stay with them. 'You know we're going into enemy-held territory.'

'Of course I know, Peter.'

It was the first time that she had used his Christian name, and now as her angry eyes met his own he felt another twist in the complex thread that bound them ever closer together. 'All right. If you're certain, you can come with us. But if you hold us up, if you can't manage it, then you must leave.'

'Yes. I understand perfectly.'

'We leave tomorrow in the morning. Nine a.m. In a truck. Can you be there on time?'

'Of course. Now go away and command your men while I try and save these ones.'

* * *

Major Kessler had heard the firing from further along the canal. He was standing against the armour-plated hull of his command tank reading the latest issue of *Die Wehrmacht* when one of his lieutenants, Faller, an Austrian, came up to him looking agitated. 'Sir, don't you think we should go and do something? I mean, we might be able to help. We have tanks. That could turn the firefight.'

Kessler shrugged. 'Maybe we should, but it's not our fight. I was told to deny the canal to the British, not to attack it. Remember? General von Rundstedt's order was quite specific this morning. "Do not attack. Allow the infantry to catch up." So we sit tight here. Besides, that's not our sector. That's the SS up there. Totenkopf Division. Theodor Eike's men. The precious SS. Do you want to help them? Would they help us?'

Faller looked away, 'I don't know. But they're still Germans. And they're dying, sir. Don't you think we should . . .'

'I think perhaps that you should shut up, Lieutenant. We'll help them when we're told to, not before. I don't want to risk my tanks in some other man's battle, and neither does the Führer. I'm sure the SS can handle the situation quite well. The general is saving us for the big attack on the Somme. Save your energy, you'll need it soon enough.'

11

The moment had come which he had been dreading, and it was no easier than he had imagined. Standing outside the little office at the rear of the town hall, he felt as if he were thirteen again, waiting outside the headmaster's study at Tonbridge, knowing full well what would happen when he entered. Fearing the worst, he had placed Bennett and the rest of the men in key positions around the town close to the town hall and had entrusted Madeleine to Corporal Mays. His stomach felt hollow and his mouth dry. He knocked on the door.

From within came an imperious voice. 'Enter.'

Lamb turned the handle. Thirteen again.

Captain Campbell was seated at what had been the mayor's desk, writing a report on the situation that morning. He looked up and saw Lamb. 'Oh, Lieutenant. It's you. That was damned good work your men did yesterday. First class. We'll be ready for them when they come again, eh?'

Lamb smiled. 'Well, that's just it, sir. You see that's why I'm here.'

'What do you mean, that's it? Why *are* you here?'

'I'm afraid I have other orders, sir, and much as I'd

love to stay and help with the defence of the town, and I appreciate how much you need our support, those orders state that I must move west.'

The captain stared at him, open-mouthed. 'What? What exactly are you trying to tell me?'

'Simply that I have orders to proceed to the south west, sir, with a message for General Fortune who commands the 51st Division. That division should by now be in position on the Somme.'

Campbell laughed. 'Lieutenant, if this is some sort of a junior officer's joke then it's in very poor taste.'

'This is no joke, sir. I'm afraid that we have to go.'

'We?'

'Me and my men, sir.'

The captain shook his head, 'No, no, no. That's simply not possible. We need every man we can get here. I have forty-eight miles of canal to defend with barely 100 men. Your orders are to remain here and assist in that defence.'

Lamb shook his head. 'I know, sir, and I'm really very, very sorry, but I am obeying a direct order from a colonel attached to the General Staff.'

Campbell narrowed his eyes. 'Which colonel? What's his name?'

'I'm afraid I don't know that, sir. I only know him as "Colonel R".'

'Lamb. Now I know you're pulling my leg. That's a character from a bloody cheap novel, isn't it? You surely don't expect me to believe that, do you? Credit me with a little more intelligence.'

'I've never been more serious, sir. It was an order given to me in Arras by a man who told me he was a colonel on the General Staff, and I have no doubt that it was genuine. His 2iC was a Major Simpson, if that means anything.'

Again Campbell shook his head. Then he stared hard into Lamb's eyes. 'Show me the order.'

'Sir?'

'The written order, man. Show it to me, and perhaps I'll start to believe you. Mind you, it'll make no difference to my orders.'

'Sorry, sir, but my instructions are to show that order to no one but General Fortune.'

Campbell shook his head. 'You're in the realms of fantasy, man. General Fortune commands 51st Division and he's moving south, last I heard. Doesn't make sense. This is the worst pack of lies I've ever heard and the worst excuse I've heard for anyone trying to shirk a fight with the enemy. You Territorial johnnies have no stomach for a fight. I've seen enough of you – weekend soldiers who can't believe their bad luck. That's what it is, I tell you. You saw some blood spilt yesterday and that put the wind up you and now you want out of it. Well, Lieutenant, that's not going to happen. And now I am giving you a genuine order, a counter-order, and that is to stay here and help defend this position.'

'Sir, with due respect you know that you cannot possibly countermand an order from a superior officer.'

Campbell shrugged. 'I've told you, Lieutenant, I don't believe you. I believe you are attempting to desert in the face of the enemy. You're a coward, man.'

Lamb bristled, his years as a lawyer suddenly returning to him. 'Sir, if that is an accusation then I refute it categorically. I have just helped you repel an attack by the enemy, risking what few men I have left under my command. I would ask you to retract your accusation, sir.'

Campbell stared at him. 'I really don't know what to make of you, Lamb. I can only conclude that you're mad – mad to even contemplate getting through the German lines on some wild goose chase to find a general who may not even be where you are told he is heading for. Or mad enough to try getting through enemy territory to save your skin. I think I'm inclined to believe the latter.'

'I'm very sorry to hear that, sir, because whatever your opinion of my story I'm leaving, with my men.'

Campbell, his face red with anger, stood up and pressed his fists hard down on the table. 'Then I shall have you arrested for desertion.'

'I don't think so, sir.'

'No? How the devil will you stop me?'

'I have sixteen men, sir, all armed, at strategic points around the centre of the town.'

'You're threatening me? That's mutiny. You'll all be shot.'

'No, sir, I'm making a request to be allowed to obey an order from a superior officer. I'm simply doing my duty.'

Campbell began to move around the desk. 'I'm going to find my Sarnt-Major. You'll see how we deal with mutiny in the regular army.'

Lamb drew his pistol. 'That would not be wise, sir.' He shouted, 'Sarnt Bennett.'

The door opened and Bennett entered, his rifle at the ready. 'Sarnt Bennett, place Captain Campbell under arrest, please. The charge is preventing an officer from doing his duty. If he tries to escape you have my permission to shoot him.'

Bennett rested his gun on his hip, its barrel pointing directly at Campbell's chest. 'Very sorry, sir. Orders is orders.'

Lamb left the room and closed the door, then, moving quickly out of the town hall into the yard at the rear of the building he found that, as he had ordered, Madeleine was already sitting in the central position in the cab of a three-ton truck. 'Right. That's the first part done. I'm off to get the others.'

Systematically he moved around the town centre, pausing beside each of his men to whisper the order to get back to the truck. Finally he returned himself and found them all safely in the rear. He went back into the town hall and found Campbell still under guard. 'Well done, Sarnt. Any trouble?'

'No, sir. The Captain's been very good.'

Lamb reached into his pocket and found the length of rope he had scrounged earlier from a neighbouring office, then, reaching behind Campbell, he bound his hands together at the back of the chair. The captain made no attempt to resist, but, red with rage, hissed at Lamb: 'This is an outrage. You won't get away with this, Lamb. I'll have you shot. The lot of you. Damned amateurs. You're no more than common criminals.'

'I don't think so, sir. I really hope that you make it out of this mess. If I know the enemy, he'll probably try to outflank you. Have a look at your map and see if there's a narrow crossing anywhere up or downstream of the canal. That's where they'll try for, then work their way along the bank. That's my guess anyway. Just a bit of advice, sir.'

Campbell stared goggle-eyed, unsure what to make of what he was being told, and as he did so Lamb stuffed a piece of torn shirting into his mouth as a gag. 'Sorry, sir, but we need a few minutes to get away. I'm sure they'll find you before long. I do apologise, sir. I really wish you had believed me. It's perfectly true.'

They left Campbell, red faced and fuming, trying to edge his chair towards the door, which Lamb then closed and locked, pocketing the key.

'They won't find him for a while. Should give us enough time. Right, into the truck.'

Lamb climbed into the driver's seat and Bennett into the left side of the cab, squeezing in beside Madeleine, who smiled at them both, relieved at their return. Lamb pressed the starter button and pushed down on the accelerator and the vehicle roared into life. 'All right, here we go. They'll wonder where we're off to, but don't worry, no one will try to stop us.'

He inched forward up the street and turned from the town square onto the road which led south, past two sandbagged positions. The men peered out at them, but did and said nothing. Lamb opened up the throttle, changed from second to third with a whine of gears, and pushed the truck faster down the road away from the town hall past more groups of soldiers, just as puzzled as the first. Within minutes they were out of the town and driving through tree-lined terrain on the north bank of the canal.

Bennett turned to Lamb. 'Well done, sir.'

'Thank you, Sarnt. I do feel sorry for Captain Campbell, though.'

Bennett smiled. 'Perhaps you should have shot him, sir. Calling us amateurs like he did.'

Lamb returned the smile. 'Thank you, Sarnt. I'll pretend I didn't hear that last remark.'

'Very good, sir. But you might have done us all a favour.'

'You do know that I would never actually have done it, don't you?' He smiled again, and Bennett grinned, unconvinced.

The truck was moving faster now, passing isolated groups of infantry dug into the bank, and on their left machine-gun and mortar pits.

Lamb had devised a new plan to get to General Fortune, presuming that his division had by now actually made it to the Somme. They would drive down the canal on the British side and cross when the opportunity showed itself. That would be the tricky bit, driving across the bridge observed by the enemy. But they had not heard any firing from the left of the line and he wondered whether the Germans had yet stationed anyone in that sector or whether whatever unit was there might be under orders to rest and recuperate until attacked. Also, he hoped that they would be so nonplussed to see a British truck driving towards them that it would be a little time before they opened fire. Whatever the case it was worth a gamble, and really their only hope of breaking out. To have gone on foot would have been hopeless: slow and vulnerable. The truck at least gave them speed and surprise. Once through the forward enemy lines, his plan was to go hell for leather through the reserve and make now not for Etaples but the town of Hesdin, further to the south. There was no point trying to get Madeleine to her cousin. She would just have to come with them. On foot, even before he realised they were behind enemy lines, he had calculated that the journey via Etaples would take them a good three days. Now, with the transport, they might be able to cut that in half, even with Germans all around. Of course, if they could pinch an enemy vehicle, that would be the best solution. In an olive green Bedford they would stick out like a sore thumb.

He turned his head slightly, keeping his eyes on the road. 'Everyone all right in the back?' There was an answering groan. He knew that his driving was more suited to his beloved old Triumph motorbike than this truck, but he was determined to push her to her limits and make every second count. 'That's fine then. Right, hang on all of you. Hesdin here we come.'

It was approaching noon when Major Manfred Kessler sat down to eat. Today, 26 May, was his birthday, his twenty-fifth, and he had decided, given the lull that had descended on their sector of the battlefield and their order not to engage the enemy, that it might be appropriate to

140

have a little celebration. So the Major's batman, Hans, had set up a table made from two ammo boxes alongside the command tank, and at this Kessler now sat, a full glass of good local red wine in his hand, the bottle on the table. The news was good from the northern front. The Belgians, it seemed, were about to surrender, and then they would sweep across and cut the British off from the sea. France would be in the bag and he, Manfred Kessler, would be covered in glory. He would take his Panzers away from this stinking canal and down to the Seine into the green fields of Normandy.

His second-in-command, Hauptman Fender, had just proposed a toast to his health and the other officers present, his three lieutenants, were giving three cheers. How clever of Hans, he thought, to find a chicken. The man was a miracle worker. The plump bird now sat, perfectly roasted, in the centre of the table and the men eyed it greedily, waiting for their commander's order to eat. Kessler smiled at them all, put down his glass and was on the point of giving the command when the most extraordinary thing happened. There was a sudden shout from the picket he had placed on the narrow bridge to their front over the canal, and suddenly, on the road to their left, there appeared a British army truck, travelling at a speed which suggested its driver must have some experience with racing cars.

Kessler stared at it for an instant as it hurtled past and then sprang to his feet, knocking both the wine and the precious chicken onto the ground. 'Did you see that? What the hell was that? They were British. My God. Open fire, you fools. Stop them.'

But it was too late. By the time the tank commanders had climbed aboard their vehicles and the turrets had even begun to traverse, the olive-green truck had long left the laager behind.

Kessler swore at the wine which had stained his neatly pressed uniform breeches and shouted to Fender, 'Quick, radio through to Brigade. No, call Divisional HQ. Tell them that the British are breaking out. No. Tell them that they have broken out.'

'How many shall I say, sir? In what strength?'

Kessler looked at him. 'I don't know.' He ran across to the guard post. 'Are there any more? How many? Any tanks?'

A voice answered him from the sandbags, 'Nothing, sir. It's all quiet.'

What the devil were the British doing? One solitary truck, hurtling through their lines at breakneck speed, straight into the rear echelons of the Corps? It was madness. Unless of course it was some sort of secret weapon. Or an assassination team, making for the General Staff. His mind was racing.

He turned to Fender. 'Have you got through to Division yet? Tell them that one British truck just passed through our lines, heading west. Tell them that. Just the one truck.'

12

The sun rose low and golden-pink far away across the vast flat plain of northern France, bathing the fields in the hopeful light of a new day, and Lamb wondered what it might hold for them. He shivered in the early morning cold and, with Madeleine's sleeping head still resting on his shoulder, pushed down again on the accelerator pedal and tried to coax a little more speed from the truck, urging her on towards the south and safety. It was the morning of the second day since they had left Essars, and not for the first time he wondered what the reaction of Lieutenant Petrie might have been on finding his furious captain tied up and gagged in the office. Outrage, he presumed, although perhaps tinged with a little amusement, especially when he heard Campbell's tale of what had happened.

They would not have sent out a party after them. Of course not. Lamb knew that another German attack must be imminent and that it would be furious when it came, seeking revenge for the SS men lying dead in the canal. But, he argued to himself, what else could he have done? What else would anyone have done but follow the course he made for himself? He felt guilty too about immobilising the remaining two trucks by removing their starter motors. But there again, he argued, Petrie and his men were not going anywhere in a hurry.

The quiet French countryside slid past them as they travelled ever further towards the south west. He had no idea how much petrol was left. He had not had time, as he had hoped to do, to siphon off fuel from the other trucks. The gauge read that there was barely a quarter of a tank left even now, but he was sure that it had said that for the past ten miles at least and knew from experience in the garage at home that such gauges were notoriously unreliable. They must find a petrol station soon, and Lamb had a trick up his sleeve. The map he had been using since arriving in France was not army issue but a chart produced by Shell and Foldex that he had acquired privately in Stanfords in London when on leave. It showed the French roads much more clearly than any official map might; better still, it showed the locations of all Shell petrol stations. One thing he had been told time and again by the old sweats in the battalion, Bennett included, back at the depot in Kent, was that it was generally better to buy your own kit: boots, maps, anything really, even pencils.

He looked across now at Bennett, who was slumped in the other passenger seat, dozing fitfully but trying to pretend that he was awake. Lamb had let him sleep for the past three hours, but now he turned to him. 'Sarnt Bennett.'

Bennett started and attempted to get as close to an expression of 'attention' as he could, sitting squashed into the cab of a truck, but just ended up looking dazed. 'Sir?'

Lamb smiled. 'I think we'll stop in a few minutes. Then it might be time for you to take a turn behind the wheel, Sarnt.'

'Very good, sir.' Bennett sat up and shook himself awake. 'Any idea of where we are, Mister Lamb?'

'Well, if my calculations are correct and we're on the right road we should be about ten miles north of Hesdin.'

'Is that good, sir? I mean, how much further do you think we have to go?'

'Well, once we reach Hesdin we have two options. Either we travel to the coast and then down along it until we reach the mouth of the river, then we head back inland and hope we find the 51st, or we just keep pushing further south, but that might be more tricky. Depends on where we reckon the Jerries are most in force.'

Bennett nodded. 'I see, sir. So then we deliver the message to the General, and then what, sir?'

'Then it's anyone's guess, Sarnt. I suppose we fall in with whoever we find ourselves with and hold the line until we receive further orders. I'm afraid we should give up all hope of finding the Battalion, or even the Division. We're on our own now.'

It was true, and he had never felt more alone and vulnerable. They were well behind enemy lines, caught between the two bisected halves of a decimated BEF, a very long way from their friends in the north and still with some way to go to the safety of those he had been told remained in the south. Lamb knew that at any moment they might go careering into a German unit: infantry, trucks or tanks. His main aim now, though, was to get them down to the coast as quickly as possible. Once there, he thought it might be an easier journey to push down to the mouth of the Somme estuary. They would wait there until nightfall and then go on foot across the mud flats to the opposite bank. He only hoped that the colonel had been right and that by the time they got there the 51st or what remained of them would be in position along the Somme.

He had chosen a deliberately rural route, which took them through as few villages as possible. True, the quality of the roads had not been as good as some others, which seemed more direct, but if that meant they stood less chance of encountering Germans then so much the better. As for the exact location of the mass of the enemy, he was quite in the dark. He knew that one front line ran the length of the canal to the north and could only assume that the other might do the same in the south.

Four times in the last day they had heard vehicles. Twice they had spotted tanks moving across fields, once dangerously close to them. They had stopped and hidden the truck in cover until the threat had passed. At one point a German motorcycle dispatch rider had roared past them, but he had not stopped. Whether out of fear, or because he simply could not believe his eyes, they never knew.

The closest squeak, though, had been when a squadron of Stukas had passed high overhead. Bennett, his ear attuned to their hum, had heard them even above the noise of their engine, and Lamb had swerved off the road and into the cover of a tree-lined hedgerow. They had passed over, doubtless *en route* to bomb a specific target and presumably under the impression that no British units could have remained in this sector. So far their luck had held.

Now though, as they reached their objective, Lamb was ironically feeling more uneasy. It had all been too simple and straightforward. Something was bound to go wrong. Most of the tanks and motorized infantry they had seen had been moving north, so he presumed they were concentrating on going in that direction and pushing the mass of the BEF into the sea, as the colonel had said. He knew, though, that some German armoured divisions had pushed down to the south west. According to

Campbell they had already reached the sea, but in what strength and exactly where they were, Lamb, like the high command, had absolutely no idea.

He felt Madeleine stir again on his shoulder and decided that the time had come to pull over and let Bennett do some driving. For the past few miles, since leaving the hamlet of Eclimeux, they had been travelling through wide open countryside with fields stretching out to either side, and Lamb knew that was one of the reasons for his unease. Now, though, as the sun began to climb he could see trees up ahead, and tall banks of hedges on both sides of the road. There was a farm to their left, but he could see no sign of any military presence, or indeed any sign of life at all. It was as good a place as any to stop.

Lamb slowed down, applied the brake, then gently coaxed the truck onto the side of the road. The question of fuel troubled him. He reckoned that they might manage the ten miles to Hesdin and knew from his map that there should be a station there. There was another marked in a village close by. They would make for that first and hope that the enemy was not in evidence. They would face that problem if they came to it.

He switched off the engine and turned to Bennett. 'There we are, Sarnt. All change.' Gently, he shook Madeleine's arm and she mumbled something, then opened her eyes. Lamb smiled at her. 'Sorry, we're just changing drivers. You'll have to move for a few minutes.' She looked at him, puzzled at first, and then, as she remembered his face, smiled. 'Of course. Thank you. Where are we?'

'Close to Hesdin, I think. You've been asleep for a few hours.'

She let him move away from her and pushed herself back into the seat.

Lamb climbed out and met Bennett at the front of the

vehicle. Both men listened, but there was no sound on the empty road, merely the chirruping of birds. It was strangely quiet after all they had been through.

Lamb opened his cigarette case and tapped an oval against the metal before lighting it. 'One of mine, Sarnt?'

'Prefer my own, sir, if you don't mind.' Bennett took a pack of Woodbines from his pocket and lit up.

'Better check on the others. You stay here.'

Lamb walked to the rear of the truck and lifted the tarpaulin. The smell inside was appalling, though familiar: stale sweat and fart and foul breath. He peered in. 'Everyone all right?'

There was a general groan of assent.

'That's fine, then. We're almost there, chaps. Not long now.'

A voice answered, 'Where are we, sir?'

'In France, Smart. Somewhere in France. Don't worry. We're heading for our own lines.'

He dropped the tarpaulin as the usual round of wheezing, coughing and swearing began and returned to the front of the truck. 'They seem fine, Sarnt. We might need to scrounge some rations before Hesdin, though. Water too. And fuel for this baby.' He patted the bonnet of the truck. 'There's a village not far from here.'

'Think there'll be Jerries there, sir?'

'I don't know, Bennett, but we should probably assume that there will be. Safer that way, anyway. We'll pull up outside the place and recce it on foot. Then we can decide what to do next.'

Lamb stubbed out his cigarette on the ground and Bennett did the same, then both men climbed up into the cab of the truck and Bennett took the wheel. Lamb reached inside his valise and took out the map. By his reckoning they were nearing one of the few villages through which they had to pass, almost the last before Hesdin. Incourt, it was called.

'Take a right turn here, and then left. We'll stop at the edge of the village.'

He nodded to Bennett, who started the engine, and they rolled off along the road. Sure enough, within 400 yards they reached a signpost for the village.

Lamb signed to Bennett and the sergeant switched off the engine. Winding down the window, Lamb listened, but heard nothing save the sounds of rural France. They would make a run for it. Changing his mind about the foot patrol, he nodded to Bennett and again the sergeant switched on. Then, revving up, he drove the truck into the village without stopping. The people of Incourt saw nothing. Half of them, probably, had already long since fled to the south, but in the houses of those who remained a few lace curtains twitched, and in a yard a dog barked, but the truck moved so fast that they presumed it must be yet another of the lorries full of German soldiers that had already passed through their quiet little village, and they turned back to their own sad lives in their newly invaded country.

Lamb looked at the map again. It would be foolish to head for the centre of Hesdin. They would make for the village to the south with the petrol station and go on from there. He turned to Bennett. 'We'll head for the centre and then carry on through this village to the south of the town, Saint-Austerberthe.'

It did not take long. They drove quickly past quiet red-brick houses and whitewashed farm buildings, and within minutes they had come to a crossroads. To their right stood a pretty little village church, on the left an enclosed farm. Dead ahead, on the road leading away from them, Lamb saw what he had been praying for: a fuel station with a single pump.

He nodded at Bennett, 'Thank God . . .' but had not finished the sentence when he froze. For in a yard, not fifty

149

feet from the pump, stood a German truck. An Opel Blitz, German infantry transport.

Lamb yelled at Bennett: 'Christ, man. Reverse. Back up the road.'

Bennett slammed the gears into reverse and the truck slewed backwards up the road as he tried to keep her steady with the steering wheel. There was no way, thought Lamb, that whoever was with the German truck could not have heard the gears crunch or the engine over-rev. He watched to see how many men would appear. But, miraculously, not one did.

As the truck continued on its backward roll cries and shouts of protest came from the men in the rear. Madeleine woke with a start and muttered something in French before sitting up. 'What's happening? Peter?'

'German truck. They must have seen us.'

Bennett kept his foot down and, eyes on the mirror, prayed that he wouldn't hit anything. He had never been a particularly good driver at the best of times, and reversing at speed was not something he had imagined he might be called on to do. But he was doing his best and, aside from a glancing blow at a low brick wall that drew louder cries of protest from the rear, he managed to control the three-tonner until eventually they veered around a corner and lost sight of the German lorry. Bennett pulled up behind the corner of a large house with blue shutters and a painted advertisement on its wall for Dubonnet.

Lamb made a sign and Bennett switched off. Lamb looked at him with wide eyes. 'Well done, Sarnt.'

'D'you think they saw us, sir?'

'No idea. But we'll know soon enough.'

The men in the back were groaning now. Lamb stuck his head through the slit behind the driver's seat: 'Keep it down in there. Jerry lorry.' The voices subsided, and then Lamb and Bennett listened and waited. Madeleine reached out and clasped Lamb's hand in hers, and although he realised that Bennett might see he did not push her away. The street was curiously silent. They must have heard us, thought Lamb, but still no sound came from the direction of the enemy truck.

After a few minutes, which seemed to last an eternity, he looked across at Bennett, and as he did so, as gently as he could, he let go of Madeleine's hand.

'Right, that's long enough. We should take a look. If they have seen us we're just sitting ducks here. Get the men out and stay in cover.'

Slowly and silently the two men left the cab and moved to the rear. The flap of the tarpaulin was up and the men were recovering from their unexpected journey, rubbing bruised arms and legs. But no one seemed badly hurt.

An educated accent came from the blackness. Valentine. 'Have we stopped, sir? Pity. I was starting to enjoy that. Just like the dodgems at Margate.'

Bennett growled at him, 'Put a sock in it, Corporal, or I'll have your stripes. There's a Jerry truck up there and we don't know if we've been spotted, so we're leaving the bus here. Right. Everybody out.'

The men clambered over the tailgate and down onto the cobbled road, making as little noise as possible. As Lamb was moving towards the wall of the house something caught his eye and he cursed. Where their truck had collided with the brick wall, the rear axle had been bent so badly that the near-side tyres stood at an angle. The damage was beyond hope. He called to Bennett and pointed: 'That's it then. Truck's US.'

Bennett gawped. 'God, I'm sorry, sir.'

'Not your fault, Sarnt. You did your best.' He went to the cab and looked in. 'Madeleine. I'm afraid the truck's kaput. You'll have to come with us.'

Now they would see if his judgement had been right to allow her to come. She would have to keep up and perhaps even go with them into combat. She climbed down from the cab and followed Lamb and the others to the shelter of the wall. They were in single file now, with Mays and two others at the front, then Lamb, Smart and Bennett, with Valentine and the odds and sods bringing up the rear. Slowly, with rifles at the ready, they walked to the end of the house. Mays went forward and, crouching on one knee, peered gingerly around the corner.

The German truck was still there. A soldier in a forage cap was leaning against the side of the truck, looking quite relaxed. The driver, presumably. As Lamb watched, another man, with short, wiry fair hair, appeared from the doorway of a small house next to the fuel station. His tunic was half unbuttoned and he had a flagon in his hand. He laughed and shouted to the man by the truck, and although Lamb could not make out his words it was clear that he wanted him to join him. Mays whispered: 'Christ, sir, he's bloody drunk.'

It was true enough. The man in the doorway looked four parts gone. Clearly whatever men were in the truck had temporarily lost their unit but had found a store of local wine or cider. Again the man in the door shouted, and this time the driver shrugged and walked across to join him. Both of them went into the house. Lamb ran back to Bennett.

'Jerry's in there right enough. Probably no more than a platoon of them, though. And by the look of them they've had a skinful of local plonk. We're going in, fast, while they're still on the sauce. We'll take both flanks at once. You and Valentine's mob take the left flank, I'll take the right with Mays. Smart can stay here with the girl.'

Bennett nodded and silently motioned to the men to his rear to follow him. Then at a running crouch he crossed the road and they followed. Lamb looked behind him,

152

signalled to Smart to stay where he was with Madeleine, and waved his hand forward for the others, then he rejoined Mays on point and, leading from the front, pistol in hand, moved fast across the road towards the truck.

From inside the house they could now hear the sound of voices and music. A crackling gramophone was pumping out some jolly French dance-band song. Someone shouted louder. Others laughed. Lamb and his men had reached the door now, and as he looked round to Mays, ready to attack, another voice spoke from their front, in German, getting closer, and then the driver walked out of the building, laughing and looking back the way he had come, with a parting word. It was the last thing he ever said. As he turned and glimpsed the khaki figures, Mays rose and clamped a hand over his mouth, at the same time sliding his bayonet neatly into the German's side. Then, as the man fell in agony, he twisted his neck for good measure. Lamb heard the crack. He looked at Mays and nodded, surprised at his efficiency. He knew the corporal had a shady history, and some said he had once been part of a Brighton razor gang. Perhaps they were right. They left the corpse, and on a count of three Lamb and Tapley hurled a grenade into the house. At the same moment Bennett's men did the same at the rear door. They turned away for a second and heard the terror in the voices of the drunken Germans as they saw the grenades fly in. Then it was too late. The explosions pushed a pocket of dust and debris out of the doorway and into the yard, instantly followed by screams. Lamb yelled 'Now', and they burst in through the door, firing as they went, into the general darkness and the dust. Bennett, he knew, would hold back so as not to get caught in their fire.

Their surprise was complete. Coughing, they continued firing until Lamb yelled for them to stop. The interior of the house was a shambles. What the drunken Germans had not wrecked in their search for booze, Lamb and his men had done with their grenades. Shattered possessions lay everywhere in what had been the house's dining room. On a bullet- and shrapnel-scarred table in the centre of the room four German soldiers lay slumped in death. One was missing half of his head; another, a sergeant, had a hole clean through his forehead, although the exit wound had taken away the back of his skull. Another two lay sprawled across the terracotta-tiled floor in pools of their own spreading blood. Their booty, a dozen bottles of wine and several flagons of cider, lay shattered around the room, the red wine mixing with the blood on the floor. Gradually the dust settled and Bennett and his men came in from the back of the house.

Lamb saw him. 'Any more?'

'Two dead in the kitchen out the back, sir. Grenades got 'em.'

'Good. That must be the lot. Tell the men to watch out, Sarnt. We can't be sure there aren't more further into the village.'

Lamb took a second look at the corpses and was struck by a thought. That truck out there was now theirs for the taking. And if the driver was worth his salt and a good, efficient German, it would also be full of petrol. If not, there was more in the pump waiting to be taken. Corporal Mays and his men moved through the house and into the yard. Lamb gazed around the room. Although the grenades had torn into some of the corpses, some of the uniforms had hardly been touched at all.

He turned to Bennett. 'Help me get these Jerries out of their clothes. Just three of them will do.'

Bennett stared at him. 'Do, sir?'

'Camouflage, Sarnt. We're taking that lorry out there and we're going south, and we can't very well do that dressed in this, can we?' He tugged at his sleeve. 'You, me and one of the others. They look about the right size.'

Bennett started to help him unbutton the uniforms of the sergeant and another of the men at the table. It took a matter of minutes.

Lamb called across the room, 'Stubbs, take the clothes off that man there and put them on.'

'Sir?'

Bennett spoke. 'Just do it, Stubbs.'

Lamb unbuttoned his own tunic and trousers and within minutes was pulling on the German NCO's uniform. It was reasonably neat, with a single shrapnel rip on the arm and unexpectedly crisp and hard after his soft British army battle-dress, which he had had made at some expense. The grey trousers were narrow, allowing them to be tucked neatly into the jackboots; the tailored tunic fastened, he felt like he was wearing a corset. He did up the collar and placed the hat on his head, just as Bennett and Stubbs finished adjusting their own dress. Lamb picked up the leather belt with its eagle badge and the inscription 'Gott Mit Uns'. As he did so he took a moment to survey the piece of equip-ment which had caught his eye when he had first seen the dead sergeant: a holster, and within it an .08 Luger pistol. He clipped it around his waist, undid the button and slid the Luger from the pouch. It fitted nicely into the palm of his hand, and instinctively Lamb opened the breech in the handle and checked the ammo. Seven bullets.

Bennett looked at him, grinning. 'You look a proper sight, Mister Lamb, sir, if you don't mind my saying so. A really proper nasty Nazzie.'

Lamb laughed and moved his shoulders around in the unfamiliar jacket. 'Thank you, Sarnt. Just doesn't feel right. Not at all.'

He straightened his cap, catching sight of it in the cracked mirror above the fireplace, until its peak was over his eyes. His temporary demotion in rank amused him. He handed his own uniform to Smart with instructions to stow it in his pack. 'Come on then. Let's show the others before they take us for the real thing and shoot us.'

With Bennett's men following on they walked through the ruined dining room and into the yard, where the remainder of his small command did a double take.

Tapley sniggered. 'Blimey, sir. You don't 'alf make a good Jerry.'

Bennett growled: 'That's enough now.'

'But, Sarge, you can see as well as me . . .'

'You heard me. As you were.'

Lamb spoke. 'Right. Here's what we're going to do. We're taking that truck there and we're going to drive hell for leather towards the Somme. You lot are going to sit in the back and keep very, very quiet and look after our French guest, and Sarnt Bennett, Stubbs and I will sit in the cab and pretend to be Germans. Just pray that we don't get caught. Corporal Mays, see what's in the back of the truck.'

Mays pulled up the tarpaulin covering the wooden rear transport section of the Opel Blitz, and gasped. 'Blimey, sir. I think you'd better come and have a dekko at this.'

Lamb walked across to the truck and peered in. Inside lay four German machine guns, MG34s, attached to bipods for light use, and with them several unopened boxes of drum ammunition. Lamb whistled. 'Quite a catch. They should make nice present for our chaps on the Somme. They can kill the Jerries with their own guns. Stack them in the centre of the truck and arrange yourselves around them. Might be a bit of a squash, but I promise I'll be as quick as I can.'

He knew it was not a promise he was likely to keep. Their new acquisition had changed his mind from the route he had planned to take to the sea and by foot across the estuary flats. The quickest route to the Somme was obvious: straight down the D928 to Canchy and then on to Abbeville. Then across the Authie and on to the Somme. But Lamb knew that, just as before, to take the obvious route would mean encountering German units *en route*. The only option, once again, was to go across country.

He opened out his map on the bonnet of the German truck and called over Bennett, Mays and Valentine. 'Right. This is where we should go.' He moved his finger down the long straight road to the south. 'At least it's where we would go if there weren't so many Jerries in the way.' He moved his finger to the left. 'And this is where we're going to go.' He traced his finger down the line of a smaller road. The men peered at the map. It was not hard to see the lack of settlements as it made its way through open countryside and woodland. 'There are fewer towns along there, and if we're lucky there won't be any road-blocks. That's what we want to avoid at all costs. Being stopped. My German's not worth a shilling.'

Mays said, 'Sir, Corporal Valentine speaks German.'

Valentine scowled at him, furious at having a confidence betrayed.

Lamb frowned. 'Do you, Valentine? Do you speak German? You haven't mentioned it before.'

Valentine smiled in that particular, insincere way of his. 'Well, I do have a smattering, sir. Not much. Schoolboy really.'

'Not much is ten times better than mine, Corporal.'

He turned to Stubbs. 'Right, get out of that Jerry uniform and give it to the corporal here. You're changing places.' He looked back to Valentine. 'We'll have you up with the Sarnt and me. You're travelling in the cab, Valentine.'

'Only too happy to help, sir.'

Lamb wondered why Valentine hadn't mentioned his ability before, and also how Mays had come to learn

157

about it. He was sure there could be nothing sinister about it, but all the same Valentine was a rum sort and if he had abandoned his roots, as it appeared he had in refusing to accept the responsibility of a commission, then who knew what else he might betray? He would tackle Mays about it when they next had a chance to talk.

Bennett interrupted his thoughts. 'So are we planning to drive in daylight, sir?'

Lamb nodded. 'Absolutely. We've got to bluff it out. Time is everything. Besides, I'm not worried about being spotted from the skies. We look like the real thing from above now. Whoever we might fail to fool will be on the ground.'

Lamb climbed up into the cab and eased himself into the driver's seat. It felt strange to be sitting on the left of the vehicle, and he took a moment or two to acquaint himself with the controls. The German machine felt very different to the Bedford. For one thing it was a fraction higher and longer, although the driver's seat was ranged lower. But the main thing he noticed was the gears. There were five of them, plus reverse. The speedometer, too, extended over a different range. Of course it was in kilometres, but even working that out Lamb could see that it was set to gauge a good fifteen kilometres an hour more than the maximum speed of the British truck. It was no great surprise. Anyone with a modicum of mechanical experience knew how good German engineering was. Perhaps, he thought, that's partly how they had managed to come so far into France in so short a time. He pressed the starter button and the machine kicked into life, over-revving as he pushed on the accelerator. He turned to Bennett. 'I should hold on, Sarnt, if I were you. It might be a bit of a bumpy ride.'

He edged out of the yard and onto the road, past the body of the German driver, and into the village street.

He felt as uncomfortable as he had ever been. He was wearing an enemy uniform and driving an enemy vehicle in enemy territory. And he was only too aware that if they were captured he for one would be shot out of hand as a spy. But he told himself again that when he had started off on this mission he had suspected it was going to land him in challenging situations. As far as he was aware he was the only man with any chance of getting word to General Fortune that if he was forced to retreat the only way home would be from the port of Le Havre. And it occurred to Lamb that, if that did prove to be the case – if Fortune were pushed back by the might of the German advance – then for the entire 51st Division, all 10,000 men, he was probably now the only hope.

13

Bennett was at the wheel again and the truck was moving smoothly. Lamb had laid the map out in front of him, spread across the shallow dashboard, and was plotting their course for the umpteenth time. How, he wondered, could he possibly have any idea where the enemy might be? He presumed they would have occupied and garrisoned all of the larger towns they had overrun in the lightning advance to Abbeville, so those would be out of the question as points on their route. But tanks were cross-country vehicles. They might be anywhere, ready to lob just one shell at their truck and send them all to oblivion.

Lamb's dread of tanks preyed on his mind and he could not expunge the image of the poor, half-mad infantryman in Arras who had seen his friend crushed to death in agony, beneath the tracks of a Panzer. Trying to divert himself, he traced their route in the truck with his fingernail across the map.

As he was studying the possible alternative roads, of which there were precious few, Valentine began to hum. It was not the song itself that irritated Lamb. 'Where or when' really wasn't half bad. In fact he had bought the

160

recording from the local music shop in Tonbridge shortly before embarking for France. Nor was it the tunefulness of Valentine's version. In fact, annoyingly, Valentine was pitch perfect. No, thought Lamb, it was more the way in which he hummed it, as if he wanted to keep it to himself, and the fact that he did so over and over again. Lamb wondered that he had never noticed it before, and whether the others had been aware of it. Or perhaps, he thought, it was something Valentine had just started to do merely to irritate him, in what seemed increasingly to be a personal vendetta. Whatever the reason, in the past few hours in which the two of them and Bennett had been sitting together crammed into the cab of the Opel, Valentine's presence had really begun to annoy Lamb. It was the very fact that his self-control should be compromised by such a man which irked him more than anything. The corporal had not yet had to use his German and had not said a word. But, still, he had somehow got under Lamb's skin. Now he began to hum again.

Lamb snapped, 'For Christ's sake, shut up, Valentine. If we've heard that bloody tune once in the last hour we've heard it ten times. Don't you know anything else? Or, better still, why don't you hum nothing at all?'

Valentine looked at him and smiled like a crestfallen schoolboy told off by a favourite master. 'I'm terribly sorry, sir. I had no idea it was annoying you so much. I'll stop then, shall I?'

Lamb said nothing and had to exercise self-control to stop himself wringing the man's neck. Bennett saw it. 'That's right, Valentine. You just change your tune. That'll suit us all, sir, won't it?'

Lamb smiled at the joke and, still saying nothing, stared at the map, unable now, despite the fact that Valentine had stopped, to get the song out of his own head.

'. . . but who knows where or when? . . .'

At least his hunch had been right. The road, which was really no more than a tiny rural track to the east of the D12, had hardly passed through any built-up areas. Now, though, they were nearing the one village that they could not avoid, and to his amusement he realised that it bore the name of Crécy en Ponthieu. He was wondering whether any of the others might spot its significance when Valentine, whom he had been aware was also looking at the map, spoke.

'It's really terribly clever of you, sir.'

'Corporal?'

'Well, to take us on such a very clever route. To give us all another history lesson.'

Lamb smiled. Trust Valentine to have noticed it. He responded grudgingly, 'Well done. I was wondering who'd be the first to spot it.'

Bennett looked puzzled. 'Beggin' your pardon, sir, but can I ask what you're talking about?'

'Well, Sarnt, the corporal here has spotted that the only village on our route is a place called Crécy. Just as we found ourselves at Waterloo, we've stumbled across another battlefield. We beat the French here too, in 1346.'

Valentine stared straight ahead and declaimed in Shakespearean tones: 'The English archers stepped forth one pace and let fly their arrows, so wholly and so thick that it seemed snow.' He turned to Lamb. 'Sorry, sir, that's Froissart. John Froissart. *The Chronicles.*'

'Yes, Corporal. I am aware of the book. Very poetic.' He looked back at the map. 'If you really want to know, I didn't intend to bring you here. It was pure fluke.'

They were nearing the town now, and on either side of the road the countryside was lush grassland. To their left Lamb spotted a small wooden notice. 'There you are. We're on the battlefield now.'

Bennett looked around as he drove. 'Hardly seems possible, sir, does it? What was it then, five hundred years ago?'

'Six hundred, Sergeant,' Valentine corrected him.

'Yes, six hundred years, near as dammit.' Lamb scratched at an itch on his leg, presumably from the fabric of the German trousers. 'I wonder if people will come here after we've gone and say the same about us.'

Valentine said, 'Well, we're not actually fighting here, sir, are we?'

At that moment there was an all-too-familiar noise in the sky above them and a vibration that shook the truck, almost making Bennett swerve. Then, seconds later and 200 yards away to their right and it seemed almost directly overhead, three huge aircraft came in low over the fields.

In his surprise, Bennett barely managed to hold the truck steady and swore as he wrenched the wheel. 'Jesus Christ. Bloody hell. Sorry, sir.' He cast a glance at the massive grey shapes, and saw the double black crosses on the fuselage. 'They're bloody Jerry.'

They slowed down and Lamb watched as the three planes, snub-nosed ME110 fighter-bombers, dipped below the tree line off to their right and reached the ground. He looked at the map, searching for the road and a relevant sign. 'Must be an airstrip.'

'A Jerry airstrip?'

'Well, it is now.' He was pointing to the sign on the map. 'Up till a few days ago it was French.'

Lamb could hardly believe it. They had come this far, and despite all his best efforts to take the most obscure of routes they had stumbled into a hotbed of enemy activity. He marvelled at the efficiency of the Germans. They could not have been here for more than a few days, yet already they had managed to locate and take over an Allied airfield and were apparently flying bombing raids out of it. He also realised that it was likely that around the next bend they would run slap bang into a Luftwaffe roadblock.

He turned to Bennett. 'Kill the engine.'

The sergeant stopped the truck and pulled up at the roadside. 'What do we do now, sir?'

Lamb did not have a straight answer. They had two options. They could carry on regardless and push through, by force or guile, any enemy roadblock in the town. Or, he thought, they could stop here and use the captured machine guns to wreak as much havoc as possible on the airfield. Choose the first option and he would be carrying out his orders and getting the message to Fortune. If he managed to do that in time and if he could find the general, and if Colonel 'R' had been genuine, then perhaps, just perhaps, his action might save thousands of British soldiers from death or captivity.

Choose the second way, though, and Lamb knew that, even by knocking out one or two of the bombers and disrupting the base, they would definitely have a direct effect upon the immediate course of the battle raging either side of them in the north and the south, and there was no doubt that their action would save the lives of their comrades in both sectors. It was a terrible dilemma, and for some minutes Lamb sat silent, saying nothing. Even though his faith in the colonel had already provoked him into a court-martial offence and brought him here, endangering the lives of his men, it was hard not to see the absolute logic now of using their new-found resources in direct action. Aside from that, his conscience was still aching from having abandoned Petrie and the men at the canal. He wondered what their fate had been, and part of him felt that he must atone for his actions. He looked at Bennett and saw from his expression that he understood.

However, it was Valentine who finally goaded him

164

into action. 'Funny, sir, isn't it? If we hadn't come here to find your battlefield, we wouldn't be in such a pickle. Do you think history's trying to tell us something?'

Lamb, finally snapping, turned on him. 'Shut up, Valentine. I didn't bring us here to find a bloody battlefield. I came here on orders. Do you think this is easy?'

But he knew that, for all his insolence, the corporal had hit on something like the truth. If they ignored their circumstances they would be betraying not only their comrades, cowering in their front-line trenches under bombs delivered by these planes, but betraying an entire tradition of British military might that stretched back to the bowmen who had stood their ground on these very fields six hundred years ago. He turned to Bennett. 'We've got to do something here. You know that, don't you? We've got to stop those bloody bombers taking off again. It's our duty.'

Bennett smiled, 'Yes, sir. Anyway I'd had enough of running away for the moment.'

Valentine shook his head, unable to believe that Lamb wanted to attack a German base. Lamb reconnoitred the road around them.

Aside from the row of trees alongside which they were now parked, it offered little if any cover. Clearly the entrance to the airfield must be no more than a few hundred yards down the road and off to the right. He thought fast. Apart from the four MG34s in the back of the truck and the mortar, their chief weapon was surprise, and if they were to have any reasonable effect, and also have any chance of getting out alive, they would have to use it to the full.

He turned to Valentine. 'Stay here, and if anyone comes up, use your German. I'm going into the back.'

Lamb got out of the cab and walked round to the rear of the truck, then, lifting the cover, he climbed inside. Fourteen pairs of eyes looked at him anxiously.

'Look, this is what's happening. That noise you heard was Jerry bombers. ME110s. There's a squadron of them, perhaps more, in an airfield over to the right, and I mean to destroy them.'

He let it sink in. 'Corporal Mays, I want two of those Jerry guns, three if you can do it, set up pointing out of the tailgate. Two-man crews on each of them. Perkins, Butterworth, Hughes and Tapley, you'll do. And make sure you have plenty of ammo to hand. You others can help feed them. We're going to bluff our way into the base. Then wait till I give the word, and when I do, two of you lift the flap at the back and let them have it. Stubbs, how many mortar bombs have we left?'

'Three, sir.'

'Right. When the balloon goes up, you and Parry stay in the back half of the truck near the cab. Get rid of that tarp and use your bombs. And make them count, Stubbs. Right, everyone got it?'

They all nodded, and Lamb looked at Madeleine. Her eyes were wide and bright – not, as he had expected, with fear, but with real excitement. He had thought to leave her in cover at the roadside, but seeing her he realised at once that if anything went wrong this would be the best place for her, with the men and in the thick of it. A good enough place for anyone to die. He started to drop the flap and go back to the cab, but then quickly he turned back. 'Smart, give me your bayonet.'

'Sir?'

'Your bayonet, man. I have a feeling that I might need it.'

Clutching the long knife, Lamb dropped the flap of the lorry and walked back to the front of the cab. Carefully he slid the thin blade of the 17-inch infantry bayonet down the side of his right jackboot and then, climbing back in, he changed places with Valentine, placing him

166

in the outside passenger seat where he would be able to speak to any guard. Then he nodded to Bennett and they started off.

They drove along the road and past the long line of trees until they reached a slight bend from which a fork went left and right.

Lamb looked at Bennett. 'Here we go. Turn right, Sarnt.'

Bennett turned the wheel and moved the Opel slowly along the smaller of the two tracks to the right, around the north end of the woods, which up till now had shielded their right. As Lamb had suspected, ahead of them lay a simple wooden gatehouse and beside it a red and white striped barrier pole. A single German sentry stood guard with a slung rifle, but Lamb was sure that there would be more men inside the guard hut. He shot Valentine a glance. 'Do your best, Corporal.'

Valentine said nothing and the truck rolled on towards the barrier. As they approached, the guard unslung his rifle and levelled it at them. '*Halt. Wir kommen?*'

Valentine stuck his head out of the window and smiled, then spoke in fluent German. The two men had a brief conversation, during which the guard smiled and nodded.

Christ, thought Lamb, it looked as if the man had bought whatever tale Valentine had spun. They were in the clear. He smiled at the sentry and Bennett began to move towards the barrier, on which the man had placed a hand. Lamb whispered to Valentine, 'What on earth did you say was in the back?'

'Supplies. Very urgent. The commandant's wine from Abbeville.' Lamb smiled, but just as the guard was beginning to raise the barrier he dropped it back into place. Lamb swore under his breath. The man frowned and peered into the cab, then muttered something else.

Valentine turned to Lamb. 'He wants you, sir.' The

guard looked uneasy and motioned them out of the cab. Valentine replied in German, 'All right, we're coming.'

He jumped down, and Lamb followed. He cast a backwards glance at the guardhouse but saw that no one had emerged to follow them. Then he caught Bennett's eye and jerked his head towards the door.

Lamb was sweating now. Perhaps this wasn't going to be such a piece of cake. Still talking to Valentine, the guard moved with him to the rear of the truck, with Lamb following. They stopped, and as Valentine moved forward to lift the tarpaulin he looked at Lamb, who fell, fast and silent, upon the guard. Covering his mouth with the palm of his hand, he slipped the bayonet up from his jackboot and drove it hard into the man's side as he had been taught in hand-to-hand combat classes – not perhaps with as much street gang style as Mays, but certainly hard enough to do the job. The guard's eyes widened with pain and terror and then clouded over as he slipped limp to the ground.

Lamb and Valentine swiftly dragged his lifeless body into the trees and pushed it beneath the undergrowth before moving back round to the front of the truck. Lamb looked up at Bennett, who shook his head and nodded towards the guardhouse. As he did so another guard emerged through the doorway. He looked startled and clearly alarmed not to see his friend. Then he saw Lamb in the German sergeant's uniform and nodded respectfully at him before saying something which he did not understand. Valentine intervened, pointing to the man's tunic, on which a button was undone. But it was too late. The man had noticed the rip in the sleeve of Lamb's uniform, where its previous owner had taken a piece of shrapnel, and, worse than that, the fresh blood, which shone on the left side of Lamb's tunic. He began to raise his rifle and Lamb watched in horror as he opened his mouth to shout the alarm to the base. Lamb began to reach for the bayonet, but from nowhere, it seemed to Lamb, a blade shot out of the darkness and fixed the German in the chest, penetrating his heart. As the man fell to the ground, Lamb looked at where it had come from and saw Valentine, grinning and staring at the dying guard.

After a few seconds Lamb spoke. 'Come on, let's get this body shifted.' They dumped the dead man in the guardhouse, and as they did so Lamb said, 'Thank you, Corporal. That was a bit close for comfort.'

'Quite all right, sir. Would have done the same for anyone.'

Again Lamb wondered at the man, belittling his own action in saving the life of his officer just to maintain that irritating façade of cynicism.

While Lamb and Valentine pushed up the barrier, Bennett jumped into the Opel and started her up before they climbed aboard. They continued along the road, and very soon the trees had given way to open fields stretching flat into the far distance. Directly ahead of them lay two huge hangars and the shell of a third, burnt out, and close by the wreckage of four destroyed Bristol Blenheim fighters. So the RAF had been here too, with the French, before the Germans had come.

To the left of the hangars stood half a dozen wooden sheds – barrack blocks, he presumed – and a smaller structure which still bore a sign in English: 'The Ritz – Officers Mess'. All were lit up from the inside, and from the smaller hut they could hear the sound of music. To their right six ME110s lay on a grass landing strip, the pale moonlight glancing off their hulls. Two were being attended by refuelling trucks, while a third was surrounded by ground crew refitting her with ammunition.

Bennett carried on driving until they had drawn level with the first of the barrack huts and then Lamb looked at him and gestured to the right. The truck veered off the track and across the runway till it was behind the farthest of the aircraft. A few of the ground crew looked round in surprise before returning to their work and no one moved from either the barracks or the mess hut. Bennett drove alongside the planes for about thirty yards and then, when Lamb saw that they were perfectly placed to cover all six, he gave the word and Bennett turned a sharp left and stopped the truck, being careful not to switch off. As he did so, Lamb yelled to his rear: 'Right. Now. Let them have it.'

Behind him Perkins and Hughes pulled hard on the sides of the rear tarpaulin and the flaps flew up to reveal the three machine guns and their crews. At the same time Parry threw off the rear of the canvas and dropped a bomb into the muzzle of the mortar. Then all hell broke loose.

The machine guns, as yet unfired in war, rattled off their deadly load and bullets slapped at a rate of 900 rounds per minute into everything in their path: metal, wood, canvas and flesh.

Some of the rounds found their home in the ground crew, and within moments most of them were dead or dying. Several hit the two petrol tankers, sending them sky high in explosions that tore apart the night sky, and these were instantly followed by three of the aircraft themselves as their newly filled fuel tanks ignited and blew them to pieces. There was a thump as the first of the mortar rounds hit another of the planes, splitting it apart.

Lamb jumped out of the cab and rushed to the rear of the truck and watched as the world in front of them dissolved into a sea of flames and death. The wounded came rushing towards him, out of the inferno, human torches, their terrible shrieks barely audible, only to be mercifully despatched by the machine guns. Still Lamb's men kept the ammo coming. And in the orange light of the burning aircraft he saw Madeleine too now as she pulled open one of the crates and handed the circular metal cartridges to the men on the guns. The barrels were getting hotter now and Lamb knew that it would not be long before he would have to order a ceasefire. It had only been a matter of minutes, but already they had done all that he had hoped they would. But he knew that at any moment the barracks would spill out the enemy.

Lamb shouted to Mays, 'Hold your fire. Get the infantry.' Two guns were silent and he heard the third stop shooting as he ran along the side of the truck. He yelled up to Bennett: 'Get going. Turn her round against the barracks.'

The truck drew away and turned a full circle in a tight angle. Lamb stepped out of its way. He had drawn the Luger now and prayed that it would live up to its reputation. As he watched a dozen Germans in various states of undress rushed from the first of the barrack buildings, to be joined by officers piling out of the mess block, pistols and sub-machine guns in their hands. Lamb took careful aim with the captured Luger, resting it on his left forearm for support, and focused it centrally on the chest of the leading officer, a big man with an open tunic who was shouting words which could not be heard. He squeezed the trigger and the pistol came back against his hand. Simultaneously, it seemed, the officer's chest opened in a spray of blood and he flew back against the side of the building just as Bennett stopped the truck.

The men in the rear had managed to keep their positions, but only one gun crackled into life. Yet it was enough to stop the tide of grey surging from the barracks. Some of the officers, however, had stopped and were taking aim. As Lamb watched they opened fire on the rear of the truck, and he saw Tapley fall. Slipping the Luger into his holster, he ran towards the tailgate and heaved himself aboard, then crouching down amid the bullets managed to pick up one of the machine guns from the floor where it had fallen and lever it back onto its bipod.

He turned to Madeleine, 'Get down. Hit the floor.'

More of the infantry had got out of the barracks now, and even Butterworth's steady fire could not wholly stop them. Lamb saw Parry, blood seeping from his shoulder, lob another bomb into the mortar before it flew towards the barracks block. It missed but exploded on the ground in front, sending shrapnel fragments towards the officers. Three of them fell, and now Lamb was at the second machine gun himself. Perkins crammed another magazine round onto the mechanism and Lamb pressed the trigger, spraying the infantry and stopping them in their tracks like a deadly hailstorm. More explosions from behind told him that another plane had gone up and he knew that it was time to leave before they met the same fate. Surprise had gone now, and with it most of their ammunition.

Lamb handed the grip of the gun to Perkins and leapt from the tailgate, then ran to the cab. 'Go, man, go on. Get us out of here. Come on.'

He hoisted himself up using the door and the seat, and as Bennett began to move off swung himself down into the passenger seat. Bennett turned to the left and pressed his foot hard down on the accelerator pedal, revving it up and pushing it towards its maximum speed. The engine complained but carried on, and the truck sputtered then shot forward to clear the edge of the mess hut before hitting the track to the gate. From behind them he heard the guttering rattle of semi-automatic fire and then a shriek and a groan, and Lamb wondered who had been hit. He prayed that it wasn't Madeleine and then felt guilty for valuing her above a member of his platoon. The sweat was pouring off him, making dark marks on the grey serge of the captured uniform. He felt sick with excitement and fear and noticed for the first time that he had been hit in the left forearm. No more than a glancing blow. He had also lost his peaked cap. The Luger, though, was still in his belt. The truck carried on down the lane, passing the barrier and the dead guards, and emerged on the main road.

Bennett looked at Lamb. 'Sir?'

'Take a left and keep driving. We need to make some miles away from here. Fast. Every bloody Jerry in the district will be on our tail soon.'

They swung to the left and Lamb looked out of the cab window. Leaping flames and columns of thick black smoke marked the location of the airfield, and more explosions still rocked the night. Good, he thought. He imagined that would be the fuel dumps going up as the fires spread. It was a job well done.

He turned to Valentine, who was sitting with a blank expression, staring out at the night. 'Where the devil did you learn to throw a knife like that?'

'It's not that hard. A few years ago I was part of an act. You know, sir, a stage act. Variety. Music halls, mainly. Just after I left university. I was drifting a bit. We played the south coast. Actually, we supported Max Miller once. You know, sir, the comic. Now there's an interesting man. I knew it would come in useful some time.'

Lamb stared at him. The man was an enigma. 'Come in useful?' He shook his head. 'Is there anything you haven't done, Valentine?'

Valentine smiled. 'Well, yes, there is actually. I've never been an officer, sir.'

They drove on through the night, sticking to the minor roads, even though it did not make things easy for them as Lamb had ordered Bennett to drive without lights. Looking across the fields to a major road which ran roughly parallel with their own, Lamb could see enemy trucks and smaller vehicles racing in the opposite direction, presumably towards the base. A whimper from the rear reminded him of the casualties, and finally, when they were a good five miles clear of the base and in the midst of a thick forest, he told Bennett to stop.

Opening the door and rushing round to the rear, Lamb pulled himself up into the truck. The wooden floor was slick with blood and four bodies lay slumped against the rails. Archer and Mitchell were obviously dead, their sightless eyes staring to the heavens. Lamb searched quickly for Madeleine and was happy to see her in the back of the truck tending the wounds of a fifth casualty, Sergeant McKracken. He looked at the others. Driscoll and Blake were goners too. Tapley was mumbling something about his mother and didn't look long for the world. Of the other eight men, miraculously none had been badly wounded. He found Mays.

'Well done back there, all of you. There'll be a few less bombs falling on our chaps tomorrow. We need to ditch the dead here, I'm afraid. And we've no time to bury them properly.'

They placed the four men in the woods to their right, and covered them as best they could with brambles. Lamb stood for a few moments beside the sad, makeshift tombs and muttered a few words of commendation, then they all piled back into the truck. Madeleine was cradling Tapley's head in her lap. Lamb looked at her and there was no need to speak. He could see the tears running clear down her face in the moonlight. He shook his head and she lowered hers.

Lamb turned away, jumped off the tailgate and climbed back up into the cab, closing the door. 'Let's go, Sarnt. They're sure to be right behind us.'

Peering at the map by the light of a small torch, Lamb

took them through the woods and south again, skirting a small hamlet, until once again they were in open fields. They were on nothing more than a farm track now, and Lamb was pleased. He knew that they were almost there, but at the same time was well aware that this would be the hardest part of their journey.

He was in two minds about what to do. Very soon he knew they must hit the rear echelons of the German front line. It stood to reason that if the 51st had drawn a line from the coast along the Somme, as the colonel had told him they would, then the advancing Germans would be directly opposite. So their task now was to break through the German lines once again but this time from the rear, pushing their way out. That at least would take the Jerries by surprise. Then, however, they would have to make it to the safety of their own lines.

Well, thought Lamb, one thing at a time. The choice now facing him immediately was whether they should carry on at night and risk all for speed and the cover of darkness, or whether they should lie low and wait for day, then bluff it out. In the dark a fast-moving lorry would undoubtedly arouse suspicion, and he was unsure, given their mental and physical state, if the men in the back would be able to win another encounter with a pursuing enemy. But to wait for the day also had its own pitfalls. First and foremost, the truck was in a sorry state. The tarpaulin was ripped and half gone and it was not hard to see from the rear the khaki-clad men and weapons in the back. From the front, however, he presumed that the truck still had a veneer of correctness. If they could guarantee to meet their enemy head on before blasting their way through, that might be the way to go.

But at this stage in a campaign where the British army had been out-manoeuvred, if not entirely out-fought, he knew that nothing could be guaranteed. They were moving fast now, as fast as the truck could manage, touching the 45-kilometre marker, and she was shaking. Those in the back, Madeleine included, had stopped making any sound, and none of the three men in the cab had spoken for a while. Lamb felt his eyes beginning to close and, waking with jolt from a second-long doze, shook himself awake, but just as he did so he was aware that Bennett too had taken his eyes off the road for a second and that the truck, arriving at that moment at a junction where a major road crossed their own, was taking the wrong turning and joining the highway.

Lamb came to his senses: 'Christ, Bennett. This is the wrong way. We're heading for that bloody town.' But it was too late. Sergeant Bennett pressed hard on the brake, but not before the truck had gone blundering into the outskirts of the village of Buigny-Saint-Maclou. The usual brick-walled farms rose on either side of them without any perceptible signs of life. Then, without warning, the street opened out into a wide crossroads and before them stood a pair of wrought-iron gates edged with verges of shorn grass. Beyond them, on a slight rise, Lamb could see the twinkling lights of a large château. On either side of the gates stood a German lorry. Half a dozen infantrymen stood smoking beside them, and with them, seated on his bike, with his mate in the armed sidecar, was a great-coated motorcycle outrider. As the Opel screeched towards them the Germans looked up in alarm.

Lamb yelled at Bennett, 'For God's sake, man, put your foot down. And turn right. Go right here. Now!'

Bennett spun the steering wheel and turned the truck to the right so fast that she almost went onto two wheels, and for a moment Lamb was convinced that she would topple over. But she bounced back onto the road. Behind them now he could hear the revving of engines and the unmistakable sound of a motorbike roaring into action.

He pushed across the seat, past Valentine, and got to the window. 'Move over. There's only one way to do this.'

Lamb drew the Luger from his holster and waited. He could hear the motorcyclist approaching now, changing gear from third to fourth as he neared the driver's cab. Lamb pictured the man's face under speed as he approached, accelerating fast, his features drawn back in a rictus by the g-force as the speedometer crept steadily up the gauge. He knew those bikes. The BMW R12. 745 ccs of pure power. He had seen one in action just before the war, racing at Brooklands. Lovely machines, capable of 120 kilometres an hour. For the Wehrmacht they had been mounted with an MG34 on the sidecar. And now one of them was closing in on them – fast.

The man in the sidecar was shouting now. Orders to them to stop. He would have seen the men in the back in their khaki by now. Lamb waited for the first smack of the machine-gun bullets to hit the cab, but none came. Instead the man kept on shouting. Then there was a burst of machine-gun fire from the MG34 on the sidecar. Not at the truck, but a warning shot well placed into the road a hundred yards ahead of them, tearing up pieces of earth and cobblestone. The man shouted again. Lamb did nothing, and waited. Waited until he could see the front of the bike and then the German's hands on the handle-bars and his rubberised coat flapping in the wind. Then he leant out of the window, pushing his arm out across the lowered glass. He knew that he had only a split second, and quickly, without aiming, squeezed the trigger. He was briefly aware of the bike rider's face and goggles exploding in a spray of blood before he pulled his arm back into the cab. There was a scream and then the sound of the bike swerving and then crashing. Lamb stared ahead and realised that he was breathing heavily.

Valentine stared at him. 'All right, sir?'

'Yes. They won't give us any more trouble. But you'd better keep her floored, Bennett. Those Jerries in the trucks will be up here soon enough.'

Lamb looked at the map and saw that their present route would take them directly to the Somme canal. He estimated that they might be there in twenty minutes. There was only one problem. The canal was sure to be patrolled by Germans. In fact, if the colonel's word was anything to go by it might well form the German front line, flowing parallel as it did with the river itself, which he knew was to be the British position. They were caught between the Germans now pursuing them, who would have found the dead bike rider, and those in front. It also occurred to him that if the two front lines were close, then, were they to crash the German lines from the rear as he had intended, they would be shot to pieces by the British before they reached their own men. It seemed perverse, but the best thing they could now do was to abandon the truck.

They were approaching another small hamlet. It was as good a place as any. He turned to Bennett. 'Sarnt, stop the truck.'

'Sir?'

'Stop the truck. We're going to leave her here. We'll be safer on foot.'

Bennett pulled over to the right and switched off the engine. The night was still, and Lamb heard no sound of approaching engines. Either they had lost their pursuers or they had given up the chase, but he did not hold out much hope of the latter. He climbed down from the cab, followed by the others, and walked to the rear. The back of the truck, lit up by the moonlight, was a shambles of spent ammunition, blood, vomit and discarded equipment. Lamb flipped down the tailgate and began to help the men out. Smart, Perkins and the others seemed remarkably robust, considering what they had been through, and he felt a wave of pride in his platoon sweeping over him.

His platoon. Christ, he thought. Was this all that was left of them? Eight men, plus Valentine and Bennett. That was it. Of the twenty-eight men he had led in Belgium two weeks ago, only ten remained, plus the four wounded whom he hoped were still in France or even back in Blighty. They had lost half their strength. And what had they accomplished? Damn little, he thought, although at least these few were still alive. Had he been a good officer, he wondered. Had he cared for his men or spent their lives foolishly? Now was not the time, though, to examine his conscience.

Butterworth had injured his leg when the truck had swerved, and Lamb helped him down from the back and then jumped up to find Madeleine sitting at the back, up against the cab, cradling Tapley's dead body. She looked at him. 'He asked for you. Then for his mother.'

'It's often that way. At the end.'

Lamb leaned down and gently took the dead boy away from her, before carrying him to the tailgate and handing him down to Bennett. 'Put him somewhere shady, Sarnt. Out of harm's way.'

He helped the girl down, then looked at the men. 'You've probably guessed. We're leaving the vehicle here. We're almost at our lines, and we'd be sitting ducks in that truck as we are. My plan is that you are our prisoners. We'll pretend to the Jerries that we're taking you in. And the girl. If our chaps are really so close, it will seem quite possible. Valentine can speak German. But if they talk to me the game's up and we let them have it. We'll have to leave most of the rifles, but Corporal Valentine and Sergeant Bennett will each take one of the machine guns and some ammo, and I want each of you to make sure you've got something on you: a bayonet, a knife, a grenade. Anything. Something to fight with.'

179

He hoped to God that his plan would succeed. And he prayed that the colonel had been right and that Fortune and his men had established a line at the Somme. If he had not, then for all Lamb knew they were simply walking deeper into the German lines – towards captivity or death.

14

As quietly as possible, Bennett moved the truck off the road to the left, where it was partly hidden by a coppice of trees at the far edge of a field. Beside it, in the shelter of the trees, they buried Tapley in a shallow grave, leaving his helmet resting on the mound of freshly dug earth to show where he lay. Lamb said a few words and then they turned away and followed him back across the road, without their rifles. Lamb was the last to leave the graveside. How vulnerable they looked, he thought, soldiers with no means to defend themselves, and no means of attack, except the few weapons he had told them to keep hidden. Perhaps it had been foolish to leave the rifles and machine guns. It went against everything the rule book dictated. But what alternative did they have? he asked himself. If they were seen by the enemy, armed and in British uniform, they would be shot. At least this way, masquerading as his prisoners, with Valentine's German, they had a slim chance of bluffing their way through.

The road stretched out ahead of them on the left, leading directly west and to the Somme canal. He looked at the map. There were two bridges across the canal, one directly ahead of them and another off to the north west.

The closer one was in a town and would be buzzing with Germans, even at this time. The smaller, more distant bridge would be less frantic, he was sure. It would, however, mean a two-mile walk across open country and, with all their injuries and wounds, not to mention their general exhaustion, he hoped that they, and not least Madeleine, would manage it.

He prayed too that the word had not yet got out of what had happened at the air base and knew that every moment now was precious.

They fell in at the roadside in the lee of an embankment, beyond which fields rose above the road, and as he watched them Lamb's mind wandered back to the colonel's words: '. . . gutter scrapings . . . underfed and ill-educated'. He knew that it had been true of a few of them, but they were his men, his platoon, and they had done damn well to make it this far. He knew, whatever the colonel thought, that the men who made it back to Britain would have to form the backbone of the new army that would strike back into France and defeat Hitler. They had unique experience. They had withstood the maelstrom of the German *blitzkrieg* and survived. They knew the odds and would, he guessed, soon be NCOs, if not officers – like Valentine. For that reason alone he knew that, as soon as he had delivered the message to General Fortune, it was his duty to get them home.

He turned to them. 'Right, lads, we're almost there. By my reckoning, four or five miles down that road, across the Somme canal, there's a British division. We're heading for a bridge at a place called Petit Port. We've made it this far, and whatever happens now, whatever danger lies ahead in the next few hours, we're going to make it all the way. Remember, you're my prisoners now. I know it's hard, but try to look like it. No smiling , Wilkinson. And no wisecracks. And any man who addresses me as sir

182

will be on a charge.' They laughed at that one. 'Got that, Sarnt Bennett? And for God's sake no one call Sarnt Bennett "Sergeant". He's a bloody Jerry now. Pretend to be frightened of him.' They liked that too. 'And Valentine too for that matter.' Then he had a brilliant idea. 'Valentine. Change uniforms with me. Quick as you can, man.'

'Sir?'

'Your German's the best. It stands to reason that as the NCO you're the man in charge. Why should they want to talk to me if you're in command? Change uniforms, man. Now!'

The two of them moved to one side and both began to unbutton their tunics. Soon they were each wearing the other's uniform. Lamb gave Valentine his captured belt and holster and the precious Luger: 'That's only on loan, Valentine. Understand?'

Valentine gave Lamb the machine pistol he had liberated from the dead guard. 'Very good, sir.'

'And for God's sake don't call me sir. You're in command now.' Lamb smiled, conscious of the irony of the situation. Valentine said nothing, but shrugged.

Lamb turned back to the men, 'Right. Corporal Valentine is now a Jerry sergeant and I'm a private. Try to behave as if that's the case. And remember, if any Jerries do start to talk to me the game's up and we give it to them. Right. Let's get going. I want to have my breakfast with the Highlanders. I hope you all like porridge.'

His talk had the desired effect, and they set off in good spirits. Valentine led the way, his captured German sub-machine gun at the ready, while Bennett marched at the side of the column of prisoners with an MG34 on his shoulder, and Lamb made up the rear. The men marched in twos, and with them, at the rear, next to Lamb, came Madeleine.

After thirty yards Lamb gave the order. 'Right, up this slope, we'll cross the fields and make for the woods.'

They scrambled up the embankment and found themselves in a field of waving wheat. They were totally exposed high up above the road, although screened from the village by a thick hedge of trees and undergrowth that marked the field's southern boundary.

Lamb said, 'Right, run for it. Into the trees.'

They pushed their way as fast as they could through the wheat field towards the spinney on the far side. After a short time the first field ended at a sunken road. Lamb didn't bother to look, but jumped down and dashed across and into the adjoining field. Another hundred yards and they were scrambling through the hedgerow, stamping down the undergrowth. Lamb raised his hand to indicate that they should stop, and they crouched down, regaining their breath. Lamb looked around and saw that the wood was in fact a thin strip of trees, beyond which lay the lawns and gardens of a modest country house. He motioned them on and, sticking to the woods, they skirted the house and its grounds and moved into denser woodland. He had no doubt that the ever-resourceful Germans were already in possession of the big house, and at any moment fully expected to be confronted by a sentry. After a short distance he saw the edge of the wood and the night sky. The moon shone through the trees, and every crunching twig or scurrying animal resounded into the night. Lamb was the first to reach the edge of the wood and pulled up fast just before he almost tumbled down a steep incline which fell away onto the road below. He scrambled down the bank, followed by the others. Butterworth cursed as he landed at the roadside, twisting his injured leg, and Lamb saw Madeleine bend down to help him up.

On the lower road he signalled that they should resume

their formation, with himself, newly demoted, still bringing up the rear, and once again they set off. They turned right and Lamb saw to his relief that to their right a railway line ran parallel with the road. They would have to go up this road for around one and a half miles before they hit the bridge, and then they would see what happened. With every step he was becoming more frustrated by the fact that they should now be so close to the British lines and at the same time so far in real terms.

They had not gone far along the road when Lamb picked up a noise, the unmistakable sound of an engine coming towards them from the rear. It sounded like a lorry. Lamb's first reaction was to bolt, but there was no cover here, merely the embankment to their right and the railway line on the left.

He yelled to the men in front, 'Hold fast. Stick it out.' And then the lorry rounded the corner behind them, lighting up the road with its full headlights. Lamb motioned the men into the side of the road and they pressed up close to the bank as the vehicle approached. It drove past them for some yards, and for a moment Lamb thought that it would carry on. But then it pulled up and stopped and the driver switched off the engine, but left the lights on. Butterworth turned and looked anxiously at Lamb, who waved him back into line with a quiet shake of the head. Both of the cab doors opened and two Germans approached them, the passenger armed with a machine pistol. Valentine stepped forward, and the armed man began to talk to him. Lamb could hear nothing of their conversation but saw the German nodding his head. Then he looked closely at the line of prisoners and smiled. The driver walked over to the lorry and opened the flap of the tarpaulin before turning and indicating to the men to get in. Lamb could hardly believe it.

Valentine walked back to him and said quietly, 'They've

bought it, sir. I told them we were heading for Petit Port with prisoners for the SS. They've offered to give us a lift.'

Lamb stared at him, incredulous. 'Is it a trick?'

'I don't think so. They are a bit gormless. But when I said we were taking them to the SS they seemed very willing to help.'

'Well done, Valentine. Let's get going then.'

With the German pushing them on, the remnants of Lamb's platoon climbed aboard the lorry, followed quickly by Madeleine, then by Lamb and Bennett, masquerading as their guards. The German said something to Bennett, who smiled and nodded. It must have been the right response, for the man wandered back to the cab with Valentine, whom he had invited to travel with him and his mate. Lamb hoped that Valentine's German would prove to be better than schoolboy. No one spoke. The truck started up and they began to roll forward along the road towards Petit Port. Lamb looked around the darkness, his eyes gradually becoming accustomed to it, and saw the faces of his men. He smiled in an attempt to reassure them but was not sure that it had worked. Madeleine was sitting close to him, but among so many of his men she did not again attempt to hold his hand. He marvelled at her strength and determination, and her ability to cope with all they had been through in the last twenty-four hours. She would no doubt make someone a wonderful wife some day, he thought. Or perhaps she would go on to fight the Germans herself in this war. He was staring at the side of her face in the dark. Perhaps it was just as well that he had not finished that letter, or sent any of his thoughts. Perhaps providence had placed Madeleine in his way out here, so far from home. But if that was the case, if anyone in this mad world still believed in providence, or some all-controlling force of destiny, then had she been sent to test his loyalty to Julia, or as a solution? Might Madeleine be his future? He was still admiring the line of her delicate profile when she turned and realised that he had been staring. Lamb looked away, but she had seen the look, even in the darkness.

Still no one spoke. From the cab in front came the sound of conversation. It sounded as if Valentine was making a good thing of it. For all his faults and his sheer bloody impudence, the man had again somehow saved the day. The only problem that faced them now was how to disentangle themselves from the complex mess they would find themselves in when they reached Petit Port. Lamb had no idea whether there were any SS at their destination and what they would do if whoever was there did believe Valentine, and would expect him to hand over the platoon. He tried to think round the problem. His old instructor at officer training school had often told him that the best way to solve a problem was to imagine that someone else was faced with it. Someone he admired – a great general, or even just a company commander. And so sitting in the back of the truck he began to ask himself what the Duke of Wellington might have done faced with a similar problem. But the trouble was this was not the sort of problem that would ever have faced Wellington, or Napoleon, or Alexander or Marlborough. It was the problem facing him, Lieutenant Peter Lamb. A platoon commander in German uniform who was about to be asked to deliver his own men into the hands of the enemy and who stood a pretty good chance, when he was found out, of being shot as a spy. The lorry lurched and turned left, then bumped across what must have been railway tracks. They were heading west again, on the road to the canal. He would have to think fast. They were slowing down now and Lamb guessed that they must be approaching Petit Port. Perhaps he would find a course of action once they were out of the lorry.

He turned to Bennett. 'This will be tricky. We'll have to play it by ear. See what their strength is. The minute we get out there do a quick head count to the right. I'll do the same on the left. We've got to get across that bridge and we'll have to take our chances where we can.' He turned to the rest of the men. 'That goes for the lot of you. Good luck.' Turning back to Madeleine, he smiled and said, 'Stay close to me. I'll have my gun on you, but with the safety on. When the bullets start flying . . .'

She nodded and cut him off. 'I know, stay low.'

'Sorry. You learn fast.'

The flaps at the rear of the lorry opened and a German smiled at Lamb and then motioned the prisoners out. Lamb jumped down, as did Bennett, and both men moved to opposite sides of the lorry. Lamb, on the left, closest to the bridge, tried to take in their surroundings as quickly as he could and to get an idea of how many of the enemy there might be. The lorry had drawn up before a wooden bridge with thin metal railings. The wooden barrier onto the bridge was raised. The canal itself could not have been more than fifty feet wide, and to either side of the bridge the ground ran away in a narrow embankment lined with poplar trees. To Lamb's surprise both sides were devoid of the enemy. But he could see that they had fortified the entrance to the bridge itself with a wall of sandbags five high, behind which two MG34s were firmly dug in, each of them manned by a team of two. He looked to the rear, back the way they had come, and saw, some distance off up the road, a group of German infantry with an officer. The man was eyeing them quizzically and looked as if he might be about to approach.

Clearly the bulk of the enemy force was back in the village itself, as one might have expected at this time of night. Lamb was wondering why the truck had not stopped back there at the local HQ when Valentine wandered up and spoke quickly and quietly. 'I told him we were meeting contacts at the bridge.'

Lamb nodded and, handing Valentine the machine pistol, held his hand out for the Luger. Reluctantly, Valentine handed it over and Lamb began to herd his prisoners towards a small brick house, which stood a few yards back from the canal.

Bennett appeared from the other side of the lorry. 'Three men. Pickets. Sub-machine guns.'

Lamb realised that they would have to act at once, or all would be lost. He nodded at Bennett and then inclined his head towards the machine-gunners on the bridge and, raising his hand to his mouth, whispered, 'Grenades there. You and Valentine take those three. I'll do our two.'

Still motioning his men and Madeleine towards the bridge-keeper's house with the Luger, Lamb looked round to find the driver and guard from their lorry. The two men were standing by the bonnet, puffing cigarettes and chatting. The guard's rifle was slung on his shoulder. The driver looked up at him and then towards where Valentine was standing lighting a cigarette, and gestured to his mate with a puzzled look. The other shrugged. This was it. Leaving Bennett standing beside the men, Lamb took a cigarette from his case and walked casually over to the driver, raising it in the air in his left hand, as if he wanted a light. The German smiled and delved into his pocket for a match, and as he did so, without any hesitation, Lamb brought up the Luger and shot him between the eyes. As the driver crumpled to the ground, his cigarette falling from dead lips, the other German turned on Lamb and attempted to get the rifle off his shoulder. It was a futile gesture. Lamb shot him in the same place with cool precision. The pistol was as good as they said, and better. In the split second between Lamb shooting the driver and the guard, Bennett and

189

Valentine had acted. As the second man fell to the ground, a grenade exploded on the bridge, tearing into the sandbags and the four men around the machine guns who had looked back in alarm but all too late. Another finished the job. Bennett had turned the MG34 and he was firing it from the hip, using it like a Bren, on the three men on picket duty. They died instantly, their bodies torn by round after round.

The smoke cleared from the bridge and Lamb saw amid the carnage that, aside from the fact that the grenades had taken off a section of the railings and blown a neat hole in the left side of the planking floor, the structure was still intact. He turned to the men. 'Run for it. Over the bridge.'

As one, they raced for the canal and clattered over the wooden planks, Madeleine with them. Lamb took a last look behind him and saw that a platoon of German infantry in the town was now running down the track towards them, led by the inquisitive officer. Two of them stopped and, raising their sub-machine guns, fired off a burst towards him, but the rounds fell hopelessly short. Two other men were kneeling down now, taking aim with their rifles. Lamb did not bother to wait around but turned and ran after his men. One bullet whistled past his ear and he expected another to hit him in the back, but although the fire continued nothing connected.

Rounds began to smack into the wood of the bridge and rebound off the metal railings, and then he was across and racing after his men up the road on the other side. They were running hell-for-leather, running for their lives, and now he could hear the officer on the other bank shouting orders. He half turned and saw a few of the Germans starting to run over the canal bridge. Still the bullets sang about him. Just ahead of him one ricocheted off the road and hit Bennett a glancing blow on the leg.

The sergeant swore and stumbled for a moment before carrying on. They were crossing another, smaller bridge now over a thin water course and then they were among houses, in a small village. The firing behind them continued and the shouting was more distant now as they ran among the abandoned houses.

Lamb turned and saw to his relief that the Germans had not followed them. And, he reasoned, how could they? Who in his right mind would run into the no man's land between their lines and those of the enemy in the dead of night? At least it seemed to confirm one thing. This must be the furthest extent of the German advance. There was no other reason to explain their lack of pursuit. Lamb turned and ran on, trying to catch up with the men before they should go too far and stumble into British or French positions. They crossed a narrow railway line and he managed to shout, 'Stop. Wait.' Mays and Smart stopped, doubled over and out of breath, at the corner of what appeared to be a signal box. Bennett turned back and stopped, yelling to the others ahead to pull up. Lamb waited until they had assembled around him and did a head count. They had all made it.

He grinned at them. 'Well done, all of you. I think we've lost them. Sarnt Bennett?'

'Yes, sir. Can't see anyone following.'

They were standing at a level crossing, and the signal box was one of two buildings, the other being a small country station with what looked like a waiting room attached, on the opposite side of the tracks. Both seemed empty, and Lamb could hardly believe their luck. He knew that the next few minutes, or hours or however long it might take for them to reach the front line and the 51st Division, were going to be tense. What he hadn't explained to the men, of course, was that once they were through the German lines they would have to hide somewhere

191

until daybreak when it would be safer for them to walk into the British lines.

'Right. We'll wait here until after dawn. Then we're going to go in and find our lines.'

They were all thinking it but only Corporal Mays gave voice to their feelings. 'Can't we carry on now, sir?'

Lamb shook his head. 'I know a night in no man's land is something none of us would relish, but there's nothing else for it. It would be bloody madness to try to get through our lines to night. We'd be taken for a raiding party. Our own chaps would shoot us before we had time to speak – let alone surrender to them.' There was a ripple of laughter, and he carried on. 'Mays, you and Smart take position in the top floor of that signal box. You'll have a good view of the area from up there. The rest of you, try and get some kip while they're on stag. Sarnt Bennett, change the picket after three hours. How's the leg?'

'Nothing, sir, just a scratch.'

'Rest it now then. And you, Butterworth. Everyone else all right?'

They nodded and a couple attempted a smile.

'Right, let's turn in. I'll take the waiting room with Mademoiselle Dujolle and two others. The rest of you, bunk down with Sarnt Bennett and Corporal Valentine in the signal box. And remember not to switch on the lights. We don't want to attract attention to ourselves, from either side.'

The waiting room, half-timbered and whitewashed, was typical of the area and looked more like a farm building than a station house. Lamb pushed open the unlocked door. The inside smelt of generations of travellers and perhaps more recent passers-by: a subtle blend of garlic, stale sweat and urine. In the moonlight he could see that the walls were lined with four wooden benches.

Lamb walked through the waiting room and opened

the door to a back room. He switched on his torch and by its faint light peered into what presumably had been the stationmaster's office. It contained a small, cast-iron wood-burning stove, a desk and three chairs. On the walls hung a framed photograph of President Lebrun, an illuminated certificate of railway proficiency and a map of the area. Lamb felt the stove. It was quite cold. He returned to the waiting room. 'Perkins, Stubbs, shift that bench into the back there. Mademoiselle Dujolle can sleep in there. And let's see if we can get that stove working. Don't try the lights, though.'

It took Stubbs, the farmer's boy, less than half an hour to get the stove working. And although it gave out unpleasant, acrid fumes its heat was welcome. Lamb found a French tricolour folded up in a drawer of the desk and used it to make a makeshift blanket for Madeleine, who occupied the back room. Their only light was from the moon, although the stove gave out a faint orange glow through its doors. Lamb lay, like the other two men, on the hard wooden bench in the waiting room, and stared at the ceiling with its dancing moonlight shadows. For the first time in days he had a moment for reflection, and thoughts tumbled pell-mell through his mind. The image of Captain Campbell, gagged and red-faced with rage, was the most powerful, but he thought too of the colonel, of the dead civilians on the bridge, and of poor young Tapley, calling for his mother. As he began to drift off to sleep the image of Madeleine entered his mind and he half imagined that he could hear her voice: 'Peter. Peter. I'm so cold.'

Then he turned and saw her face. She was kneeling on the floor beside the bench. Lamb sat up and placed an arm around her shoulders: 'Go back next door, Madeleine. You should get some sleep.'

She smiled at him in the moonlight. Then, very slowly,

she took her right hand and placed it on his. It was smaller than his own and fitted inside the outline like a second skin. 'I'm cold.' She paused, 'Come and warm me.'

He looked at her and knew that this was what they had both wanted since they had first met. He got up very slowly, careful not to wake the two sleeping soldiers, followed her into the office and closed the door.

The sun came up low on the horizon and cast its light through the unshuttered windows of the little back office, falling across Lamb's body and waking him with its warmth. But that was little compared to the heat he felt from Madeleine's softly breathing, half-naked body, which lay entangled with his own on the narrow wooden bench. The stove had long since gone out, but the stench remained. Lamb opened his eyes and felt her body on his and for a while did not, could not move. He lay there luxuriating in the intimacy, unable to believe that in the midst of such a war he should have found a feeling that had eluded him for so many years. He looked down at Madeleine and wondered if what they shared would end now, or if it might last. Was it too much to hope, at a time when for so many people all hope had vanished? Perhaps she was the person who would at last make sense of his twisted mess of a life, who would give some meaning to an existence brightened only by the passing, adrenalin-driven elation of soldiering and racing motorbikes. For, stronger even than his desire to be a good officer, there burned within him a need to give, to be a part of someone else, and through her to make him whole. He had sensed that she felt the same, and wondered if he was right.

At last he gently pushed Madeleine's half-clothed form away from his own. She tried to open her eyes and he bent to kiss her, then climbed off the bench and straightened his uniform before opening the door to the waiting room.

Stubbs and Perkins were still asleep on the benches, even though the sunlight was flooding the room.

Lamb stepped outside the door. Bennett was up in the signal box with Hughes, and he raised a hand to him, swiftly following it with the 'thumbs up' to indicate a quiet night. Lamb walked over the railway line and opened the door. The six men were seated at a wooden table eating dry biscuits, all that was left of their rations. They had, however, managed to make some tea and, seeing him, Smart offered Lamb a mug. He took it and sat on the edge of the table, drinking the hot, sweet tea: 'Ten minutes till the off. Valentine, you, Sarnt Bennett and I should change back into uniform. Don't want to get shot by our own side, do we?'

Valentine smirked. 'No, sir. We certainly don't.'

Lamb turned to his batman. 'Smart, I'll need my uniform.'

Smart smiled at him uncomfortably. 'Well, you see, Mister Lamb, sir, I do need to talk to you about that.'

'What about it?'

'Well, sir, the fact is I've, er, mislaid it.'

'Mislaid it? For God's sake, man. Where?'

Smart looked downcast. ''Fraid I couldn't say, sir. Must have been back in the truck in all that hoo-ha.'

Lamb shook his head. 'I'm surprised at you, Smart. You're normally so careful.'

'Sorry, sir.'

'Well, there's nothing for it. I'll just have to stay like this. Can't say I've got used to it. Not right. One of you will have to cover me. Pretend that I'm your prisoner.' Then he added, 'Just make sure that you don't let your finger slip and shoot me.'

They all laughed, except for Valentine, and for an instant it crossed Lamb's mind that the man might actually be tempted. But no sooner had it come to him than he banished the ludicrous thought and, putting down the empty mug

195

on the table, left the room. Outside, by the railway line, he found the other two and Madeleine up and dressed, and looking surprisingly neat. She smiled at him. But it was not the smile of yesterday. This was a different look. A look that spoke of a newly shared happiness and of hope.

They set off from the railway towards the west, away from the sun and down a road lined on either side with dense foliage. A narrow stream gurgled past them parallel to the road, down a slope to their right. They walked in single file, with Wilkinson in front and behind him Bennett, Perkins and Stubbs. Then came Lamb, disarmed again, with Valentine and Smart as his escort, and directly behind them Sergeant McKracken, Hughes, Butterworth, Madeleine and the others, with Mays bringing up the rear. The early morning sunshine dappled the road through the trees, and songbirds thronged the branches above them. They came to a crossroads and, put at ease for a moment by the glorious morning in which the war seemed a distant nightmare, walked straight across, forgetting any dangers, past a deserted farmyard. Lamb felt curiously liberated, almost euphoric, and, struggling to bring himself back to the task in hand, began to think about soldiering and the fact that the Somme had been where his father had fought twenty-five years before. Of course he was well aware how very different the terrain was here to the old battle-field of 1916 of which he had been told so often, where the river lay so still across the flatlands to the south west.

They had walked about three hundred yards from the crossroads; on the left side the road was bounded by the edge of a great wood, which stretched for as far as the eye could see. Lamb stopped, and the others followed suit. Bennett walked back to him. 'Sir?'

'That wood, Sarnt. It's as good a defensive position as I've ever seen. I'm willing to bet that the front line is somewhere in there.'

'You want us to go through it, sir?'

'No, it's too dense for us to keep formation. We should carry on up the road. But just be alert. If they see us coming they'll jump us before we see them.'

'Sir.'

They had gone a little further when there was a rustling noise in the woodland off to their left, immediately followed by a shout: 'Halt. Who goes there? Friend or foe? Don't move.'

They froze. It was a British voice, a deep, growling British voice, with a heavy Scottish accent. And to Lamb, at that moment, it was the sweetest sound he had ever heard.

15

Ahead of them, in the trees, they heard the unmistakable, gut-wrenching sound of the bolt of a rifle being drawn back. The voice came again. 'Who goes there? Answer or I'll shoot you.'

Bennett replied, 'Friends. We're British, with a Jerry prisoner.'

'Who are you?'

'The Jackals, mate. We're a bit adrift.'

There was a short pause, and then another voice, English this time. Home counties. An officer, thought Lamb. 'Advance and be recognised. And no funny business. We've got you all covered.'

For the first time in days Lamb felt himself relax. Which was a little absurd, as at that moment several guns were apparently trained on him. He hissed an order at Bennett, and slowly they walked from the road across and into the edge of the wood. It seemed that, against all the odds, they had made it to the Scots. They walked forward carefully through the undergrowth, still keeping up the pretence that Lamb was a prisoner, until at last the branches ahead of them parted to reveal two British infantrymen and an officer, a lieutenant, standing with their weapons pointed directly at them.

The officer spoke. 'If you're part of the Jackals, I should say you're a bit adrift. They're up at Dunkirk, last I heard from the French, with the rest of the BEF. Everyone apart from us. The Navy's trying to get them off and back to England.'

So it was true, thought Lamb. They were going to try it, just as the colonel had predicted. Now he realised just how important his own message was. For soon, apart from POWs, the 51st Division would be the only British troops left in France.

Bennett spoke. 'Yes, sir, we lost our battalion up at Wavre, two weeks ago.'

'I say, then you are lost. But what the devil are you doing down here, and how did you acquire that?' He pointed at Lamb.

Lamb realised that now was the time to reveal himself. He walked forward and said, 'Actually I acquired them, Lieutenant, in Kent, about a year ago. Lieutenant Peter Lamb, Royal North Kents.'

The Scottish officer gawped. 'Good God. You're English.'

'Yes, I'm afraid so. And, by the sound of your men, you're Scots.'

'Geordie Crawford, 1st Black Watch.'

'So you are part of the 51st?'

'That's us. Strung out along this bloody river. Sorry, seems strange telling that to a German. Where's your uniform?'

'Missing. I don't suppose you could fix me up?'

'I'm sure we can scrounge something for you at Battalion. We'd better take you in for debriefing.'

'Well, actually, I was rather hoping to get to General Fortune.'

Crawford laughed. 'You want to see the General? I'm

afraid he's not here. Why do you need to see him? Perhaps you are a Jerry after all.'

Lamb ignored the comment. 'I have a message for him. Rather important.' He felt impatient but knew there was nothing he could do about it.

Crawford seemed both intrigued and amused. 'Well, let's start off with the colonel, and perhaps then, after he's seen you, we can work our way up to the top brass.' He looked at the motley group of men. 'Is this all you've got?'

'All that's left of my platoon, yes, and a few odds and sods. We had a bit of a rough time getting here.'

He noticed Madeleine. 'And a girl. Good God. Who's she?'

'It's a long story. The SS murdered her family.'

'You'd better come along to HQ. We're pulling out of here anyway later this morning.'

Leaving one of the privates on picket duty, Crawford and the other man led them further into the woods, here and there encountering other Highlanders in their distinctive Balmoral bonnets. The position seemed very sparsely occupied, and Lamb thought of the mass of German men and vehicles they had recently passed through.

Crawford turned to Lamb. 'So, extraordinary journey you must have had.' He paused. 'You're from Kent, you say?'

'Yes.'

'I'm a bit of keen cricketer. Went to see them play a few times at Canterbury when I lived in London. What was the name of that tremendous wicket-keeper of yours? You know. He played in the last test against South Africa last year.'

Lamb was aware that this was a test, but he didn't mind. The lieutenant was only doing his job. In fact he was rather flattered that he made such a passable Nazi. Luckily he knew the answer. 'I think you mean Les Ames.

The only man to score 100 runs before lunch. He's in the RAF now.'

Crawford smiled. 'Yes, of course, Les Ames. How could I forget that name?'

They left the wood after a few hundred yards and, slipping down onto the road, carried on for more than a mile until they came to a village. Save for the cricketing conversation, Crawford had said nothing throughout the journey and had ignored the curious looks they were given by the few British soldiers they encountered.

Now, though, he turned to Lamb. 'This is Lambercourt. Our front line proper starts here. I shouldn't really tell you any of this, as you haven't been debriefed, but I reckon you're who you say you are. And in any case, if we decide that you aren't, we'll just shoot you.'

Lamb hardly felt reassured. 'Thank you.'

They found the Battalion HQ established in the town hall. Crawford left the private outside with Lamb's men and Madeleine, and took Lamb into the building.

The CO, Colonel Honeyman, a genial-looking man with huge eyebrows and a moustache to match, was sitting at a desk in the mayor's office, with his batman, a signals officer and the RSM standing close by. He looked up. 'Geordie. Good to see you. I say. Bagged a Jerry?'

'Not exactly, sir. This is Lieutenant Lamb, of the Black Jackals.'

'Good heavens. Are you sure? Looks damn like a Jerry.'

'In my opinion, sir, he's the real thing. He knew that Les Ames was wicket-keeper for Kent.'

The colonel shrugged. 'Where have you come from, Lieutenant?'

'From Wavre, sir, by way of Tournai and Arras.'

'Arras, eh? Did you see the counter-attack?'

'Yes, sir. We took part in it.'

'Did you, by God? Bloody shame. That's quite a march. How long did it take you?'

'Two weeks, sir, almost to the day.'

The colonel rubbed at his chin. 'Sarnt-Major, ask this man a question. One of your good ones.'

'Righto, sir.' The RSM thought long and hard, and after a couple of minutes turned to Lamb. 'All right, sir. Please would you be so kind as to tell me the name of the cleaner in ITMA?'

The colonel looked heavenward.

Lamb laughed. 'Mrs Mopp, of course. "Can I do you now, sir?" Got any more, Sarnt-Major?'

The RSM blustered. 'Who plays Sophie Tuckshop then, sir?'

'Hattie Jacques.'

The colonel looked at the RSM. 'Well, is he right? You don't suppose that I listen to that bloody show?'

'Quite right, sir. He's quite right.'

'Thank God for that. Now, Lamb, tell us how you got here. And make it quick.'

So in the space of the next twenty minutes Lamb gave a somewhat condensed account of their journey south. He mentioned the fight at the Dyle, his meeting with the colonel, although not the content of the message, the fight at Arras and his capture of Kurtz, the atrocity at Aubigny and meeting Madeleine, and lastly the raid on the air base. He was careful, of course, not to include mention of the civilians on the bridge or his treatment of Captain Campbell.

He finished and, as soon as he had, thought to himself that the whole story sounded so far fetched they would probably not believe him and shoot him as a German spy.

Honeyman looked at him. 'And the Jerries you came through, how many would you say? What sort of strength are we up against?'

Lamb thought for a moment. 'Hard to say, sir, but

202

they're pretty thick on the ground. Must be at least two divisions, perhaps more.'

The colonel nodded and looked serious. 'You are an extraordinary man, Lamb. And I don't know why — your story sounds more like some Boy's Own adventure rather than war — but I'm inclined to believe you. And if the RSM and Lieutenant Crawford here both vouch for you then you're probably who you say you are. You say you have a message for General Fortune from this colonel in Tournai?'

'Yes, sir. It's absolutely vital.'

'Well, General Fortune's down at St Leger. That's some seven miles south of Blangy. About thirty miles from here.'

'How soon can I get to him, sir?'

'Can't you just give me the message, Lieutenant?'

'I'm sorry, sir. The staff officer who gave me the message told me that it was only to be delivered to General Fortune himself.'

The colonel bristled. 'Then I'm afraid I can't really help you at the moment. I have the very pressing matter of holding the line against the enemy.'

'But sir, with respect, I don't see what that has to do with my getting the message to General Fortune. If you could just spare a man to show me the way, and perhaps a truck or a car.'

The colonel smiled indulgently and sighed. 'Lieutenant Lamb, the 51st Division is currently holding eighteen miles of the front line. Do you know what that means? Normally we would expect a division to hold four miles. We have to do more than four times that with no prepared positions. My battalion is holding two and a half miles of that front, all the way from Toeuffles to Miannay.' He indicated the two towns on the map. 'That's proportionately the same. And we have another problem here. We are under French command. Now the French are not all bad. I'm not saying that. Fought alongside them in the last show. But how can I be expected to work under French command? I'm sorry, Lamb, I just can't spare anyone at present. In fact I was rather hoping that you and your men might join us here. We can use everyone we can get.'

'Sir, with respect. This message . . .'

The colonel silenced him. 'Lieutenant. I have said my piece and you have had your time too. And that's an end to it at present. I have promised to try to get you to GHQ just as soon as it becomes possible. I can do no more than that.'

Crawford coughed. 'There is the girl, sir.'

'The girl? Oh, the girl. Well, she'll have to stay here at HQ, of course, and take her chances along with the rest of you.'

Lamb spoke. 'There is the question of my uniform, sir. I lost it in the fight at the airfield.'

'Oh yes, can't have you wandering around dressed like that. Might get yourself shot, eh? The RSM here should be able to fix you up with something. Won't be Savile Row, of course, and we don't have hyenas on our buttons, either, but at least it will look better than that rubbish you're wearing.' He turned to the RSM. 'The lieutenant here looks about Mister Watson's size, Sarnt-Major. Wouldn't you say?'

'Very good, sir.'

Lamb knew that it was futile to continue pleading his case. And he was weary too. He had done everything earthly possible to get the colonel's message through to General Fortune, and he had fallen, it seemed, at the final hurdle. Of course he would do it. But he could see that it was quite impossible to achieve anything now. Nor could he simply run off to the GHQ at St Leger, as they had done at Essars. For one thing he had no idea how to find it, despite his map; for another he knew that without someone from Honeyman's command to accompany him he would simply have no hope of getting to the general. Better to stick it out here for another day or so, get some rest and endear himself to the colonel in the hope that it might speed his actions.

Together, he and Crawford left the little office and walked into the street. The sun was high in the sky now and the others were sitting on the steps of two houses and on their packs on the cobbles near the entrance to the town hall. Seeing Lamb, they got to their feet.

'Sarnt Bennett, looks as if we'll be staying here for a few days. Try and find the men billets and something a little more private for Mademoiselle Dujolle.'

Crawford nodded. 'We can find you somewhere. I'll have a word with the battalion quartermaster. I'm sorry, Lamb. I know how important it is to you to get to the general, but you can see the situation here. The colonel has his hands tied. Don't worry, stick with us, we'll find some way of getting you to him. And you'd best take Mademoiselle Dujolle with you when you go. This is no place for a woman.'

Lamb smiled. 'Yes. I know you're right. But you haven't seen her in action. I've seen grown men take fright more easily.'

'Well, you might as well keep her with you here for the present. As the colonel said, we're sitting in reserve so the French can attack the bridgehead with their tanks. It's General de Gaulle's idea. He's one of the better French commanders. So that why we're here, strung out like washing on a line. Holding the sector. That's why you bumped into our pickets out in the wood. We're pulling back to the village. Haven't the support weapons to do anything else. We're only good for a reserve. Mind you, if the attack fails then ten to one the Jerries will counter-attack us here.' He fell silent, contemplating the unpleasant prospect of being outnumbered. 'Still, I expect that General Gort will send reinforcements over soon enough. That's what we're counting on, at least. If we can just hold the Jerries off that long.'

Lamb could not help but admire his optimism, but with the colonel's words in his ears he knew that Crawford's hopes were probably not what the War Office had in mind for General Fortune's command.

Crawford turned to go. 'Well, I'd better get back and pull the platoon out of the wood. I suppose you're with us now. Glad to have you. I'll see you back here then. And Lamb, I really should get that British uniform from the RSM if I were you, before someone takes a pot shot.'

Lamb laughed. 'I meant to ask you. Who's Mister Watson?'

'Jimmie Watson. Subaltern in C Company. That is, he was. Bought it at the canal three days ago. Shot through the head by a sniper. But I think the colonel was right. His battledress should fit you perfectly.'

Standing in the little village square of Lambercourt, Lamb adjusted the sleeves of his newly acquired battledress top and straightened his tie. The colonel had been right. Apart from the sleeve length being a little short, it was a perfect fit. Lieutenant Watson had been a tall, fit rugby player from the Scottish borders with broad shoulders and the long, athletic legs of a full-back, and his physique exactly matched Lamb's own. It felt a little eerie, though, wearing a dead man's clothes, even his shirts and his boots. The tin hat they had scrounged from the battalion stores in exchange for Smart's last packet of Woodbines. The batman felt it was all he could do to atone for the loss of Lamb's own uniform. But even if the uniform had not fitted, Lamb would have worn it, for he had had enough of wearing the grey drab of their enemies.

Madeleine had helped him to dress in the rooms they had found for her in an abandoned house in the centre of

206

the village. He did not really care any more whether the men knew of their relationship and thought that they must have guessed, although no one had said anything. She and Lamb were not outwardly affectionate, but it was surely obvious to anyone who knew him. He felt changed in a way so fundamental that he sensed it might have affected his very appearance. And the change went deep. He was filled with a new resolve. The war, it seemed, was about to take turn against the Allies, and soon Britain might be standing alone against the German invader. Now he knew that every second, every moment would count for them. He was acutely aware that whatever it was that he and Madeleine had found might be snatched away from them in an instant. Fate had played them a cruel trick, but he did not intend to allow fate to win, any more than he intended to let the Nazis subject Britain and Europe to a new dark age of barbarity. He would fight for both. For love and for mankind and he would win, or would die trying.

Lamb looked at his watch and saw that it was 2 p.m. The watch, which had been his father's, was one of the few things of his own that he still had. He had lost everything else save the map, his torch and his cigarette case along with his uniform. Even the draft of the letter to Kate had gone, and he felt well rid of it. He wondered whether he had been living in a dream, deluding himself that she really loved him, that he could ever have forged a new life with her after she had been the catalyst in destroying his marriage. No, Madeleine was everything now. He wondered where she was and was about to find out when he saw Crawford walking in his direction with a face like thunder. B Company had been clear of the wood for four hours now, and the lieutenant came fresh from a briefing with the colonel. He was shaking his head.

'I don't bloody believe it. I thought de Gaulle was a good Frenchman. But this now, this is just madness.'

'What? Tell me.'

'The colonel's just got the order through. We've got to take that wood at Cambon. Le Grand Bois.'

'Not the one you've just abandoned?'

'The very same. Except now intelligence reports suggest that the Jerries have begun to occupy it. And the French want it back. The order was direct from General de Gaulle. The colonel's hopping mad. Keeps saying that they've gone behind General Fortune's back. But what can we do? We're under orders from the French.'

'When do we go?'

Crawford looked surprised. 'We?'

'We're with you now. Remember?'

Crawford smiled. 'Thank you, Lamb. Well, the attack was scheduled for 1600 hours but the colonel's managed to postpone for fifteen minutes.'

'What? In two hours' time? That's absurd. What about reconnaissance? Does anyone have any idea what they've got in there?'

'None at all. Just sightings of enemy movement. And we've no time now to appeal to Brigade or Division. We'll have to leave your girl here.'

Lamb replied quickly. 'She's not my girl.'

'Oh really, I rather thought . . .'

Cross with himself for having been so quick to deny her, and puzzled as to why he had, Lamb moved on. 'She'll be fine here with the colonel and the reserve platoon. And she can make bandages. But not tea, I'm afraid. She's French, remember.'

Crawford grinned. 'Well, coffee then. We'll need it when we get back. God knows what we'll find in there.'

It was almost 4.30 when they began to advance into the wood. They moved cautiously, strung out in a line, with three yards between each man. Lamb had reclaimed the

Luger and led his ragged command on the right flank of B Company. No sooner had they moved the first twenty yards than two shells crashed in to their front.

Lamb yelled, 'Take cover,' and ducked down, and the men fell to the ground, finding what protection they could among the roots and natural potholes.

Crawford shouted across to him, 'There's an eighty-eight on the ridge up there, near Grand Laviers. About 2,500 yards away. They haven't got our range yet. Just listen out for the whine.'

They stood up and began to walk forward again. Three minutes later Lamb heard the whine. 'Take cover.' They dropped as before, and as before the shells fell short. Next time, he thought, they won't get it wrong. Slowly, they moved on again. It was heavy going underfoot and the roots and brambles threatened to catch the unwary. When five minutes had passed the whine came again and again they dropped to the ground as two more shells crashed through the trees. This time, as Lamb had predicted, the gunners' aim was better and one of the shells hit the centre of the line, in B Company. There was a huge explosion and a scream as the earth flew and trees splintered, but he could not tell the extent of their casualties. As they walked on he was aware of a desperate call from his left for stretcher-bearers.

He shouted across to Crawford, 'You all right there?'

'Yes. One of my corporals bought it, though, and we've another man down.'

They were deep in the woods now. About half way through, thought Lamb, but still they had seen nothing of the enemy. He turned to Bennett. 'Keep your eyes peeled, Sarnt. Don't know what they're up to, but judging by the incoming fire it's my guess they've scarpered.'

Bennett nodded.

Valentine called to him, 'Sir, look over there.'

209

He was pointing to what looked like a tree stump.

Lamb walked across to it and discovered a small slit trench. His eye was caught by a small shiny object. He bent down and, after checking carefully for wires which might suggest a booby trap, picked it up. It was a spent cartridge case. He turned it over and saw German writing. Stooping again, he picked up a cardboard packet. The label read 'Hartkeks' in a Gothic script.

Valentine saw it. 'It's crispbread. German rations.'

'Well, they've certainly been here. Intelligence was right after all.'

Bennett spoke. 'But your guess was right. They're not here any more, sir.'

Valentine chimed in, 'This seems a little mad. We're risking our lives for a wood that no one wants.'

Lamb replied, still looking into the trench, 'The French want it. And we're here under French orders.'

Perkins joined in, 'Never thought I'd see the day. Taking orders from a Frog.'

Bennett snapped at him, 'Shut it. Orders is orders. Doesn't matter who gives them. Isn't that right, sir?'

'Quite right. We just do the job. Come on. And spread out.'

Another shell came through the foliage and crashed behind them this time.

Perkins laughed. 'Couldn't hit a barn door.'

Hughes yelled at him, 'Don't tempt fate, you silly bugger. You'll get us all killed.'

They were almost at the far edge of the wood when, as abruptly as they had begun, the shells stopped.

Bennett said, 'That's queer, sir. Doesn't make sense.'

'Perhaps they're saving their ammo for later.'

Looking out from the woods they could see the German positions on the ridge above them, but otherwise there was no sign of the enemy. Exhausted, the men collapsed on the ground. Perkins slipped, and his leg fell through a hole in the undergrowth. 'Bloody hell.' He brushed aside the twigs and found himself half sitting in an abandoned slit trench. 'That's handy, Sarge. They must have known we was coming.'

Valentine stood over him. 'Don't move. It might be booby-trapped.'

'Shit.'

Valentine stretched out an arm. 'Here, take my hand. Carefully now.' Gently, Valentine pulled him out of the hole and quickly to one side.

'Thanks, Corp. Pity. Seems a waste.'

Bennett spoke. 'You won't be saying that when your arse gets blown over the trees.'

Lamb looked at the trench. 'All right, all of you. Be careful not to fall into one of these holes. Corporal Valentine's right. They might be rigged.'

So they sat in the undergrowth, away from the trenches, huddled as close to the ground as they could get. There was always the chance of an enemy sniper seizing the moment, and Lamb did not intend to lose anyone else.

Bennett was close to him. 'Now what, sir?'

'We wait for more orders. I imagine they'll want us to hold the wood, now we've taken it. So we might have to dig in. Just tell the men to remember to dig away from the Jerry trenches.'

They could hear firing now from further over on their right, well beyond the wood at the nearby town. Cambron, Crawford had told him it was called. Heavy rounds were coming in from the direction of the bluff at Laviers, and explosions that suggested they might have found their targets.

Crawford came across to them through the trees. 'Looks like the French are getting shot up pretty badly over there at Cambron. I don't think their intelligence chaps can have got it quite right, do you? They weren't exactly on the ball in here, were they?'

'Where are the French tanks? I thought they were meant to be pushing through with us on their flank.'

'Those are their tanks. Sounds like they're being blown to buggery.'

A runner came up from the rear. A Frenchman. 'You are the Black Watch?'

Crawford answered, 'Yes, that's us.'

'You are to retire.'

'What?'

'You are to retire, sir. Pull your men back to the village.'

'You must have the wrong man, old chap. We've just taken this wood. I've lost four men doing it. I'm not giving it up now.'

'Those are your orders, sir. From the General.'

'From your general. Not mine.'

The Frenchman shrugged. 'Those are the orders I have. Now you have them.' He nodded politely, turned and ran at a trot back through the woods.

Crawford turned to Lamb. 'What d'you make of that?'

The RSM came over. 'The French have been beaten back on the right, sir. Jerry's pushing on over there too. Past Cambron. If we don't get out of here pretty sharpish we'll be left up in the air with the Jerries on our flank.'

'So that's the reason we're off. No wonder that runner didn't want to explain it.'

He turned to the men. 'All right, lads. Pack up. We're falling back.'

Bennett came up to him. 'Is that right sir, that we've been told to pull out?'

'That's it, Bennett. Can't help feeling as if we've been here before.'

'Just like at the Dyle, sir.'

'Just like at the Dyle. What I don't understand is . . .'

212

His words were lost in a great whooshing noise as an 88-millimetre shell came in low over their heads, smashing through the treetops, and Lamb just had time to yell 'Cover'. It hit the trees at 1,000 metres per second and tore two of them up, exploding in the centre of a group of Highlanders who were putting on their kit. It took the left leg off one of them, decapitated another and made a hole in the torso of the third, killing him. The maimed man screamed, and his noise was drowned by the roar of a second shell.

'Christ, their aim's better now. Run. Run for it.'

The men turned and began to run through the undergrowth as fast as they could. More shells began to fall, and Lamb was aware of men falling to his right, tripping on the hidden roots. There were screams from the Highlanders, but there was no turning back to help. The woods were a mass of flame and falling trees as the 88s continued to plough in. Lamb emerged, panting and dripping with sweat at the far edge, just out of range. He saw Crawford close by, doubled over with the effort, as the men began to come in.

Crawford straightened up and yelled at one of them, 'Get a runner back to the colonel and tell him we've taken casualties in the woods. And tell him that we were ordered to pull back by the French.'

Still panting, he turned to Lamb. 'I'd like to hear the general's comments when he finds out where we are. Trust the French to renege on their agreement. De Gaulle went behind his back. We were strictly not to be used in an attack. And now this happens. It's a bloody mess. Who the hell can we trust?'

Lamb shook his head. He was damned if he knew any more. But the biggest question on his mind was why, if Colonel Honeyman could send a runner to the general, he had still not got through to HQ.

16

Lamb sat in the Battalion HQ of 1st Black Watch in Lambercourt and puffed at a Craven 'A' as he tapped his fingers against the table top. He was frustrated beyond imagining. For three entire days, ever since they had pulled out of the wood, they had been waiting here. Three days. Days in which he could have moved closer to General Fortune and closer to getting his men home and back to the regiment. He had decided now that, whatever happened, that was his duty. Once the message had been delivered his mission in France was complete and it was paramount that he should return with what was left of his command to Britain. But first he had to reach General Fortune. He drummed his fingers harder and tried to think of a plan. Twice he had approached Colonel Honeyman and twice had been rebuffed with the answer that he was unable to spare the man necessary to guide him safely to Fortune. Whatever credence the colonel gave to Lamb's story, he knew that Honeyman's prime concern was to hold the front line and he knew too that he did not want Lamb to take his men with him when he went. Even ten men were a bonus here, where the line was stretched to capacity. Nor of course would Lamb have dreamt of attempting to reach GHQ without them, particularly after what he presumed had happened to Briggs's section.

There was something else too. Honeyman had asked Lamb if he would assume temporary command of 'A' company, which had now lost every one of its officers, killed and wounded, supporting 'B' company on their left flank in the past few days. Of course he had accepted and had met his new command that morning.

They were a friendly bunch, if hugely reduced in strength over the past few weeks. There were only forty-eight of them remaining now, led by Sergeant-Major Dodd, a huge farmer from Fife, and two other notable NCOs, Sergeants McNulty and Graham. Lamb had been more than a little apprehensive as to how he would be received. To place a Sassenach in charge of a bunch of Highlanders, rather than promote the leading NCO, seemed to him to amount to heresy. But Honeyman had insisted that the men would accept him, and to Lamb's surprise the colonel had been right. They welcomed him as if he had been a Highlander himself, and now he was fully committed to staying. His own men, including Sergeant McKracken, had of course been integrated as an independent platoon within the company, bringing its strength up to fifty-seven. In truth he was excited by the challenge of leading a company, but knew too that when the opportunity came he must immediately find General Fortune.

His only hope lay in the possibility that a messenger might come from GHQ, but thus far the only orders had been those received from the French. Honeyman had sent a runner back on a civilian bicycle with the news that they had been attacked in the wood, but the man had not returned and they did not even know if the message had got through. There was worse, though.

From the French they had got wind of the fact that if

the Germans overran their current position the division was to pull back to Rouen, in the opposite direction to Le Havre. Lamb realised that if that were to happen it would in all probability be cut off from the sea, and given the French defeatism such a move could only result in the loss of the division. It made his message all the more vital, but how could he explain that to Honeyman? A withdrawal from Le Havre was in contravention of all general orders to date, and Lamb knew that the moment the French found out about their intentions, they would scent treachery, which was the last thing he wanted to engender.

He stubbed his cigarette out in an ashtray, then got up from the table and left the room. Madeleine and the Battalion MO, a bluff Glaswegian doctor named Macwilliam, had established a rudimentary first aid post across from the Mairie in what had been the village hall. Lamb crossed the road and went inside. She smiled at him, and instantly his spirits rose. They had not had a chance to be alone in days, save for the occasional furtive embrace, but he knew that nothing in either of their feelings had changed. She was washing bandages in sterilising liquid, wringing out the bandages and laying them to dry on the old stove at the end of the hall. Dr Macwilliam was not to be seen, and unusually there were no patients. Lamb walked across to her and was about to wrap her in his arms when behind him the door opened and she pulled away.

It was Crawford. 'I say, Madeleine, don't suppose you've anything for gyppy tummy. Two of my men have gone down with it. Reckon it was that half-cooked chicken they scrounged. Oh, hello Lamb.'

Madeleine looked at Lamb, 'Gyppy tummy?'

'He means an upset stomach. The runs.'

'Oh. I see. No, not really. But my mother used to say eat plenty of bananas. Perhaps the doctor can help.'

216

'Not to worry. No time. In fact, glad I found you, Lamb. Have you heard?'

'Heard?'

'We've been ordered to attack.'

'Attack? You are joking?'

'No, I'm in deadly earnest. Order just came through to the Colonel.'

'From General Fortune?'

'Hardly. From de Gaulle. But the old man says that Fortune's been given command.'

Lamb brightened. 'Is he coming to the front?'

'I hardly think so. We're only one battalion out of nine in the Division, old boy. He's better off back at St Leger.'

Lamb had known it would be the case. Once again he found himself moving further away from Fortune in another futile attack that would get them nowhere and only served to appease the French generals. He wondered at the logic of it. But just as quickly he realized that there was no logic and that the French generals were desperate. They could only do what they had done time and again in the Great War, and throw more and more men into the meat grinder. For a moment he considered refusing to join the attack, but he realised that would be not only ridiculous but tantamount to cowardice, particularly given his new command. The only answer was to go as ordered and to tell Madeleine the gist of his message and importantly who she should say it was from. If he should be killed or lost then at least she could try and get the message to Fortune, and he prayed that she would be believed.

He turned to Crawford. 'When do we go?'

'Three thirty in the morning.'

Madeleine looked alarmed. 'Tonight?'

'Yes.'

She looked down and pretended to busy herself with the bandages.

217

Crawford continued, 'The objective's a patch of ground from Caubert to Cambron, about six miles. They're planning a stonking great barrage before it. Should be like Guy Fawkes Night. They say nothing will stand under that. What do you reckon?'

Lamb thought back to tales of the Great War and to another huge barrage, the largest ever seen back then, which had happened a month later than this, in July 1916, along a different stretch of the same river. The troops had also been assured then that nothing would be alive when the barrage lifted, yet it heralded the worst day in British military history. 'Well,' he said, disingenuously, 'you never know.'

Colonel Honeyman had generously arranged a supper for all the battalion officers in the Mairie at 11 p.m. that evening, and they sat down together in the large anteroom at an improvised table. Smart joined the other batmen in serving, and for a moment it was as if Lamb, in his borrowed uniform, had been transported back to Kent, to the officers' mess. There were eight of them at the table, including the colonel, and the conversation flowed as easily as the wine. But Lamb realised that, cheerful as it was, this would be the last time they would be together like this. It was almost as if the dinner became a wake for the battalion, and he hoped his presentiments were ill founded.

As they ate, Honeyman went over the basics of Fortune's plan. The French tanks were attacking in the centre, with the Scots on either flank and the Seaforths in support with the few British tanks from 1st Armoured, attached to Fortune's command. To the right, the Camerons would take Caubert and the wooded ridge known as the 'Hedgehog', while the Gordons on the left would take Cambron and the troublesome bluff overlooking the wood where the 88s were positioned. The Black Watch were to support the Gordons and take the wood.

Lamb could hardly believe it. He turned to Crawford. 'Not that bloody wood again.' Crawford smiled but could not disguise his unease. He said in a whisper, 'D'you want to know something? The adjutant told me that if the enemy aren't destroyed by the barrage they'll be able to enfilade us. And didn't the French fail in exactly the same place three days ago? And there's one more thing. We haven't rehearsed with tanks, have we?'

Lamb nodded. 'You're right. I remember a Tank Corps commander lecturing us at Aldershot. Tanks and infantry just don't mix, he said, unless you rehearse. Otherwise you're going to fail. Just like in 1918.'

At that moment Honeyman rose to his feet. 'Gentleman, a toast. To the King.' They echoed his words and drained their glasses, which were quickly refilled. 'And to our success in tomorrow's attack.'

At a quarter after three on that morning of June 4th the valley of the lower Somme was shrouded in mist, and Lamb was thankful for it. Behind it the men were well hidden from enemy observation. Lamb looked at his watch, and at precisely 3.20 the guns began. From their start point on the far north-west edge of Lambercourt, he looked away from their own objective, south east across the valley in the direction of the villages of Bienfay and Villers, and saw smoke rising as explosions shook the ground. There were known to be enemy posts there at least, even if the reconnaissance had not done its job anywhere else. There were other, smaller explosions from the wood in front of them, their own objective, and that of the Gordons a little further on. For a full ten minutes the barrage continued and the air high above Lamb's head seemed to turn into a continuous mass of whistling metal.

He began to think that no man could possibly survive the torrent of explosive raining down upon the German positions. But then it stopped, and all he could hear was the rumble of tanks and the murmur of the men around him, heightened with apprehension. Curiously, the tanks appeared to be behind their position, and at first he thought he must be mistaken. But then he saw them, advancing to the north west of the village: French heavy tanks. Surely that was wrong. They were meant to be with the Seaforths in the centre of the line. As he watched, the column halted and began to reverse and then turned and withdrew. It was not hard to see that something had gone wrong.

He looked at his watch again. 3.29.

Off to his left and behind, a whistle blew to signal the attack and Lamb put his own to his mouth and followed suit, along with the other officers. Together the men entered the woods. Lamb looked both ways, making sure that none of them were going too far ahead, keeping in a line abreast, like a pheasant shoot walking through a copse. It had been the British artillery, 25-pounders and 6-inch howitzers, not the French, that had shelled the wood, and where the shells had struck home trees were still smouldering. Others had been ripped up by the roots, or simply blown to pieces. As before, there was no enemy opposition, and while he could hear machine-gun and artillery fire on both flanks, in the wood itself there was nothing. The company walked on until it reached the far fringe of the wood, where the trees gave way to fields once more, before the huge green mass of the Bois de Cambron rising before them. That was where the Gordons were heading. It was his job merely to sit tight here in support.

Lamb watched as the Gordons began their attack on the wood. Advancing with fixed bayonets along a narrow

220

sunken lane, they marched in regular formation, looking like something out of the nineteenth century. Then half way up the right face of the wood they turned and began to advance inwards.

It was then that the German machine guns opened up, and he saw the Jocks begin to fall. But still they went in.

After a few minutes of the slaughter, Lamb turned to Bennett. 'I don't know about you, Sarnt, but I can't sit here like this watching them being mown down. Come on.'

Together they walked forward and were instantly followed by the rest of Lamb's original platoon and then by the company.

Company Sergeant-Major Dodd came hurrying up to Lamb. 'Are you sure this is right, sir? I mean, we're goin' against orders.'

Lamb looked at him. 'Sarnt-Major, do you propose to sit there and watch your countrymen being cut down like corn? For I most certainly do not.'

'No, sir.' Dodd nodded at the remaining Highlanders and they surged out of the wood behind Lamb and followed him across the field and into the lane.

He shouted to the sergeant-major, 'I'll take the right side, you go through and round. I'm going to try and get some of those MGs.'

Ahead of him a thick wall of gorse rose up, cladding a bank of earth and foliage. The wood lay at the top of the bank, through a number of narrow paths. Lamb called the men forward and as quickly as they could manage, cursing as they tore their trousers and themselves on the gorse, they made their way up and onto the higher field. A few steps and they were among the trees now. There was a noise, and in front of Lamb the undergrowth suddenly parted. A German jumped up from a foxhole and lunged with his bayonet at him, scraping him on the

221

arm and drawing blood in a long, shallow cut. Bennett gave the German a burst of the Bren and the man fell to the ground, his body traversed by a line of bullets. There was a cry from Lamb's right and a Highlander fell, shot from above. There were Germans in the trees above them, shooting down.

Lamb pointed the Luger upwards and fired, and one of them fell with a scream. 'Fire upwards. Into the trees.'

There was a rattle of gunfire, and more of the snipers fell. Ahead of them he could see a machine-gun nest well dug in and rattling off fire towards the Gordons on the left. He waved his hand to signal halt, then put his finger to his lips and pulled a hand grenade from his pocket before pulling the pin and holding the detonator. 'Come on, Sarnt. Who else is with me?'

Together, Lamb, Bennett and two of the Highlanders rushed the nest. The gunner saw them coming form the corner of his eye and tried to traverse the gun, but it was too late. Lamb hurled his grenade, as did one of the Scotsmen, and Bennett opened up with the Bren. The position exploded. They rushed past it, followed now by the whole company. Ahead of them they could see the Gordons, fighting with rifle butts and bayonets as the German defenders surged around them. Men were everywhere in the trees and it was hard to know who was friend or foe. Lamb looked across to his left. Four men of his company had captured a slit trench, and the Germans had their hands up. He yelled to them, 'Well done.' But as he did so he saw a German throw something at the Jocks. A second later it exploded, hurling all four of them to the ground. Lamb ran over and fired the Luger straight at the man who had thrown the bomb, and then without thinking did the same to the man beside him. The two others yelled for mercy, but one of the three Jocks had not been killed and, managing to get to his feet, let rip with a burst of fire from a captured sub-machine gun, cutting them down where they stood before collapsing himself. Lamb yelled for a stretcher-bearer, and turning to find his men saw Bennett, Valentine, Mays and the others were close on his heels, and the rest of the Jocks, apparently unscathed, following too. 'Come on,' he shouted and began to run further along though the edge of the wood.

He reloaded the Luger with precious ammunition and checked that he had also brought the standard British service revolver that Crawford had supplied him with as a back-up, his own having been lost with his uniform. Suddenly their part of the wood seemed to be clear of the enemy, and they moved on steadily. Over to the left he could hear the sound of firing, and to the right, beyond the wood, heavy shelling as the other attacks went in further down the valley. Then the rattle of machine-gun fire seemed to recede for a moment and Lamb found himself and his men standing at the edge of a very wide ride through the centre of the wood. It was perfectly quiet, no birds singing and no rabbits moving, as there had been through the rest of the wood. In happier times he thought this would have been a place of shooting and hunting parties; today, though, it was a potential death trap – ten yards of open ground over which any attempt to advance might spell certain death. He knelt down and spoke to Bennett in a whisper, raising his hand and fanning it down to indicate that the rest of the company should follow suit. 'Ten to one there's a Jerry machine gun covering this ride, Sarnt. What d'you think?'

Bennett was flattered at being asked his opinion. 'Reckon you're right there, sir. Anyone can see it would make the perfect place.'

'Well, we're not going to give them the satisfaction. Where would you place your men if you were the Jerries?'

Bennett pointed to a slight clearing across the opposite side of the ride. Lamb looked at it. The man was absolutely right. There was a clear arc of fire, almost as if it had been cleared deliberately of any undergrowth. 'Yes, I think you're spot on. All right. On my command.'

He pulled a Mills bomb from his tunic and primed it. Bennett did the same. 'One, two, three.'

Both men lobbed their bombs at the same time, full toss, straight into the clearing. The grenades exploded, but there were no cries, no men running for cover.

Lamb looked at Bennett. 'Come on. Sarnt-Major Dodd, with me.'

Together the three of them ran crouching across the ride. Then Lamb stood up and laughed out loud: 'Christ. They've gone. Look.'

Sure enough, there was a slit trench exactly where the sergeant had predicted, but instead of being filled with surrendering Germans it contained only their equipment: four MG34s and a deal of ammunition along with the other detritus of trench life, spent ammo and old food and drink containers.

He shouted the all clear across the ride to the others, and the company crossed over and into the far side of the wood. They checked the trenches as best they could for traps, and when Lamb was satisfied Mays and two of the Highlanders reached in and picked up five heavy machine guns and five cases of ammunition.

Bennett said, 'Beats me why you'd leave these. Lovely weapons, they are.'

Valentine had found them and was looking at the mechanism of one of the guns: 'They must have been in a hurry to get away. Perhaps it was the Highlanders they didn't like.'

Sergeant-Major Dodd grinned. 'Aye. You could be right, lad. We've a terrible reputation.'

Lamb laughed. 'How many men have we lost, Sarnt-Major?'

'At my count, sir, we're ten men down, eight dead.'

'Our mob all right, Sarnt Bennett?'

'All present, sir. What there is.'

It was nearing 10 o'clock in the morning. They had been attacking for a good six hours but the time had flashed past.

Lamb had decided that it would be best if they dug in while the Gordons pushed on. They were setting up an arc of fire for the Bren gun when they saw a figure dashing through the wood from the flank, heading for their lines. At first Lamb thought the man must be a deserter, but then he saw that he was an officer and that he was waving at them not to shoot. He came tumbling into the position and stood before Lamb, shaking with exhaustion. Lamb grabbed him. 'Are you all right, man? What is it? Who are you?'

The man managed a couple of words through his panting breaths. 'Lieutenant Jackson . . . message . . . Brigadier' were all that Lamb could make out. He gave him a swig from his water bottle and was rewarded with 'Thanks'.

'What news? Have we broken through?'

The man stared at him. 'No. Hardly.' His face looked a picture of despair. 'The 2nd Seaforths and the French armour with them have been hit hard.' He took another swig of water and sank down on a tree stump. 'The Seaforths managed to clear the forward posts in the woods on their own, but when the French tanks arrived they came late and our barrage was long past. They drove into a minefield between the road and the woods. It was bloody carnage. They got shot up by Jerry anti-tank guns. The Jerries machine-gunned the men trying to get out of the hatches. They've taken heavy casualties and lost dozens of tanks. I've got to tell the Brigadier. Radios are all kaput.' The man staggered to his feet and handed the water bottle back to Lamb: 'Thanks awfully, old man.' Then without another word he went on his way in a daze and after a while began to run back through the lines.

Lamb could hear the words of the Aldershot instructor again. He turned to Bennett. 'Did you hear that? This is madness. How can we coordinate an attack when more than half of our officers don't speak French and even fewer of theirs speak English?'

'Perhaps we should try Gaelic,' Valentine quipped, but Lamb ignored him.

Bennett shook his head. 'Well, we've done what we were asked to do here, sir. We've secured the flank of the Gordons. We've got the wood.'

'Yes, that's right, Sarnt. We have. Perhaps they'll even push on from here.'

But when word arrived from Brigade an hour later it was not what Lamb wanted to hear. Its bearer was a short, sinewy lieutenant with a fixed grin and a bandage over one eye. He approached their position from the rear at a crouch and tucked himself in beside Lamb. 'Lieutenant Lamb?'

'That's me.'

'You're to retire, sir.'

Lamb gazed at him. 'What?'

'Orders to pull out, I'm afraid.'

'What in God's name is going on?'

'The French have lost half their light tanks and fourteen of their twenty heavies. The 4th Camerons have failed to take their objective. The whole position's just too well covered by dug-in machine guns. Two platoons are cut off, and the Brigade's lost twenty officers and over 500 other ranks.'

'But fall back? That's just madness.'

'Point is, 1st Gordons might have kicked Jerry out of the Grand Bois, but they can't hold it. Not without French tank support. The high ground overlooking the Somme north west of Caubert is still in enemy hands. He's got his guns zeroed in on the Gordons. They're being blown to bits. They've been ordered back to the starting point.'

Lamb shook his head. 'I just can't believe it. What the hell is the bloody point? All that effort, all those men lost, killed and wounded, and for what? It just doesn't make sense.'

17

Yesterday was a nightmare best forgotten. Yet it was one day of his life that Lamb would not, could never forget. He stood in their new position, at the edge of a broad sweep of marshland, and tried to think positively, but it was well nigh impossible.

He was astonished at how quickly it had happened. Three days ago they had been holding their positions on the Somme, although admittedly under pressure, and had seemed capable of holding off the advance for some days if not weeks. Today they were behind the Bresle, ten miles further to the south west and pinned down from the south by the German advance to the sea.

In this entire campaign it had been the swiftest retreat yet, and that he thought could not be good. It was as if they were being suffocated by an unstoppable tide of German troops. As if a sea was pouring through the gaps in the line, gradually making them wider – a sea that would very soon drench them all. He was determined that neither he nor his men should be drowned by it. The received wisdom filtering down from high command was still that they were falling back on Rouen – retreating inland, in other words. The sooner he got to Fortune and reversed that decision – made sure that they were moving towards the coast – the better.

They had halted at the edge of what had been a causeway across the marshes at a place called Lieu Dieu near the major crossing at Gamaches. It had been destroyed by the sappers earlier that day after the last of their retreating units had managed to get across. At least Lamb hoped that it had been the last unit.

He knew that General Fortune's HQ had been near here, in some requisitioned château, Crawford had said. La Grande Vallée, he remembered it was called. Funny how in all wars the generals automatically took over the big country houses while officers ended up in *estaminets* and the men in stables, if they were lucky. He supposed it was all part of the army hierarchy, and that he knew was vital. It was what made the British army work – the respect of the lower ranks for the senior. The men, his company, were sitting in their hastily dug gun pits eating what rations they had managed to share out. The Highlanders had been generous to their newly acquired comrades, though Lamb was not sure that the few men of his platoon shared a liking for thick porridge. Nevertheless, it was food, and he gratefully took another spoonful of his own portion as he stared across the marsh towards the German lines.

Finishing the remains in his mess tin, he walked back to where Bennett was sitting on a tree trunk. 'Sarnt, have the men stand to. We don't want to be caught with our pants down. I'm going to find Lieutenant Crawford.'

Swilling out the tin with a few drops of water, he wiped it with a cloth and gave both to Smart to stow away before walking back through the lines to where he knew C Company were encamped. He saw Crawford, hunched over a map on the bonnet of an abandoned civilian car, and hailed him. 'Morning. Quiet night?'

'Yes. I hadn't expected that. Thought that Jerry might push on. Lucky he didn't. My lads are all in.'

'Mine too. Listen. You know how badly I have to get this message back to the General. Now I think this is my best chance. We must be close to HQ here. I have to go from here. It's my only hope. Our only hope. Will you help me?'

Crawford thought for a moment. 'The colonel won't like it much, particularly after giving you the company, but I'll stand up for you. It must be bloody important if you're willing to risk your neck for it, and your career.'

If only you knew, thought Lamb.

Crawford went on, 'Of course, I can't take you there myself. That would be desertion. But I think I can help. One of my men, McEwan, has been to the château before, twice, with sit reps, and the guards there will recognise him. You can take him along with you. Can't supply any transport, I'm afraid. Need all we've got if Jerry comes on again as fast as he did yesterday.'

'I didn't expect you could, but your man will do perfectly. Thank you, Crawford.'

Crawford smiled and thought for a moment, then added, 'I don't suppose you could tell me the message?'

Lamb looked at him. 'Well, you've helped me, so I will. The plan is for the Division to fall back on Le Havre. The Royal Navy's primed to evacuate from there. But the General will have no idea of that yet. That's the whole point. We've got to start moving towards the coast before it's too late and the Jerries cut us off.'

Crawford was dumbfounded. 'What, the whole Division? Off the coast?'

'If possible. At least, that's the plan. It worked at Dunkirk.'

'Christ. How long have you known this?'

'More than a week. That's why I've got to get it to Fortune soonest. It was a contingency plan but it looks like it's becoming a reality. So now you know why I've got to get that message through. If I don't the General will order everyone back on Rouen. That seems to be what the French intend to order, and then there'll be no hope for the Division.'

'You'd better go. Of course you can't take the company. I'll get Sarnt-Major Dodd to take over. I know he wanted it from the start, though he'd never have said anything.'

Lamb nodded. 'He'll do a good job. I'll be sorry to lose them. I'd like to say I've enjoyed my time with your Jocks but I don't really think that "enjoy" is the right word for what we've seen in the last few days, do you? They're great lads, though. Some of the finest.'

'I know. They don't deserve to be taken prisoner.'

'Who does? Let's just hope I'm not too late. I'll take my own men with me, though. And McKracken. And Madeleine.'

Crawford smiled. 'Of course. You're a lucky man, Lamb.'

'I am?'

Crawford laughed. 'It's as plain as day. Anyway, it's been a pleasure having you all aboard, Lamb.'

'If we both get out of this, why don't we meet back in England?'

'Or Scotland.'

Lamb laughed. 'I'll stand you a pint in the Fox and Hounds at Toys Hill. The loveliest pub in England.'

'And I'll buy you dinner at my club in Edinburgh.'

'Done.'

'Good luck, Lamb.'

'Good luck, Crawford. See you in Blighty.'

They shook hands, and as Lamb walked back to find Bennett and the others he wondered whether they would manage to keep their promise, and whether Crawford and any of his men would make it back.

The men were settling into their slit trenches and rifle pits.

'Sarnt Bennett, we're packing up.'

'Right away, sir. Right, you lot, get your kit together. We're moving off.'

There was a collective groan from the Black Jackals. 'But we've only just got 'ere, Sarge.'

'And now we're just leaving here, Perkins. You heard me.'

'Where are we going, Sarge?'

'That's for me and the officer to know, Hughes, and you to find out. And don't call me Sarge.'

'Sorry, Sarge.'

Bennett slung his own pack and walked over to where Lamb and Smart were busy packing up. 'Beggin' your pardon, sir, but where are we off to?'

'We're going to HQ, Sarnt. Mister Crawford is lending us a guide. Just us. Not the Jocks.'

'Sorry about that, sir. Thought you'd rather taken to having a company.'

Lamb shrugged. 'Easy come easy go, Sarnt.'

Lamb walked over to the men. The Highlanders had begun to move too, and he waved a hand to signal them all to sit down. 'All right. It looks as if we're parting company with our Scottish friends. Sarnt-Major Dodd, I believe that Mister Crawford might want to see you. I'd like to thank you all for what you did yesterday. It was more than anyone could have asked of you. You were faced with impossible odds and you managed to pull back in proper style. I shall miss you, Black Watch. I hope we meet again in happier circumstances.'

The Highlanders muttered thanks and returned to their rifle pits.

Lamb went on, 'You others, men of my old platoon, it looks as if I'm finally going to get to the General. You've been with me through all of this, and thank you for it. It won't take long. It's only five miles, lads. Not far. And then we should know where we stand.'

He turned and walked to the house where he had

billeted Madeleine the previous night. He found her at the kitchen table looking at a framed photograph that she had taken down from the wall. It was of a family, dressed in their best clothes: a father, mother and two children, a son and a daughter. Seeing him come in, she turned and smiled. He could see that she had been crying. She said, 'I wonder where they are.'

'They must have fled. Probably with family.'

'Not like me. I have no family.'

'You have me.'

He leant over her and cradled her head in his arms. 'We're moving out. Crawford's sending a guide to get us to the General.'

'What then?'

'I don't know. We'll wait and see.'

'Peter, I don't want to leave you.'

'Let's just wait and see what happens, shall we? Come on. We should be on the road.'

Outside the men were waiting. Sergeant-Major McKracken came up to Lamb. 'Sir, I've been thinking, and if you don't mind I'd really like tae stay on with the other lads. I feel more at home here. I'd rather take my chances with them, if you know what I mean, sir.'

Lamb smiled. 'Yes, I thought you might, and I know what you mean. Thank you for your help, McKracken. We've come through a lot together. I hope you make it back.'

'Thank you, sir.'

McKracken saluted and walked away towards the Black Watch. Lamb turned back to the men and was surprised to find, standing right behind him, a small, ferret-faced man in Highland headgear, wearing a broad smile. 'Private McEwan, I presume.'

'Aye, sir, the very same.'

They set off away from the centre of the little hamlet, heading south west and then turning right and skirting the marsh which defined the area. On the outskirts of Gamaches they took a right turn and hit a main road. McEwan, walking beside Lamb, said nothing. They could hear shellfire to their rear now and McEwan looked back towards his friends. 'Jerry's attacking again, sir. Poor lads.'

There seemed no end to the Germans' resources, and Lamb wondered how long the General's HQ would remain at the château and indeed if when they got there they might not find that it had already decamped.

It was an easy march in comparison with what they had been through over the past two weeks. Here, within the British lines, there was less evidence as yet of destruction – a few houses destroyed by bombing and some shell holes, but nothing compared to the wholesale destruction they had witnessed. Not for much longer though, thought Lamb. When the Highlanders finally retreated through here, as he knew they must, the German bombs and shells would fall with as much unrelenting fury as they had through the rest of northern France. The houses gave way to open fields, flanked on their right and left by small woods where they could hear songbirds in the trees. It was not until they had been on the road for two hours, as they entered the village of Guerville, that McEwan spoke again, pointing off to the left. 'It's doon there, sir. Doon that wee track, o'er there, see. The château.'

He led them off the road and onto a farm track, which ran between two gateposts topped with heraldic beasts. The track snaked round and entered a wood, and as they walked through the trees Lamb began to see evidence of occupation. Two armoured cars of the Lothian and Borders Horse stood out in the fields beyond the woods, and then directly in front of them their path was blocked by two armed sentries. They levelled their bayonet-topped rifles at Lamb and his party. 'Halt. Who are you?'

234

McEwan stepped forward. 'Private Hamish McEwan, Black Watch. From Colonel Honeyman with a message for General Fortune.'

One of the sentries looked at him and seemed to recognise him, but kept his rifle levelled. 'What's the password then, Private?'

McEwan smiled and hissed, 'Bannockburn, you daft numbtie, Macgregor. And have you no seen there's an officer present.'

The guards lowered their rifles and then brought them up smartly to present as Lamb and his men passed between them. They walked on and Lamb noticed that the path was steadily rising and veering round to the left. He was aware too that the trees grew up a slope and that they were making their way up a hill. Then the trees fell away and the path opened out to a courtyard, on one side of which stood a large château.

Lamb thought it might date from the mid-eighteenth century. It had three tall chimneys and a façade of eighteen tall windows, and on the flagpole which jutted out from the front someone had hung the blue and white saltire of Scotland. The main block was surrounded by a complex of outbuildings and stables, and in the cobbled courtyard stood an assortment of military vehicles: staff cars, dispatch riders' motorbikes, a Bren carrier and a three-ton truck. They walked across to the main entrance, accessed by a sweeping staircase. Officers of all ranks were standing in groups and pairs, or entering and leaving.

Lamb sensed that his men, not to mention Madeleine, stood out somewhat. He turned to them. 'You'd better wait out here. McEwan, help me get in there.'

The two sentries on the door recognised McEwan and on his word brushed the two of them through. Inside a large airy, tiled hall was alive with activity. Radio sets, stores of all sorts and furniture were being carried in various directions while officers bearing sheaves of papers walked hurriedly across their path.

Lamb stopped and accosted a captain. 'Excuse me, sir, can you direct me to the General?' The man looked at him. 'He's in his office. Through the big room on the right, and turn left. Can't miss it.'

Major General Victor Fortune paced the floor of the grand salon in the Château de la Grande Vallée, and once more tried to make sense of the situation. Close beside him stood his immediate superior, Lieutenant General Sir Henry Karslake, who had arrived half an hour ago bearing a communiqué from London.

Fortune turned to Karslake. 'You say that London has told you we must stay with the French. No matter what happens? That any withdrawal must be to Rouen?'

'I'm afraid so, General. It would seem that General Altmayer says he has no reserve with which to replace us. We're to stay put, sir, until the French tell us to move.'

Fortune was fuming. 'It's madness. You mean, sir, I just have to sit here? I've just been told that there may be two divisions of Panzers at Buchy.' He pointed to a large map pinned to one of the panelled walls. 'That's here, fifteen miles north east of Rouen. It stands to reason that we must keep our lines of communication open to the coast.' He turned to the one other man in the room, Major General Beauman: 'Am I right, Beauman?'

'Quite right, Fortune. I've always thought we should prepare to evacuate if necessary. Of course, Dieppe would have been my choice. Or Le Havre. To retire towards the Seine seems nonsensical.'

Karslake nodded to Fortune, 'I agree, Victor. And from what you say and information I have received it does seem that an outflanking manoeuvre is more than likely.'

Fortune went on, 'If the Navy managed to get 300,000

236

men away at Dunkirk, why the devil can't they come in and save our mere 12,000 and a few French?'

'I'm only going by the orders from the Ministry, Victor. London says that we should sit here and take our orders from the French.'

'If you want my opinion, sir, it is the Prime Minister's view that if we are allowed to retire to the coast and even seem to be looking to a possible evacuation then the French will not view that well. The French already consider us perfidious, apparently. To pull out the Division now might look like treachery.' Fortune wrung his hands.

A clerk appeared at the door. 'Sorry, sir. Signal from General Vyse, sir, liaison at French HQ. Came from London, sir.'

Fortune took the note. 'It's from the War Office, to Vyse. "You are to represent to the French Commander-in-Chief in the strongest terms that evacuation between Dieppe and Le Havre cannot be contemplated." Well, I'll be . . .'

He placed the note on the table before him and stood, palms resting on its surface. 'Gentlemen, if we stay here or retire on the Seine I shall lose the entire Division. What the devil are London playing at? What does Churchill want me to do?'

There was a knock at the door and an aide-de-camp entered. 'Sir, I have a Lieutenant Lamb, here, sir. With an urgent message for you.'

Fortune turned to the ADC. 'Lamb? I don't know a Lieutenant Lamb, do I, Thompson?'

The aide shook his head. 'No, sir. Never seen him before. He did say that he came from Colonel "R".'

Fortune looked up. 'Colonel "R"? Well, what are you waiting for? Show him in.'

Lamb entered and, seeing the three staff officers in the room, was unsure at first which was the man he had come so far to find. Then the figure in the centre walked towards him. He was a well-built man, in his late fifties, with piercing eyes and a neat grey moustache. An unremarkable-looking man, Lamb thought, for one who had come to mean so much to him over the past days.

The man said, 'Well?'

'General Fortune, sir?'

'Yes, and you are?'

'Thank God. Sorry, sir, I mean, Lieutenant Peter Lamb, sir. North Kents.'

'Are you, by Jove? The Jackals, eh? You've a message from "R", you say?'

'Sir.'

'Where did he give you this message?'

'Twenty days ago, sir, in Tournai. That was the last time I saw him.'

'How did you get it here? Why has it taken you so long?'

'It's a long story, sir.'

'Well, what's the message?'

Lamb reached into his battledress pocket and drew out the piece of paper, folded and creased, which he had transferred from one uniform to the other over the past week. He unfolded it and handed it to Fortune.

'He said to tell you, sir, that no matter what happens you will be evacuated. That should the line fold, or should you be outflanked, you must fall back on Le Havre.'

Fortune read the message and then looked Lamb hard in the eyes. 'He said that?'

'Yes, sir. And he said that this will be the case no matter what else you hear. In particular what you might hear from the War Office, sir. Ships have already been assembled to evacuate the Division.'

Fortune looked down at the message again, then smiled at Lamb. 'You have no idea, Lieutenant, how good that news sounds.' He turned to Karslake. 'What d'you say to that, sir?'

'It would seem that what Whitehall tells us is somewhat different to other information. "R" never gets it wrong.'

Fortune walked across to the map, 'In that case my mind is made up. We fall back on Le Havre.'

Karslake looked at him. 'Would it perhaps be prudent, Victor, to at least listen to what the French have to say?'

'No, sir. It is imperative that we move with the utmost speed. If we sit here we will be surrounded and the entire Divison will be taken prisoner. We move now.' He paused, reflective. 'But I will talk to General Altmayer, as you suggest. I will ask him to place us in reserve.

Lamb had listened to Fortune's conversation with astonishment. He had presumed that the Prime Minister and the War Office were the ultimate authority, but now it seemed there was some other high command whose orders carried more weight. He was staggered too by the very fact of the internal politics. How could they hope to win a war if they had different objectives and goals. Goals which ultimately would cost thousands of lives.

Fortune was speaking 'We'll send a signal now and pray that it gets through. You've done well, Lamb. What will you do now?'

'I don't know, sir. My men are all in. But we can still fight.'

'How many of you are there?'

'Myself and nine men, sir. And a French girl we rescued from the SS.'

Fortune's eyes widened. 'That's all that's left of your platoon?'

'Yes, sir. We have come all the way from the Dyle.'

Fortune stared at him. 'You're quite a man, Mister Lamb, aren't you? You and your Jackals.' He thought for a while, then walked over to Lamb and clapped him on the back. 'Why don't you stay here tonight? Mess with us. Get your French girl a bath. Simpson will find her a room upstairs, and I'm sure there's room in one of the officers' cottages for you. Your men will find billets. But don't get too comfortable. I'll think of something for you to do by the morning.'

Lamb found Bennett and the others waiting outside in the garden. 'Right, Sarnt. Twelve hours' leave. Here. See if you can find a billet for the men. Miss Dujolle will be staying in the house.'

'What's the plan, sir? Are we going to try and find the Battalion? Are we going home?'

'I don't know, Bennett. I just don't know. It all depends on the General.'

He took Madeleine by the hand and led her towards the house, up the stairs and past the guards. She looked around, taking it all in, bewildered to be inside such a grand country house. 'Have they just taken it over?'

'Yes. It's what happens in wartime.'

'It's so big, so grand. My grandmother worked as a maid in such a place. I never thought I would stay somewhere like this.'

He smiled. 'Come on.'

They climbed the stairs, and at the top, as he had been told by the General's aide, turned left along a corridor hung with oil paintings of grim-looking Frenchmen, ancestors of the owners, he presumed. It reminded him a little of his ex-wife's family home in Kent, and for a moment his mind was distracted by thoughts of Julia and Kate. But then Madeleine looked up at him and their faces disappeared. Fourth room on the left, the man had said, and Lamb turned the handle.

Madeleine gasped. She could hardly believe it. The room was high and panelled in two shades of grey. Lace curtains hung at the shuttered windows, which led to a wrought-iron balcony. There was a bed with white sheets, and a bathroom. The General Staff had taken over the château and were doing their best to keep it intact in case the family returned. The reception rooms had suffered worst, being turned upside down to accommodate the needs of the General's offices, but upstairs the rooms were as elegant as when they had been left by the fugitive family. There were clean, soft towels in the armoires and piles of unopened soaps in paper wrappers.

Madeleine hugged Lamb. 'Thank you. Oh thank you, my darling. It's like a dream.'

'I'm afraid we can't stay here for long, unless you want to stay with the General Staff, and I don't know if that would be possible. I imagine even the General will be on the move quite soon. The Germans are moving fast.'

Her smile vanished and she let go of him and sat on the edge of the bed. 'Yes, of course. I know. It's only an illusion, isn't it? But can you allow me my little daydream, Peter? Just for a few hours.'

He smiled at her. 'All right. I'm sorry. For a few hours. Why don't you have a bath and then we can see what we can find to eat here.'

She went into the bathroom, and as he opened the door to leave he heard her gasp again and giggle with joy.

Lamb descended the staircase and, hearing the sound of voices and laughter, walked towards it. In one of the château's large reception rooms, he thought it must have been the Morning Room, the officers had set up a make-shift mess and bar, and one of the batmen was acting as steward. Lamb walked in. It was a surreal scene, straight from St James's. And just as they would have done in their clubs, or the mess, the other officers turned and acknowledged him politely before returning to their conversations. He went to the bar — a line of ammo boxes — and ordered a Scotch and soda from the batman. There was a distant booming from shells to the north, and Lamb knew that the front was being bombarded again. He wondered how Crawford and the others were doing, and part of him wished he had not had to leave them to come here. He felt a sudden pang of conscience at the knowledge that he would sleep in a clean bed that night, and eat well.

As he was drinking another officer entered, a Frenchman, although not of the sort he had become used to seeing on the road with the retreating army. This man was neatly dressed in the uniform of a cavalry officer, with baggy breeches, highly polished boots and a Polish-style khaki tunic rather than the normal service dress. On his chest he wore a row of medal ribbons, and at his side hung a cavalry sabre.

The British officers turned and, just as they had with Lamb, smiled at the newcomer. Lamb, at the bar, smiled too. 'Can I buy you a drink?'

'Thank you. I will have a whisky soda. Like you. You are Scots?'

'No, English. But I still drink Scotch. Like the French.'

'Excuse me. Etienne Charvet. Captain, 4th Cuirassiers.'

'Peter Lamb, Lieutenant, North Kents. Your regiment fought mine at Waterloo.'

'Of course.' The Frenchman raised his glass. 'Well, chin-chin. To old scores.'

'To the *Entente Cordiale*.'

The man shrugged. 'Is it still *cordiale*? I don't think so. You know what my general calls your General Fortune? General Misfortune. But though I know he has no respect, we have great respect for you. For all the Highlanders too. We know these men, these amazons who would rather wear their skirts than trousers.'

He drained his glass and signalled to the batman for a refill for both of them.

'Let's drink it while we can, Lieutenant. I have just delivered a report to your generals. The Germans have made a gap in the line twenty-five miles to the south, at Forges. Do you know how they did it? All morning refugees, stragglers and vehicles had been passing through Forges, and your men couldn't close their roadblocks. Some of our tanks were allowed to go through. Of course they were French tanks, but they had been captured by the enemy. Once through the defences they turned on our posts from the rear. Then they broke through behind with their own tanks. Neufchatel's in flames, and the enemy's tanks are on the road to Rouen. You know the battle is as good as lost. We have no reserves and we are outnumbered two to one. How can we win?'

Lamb said nothing. There was nothing to be said.

It was 8 p.m. At a crossroads five miles to the east of Rouen Kessler stopped and peered out of the hatch. The tanks' engines were idling. They had come so far so quickly that he had decided it was time to let them cool down before they seized up.

His sergeant called up to him from the roadside, 'Sir, we could go on and take Rouen. It's there for the taking.'

'No, Hans, I have a better plan. I have permission from General Hoth to take the bridges at Elbeuf. That's fifteen miles south west. The French and British will expect nothing to happen there, so that is where we will attack. It will take five tanks. Just five and a motorcycle company.'

Six days' rest they had enjoyed – their prize for rolling up the French at Lille. He was restless now. General Rommel had been honoured with a Knight's Cross and now Kessler had one thought in his mind. He might have been beaten to the coast but he would be first to the Seine. Then they would sweep round and trap what was left of the British with a sickle stroke to the sea. And that would be that.

18

Lamb was awakened the following morning by a strange and alarming noise. For a moment he wondered what it was, and then through his semi-conscious state it became clear. Somewhere outside someone was playing the bagpipes. He turned over and felt a soft, smooth, naked back and pushed against it with his own body, relishing the warmth.

She sighed. 'Are you awake?'

'Yes. That bloody noise woke me. Didn't it you?'

She laughed. 'Your Scottish soldiers will wake everyone with that. I like it.'

'I'm afraid I have to get up before anyone knows I've been in here. Against King's regulations, and not good for morale.'

He climbed from the bed and began to dress, hauling on his battledress trousers and braces and then buttoning his flies and his shirt before turning back to her. She had rolled over in the bed and was looking up at him half-naked, and seeing her like that and gazing into her eyes Lamb was temped to throw himself back onto the bed. But he managed to steel himself and carried on dressing, looking away, saying nothing.

'Peter.'

'Uh-huh.'

'Peter, you will take me back to England, won't you?'

He stopped. It was not something of which they had spoken before, and he had been putting off the thought.

'I don't know. I can't work out what to do.'

'You know I can't stay here, darling. The Boche will have my country, and now I have no one to live for. No one but you.'

He froze. Of course he wanted to take her back. But what then? Did she expect to get married? He was not sure if he was ready for that again, if indeed he wanted it at all. But he knew that she was quite right: to stay in France would be the end for her, and he could not let that happen. In any case, to be parted from her now . . . He looked at her. 'I'm sorry. Can we talk about it later. I'll be late for the men.'

She smiled and nodded. 'I'm sorry, I didn't mean to rush you. Don't worry. We can talk.' She looked down at the floor, but he crossed the room, bent down, lifted her chin and placed his lips against hers.

Then he turned and walked to the door. 'I have a feeling the General's going to move from here today, so I should get dressed now. I promise I won't be long.'

Downstairs the Divisional HQ was in uproar. Officers and men seemed to be rushing in all directions to no apparent purpose.

Lamb stopped one of them. 'What's going on?'

'Haven't you heard, sir? Jerry's broken through. He's only four miles away. We're moving back.'

The man broke away, and Lamb rushed outside to find his platoon. They had been billeted in the gardener's cottage and he ran across to it and pushed the door open. They were inside, cleaning their weapons, shaving and eating.

Smart looked up. 'Wondered where you were, sir. Fancy a brew? I've just got one on.'

'No time. Come on. There's a flap on. We're moving out. Jerry'll be here in an hour. Less.'

They stood up. Stubbs wiped the soap off his chin and Smart poured away the tea with a dejected look.

'Where are we going, sir?'

'Damned if I know, Mays. But I'm going to find out.'

He left and ran across the yard to where a gunnery sergeant was supervising the transports pulling out of the farm courtyard to the rear.

'Any idea where we're headed, Sarnt?'

'We're off to another ruddy big house, sir. It's about fifteen miles due west. La Chaussee, it's called. Want a lift?'

'I've eleven others with me.'

'Not a problem, sir. You can all get in one of the ammo trucks. Course, if it gets hit you'll all go up like Roman candles.'

'We'll take our chances. Rather that than get nabbed by the Jerries.'

He saw Bennett across the yard. 'Sarnt, we've scrounged a lift. Round up the men.'

Lamb ran back into the château, and as he was about to run up the staircase a voice stopped him in his tracks.

'Mister Lamb. Good morning.' General Fortune was standing at the foot of the staircase with his batman and three staff officers. 'Sleep well?'

'Very well, thank you, sir.'

'My piper woke you?'

'Yes, sir. It was very nice.'

'Don't be soft, man. It wasn't nice at all. But it woke you up. Stirred the spirits a bit, I'll bet, even for a Sassenach. You know we're pulling out of here?'

'Yes, sir.'

'You are coming with us?'

246

'Yes, sir, of course. Just getting my kit.'

'Good. I've come up with a job for you, Lamb. But it will wait until we get where we're going. See you at HQ.'

'Yes, sir.'

Lamb's mind was racing. A job for him. Oh dear God, he prayed it wasn't another mission to deliver a message. He was fed up to the back teeth with being a runner for the high command.

They rattled around in the ammo truck for two hours. No one spoke much. Valentine cracked a joke, and then even he was silent. At length they stopped and the engine died. Lamb climbed down from the back and saw that they were parked in a courtyard very similar to the one they had left, with a large château dominating the place.

The driver came round the back of the truck. 'There we are, sir. Just like home. Everybody out.'

As the men and Madeleine clambered down from the truck, a staff car roared into the courtyard and pulled up dangerously close to him. The rear window was wound down and Lamb found himself looking into the face of General Fortune.

'Glad to see you found it, Lamb. Off to a conference. Come along. You'll find it of interest. Simpson will take you. Drive on.'

As Fortune rolled away and out of the gate, another staff car arrived, open-topped this time, driven by the aide-de-camp, a captain in the Grenadiers. 'Hop in, Lieutenant. The general wants you there, for some reason.'

Lamb turned to the men, exchanged glances with Madeleine and climbed into the car. He looked at his watch. It was five p.m.

An hour later he was standing in a stiflingly hot room in the elementary school of the town of Arques-la-Bataille, temporarily transformed into the HQ of 154 Brigade. The room was filled with officers, mostly major and above. They were standing in convivial groups and chattering, and Lamb felt not a little out of place. The evening sun beat down through the windows, and Lamb looked around at the room, which seemed to have been largely untouched by the war as yet. The walls were covered with posters explaining sums and how to tell the time. There were images of foreign places, including one of London with Big Ben and Buckingham Palace and another of the Brandenburg Gate in Berlin. Lamb stood at the rear of the room, trying to blend into the sea of field officers, but still felt uncomfortable. He wondered why the General had asked him, a lowly lieutenant, to attend a staff conference, and could only conclude that it must have something to do with the task that lay ahead.

A familiar face came weaving through the crowd towards him. Colonel Honeyman clasped his hand. 'Lieutenant. Good to see you again. Thought we might have lost you.'

Lamb looked at him sheepishly. 'Hello, sir. I'm most terribly sorry about leaving you. I had to grasp the moment. Did Lieutenant Crawford explain?'

'Of course. I have to say that I was more than a little angry when I found out, but when Crawford told me about the message and how vital it was I quite forgave you. Is that what this is about?'

'Yes, sir, I presume it is.'

So Crawford had told Honeyman about Le Havre. Well, Lamb was not sorry. Perhaps it had saved his bacon.

Fortune banged on the schoolteacher's desk at the front of the room and, having silenced the officers, began to speak. 'Gentlemen, I have an announcement to make. Contrary to what some of you might think, this Division is no longer making for Rouen. We had hoped to establish

248

another line across the Seine, but it seems now that will not be possible. So we're falling back in the direction of Le Havre.'

There was a buzz in the room, and murmuring.

Fortune raised his hand and all fell silent. 'I have received a message informing me that the Royal Navy has plans in hand to send nine destroyers and numerous smaller vessels and if necessary evacuate the 51st from Le Havre, just as they managed so wonderfully at Dunkirk.'

A ragged cheer.

'So as from this moment we are making for Le Havre, and then home.'

A huge cheer. Fortune smiled.

'I have come up with a plan to hold the Germans in the east, and as it seems more than likely that they will arrive at Le Havre ere long, another plan to safeguard the security of the port, prior to our embarkation.'

He paused and pointed to a staff officer standing on his right. 'I'm creating a force for that purpose under Brigadier Stanley-Clarke, here. This force will take position between Fécamp in the north, here,' he pointed to the map, 'and Lillebonne in the south, here. It will comprise the 6th Royal Scots, 1st Kensingtons, 17 and 75 Field Regiment RA, three companies of sappers and any other unlucky odds and sods whom we might deem to be a help to it. We've called it Ark Force for two reasons. One, it's been formed here at Arques-la-Bataille, which as you all bright historians will remember is the birthplace of William the Conqueror and thus a good omen for getting us all back across the channel.' This brought a laugh from the officers. 'The other is for the obvious reason that I do feel a little bit like Noah, and I intend for you all to go in two by two.'

There was another huge burst of laughter and applause this time, but Lamb could hear its hollowness.

Fortune waved away the laughter. 'I have sent a message to the Prime Minister asking for all spare fighter aircraft to be despatched to us. The Navy too is doing everything to embark us from le Havre. Admiral James is sending nine destroyers from Portsmouth. In fact I'm told they may well already have arrived at the Le Havre estuary. The French estimate that it will take three nights to get us all off.' He paused, aware of the impact his next words would have. 'And we plan to start the embarkation on the 13th.'

A silence echoed through the room.

Someone coughed, Lamb could not see who. Another officer asked the question they were all asking themselves: 'Isn't that rather late, sir?'

'Yes, thank you for that question. Well, it's not my place to comment, but that is the schedule that's been set by the French commanders for their own men to withdraw, and as you know I've always said that in the order of battle here the French have the ultimate word. So that's the date were going with. I have agreed to it. Don't forget that quite apart from the Division and all the other chaps who've pitched up here, we are also embarking whatever we can of the French IX Corps. We're all in this together, after all. The main point is that Le Havre must be defended.'

They left the room, and Honeyman turned to Lamb. 'Well, I'll be blowed. I know the old man's loyal to the end. To the French, I mean, as well as us. But well, you heard him. The 13th? That's just absurd. By then we'll all be in the bloody bag, if you ask me.'

'I suppose we can't be seen to be disunited, sir.'

'Yes. I dare say you're right, but it's going to be a damn close call. See you in Le Havre, Lamb.'

'Sir.'

As he was passing Lamb, Fortune turned to him and stopped. 'Lieutenant Lamb? There you are. Enjoy that?

Thanks to you, you know. Well done. As a reward I'm sending you and your men with Arkforce as part of A Brigade. You should feel at home with them. We've made it up from all sorts: two battalions of the Argylls, what's left of them, 4th Black Watch, the 6th Royal Scots, and A Brigade. That's you now. We need every man we can get, and they're a real hodgepodge. No offence, laddie. In fact I think we need chaps like you with them. You've only ten men, so I'm giving you a composite company: Norfolks, Kensingtons and a few stray Highlanders. You'll be brigaded with the Sherwood Foresters and the Buffs.'

Lamb stared, dumbstruck. Promoted again to company commander. 'Thank you, sir.'

'Oh, don't thank me, Lieutenant. Just take your command, and do your utmost to stop the Jerries from taking Le Havre.'

Fortune turned to go. Lamb coughed and Fortune turned. 'Yes, was there something else?'

'The girl, sir. The French girl who is with us. Can I leave her here?'

Fortune looked at him. 'This is not a hotel or a hostel, Lieutenant. Has she no home to go to?'

'No, sir. That's just it. Her parents were shot by the SS. She only just escaped.' He thought. 'She's really a very good medic, sir.'

'I shouldn't do this but as it's you, Lamb, yes, the girl can stay. She can travel with the GHQ signallers, in their truck. But the slightest problem and she's out, Lamb. Right, you'd better get going.'

The journey back to the new HQ at the château of La Chaussee was uneventful and silent, and having thanked Captain Simpson Lamb crossed the courtyard and found Bennett and the others. 'Well, we've got our matching orders. We're off to defend Le Havre. The general's getting

251

everyone out. At least that's the plan. We're off back to Blighty.'

There were cheers and smiles, and Bennett said, 'Very good, sir. I'll say, that *is* good.'

'Have you seen Miss Dujolle, Sarnt?'

'She's up in the big house, sir. With some of the brass hats.'

Lamb nodded, 'Wait here. I shan't be long.'

He had known that at some point he would have to leave Madeleine, and he had known that it would be hard, but he had not imagined it would feel like this. Lamb cradled her head against his chest and ran his fingers through her dark hair, watching how the locks fell around them, savouring every instant. She said nothing, but her sobs throbbed against him.

'I'll be back. Very soon. And then we'll get away. Together.'

'Don't lie, Peter. You are going to fight and I am staying here with the general, as you said. And who will get away first? Your general. Isn't that how it is? And he will take me with him, as you said, and I will leave you here.'

She began to sob again.

'No. No I promise you. Of course you'll get away, but I'll come back for you. We'll go together.'

She raised her head and looked into his eyes. 'Promise?'

'I promise. I promise that I will not leave France without you. There. And I never break my promise.'

She smiled. 'Thank you. Though I don't think I believe you.'

He pressed her to him and held her hard, as if it were for the last time. Finally she broke away, and, reaching into his pocket, he offered a handkerchief, which she took to wipe her eyes. She looked at him and managed a smile. 'Go on. Go to your men. They're waiting.'

Reaching down, Lamb kissed her and then quickly

pulled away and turned, not wanting to look back and knowing that she would be looking at him until he was out of sight.

He found Bennett and the men where he had left them, outside the main entrance. With them now, though, were other men: a good forty of them, he supposed, in a variety of headgear. Bennett was talking to one of them when Lamb appeared and nodded towards him.

The man turned and saluted. 'Sergeant Buck, sir, Royal Norfolks. Orders to report to you, sir.'

'Yes, Sarnt. Well done. It seems that I'm to be your new commanding officer. For the present, at least. Who else have we got?'

Bennett said with a sigh, 'Well, sir, there's five from the Norfolks, including Sergeant Buck here, a half dozen of the Kensingtons, a couple of lads from the Buffs, four Royal Sussex and twenty-odd from the Cameron Highlanders. Thirty-seven all told, sir.'

Hardly a company thought Lamb. More an over-strength platoon. Still, a company was what Fortune had given him, so a company they were, and he a brevet captain by default.

'And the ten of us, Sarnt. That'll do. How many NCOs?'

'No sergeants, sir, save me and Sergeant Buck. One corporal of the Norfolks, and a lance-jack from the Camerons.'

Lamb thought for a moment. 'We'll make two platoons: number 1 under you Bennett, the other, number 2, under Sarnt Buck. You'll have our mob, less Corporal Valentine. I'm lending him to Sarnt Buck's number 2 platoon. All right, Valentine?'

The reply came in a weary drawl. 'Very good, sir.'

'Transports should be here any minute, so get yourselves ready. We're off to the seaside.'

*   *   *

It was forty miles to the little seaside town of Fécamp and fully three hours before Lamb and his men began to enter the outskirts. They were travelling in four open-topped Bedfords and Lamb had at first been worried that the German bombers would have a field day, particularly as the road they had taken was so packed with refugees that their advance was dangerously slow. But as they advanced down the crowded road the sky began to darken, even though the sun was high in the sky. Looking up, he saw that it was covered with a huge cloud of smoke, and with it came a smell. The stench was cloying, catching the back of the throat like tar. Lamb knew at once what it meant: burning oil. He looked south, whence the cloud seemed to be emanating, and saw more smoke curled up in a thick black pall hanging in the sky like some biblical portent. Le Havre. The Germans were bombing the port and must have set fire to the giant oil refineries there. Lucky for them. Otherwise, he thought, the Stukas would have been on them.

Then in the sky, above the cloud, he heard engines: enemy bombers off to destroy the port and make escape impossible. What, he wondered was the point of Arkforce even trying to establish a line around Le Havre if the Germans could simply block the harbour with bombed vessels? He shook his head.

Valentine saw it. 'Problem, sir?'

'No, Valentine, not really. I was just contemplating the folly of war.'

'Really, sir? I often do that. Helps pass the time.'

'You think too much, Valentine.'

'I'm sorry, sir. I'll try not to do that. Force of habit.'

'Force of habit?'

'University, sir. I was reading philosophy when the war broke out.'

Lamb perked up. 'Really? Oxford or Cambridge?'

'Neither, actually. Not smart enough. Not like you, sir. I went to Reading.'

'I'm not smart, Valentine.'

'But you are an officer, sir. And you did go to Oxford and public school.' He gave that annoying little smile. 'You must be smart.'

Lamb ignored him. 'We're almost there, I think. All right, men, prepare to de-bus.'

The vehicle crossed a bridge at the harbour mouth, drove on for a few yards and stopped. Lamb leaped down from the tailgate, followed by the others. They were in the town square, a pretty place with tall nineteenth-century houses and a few cafés. Apart from British and French soldiers and military vehicles it was now quite deserted.

In a corner of the square a group was gathering and Lamb could see what looked like a commanding officer issuing officers to his subordinates. He walked over. The CO was standing with his back to Lamb, who coughed, 'Lieutenant Peter Lamb, sir, reporting to Arkforce with . . .'

The officer turned, and Lamb stopped in mid-sentence as he found himself looking into the eyes of Captain Campbell.

'Lieutenant Lamb. What a very pleasant surprise. I had heard that you were being sent to us with your merry band. What have you been up to since last we met? Assaulted any more senior officers? Stolen any more trucks? Deserted your post again?'

Brigadier Stanley-Clarke, whom Lamb now saw standing next to Campbell, looked at the captain. 'I say, steady on Campbell. What on earth d'you mean? Lieutenant Lamb is here on the recommendation of General Fortune himself. He's an asset, Campbell. You can't go slandering a fellow officer.'

'An asset, sir? An ass, more like. And as for slander, do you know, sir, what this fellow officer did to me? He attacked me, sir. Tied me up and then deserted with his men and stole one of our vehicles. And now he has the temerity to try and escape back to England. Brigadier, I would be very much obliged if you would have this officer and his men placed under arrest immediately pending a field court martial and sentencing.'

Stanley-Clarke looked on in amazement. 'If that's what you say happened, Campbell, I'll have to take your word for it. I don't know this man, even though he claims to have been sent by General Fortune. But I do know you, Campbell and I've no cause to doubt you. Very well.' He nodded to two redcaps who were standing beside a lorry and came running across. Before Lamb knew it they were holding his arms in a vice-like grip. The brigadier looked at Lamb. 'I'm sorry, Lieutenant. I have no idea whose story is correct, but Captain Campbell is the senior officer and for that reason I shall have to place you and your men under arrest. Where are they?'

Campbell had already seen to that, and a dozen of his men were standing, their rifles levelled around the newly disembarked company. He turned to the military police sergeant. 'Sarnt, put this man in the town gaol with as many of those men as you can fit in. NCOs first. Place a guard on the door. He's extremely dangerous. Oh, and make sure you disarm them all first.'

He turned to Lamb. 'I'll deal with you as soon as we get organised here. But you know what to expect, Lamb, don't you? "Shot at dawn" is hardly the end to a glittering military career that you'd been expecting, I suppose. Take him away.'

Lamb was marched towards the others. Bennett tried to yell something to him but he could not hear. The gaol was across the square inside the town hall. They walked up the steps and into the hall, which as usual had been requisitioned as Brigade HQ. As one of the redcaps asked a clerk how to get to the gaol and where the keys could be found, an officer came crashing through the doors behind them. 'Where's the brigadier?'

Someone, a staff officer, answered, 'In the square with his O group. Why?'

'The Division's been cut off. Jerry's broken through at Rouen and got up to the coast at St Pierre-en-Port. Your job's a bit useless, old man. The general's orders are that the brigadier should make his own arrangements now for a defensive line and try to save what he can of you lot.'

'Are you serious? We've only just got here.'

'Well, you'd better jolly well get out of here before you all end up in the bag. St Pierre's only six miles away. The general says you might want to head for Goderville. There are some good old French positions down there.'

With that the man turned and rushed out into the square.

The redcap, apparently oblivious to the revelation that had just occurred, turned back to Lamb and the clerk. He was holding a bunch of keys. 'Bloke says there are six cells, Bert. Reckons might be enough for three dozen of them. That should do it. Sorry, sir, we'll have to put you in with some of the men. This way, sir.'

They walked through the hall, which by now was in a frenzy. So the Germans had broken through and were likely to be closing in on Fécamp before long, and he and his men were about to be shut up in some stinking prison. And what would he do there, he wondered, except wait for the inevitable, and then God knew how many years in a German prisoner-of-war camp. Still, he thought, it was better than being shot on Campbell's orders. And grotesquely, something inside him began to hope that the Germans would arrive sooner than Campbell was able to hold his kangaroo court. Either way, he was finished.

*   *   *

Kessler moved fast across the plain, the command tank flattening all in its path.

He might have been beaten to the sea and to Abbeville but he was damned if he was not going to take away some measure of glory from this campaign. He was going to take the town of Fécamp and cut the British off from the sea. He shouted down into the tank from his position up in the commander's hatch. 'Keep it up, Hans. Not far now. There's no one out there. No one.'

'Perhaps they've gone already, sir.'

'Nonsense. These are Scottish troops, Hans. Men in skirts. They stay and fight. My father fought them in the last war. They're waiting for us, somewhere.'

The air had become noticeably cooler now against his face atop the tank, and the fields seemed to shrink against the horizon. Then he saw it, stretching out ahead of him – a seemingly endless expanse of water. The channel. He yelled down into the tank: 'I can see it. I can see the sea.'

On either side of him now the white cliffs came into view. They had reached the coast of France. The ground dipped down below them and they began to descend towards the water, until the beach came into sight. 'Take her down to the water's edge, Hans. I want to put my boots in the ocean. We've done it. We've surrounded them. They're finished.'

19

The prison in the town hall of Fécamp had been built shortly after the French Revolution, and the fact that it housed no less than six cells was due largely to the anticipation of the new Napoleonic administration that there would be other Royalist revolts to put down and more heads to lop. For that surprising spaciousness Lamb was now thankful as he woke, stiff and sore, on the stone floor of his cell. At least they were not too tightly packed. Six men to a cell, to be precise. It was not the most salubrious of places at the best of times, but now, neglected by its absent gaolers, some of whom had joined the ranks of the army while others had either moved to Rouen or simply joined the columns of refugees, it was among the filthiest places Lamb had ever had the misfortune to spend the night. The slop pails were still full of excrement from the last prisoners before they had been moved to Rouen, and the place stank of long-dried urine.

He turned to Bennett. 'I'm truly sorry, Sarnt. I never meant to get you all into this mess. I'm sure that when General Fortune finds out about this he'll get us out.'

Bennett shook his head and managed a smile. 'Don't worry, Mister Lamb, sir. I know, we all do, that you were only trying your best. We knew that that message had to get through, and the main thing is that you did it. And you got us this far when others have ended up in the bag. I was talking to a bloke in the Norfolks who'd heard that the Jerries had killed eighty of his mob up north – just shot them against a wall in cold blood. And there's thousands of others been taken prisoner up north by Dunkirk and Calais that didn't get off last week. So I reckon we should be thankful to you, sir, for keeping us alive and out of Jerry's hands.'

'Thank you, Sarnt. I really appreciate that, although I don't know how long we'll stay out of German hands if we have to remain in here.'

Another voice spoke, in a familiar drawl. 'Of course I always suspected I'd end my days in a French prison. Just knew it, somehow.'

Mays groaned. 'Oh give it a rest, Valentine. Or I'll sock you one.'

Bennett growled at them. 'That's enough, Corporal. Both of you. But he's right. Stop whingeing, Valentine. We're all in the same fix, the lieutenant here included.'

Lamb said nothing and stared at the floor. They were cut off from the others, from the Division and from Madeleine. German tanks were on the banks of the Durdent, and where was he? Rotting in a stinking French gaol. But how, he wondered, could he have done it any differently? He had grasped the opportunities as they arose and managed to get the message through to Fortune. Yet this was his reward. Chiefly he felt sorry for his men. Their options were between trial for mutiny and capture by the enemy. And he wondered what the new additions to his command would make of him now, having spent their first night under Lamb in the cells. He was pondering their fate when there was a commotion outside. Lamb managed to smile. 'Breakfast, I expect, lads.'

But it was not breakfast. A tall military policeman opened the door to Lamb's cell. 'Someone to see you, sir.'

Lamb stood and walked towards the door. A small, rotund figure entered in the uniform of a British staff officer, and Lamb did not at first recognise him. But then he spoke and Lamb remembered: remembered a farmhouse on a battlefield, and several glasses of good claret. Dewy Meadows blinked in the half light of the early morning cell and recoiled at the stench, before he focused on Lamb. 'I say. It *is* you. Extraordinary.'

'Brigadier, what are you doing here, sir?'

'Funny thing, really. Drove west to find Corps HQ and ended up here. Got put in charge of defaulters. Saw your name on the list and I said to myself, Dewy, old boy, you know that name. That chap's no jailbird. Decent cove. Knows his wine. Had dinner with him in Belgium. Damn good conversation. Damned good claret too. Good food, as I remember. My driver cooked it. What's his name? Damned good cook. Damned bad driver. That's largely why I ended up here. Must have taken a wrong turning. Anyway. He went west a little time back. Stukas. Damn shame really. Damned good cook. Damned awful driver.'

Lamb interrupted the flow of memories. 'Sorry, sir, but if you're in charge here, is there any way you can get us out? We'd rather like to get back to the fighting.'

Meadows smiled at him. 'Course you would, Lamb. Course you would. Chap like you – ought to be hitting the Boche for six instead of rotting in here. What on earth are you doing in here, anyway? Papers said something about stealing a truck. Was that you? An officer and a gentleman?'

'I did have to requisition one, sir, to get down here with an important message.'

'Message? Ah yes, of course. I gave you that message, didn't I? Did you get it through?'

'Yes, sir. Delivered by hand to the General Staff.'

'Splendid, splendid. Of course you'd need a truck for that, wouldn't you? Must be some sort of misunderstanding. Someone's got hold of the wrong end of the stick, eh?'

'Yes, sir, that'll be it. The wrong end of the stick.'

'Stealin' a truck? Won't do. Not at all. Nonsense. And just look at this place. Good Lord, what a stench. Can't have chap like you locked up in here. I say, you seem to have a few other chaps in there. All with you?'

'Yes, sir, these are my men. And the others too. I command a company now.'

'Do you, by Jove? You see I told you you were no jailbird. Been promoted. I think it's high time we got you out of here.' He turned and shouted into the corridor: 'Sarnt!'

The redcap came running. 'Yes, sir.'

'Have this man released immediately. And all his men. There's been some sort of balls-up. Wrong man.'

The sergeant stared at him. 'But, sir, sorry, sir. Captain Campbell said . . . And Brigadier Stanley-Clarke . . .'

'Arthur Stanley-Clarke? I was fighting the Boers when he was still at school. See to it, man. Sharpish. That's an order. And find his men their weapons.'

Lamb smiled at Meadows. 'Thank you, sir. I'm in your debt. You won't regret it.'

'I certainly hope not. I don't know what the devil you did to that man Campbell, but he's absolutely furious. Was it his truck you borrowed to get my message through? Keeps saying if the army doesn't shoot you he damn well will.' He rocked with laughter. 'Bit of a joker, if you ask me. Shoot a fellow officer? What can you have done to him?'

'If only you knew, sir.'

'Sorry?'

'I said I wish I knew, sir. By the way, is he still here?'

'No. Met him as he was leaving. Sent down the line to the south with part of "Arkforce". Damned funny name for a brigade. Hate this modern stuff. Not like the old army.'

'No, sir. Not at all like the old army.'

With the Brigadier leading the way, Lamb led his men out of his cell and past the others as they were opened in turn by the MPs, who were issuing the men with their rifles. The sergeant returned his two pistols, the Luger and the Enfield, to Lamb. Upstairs in the town hall the air was cool and fresh. The clerks had gone now, and with them all semblance of an HQ. All that was left was the detritus of an army: a few unfilled forms, a scattering of discarded webbing, empty cigarette packets, magazines, unwashed plates and cutlery lay on the requisitioned furniture of the town hall, scattered around in unlikely positions, where the staff had left it in their hurry to escape the German advance.

Lamb turned to Meadows. 'Hadn't we better get a move on, sir? The Germans must almost be here.'

'Yes, I dare say you're right. Probably a good idea.' He walked across to the doors and then turned back. 'Good luck, Lieutenant. Good to have you back.'

'Thank you, sir. And thank you for getting me out of there. If ever I can return the favour . . .'

Meadows nodded, saluted and left the building with another officer who had been waiting for him by the door.

Lamb found Bennett. 'Right. That was a close call. We need to get moving, fast, or we'll be going straight back into another prison.'

With his company following close behind, Lamb walked down the steps of the town hall and found himself out again on the streets of the town. He watched as the brigadier's staff car rounded a corner of the square and drove out of sight, and then took stock. Fécamp was now far from the bustling town it had been the previous day. A single British truck, its bonnet left open, stood on the opposite side of the square, which like the inside of the town hall was littered with the army's rubbish. Of any other British soldiers there was no evidence. As they stood there the two MPs came out of the town hall and brushed past Lamb.

'That's us, sir. We're finished here. We've got a lift to Le Havre. That's where the Brigade's making for now, sir: a line between Octeville and Contreville. You'd be best getting out too, sir. Jerry'll be here any minute. Last we heard he was at the sea, four miles away.'

'Thank you, Sarnt. I'll take your advice.'

The policemen ran down the street and vanished from view. Lamb turned to the men behind him. 'We'd better get moving. Stay together. Any sign of the enemy, take cover. We're heading for Le Havre.'

No sooner had he said the words than he knew them to be wrong. Why, he wondered, should he be heading for Le Havre? What earthly good would it do now? As part of Arkforce he had had specific orders, to help hold the line and defend the port to allow the Division to get away. But now that the Germans had cut them off from the Division, what point was there in holding Le Havre? If the Division, and Madeleine with them, were to escape capture and get to England, then their only hope would surely be further up the coast, back the way they had come. He knew that Fortune would have worked that one out by now. But to get there? To get back to the Division would now mean having to cut through the German lines, and that was not something he could ask his men to do. If there was a hope of getting Bennett and the others off from Le Havre, surely he should leave Fortune and his men to fend for themselves and get himself and what was left of his platoon to the port? But then there was Madeleine. While Lamb was wrestling with the problem he did not notice anything else.

Valentine spoke. 'Begging your pardon, sir, and not wishing to speak out of turn . . .'

Lamb turned to him. 'Valentine, you always speak out of turn. What do you want?'

'Well, sir, I was thinking that Le Havre is not really perhaps the place to which we should be heading.'

Lamb cast a glance at him. 'Why? What do you mean?'

'Well, sir, if we get to Le Havre and if we find Arkforce, aren't we just going to get put back into jail?'

'There is that possibility.'

'Well, sir, do you really think that wise?'

'What do you suggest, Corporal?'

'We could try to find the Division, sir. Try to get to St Valéry. It's got the only possible harbour for an evacuation, and beaches.'

Lamb stared, 'Are you mad? That would mean breaking through the enemy lines.'

'We've done it before, sir. You've done it.'

'And then what?'

'Then at least we know where we are, sir. And you might even find Miss Dujolle.' Valentine smiled.

Lamb paused. 'What of it? She's not important. Besides, she's quite safe.'

'Yes, sir. If you say so.'

Both of them were silent now, and as they walked on Lamb realised that Valentine was right. If they reached Arkforce they would end up being arrested. St Valéry was only twelve miles distant. And they had done it before – twice. He turned to Valentine. 'Thank you, Corporal.'

As they reached the western outskirts of Fécamp Lamb brought them to a halt and turned to face them.

'Gather round. I have something to say. I have decided that we are not going to Le Havre after all. I intend to take as many men as will come with me back to join the Highland Division. I'm going to head for St Valéry. That's where they are now, and that's where we should be too. Arkforce has ceased to be of any importance. Le Havre is cut off and we can do no good down there. But we might just do some good at St Valéry, perhaps as a re-arguard to help the Highlanders get away. Perhaps we might even get away ourselves. I don't know. And I don't know if there will be any ships. What I do know, though, is that I'm going to try and help, and anyone who wants to can come with me. I'm not going to order you to do so. It means going through enemy lines. All I will say is that I would welcome any one of you.'

He stopped and scanned their faces. Bennett was the first to speak. 'I'll come with you, sir. So will the rest of us. Won't we, lads.' Mays and Perkins walked forward, followed swiftly by Smart, Hughes, Stubbs, Butterworth and Wilkinson. As the last two came forward Sergeant Buck turned and spoke to his men, quietly.

Lamb waited. He was banking on the fact that, like any soldiers, they needed an officer and he needed them.

Buck turned and walked back to Lamb. 'All right, sir. We took a vote on it and we'd be happy to come with you. What we want, sir, is to get back to Blighty. We just want to get out of this mess and not get put in the bag. Anyway, it's the best hope we've got. It's pretty bloody mad, but we'll come with you.'

'I guarantee that I'll do my very best to make sure we all get away. And thank you. We're better off together.'

They were followed by the Sussex men and the Cameron Highlanders. The Buffs and the Kensingtons came next. Lamb smiled at them. 'Thank you. Thank you all.'

Finally, Valentine walked over. He was smiling.

266

Lamb turned to Bennett. 'I don't suppose you've seen any transport, Sarnt?'

'Not much, sir.'

Sergeant Buck heard them. 'There was a couple of knackered Bedfords back up along the coast road, sir, but none of us are mechanics and we couldn't get them started.'

Lamb smiled. 'I think we might give it another go, don't you, Sarnt Bennett?'

Bennett nodded. 'Yes, sir. I think we might.'

They walked back up the road and through the town, taking the route up towards the beach. Lamb posted sentries on the road to the east, the direction from which any Germans might appear, and went to find the trucks. They were sitting, as Buck had said, on the road along the waterfront. He opened the bonnet of the first truck and got to work. It took him half an hour, and with every moment he knew that the enemy would be getting nearer. At length he yelled to Corporal Mays, who was sitting in the driver's seat, 'Turn her over, Mays.'

There was a click and then a roar as the engine came to life. Lamb sighed. 'That's one. Now for the other.'

Wiping his oily hands on a rag provided by Smart, he walked over to the second lorry, its bonnet already up. Peering in, he found the problem and was just repairing a broken wire when there was a shout. 'Jerries, sir, coming up the coast road. Lorry-loads of them.'

'Christ.' Lamb tied the wires together and yelled at Mays, 'Right, let her go.'

Again the engine roared into life and the corporal kept her running. Lamb, not bothering to wipe his hands, ran to the first truck and grabbed his battledress jacket, then yelled: 'Right, everybody in. Just get in. Let's go.'

He jumped up into the driver's seat and revved up the engine as the last men scrambled into the rear of the second truck, driven by Mays. It was an almost unbearable crush, but somehow they managed to cram themselves in. They tore down the road into the town and gathered up the picquets on the way before continuing to the south, away from the Germans. As they crossed the square Lamb was vaguely aware of something out of the corner of his eye – a lorry entering from the other side. He floored the accelerator pedal and the truck careered down the street and through the southern part of the town before emerging in the countryside beyond.

Bennett, who was sitting with him in the cab alongside Smart, said, 'Do you think they'll follow, sir?'

'No idea, and I don't intend to find out. I shouldn't think so. They'll want to get into the town. We need to get out of here and back up towards St Valéry. Can you read a map, Sarnt?'

'Pretty well, sir.'

'I can, sir.'

'Right, Smart, dig into my tunic and find my map, then tell me where to go.'

They took a left and Smart led them into a maze of back roads which Lamb thought would avoid the approaching enemy.

'Sir.'

'Smart?'

'I think we have a problem, sir. The only way to get to St Valéry is through Cany-Barville, across the Durdent.'

'Yes, I'd seen that. We're just going to have to crash through the town.'

It was approaching 10 a.m. as they came into Cany along a tree-lined road. Apart from the constant drone of the bombers high above them, there was no evidence of the enemy.

'No sign of Jerry, sir.'

'Well, if he's here he's being bloody quiet about it.'

Then, turning a corner, they saw the first houses of the village, and there in the road ahead of them, to their complete surprise, a platoon of German infantry in the process of building a roadblock. Luckily the surprise was mutual.

Lamb yelled, 'This is it. Hold on,' and pushed down hard on the accelerator. The truck and the one behind it went hurtling towards the half-built pile of crates and furniture and knocked it flying into the air, and with it two of the Germans.

They careered on and pushed a motorcycle into the verge, twisting it on its chassis, before continuing into the village.

Behind them Lamb could hear the sound of small-arms fire, but now there was also firing from up ahead. Not just rifles, but machine guns, and something heavier. Lamb carried on. They were in the centre of the village now, on the main street, and German soldiers were staring at them as they sped past. A few of them managed to get off shots, but none made contact as the trucks rolled past tall houses and shuttered and boarded shops. A German officer raised his pistol and fired. The bullet shattered the windscreen and just missed Lamb's head before embedding itself in the steel framework of the cab. The firing from their front was becoming louder now and Lamb put his foot to the floor. If there were British up there capable of firing then he wanted to be with them. They rounded a bend in the road and almost crashed into the rear of a German armoured car. Lamb hit the brakes and the truck lurched to a painful halt. Beyond the armoured car, through a shattered roadblock, he could see two British light tanks. As he watched one of them fired and the shell flew from the barrel and smashed into the wall of a house, exploding on impact in a rain of bricks and masonry.

The armoured car reversed past them and headed away from the British tanks, which began to advance. The second tank fired, and this time the shell connected with the retreating German vehicle, throwing it onto its side. There were screams, and a group of enemy infantry came round the corner of a nearby house but took cover when they saw the tanks and Lamb's two trucks. At that moment there was a deep boom and the lead tank was hit amidships by a shell.

Lamb looked for the source and saw that a German anti-tank gun had been set up on the left of the road, about fifteen yards away. He backed the truck and shouted to the men in the back, 'Jerry field gun at two o'clock. Take it out.'

There was a noise as men jumped down from the rear of the truck and then Lamb saw the gunners of the German gun pointing. It was the last thing they did, as seconds later two of them died in a hail of bullets from the Bren gun in the rear of the truck. He saw a Mills bomb fly towards the other gunners and explode, making a bloody mess of them. The German infantry under cover of the houses now broke and ran towards the wrecked armoured car and then beyond it into a side street. Lamb started up the truck and moved towards the British tanks. As he neared them one of the hatches flew open and a young officer appeared. The air was thick with the smell of cordite and fuel.

Lamb pulled up alongside and yelled across, 'Who are you?'

'Hogarth, 1st Lothians. Who are you?'

'Lamb, North Kents, with a bunch of odds and sods. We're trying to get back to the 51st.'

'Well, you've found us. Well done. This is as far as we go. Just trying to clear Jerry out of the place. Carry on up this road and you can't miss the rest of us.'

The tank pushed on in pursuit of the infantry and Lamb

drove past the second tank, which was wreathed in black smoke, and sped out of the village as behind them the tank burst into flames, cremating the crew.

They passed several Bren carriers of the Lothians, and leaving the village behind they moved into dense woods on either side of the road. Rounding a huge loop in the road, Lamb sensed they were heading due north, directly for St Valéry.

Ahead of them, in the middle of the road, Lamb saw a figure − a British soldier with a Balmoral bonnet on his head. He was carrying no rifle, but instead a metal pail. As the lorries approached he moved to the side of the road and hailed them. Lamb slowed to a stop.

'Are you lost?'

The soldier smiled. 'No, sir, I'm just away tae find a coo tae milk. You havnay seen one, sir, have you?'

Lamb shook his head. 'No, soldier. No cows. Plenty of Jerries, though. I should get back to your unit if I were you. Who are you with?'

'First Gordons, sir. We're holding the centre at Ingouville. Dead ahead. Good day, sir.' And with that the man walked on past the trucks in search of his cow. Lamb looked at Bennett, and both of them burst out laughing. 'Now I've seen everything. Looking for a coo. Good God.'

He drove on, followed by Mays's truck, and the woods gave way to farmland, and very soon, at a place called St Riquier, they saw other Highlanders manning slit trenches in the fields on either side of the road. They stopped at a roadblock made of a burnt-out car, two farm carts and a collection of farming machinery.

A lanky officer of the Gordons approached the truck, his pistol drawn. 'Who are you? Where are you going?'

'Lieutenant Lamb, Black Jackals. I'm taking my company into St Valéry.'

The man smiled knowingly. 'Fair enough, but I wouldn't bother doing that. We're trying to hold the Jerries off here. You'd best join us, or keep going to the right flank and help them out over there. We're surrounded, you know.'

'Yes, I knew that. Where's the General?'

'Last I heard he was over at Blosseville at the cross-roads, directing the traffic. The Frogs are coming in from the north, fouling everything up. Some job for a General, that, eh?' He waved them on, and two of his men cleared a gap in the roadblock, replacing it after the two trucks had passed through.

'Sounds a bit desperate, sir,' said Bennett, 'if the General's directing the Froggie trucks.'

'Yes. I wonder where the French generals are. Sarnt Bennett, you take the wheel for a while. I want to look at the map.'

They stopped briefly to hand over, and as Bennett drove away Lamb studied his map, so used now that it had begun to rip along two of the folds. They were entering another village, Ingouville, and he saw that if they took a right turn rather than a left they would eventually reach Blosseville, where Fortune was acting as traffic policeman. He did not really expect to get any fresh orders from the general, but it seemed likely that Madeleine would be with him, or if she wasn't at least Fortune would know her whereabouts, and he needed at least to make sure that she was safe before he took his place in the defensive line.

'Turn right here.'

They turned into the village and skirted its southern fringes. Looking to the left Lamb saw that it was teeming with more Highlanders and vehicles of all shapes and sizes, from requisitioned civilian cars and carts to trucks and carriers. Crossing a railway line they found their route blocked by another roadblock, 4th Camerons this time. They had evidently just arrived, for Lamb saw the drivers attempting to hide the battalion transport in an orchard beside the church. Having negotiated this obstacle they entered another similar village. Lamb directed them to the north, and no sooner had they left the village than the road was inundated by a sea of refugees. It was not, however, the usual mob of civilians slowing the truck down almost to a stop, but French soldiers, wandering aimlessly towards the south, in the opposite direction to Lamb's men. They were aiming vaguely for Rouen, as they had been ordered by their commanders, and they were certain now that they were heading for defeat.

As the trucks slowed to three miles an hour, Bennett turned to Lamb. 'It's as busy as the Epsom road on Derby Day, sir. Shall I use the horn?'

'Do whatever you have to. Just be careful. I don't want a riot.'

With his hand pressed almost permanently on the horn, Bennett gently guided the truck through the crowd, making way for the second lorry.

It was slow going for three miles, before the road cleared a little and he was able to get her up to about thirty miles an hour. Within the hour they found themselves at Blosseville. And if Lamb had thought the road chaotic, it was nothing compared to the streets of the little town. It seemed as if the entire French army had converged upon Blosseville. Moreover, from the way they were heading, it looked to Lamb as if some of the French were actually making for the coast and not towards the Seine. He wondered what chance 10,000 British troops would have of being evacuated in the face of this swelling tide of French soldiery.

Bennett gawped. 'Blimey, sir. Who's in charge of this lot?'

'No one, I suspect. I think their officers have the same idea. Everyone just wants to get away from the Germans.'

They drove past the village church and were approaching a crossroads when Lamb saw General Fortune. He was standing at the side of the road, map in hand, surrounded by British officers. His expression spoke volumes. Beside him a French general was shouting and gesticulating. It was not hard to work out what he might be saying.

Lamb directed Bennett towards the group and, stopping the trucks, he jumped from the cab. 'General Fortune, sir.'

The General looked up from the map. 'Is it Lamb? I thought you were with Arkforce.'

Lamb took a deep breath and prayed. 'Thought I'd be more use here, sir. I've a company of men, sir, if you can use us.'

'You do a lot of this sort of thing, Lamb? Disobeying orders from a senior officer?'

'Acting on my initiative, sir.'

Fortune looked at him and laughed. 'Of course we can use you, laddie. Question is how.' He turned to the French general, who had not stopped speaking: 'General, I have told you, I have no spare ammunition. It has all been issued. In any case my bullets would not fit your guns. And yes, I do intend to embark my men, just as soon as the Navy can provide me with the necessary vessels.'

He turned to Lamb. 'Why don't you take yourself off west of Houdetot. 1st Black Watch are holding the line down there. Your old friends. But the French are meant to be filling the gap between them and the Camerons, and they haven't arrived yet. Recce the gap until they arrive, will you, Lamb? My men are all in. We can't get away too soon. We're going to use St Valéry. There's nowhere else. I intend to start tonight. I've got 10,000 men of the Division and another 5,000 French, but there are more of them coming in by the hour.'

'Sir, can I ask, is Miss Dujolle quite safe?'

'Quite safe, Lamb. In St Valéry helping the medics.'

'Thank you, sir. We'll get off to Houdetot.'

Lamb saluted and climbed back into the truck. 'Well, that's it, Sarnt. Looks like the game's up. They're going to try to get us all off from St Valéry.'

'Is that where we're going then, sir?'

'No. We've got something else to do first. We've got to hold the line in the south until the French get there. You'd better turn right if you can and head down to Houdetot.'

They passed a farm destroyed by shellfire and then the road opened up and they could see, it seemed, along its whole length as it stretched away to the south. The road was just as packed as those heading west and north: French soldiers, mostly, and a few civilians, infantry, artillery and armoured men all mixed into one great mass and with them black Tirailleurs d'Afrique and other exotic North African troops, some of them riding in horse-drawn vehicles. At the roadside Lamb gazed at the lines of the uniformed dead, mostly French, machine-gunned by planes strafing the columns from the air. Had they been piled up there, he wondered, or, as it appeared they had, fallen there in a straight line, to lie dead in formation?

After a couple of miles of slow and careful driving they came upon a large farmyard filled with troop transports and Highlanders carrying entrenching tools.

Lamb had Bennett stop the truck and, leaving the cab, found a sergeant. 'Are you 1st Black Watch?'

'That's us, sir. Why, it's Mister Lamb, isn't it?'

Lamb recognised the man, a sergeant. 'Sarnt. Is Lieutenant Crawford here?'

'Aye, sir. He's up with C Company and the CO at St-Pierre-le-Viger. That's about a mile up that road.' He pointed away towards the north east. 'You the reinforcements, sir?'

275

'I suppose we are in a way, yes.'

'That's good news, sir. We need every man we can get.'

Lamb climbed back in the lorry, and they drove along the road. After a mile they came to St-Pierre.

Around the outskirts of the village men were busy digging in, while from the houses came the sound of windows being smashed as the Highlanders prepared their defensive positions. The centre of the village was marked by a church, and behind it in a large rectory Lamb could see what he took to be company HQ. Bennett stopped the truck outside and Lamb, Valentine and the sergeant jumped out and walked to the door as the men in both trucks began to climb down from the rear. There was a guard on the door; recognising Lamb, he saluted and allowed him inside. The house had not been damaged by war so far, but the troops were now making up for that. They had overturned tables as extra barricades and pulled down the hangings and curtains to give clearer fields of fire. In one of the rooms on the ground floor Lamb found Crawford. He was with Colonel Honeyman.

Both men turned as he entered. 'Lamb, what on earth are you doing here?'

'General Fortune's orders, sir. We're here to help you hold the line. Until the French get here.'

Honeyman smiled. 'Yes, whenever that may be. How many men do you have?'

'Forty odd. Not many, I'm afraid. There are a few Highlanders among them.'

'Fine. Lieutenant Crawford's just come in from a recce and the Germans are coming on in force.'

'It's true, Peter. Saw it myself. We've a fight on our hands.'

'Well, all the better that we're here then.' Lamb turned to Honeyman. 'Where d'you want us, sir?'

'Crawford will find you a place. Good to have you along.'

Crawford took Lamb outside, saying as they went, 'Funny, someone said you were in the clink. Knew they must be wrong.'

'Yes, quite wrong.'

Lamb's men were standing around the two trucks, some of them smoking.

Crawford, used to Honeyman's spit-and-polish rules in all weathers, raised an eyebrow. 'This your mob? Bit of a mixed bag, aren't they?'

'Careful, Crawford, this is my company. They may be a bit rough and ready but they did just save us from going in the bag, or worse. Anyway we're all you've got. Thought we'd be more use here than with Arkforce.'

'Well, you're certainly better off here than with those poor buggers.'

'What?'

'Didn't you hear? A battalion of them were shot up just outside Fécamp. Took a wrong turn and bumped into a bloody Panzer group. Thirty survivors. Managed to get up to Le Tot in a nicked Jerry truck. Came in two hours ago. Pretty shaken.'

'Christ, which battalion?'

'2nd Borderers. Thirty left out of the entire battalion. Thirty men.' He whistled.

Lamb's mind was reeling. Campbell's command. 'The Borderers? Are you sure? Was their CO among the dead?'

'I should say so. Riddled with bullets, one of the men said. How's your girl?'

'I told you, she's not "my" girl.'

'Well, whoever's she is then. How is she?'

'Safe, I'm told. She's in St Valéry with the medics.'

'We'll all be there soon, with a bit of luck. Then back home. What will she do?'

277

'I'm gong to try to get her off with me.'

'You're mad. It's military personnel only when we go.'

'Perhaps you don't understand. She has to get away.'

Saying it, Lamb wondered if he understood himself. He realised that, quite apart from the fact of his attraction for her and hers for him, he hesitated to call it 'love' – he had a duty to her, a duty to keep her safe. It had been Kurtz who had destroyed her world, murdered her parents, and it had been he from whom Kurtz had escaped. Why, he asked himself, had he found her in the barn? What act of providence had brought them together? The answer kept coming back to him that she had been sent as a chance for him to atone for the consequences of his mistake in not having killed Kurtz at the château.

Crawford grinned. 'Yes, I do, old man. I understand perfectly. The question is, will the general, when she takes the place of one of the men on a transport?'

Lamb said nothing. Crawford was right. He knew that. He couldn't justify taking a French girl off rather than a fighting man. He only hoped that when the moment came there would be some way of saving her. And then he knew that if there was no way, if Madeleine had to remain in France, he must do the same.

He turned to Crawford, impatient now to be in position. 'Sorry, where was it you wanted my men? And can you find me a rifle?'

'Of course, we've a few to spare now. And I didn't say, actually, but I should occupy that stretch of wood over there, beyond the church. Dig in however you can. We've a bit of a dearth of entrenching tools, but see what you can do.'

Lamb led the company into the woods, and within half an hour they had scraped some shallow cover, increasing the height with fallen trees and other debris. It might deflect the odd bullet, but it was hardly going to stop a tank. But then, he thought, what would? They lay silently, checking ammunition supplies, fixing bayonets to rifles. Lamb pulled out the service revolver. Six bullets. He reached to his side and picked up a rifle he had collected from one of Crawford's men *en route* to the wood: one full magazine and another four in his battledress pockets. He felt the two grenades tucked into his webbing. That was it. No more. He prayed that it would be enough. Lying flat on his stomach, he propped it on top of the thatch of branches and scrub which topped his shallow trench and stared out into the distance. He thought back to that first action, on the Dyle; to the bridge with the civilians, and Bennett jogging from trench to trench with mugs of tea slopping on the ground. Then he thought of the others, of the dead, and he looked across to where the remnants of his platoon lay with their new comrades. He saw Valentine, who caught his eye and smiled back. Bennett was looking out across the fields, unshaven and looking more tired than Lamb had ever seen him. Smart, jittery as usual, lay silent, stroking the butt of his rifle. And then he heard it – that familiar, gut-churning noise of engines. And he knew their arrival was imminent.

20

Lamb had known all along that their position was tenuous, but this was desperate. Crawford's C Company was dug in on the forward slope of a hill, at the apex of a salient, and although he admired Crawford as an officer he thought that, had he been given such a disposition, he might have questioned it. He could see them clearly from their own lines within the woods to their right, and for the last hour what he had seen had filled him with despair. The German attack had been swift and merciless, and it was a miracle, he thought, that they had beaten it off. But since then they had come again, and Crawford had taken more casualties. He himself had lost two men, although not directly under attack, both from the Norfolks, killed outright by a mortar, with several others wounded. He wondered how much longer they would be able to hold out.

It was almost six in the evening now and the sun was painting the sky in a watercolour palette of reds, yellows and rose pinks. He lay pressed close to the ground and listened as a German machine gun rattled off to his left and another heavy mortar round landed with a crump slightly forward of Crawford's position. Rifles crackled out in reply but Lamb was concentrating so much on what was happening to C Company that he was hardly aware that directly to their own front rounds were now smacking hard into the trees.

He shouted, 'Keep down. Wait until you can see a proper target. Save your ammo until you can see them.'

Bennett took up the cry, and then Mays, Valentine and Sergeant Buck sent it ringing down the line through the woods. There was a sound like a swarm of angry hornets and a young tree inches to the left of Lamb's head was cut in two by a rasp of heavy machine-gun fire.

'Christ, that was close.'

'Mind your head, sir.' Smart smiled at him.

'I suppose it's stupid to ask, Smart, if there's any radio signal?'

'None, sir. Not for days. Even the general's using runners now, sir. Least that's what a dispatch rider told me last night. They're sending junior officers out. Gone back a hundred years, we have, sir.'

Another burst of machine-gun fire tore up the ground to their left. Back a hundred years, thought Lamb. Tell that to the men on the receiving end of that.

There was a commotion from their rear and Lamb looked round to see what at first seemed like a mirage. Dozens of men on horseback were riding into the woods. He shouted to Bennett, 'Sarnt, what the hell's all that? What's going on?'

In reply two of the cavalry rode up and dismounted. He saw now that they were French, in their distinctive brown coats, with rifles slung across their backs. One of them, an officer, ran towards him, keeping his head down as more German rounds began to sing in. He threw himself on the ground beside Lamb. 'Captain Marchand, Fifth Hussars. We're here to help you hold off the Boche.'

Lamb smiled. 'Wonderful. Lamb, North Kents. How many are you?'

'Two squadrons, about fifty men. My major is over there with your friends.' He pointed across to Crawford's men, then spoke again. 'You are not Scots? We thought . . .'

'No, they are Scots. We are here helping them.'

The Frenchman grinned. 'Now we all help each other.'

Another burst of machine-gun fire. Both men ducked.

The French officer turned and signalled to his men and, having secured their horses among the trees, a score of the Hussars came up and took cover against the under-growth alongside Lamb's men.

Captain Marchand made himself as comfortable as he could against a fallen tree, drew his pistol and checked the rounds, then unslung his rifle and propped it against the branches before turning to Lamb. 'I don't think this is going so well for us.'

'No, I don't think we'll be able to hold them for much longer.'

'And what then?'

'Then we retreat to St Valéry and wait for the boats.'

'For the boats?'

'To evacuate. Isn't that what we're all going to do?'

Another round cracked into the trees above them and both men ducked again. Away to the right a mortar round exploded and someone began to shout for stretcher-bearers.

'You mean you are going to leave us for the Germans? Like you did at Dunkirk?'

'No, you're coming with us. That's what I was told.'

'But what about France?'

'You'll fight another day and come back and set France free. But you must see, your army is finished here.'

'Tell that to my major.'

Lamb looked across and saw that the French were now dug in with Crawford's men. He could see a man standing up among them, waving his revolver in the air and shouting encouragement to the cowering soldiers. As he watched a tank shell came howling into the wood, and the world rocked. It was followed by another. Lamb looked away, shielding his eyes. There was an explosion and the trees where the French major had been standing cracked and flew into the air. As the dirt and dust cleared Lamb looked up. To his amazement the officer was still there, still standing bravely above his men who, inspired by his example, were now getting to their feet and firing back at the enemy. The only problem was, Lamb noticed, that where before the major's arm had been waving them on, the man was now only holding up a bloody stump and shredded sleeve. As he watched the major slumped to his knees, but even as medics came up to bind the bloody stump he continued to yell to his men to fire at the enemy.

God, thought Lamb, that was real bravery. If only all the French fought that way we wouldn't be in this bloody mess. It gave him hope to watch as the Hussars poured round after round at the advancing Germans. Captain Marchand uttered an oath and shook his head. The major was sitting on the ground now, but as Lamb watched he summoned two of his men. Using their rifles as supports, they managed to hoist him up and carried him to the furthermost forward of his men's positions, and there they held him, with his mangled arm, as he barked commands to his men.

There was a shout from Bennett. 'Sir, I think they're bringing the tanks up.'

Lamb listened, and sure enough heard the unmistakable grinding of slim wheels on caterpillar tracks. 'Sarnt, send a runner to Mister Crawford. Ask him if his anti-tank platoon is about. We've got company.'

Bennett sent Perkins out, and Lamb saw the boy flatten himself on the ground as he reached C Company.

A few seconds later Crawford himself was with him.

'Yes, I've seen them. There's about a dozen Panzers and they're heading straight for you and the Captain here. Our signals officer has gone off to find the anti-tank boys, but God knows where they are. We'll have to hold the Jerries off till they get here.' He turned to Marchand. 'I say, did you see your CO? Extraordinary. Brave man.'

Lamb looked puzzled. 'What about us?'

Crawford smiled at him and gripped his shoulder. 'Take your men and get back to St Valéry. Try to get out. This is my fight now, my chance to do something good. You've had yours. Done your bit. Now save yourself and your men. Get out. And don't forget your girl.'

Lamb opened his mouth. 'She's not my . . .'

Crawford waved him down. 'Shut up and get out of here before the tanks reach you. That's an order.'

'You can't give me an order. We hold the same rank.'

Crawford thought for a moment. 'What was the date of your commission?'

Lamb looked at him. '24th October '38.'

'As a regular officer or TA?'

'16th June '39.'

Crawford smiled. '14th May '39. I outrank you. Now, will you obey an order?'

Lamb grinned. 'What if I said no?'

'I'd have you put on a charge.'

Lamb shrugged. 'Do it. I've nothing to lose. I'm already on at least one.'

Crawford's face became more serious and he fixed Lamb with his brown eyes. 'But you do have everything to lose if you stay here. And more to the point, so does Madeleine. So do it for her. And do it for me.'

Lamb looked down at the ground and listened to the bullets ripping into the trees and the rumble of engines and wheels that made the ground tremble. At length he nodded.

284

'Very well. For you.' He called across to Bennett, 'New orders, Sarnt. We're pulling back. Get the lads together.'

He turned to Crawford, intending to thank him, but he was already running back to his position, and as Lamb's eyes followed him he saw the French major, still sitting on his improvised chair, his bloody stump bound up with bandages, still managing through the pain to direct his men.

The way north was worse than any road they had yet been on. Lines of British and French walking wounded meandered slowly in the direction of the sea, jostling for position with units pulling back to the new defensive perimeter, and in the other direction refugees were trying to flee the now encircled town.

To their left the night sky was lit by flames from the still-blazing oil refineries at Le Havre, and in places the moon was obscured by the thick greasy smoke that accompanied it. It was almost like a fog drifting in the sky. They were travelling again in the two requisitioned trucks, and Lamb wondered how long they would last. His repairs, though sound and examined the previous day, had only ever been intended as short term. Bennett was again in the driver's seat, and as the sad columns drifted across the road in front of them he was forced to swerve and sound the horn. No one had spoken much since leaving St-Pierre. Their spirits were as low as Lamb had seen them and he could only pray that there might really be some hope of salvation at St Valéry and not just another unfulfilled promise. They were hungry too. Hard tack and water had been their fare for the last forty-eight hours and hunger gnawed at all their stomachs.

At a crossroads they passed a British provost, a redcap, trying to control the rabble on the road without much success. At least, thought Lamb, the Luftwaffe were not harrying them, although there was evidence that they had paid a visit.

They passed a number of burned-out vehicles and scores of bodies on the verge. At one point, where the road was wider, Lamb spotted an intact car, a Renault, sitting on the grass and immediately wondered whether it might contain anything useful to scrounge, in particular food. As they neared it he fancied that he could see four figures inside, two of whom wore the distinctive round képi of a French officer.

He said to Bennett, 'Slow down. We'll stop here and have a dekko inside. God knows what this lot are doing here. Look like French staff officers. Car must have broken down. I'll see if we can help at all.'

They stopped and he climbed down alone from the cab, approaching the passenger side. He was about to lean in when he saw the driver. He was asleep. In fact they all were. Four French officers, their medals pinned on their tunics, sitting asleep in their car. Lamb wondered if he was seeing things and then looked again and saw the neat bullet holes in their bodies where the rounds had entered from the front, and the smashed windscreen. He turned and walked back to the lorry, its engine still idling. Opening the door he climbed back up into the cab.

Bennett said, 'No use, sir?'

'No, no use.'

It was ten o'clock when they entered the outskirts of St Valéry. The place was well lit, not by streetlamps but by a flickering light from the many houses that had been set alight by shellfire.

They moved slowly through streets clogged with human jetsam. Lamb was just beginning to wonder if they should abandon the trucks when the engine gave a sputter and died. He looked at Bennett. 'I think we've been told something. Right. Everybody out.'

286

They left the two trucks on a road above the harbour and began to walk down, careful to retain some semblance of formation among the rabble.

They had been wandering for the best part of two hours and were near the quay when Lamb spotted a group of Jocks and among them a man he recognised: McCade, one of the sergeants from B Company of 1st Black Watch.

He accosted him. 'McCade, isn't it? Have you any news of Lieutenant Crawford?'

The man shook his head, solemnly. 'Naw, sir. We were on the forward slope at St-Pierre-le-Viger. They came at us. Tanks. We lost fifty men in two hours. It was bloody murder. The anti-tank platoon was blown to bits, and Mister Telfer-Smollett with it. That's when Major Bradford ordered us to pull out, sir. Had to leave half the wounded out there. It was a bloody tragedy, Mister Lamb, sir. There's only 100 men left all told from the two companies. Colonel Honeyman was cut off from the battalion back at Brigade. We hav'nae seen him yet, neither. Good that you're alive though, sir.'

So, he thought, Crawford was almost certainly dead, sacrificed so that he could get back to St Valéry and Madeleine. He felt like crying, or screaming with rage, or both.

Bennett brought him back from the abyss. 'Sir, hadn't we better get down towards the harbour? If we want a chance, sir?'

'Yes, Sarnt, of course. Good luck, McCade.'

He felt strangely hollow. Up to now he had felt that in some strange way they were winning. But, with Crawford's death, somehow things had changed. The stark reality of their desperate situation took possession of him. He steadied himself. But only just.

'Bennett, we need to get down to the sea. Are we all here?'

'Apart from those we left in the woods, sir.'

'Right, let's get through this mess.'

He pushed forward and pressed against the crowd of listless men that had gathered in the main square. His men followed on. It was extraordinary and terrifying, thought Lamb, how quickly and easily a well-organised and disciplined body of men could degenerate into a rabble in which the only ethos was 'every man for himself and hang the consequences'. As if to echo his thoughts, at that moment, as they passed a small *estaminet*, three British soldiers rolled out onto the street. Hopelessly drunk and carrying bottles of wine, they were singing: 'Roll out the barrel, let's have a barrel of fun . . .' One of them leered into Lamb's face and Bennett gave him a shove which sent him hurtling back into the window of the café, smashing it as he fell inside. The other two went to help him and then turned on Lamb's men. Bennett and Mays levelled their rifles at them and the men moved back, muttering, and helped their friend up out of the smashed shop front.

Lamb walked on with the others behind him. 'Not a pretty sight, is it, Sarnt? An army on the brink of defeat.'

'No, sir. Not pretty. But we'll need them all, sir, just the same.'

Lamb knew it. This would be the core of the new army that must come back and liberate France. That was why it was so vital to get them off. Get them home.

They carried on through the mob, cursed as they went. The glow in the sky became a little clearer and Lamb caught sight of the sea, spreading out from the harbour under the blood-red night. As he looked, the surface of the water was thrown into chaos as dive-bombers came swooping down from the sky. The cacophony of voices in the town was punctuated now by explosions, and in the distance, perhaps half a mile off the harbour wall,

288

Lamb watched as a plume of smoke rose to meet the overhanging black cloud. Somewhere on the shimmering stretch of water that separated the retreating British from their homeland and safety, the Luftwaffe had scored another hit on a ship, and with its destruction another of the few strands of hope that had been offered to the desperate allies had been swept away. A pang of utter despair swept through Lamb and he began to wonder whether they wouldn't all be captured or killed. They had just turned into a small square where four streets met when there was a sudden shout and what looked like a platoon of French soldiers came running out of one of the side streets, yelling at them to save themselves.

Lamb shouted to Bennett and the sergeant, 'Get ready. God knows what it is. Tanks, probably. Get everyone into cover.'

To a man, they ducked into doorways and behind walls, waiting for the enemy.

The noise grew, but Lamb couldn't make it out. As it grew closer it began to sound like a thousand running feet. No, he thought, they were hooves. For a moment he had the ludicrous notion that it might be a cavalry charge. After all, the French were using cavalry. Why shouldn't the Germans try something so insane? Nothing would have surprised him now. But it was not a regiment of Prussian Uhlans that came screaming round the corner. As Lamb looked on, dumbstruck, dozens of mules, saddled with leather panniers, charged into the square.

Lamb stared at them for a moment, then burst out laughing. The mules rushed in and careered out as swiftly as they'd come, in all directions. Lamb turned to Bennett, still laughing. 'They must have got loose. The French use them to carry munitions. Christ, I thought we were all dead.'

The mules continued to pour into the square. 'There's hundreds of them, sir. Bloody hundreds.'

What made the sight even more comical was that the mules were being pursued by French soldiers, their long coats flapping out behind them.

The British shouted at them, urging them on.

Smart turned to Perkins. "Ere, what's donkey taste like?'

Wilkinson piped up. 'They're not donkeys, they're mules.'

'Same thing, innit. What's the difference? Anyway, what d'you reckon it tastes like?'

'How should I know? I ain't never ate a mule, you berk. Dunno, chicken?'

'More like pig, I'd think.'

'Well, either way, you're not going to find out now.'

Behind them a series of breech explosions marked the end of an abandoned British battery. They were destroying their own equipment now, thought Lamb. 'Hear that, Sarnt? We'll be away from here soon.'

The narrow, twisting streets that gave so much character to the old fishing port were now filled with soldiers of all types, and it seemed to Lamb that every second house was ablaze. As they tried to make their way through the maze, a few yards in front a chimney pot crashed to the street below from a burning building, killing one man and injuring another. On the next block some beams from a half-timbered house collapsed into the column of men, showering them with sparks and burning cinders which set fire to their coats. Lamb despaired. At this rate they would be captured by the Germans before anyone had reached the beach. And he had still not had any word of Madeleine.

He found Bennett. 'Come on. There's a side street up there. Get the men down that.'

One by one they pushed the company away from the mob and into the narrower alley. But Lamb's hunch had been right, for, small as it seemed, it debouched onto another street which the fleeing soldiers for the most part had not found, and there, down at the end, he could see the sea.

They reached the beach, and behind them the press of soldiers continued. Lamb led the way down to the shoreline and found shelter behind the sea wall. Slowly, but as quickly as they were able, the company crunched onto the awkward shingle and into the lee of the sea wall. Lamb waited until they were all assembled and then turned and faced out to sea. He could not see any ships, merely a fog drifting across the sea which reflected the glow from two tall plumes of red smoke emanating for the west side of the town. He sat down on a stone bollard, leaned against a wooden windbreak and almost without realising it fell into the deep and dreamless sleep of utter exhaustion.

He woke amid a cacophony and opened his eyes. The fog had cleared a little and he could see that out on the sea lay three ships, two Royal Navy destroyers and a huge transport.

Above them, standing on the mole, a naval officer was yelling orders.

Lamb got to his feet and walked over to him. 'Sorry, sir. Are we to get off? I've got about forty men.'

The man, the rank of Commander on his sleeve, looked down at Lamb. 'That's the plan, Lieutenant. It was planned to begin at 22.30 hours. Of course we need the transports first. And you'll have to wait your turn.' He turned back to the beach parties. 'Lieutenant Hemans, can you get those boats closer in? See if someone can get those wounded onto that tug. Find Lieutenant Scott. Take a cutter out.'

There was another man standing close to the commander.

Lamb stood and stared at him for a moment before climbing up, 'Colonel "R"? What on earth are you doing here, sir? I thought you must be dead or captured.'

The colonel smiled: 'Lieutenant Lamb. Thought I'd find you here somewhere. In the thick of it, of course. No, as you see I'm neither dead nor a prisoner. In fact I've been in England, trying to sort out this mess. You got through with the message, though. Well done.'

'For all the good it's done. I'm afraid I was too late, sir.'

'Not your fault. It was the bloody French. More precisely it's the High Command and government in London that should answer for this. But of course they won't, and it's up to us to pick up the pieces. Fortune's men were doomed from the moment they got to the Somme. At least my message gave him the chance to get some of them away.'

'Some of them?'

'You don't think they're all going to get off, laddie? That's why I'm here, seeing how many we can get away. And now I've found you, you can help. You see, while the rest of the high command seem to want to believe that the 51st are as good as dead, I'm afraid I don't. And of course I couldn't pass up the chance to clobber a few of the Boche. Don't know when we'll get the opportunity again.'

He walked a short distance away from the commander and spoke close to Lamb's ear. 'To tell you the truth, Lamb, we've got a problem. Churchill needs a scapegoat. Well, not exactly that, a sort of sacrifice. You see the French are hopping mad about what happened at Dunkirk – one in ten French to British got away – and as far as they're concerned this looks just the same. They don't see it as very fair. So Churchill came up with a plan, and it stinks. He wants us to leave the Highlanders as a sort of trade-off with the French – a pledge of support, if you like, to appease their anger about Dunkirk. But I'm not wearing it. I plan to get off as many of them as we can. These men will be the backbone of the new army. I know what I said to you about your own men before, but these men, and yours now, the ones that have come through hell together, are tougher. General Fortune hasn't cottoned on to Churchill's plan yet, and he mustn't. Of course poor Victor won't be coming back. If I know him, and I do, he'll stay with the majority of his men and be captured. But we've got work to do, Lamb, you and I. We've got to get some of them away, laddie, before it's too late.'

Lamb was staggered. This was a level of politicking the likes of which he had only guessed might have existed within the army or the government. It only seemed to confirm everything that General Fortune had hinted at. He knew that Churchill had only become Prime Minister a few weeks ago, but for any politician to be prepared to sacrifice an entire division in aid of *entente cordiale* was obscene. Particularly as everything he had heard pointed to the fact that the French would sooner accept Nazi rule than lose another million men to save their country. It was a new way of fighting a war and it made him see, more than ever, just how outdated were the principles of so many of the men who were now his superiors. Churchill's plan was clearly warped. But it was no more useless than their antiquated vision of lines of men advancing in a frontal assault against an enemy armed with weapons the power of which had never been seen. Clearly the men who were going to win this war for the allies, if it could be won, were those who had the power to mobilise the Royal Navy and attempt to get Fortune's men away. Those men who issued orders to Colonel 'R', whoever they might be. And whoever they were, Lamb told himself, these were the men from whom he knew he wanted to take orders. For at present, the only men on whom he knew he could rely were those with whom he shared the everyday dangers of the battlefield. He realised that he had been staring at the colonel.

'So what do we do now, sir?'

'Take your men towards the east of the town. See what you can pick up along the way. Any likely-looking officer or NCO, bring him along. And mind now, I only want the best. I want people who are going to count when we get back home. I'm going to do the same on the west side, and circle round.'

'And then, sir?'

'Then, laddie, we're going to get away further up the coast. There's a place I know. I came here some years ago. A bit further east. Veules les Roses. There are cliffs, but hidden gullies lead down to a beach, and the Germans won't know about those. The beach is big enough for the Navy to come in. Commander Elkins here knows all about it. Our rendezvous hour is 3 a.m.' He looked at his watch. 'That's just over three hours' time, Lamb. Think you can make it with whoever you've got?'

'Of course, sir. I'll be there.'

'Good man. Get enough men away and you might end up keeping your company.'

A young lieutenant came hurrying up to the colonel. 'Sir, there's a Jerry battery up on the cliff to the west shelling the beaches. And we have reports that they've broken through in the west woods, by Les Tots.'

'Where's the general?'

'He's moved his HQ from the west of the town, sir, about half a mile south of the railway station. Opposite a church.'

'Good. I'll remember to keep out of his way. Lamb, remember: 3 a.m.'

'Sir.'

Cool as ever, the colonel walked back over to Commander Elkins and began to talk to him. Lamb climbed down from the mole and ran over the beach to where his men were still sheltering. 'Right. We're heading up to the east. And we're going to try and get as many off as we can. The Navy's coming in and we're due to go at three in the morning. See if you can pick up any others – any men who look as if they can handle a fight.'

Wearily, the company began to move across the beach. Every few minutes a shell would come crashing into the sand and rocks. They were being fired at from the German battery on the west cliffs, and it seemed pointless to try to take cover. Lamb thought it was a sign of the men's fatigue and the dangers of the past few weeks that they just seemed to ignore them. In any case, if one had your name on it you were a gonner anyway. That was what all the old sweats said.

As he walked on, Lamb gazed at the transports moored outside the harbour. There was a whine of engines and, looking up, he saw the Stukas come in. They fell like vultures from the sky in a vertical dive, their sirens blaring out in a banshee wail, bringing terror to the soldiers on the west beach. Now was the time to take cover, he thought; French and British troops clasped their hands to their heads and pushed themselves deeper into the sand and shingle. But it was not the infantry that the Stukas wanted today, and their bombs began to fall out at sea. Two ships were hit, one of them badly. There were explosions on board. Lamb kept on walking and watching. He passed a British soldier who shook his head and looked at him with hollow eyes. 'That's the *Hebe II* blown up,' he said. 'All my mates, gone.'

A gun opened up from the cliff above them, an 88, sending a huge shell towards the transports. Lamb could not bring himself to watch any more, but heard the explosion echoing in from the sea as another of the ships, *Helix II,* with eighty soldiers on board, was hit. In front of him another man was sitting on a rock, his face a mask of tears.

Behind them a house burst into flames as the fires reached its gas supply and a huge explosion took the building away.

More shells were landing close now. One dropped fifty yards behind him and Lamb signalled to Bennett to take cover. He ran and found himself with Valentine, sheltering in the shadow of the town war memorial, a square stone base topped with a towering statue of a 1916 French *poilu*, his arm raised to heaven. Looking up at the plinth he saw the names on the roll of honour. There were hundreds of them. Good God, he thought, in the same sort of seaside town in Sussex or Kent you might find thirty or forty names killed in the Great War. But here a generation of the town's young men seemed to have been wiped out.

Valentine saw him. 'You're thinking the same as me, sir, aren't you?'

'What's that, Corporal?'

'You've just realised why the French don't want to fight any more – why we're all here in this little seaside town trying to get back to England. It's because they lost so many men last time. They won't carry on, sir. Not after that. That memorial says it all.'

Lamb knew he was right. That was why the French had collapsed, and he hoped that when it came to her turn to face the Germans, perhaps on her own soil, the British people would not have the same feelings.

They were on the east side of the town now, and after a climb found themselves by a medieval church surrounded by a walled cemetery. Lamb spotted several men in Balmorals holding the perimeter and hailed them, 'Who are you?'

A sergeant answered, 'Pretty much all that's left of 1st

Black Watch, sir. There's an ammo dump up here, sir. Rations too. But you'd better be quick, sir. We've just found it, and my lads are pretty nifty at scrounging.'

Lamb saw an officer moving between the gravestones, a subaltern from A Company whom he last recalled seeing at the regimental dinner. 'Where's your CO?'

'No idea, Lieutenant. Haven't seen him for hours. Think he was caught at Brigade. Could be in the bag.'

'What about Lieutenant Crawford?'

'Last I heard he was getting it bad at St-Pierre with what was left of C Company and then we lost touch with them.' He turned to his men, and Lamb watched with interest as he organised the perimeter defences of the cemetery, placing the men with care and fortifying whatever he could with stones, debris and anything that came to hand. He thought of Crawford. What a terrible loss he was.

Lamb had grasped at some faint hope that he might still be alive. He was sure now that Crawford must be dead. He moved through the cemetery with the NCOs close behind and found just beyond it a laager of trucks filled with food and ammunition that was being carried away by the Highlanders. 'Right, men. Sarnt Bennett, Valentine, Mays, Sarnt Buck, get what you can and distribute it to the men. We need whatever we can find.'

Turning back to the officer he shouted above the increasing din of shellfire and the hum of thousands of voices, 'You waiting for a boat?'

The man nodded. 'Yes, but it looks like it could be a long wait. A tug came in with some drifters at about midnight but the Jerries spotted her and opened up. I saw four of them go down, then they cleared off. A destroyer came in a little after that but it sailed along the coast to the east. I reckon that's our best bet. But for now we're not going anywhere.'

As he spoke a German battery opened up on the cemetery.

The men began to shelter in the lee of the gravestones and tombs while shells burst against the cemetery walls.

Lamb turned to the officer. 'What's your name?'

'Maclachlan. Jamie Maclachlan.'

'Peter Lamb. We met in your mess. Do you want to get away?'

'Of course, but we've orders to stay.'

'Don't be mad, man. The whole place will be full of Jerries in a couple of hours. If you want to get off, I've got a boat coming in. You can all come with us. But you'll have to hurry. Place called Veules les Roses, about three miles from here to the east. Go past the town and slip down the gullies to the beach.'

Maclachlan thought about it. 'Well, it would seem better than being shot or captured. All right, we're with you.'

Lamb turned to Bennett. 'Sarnt, Mister Maclachlan will be joining us. You're in command of the company until I get back. And remember, if you come across any other useful officers or NCOs try to bring them along.'

'Sir. Where are you going, sir?'

Lamb smiled. In the heat of getting the men up to the eastern perimeter he had not had time to get to the one place that had been at the forefront of his mind. But now, thanks to the colonel, he knew where General Fortune's HQ was located. 'I'm going back down to the town. There's someone I've got to find.'

21

The way back into the town was easier than the journey out had been, and Lamb was able to move quickly on his own, even against the tide of soldiers.

He walked past a crowd that had gathered around two French lorries which had been hit by shellfire and overturned, blocking the road. While the British, under a doughty corporal of the Gordons, were attempting to heave them off the road to open the way to traffic, the French were trying to pull the dead and wounded from the wreckage, and it was not hard to see that in the absence of officers or provosts a fight was about to break out. Lamb decided to avoid it and circled round as the first punches were thrown.

He hurried on down the rue des Ramparts and turned left towards the town hall. Men wandered past him in groups or on their own, some of them clutching the contraband they had found in abandoned shops: tins of chocolate, bottles of wine. One man was carrying four waterproof coats, another a whole cheese. To add to the misery it began to rain.

A piper was playing in the middle of the Place de l'Hôtel de Ville, and around him dozens of Scottish soldiers had sat down to listen. And there, among the falling shells and the pipes, Lamb felt a strange, resigned calm. As he watched two other pipers joined in a pibroch, a lament for the dead: 'The Flowers of the Forest'. The tune changed quickly to another: 'The Barren Rocks of Aden', one of the tunes that had endeared them to the French when they had landed here, only five months ago. Lamb stood and stared, and then one of the watching men stood up and began to hum. 'Come on. Gie us a reel.' One of the pipers began to play faster, and then the others joined in and soon some of the Highlanders were dancing with each other.

Lamb shook his head. Either it was folly, or it showed incredible strength of spirit. He preferred to think it was the latter. Leaving the dance behind, he walked across the bridge that separated the inner harbour for the outer and found himself in the west of the town.

A British soldier, a young lieutenant, came running at him with wild eyes. 'Have you heard? There's a ship coming in. Get out. Get down to the pier.' The man rushed past, gabbling his message, and from his vantage point Lamb looked to see if it was true or just another hopeful fantasy. What he saw was not a ship but French soldiers, hundreds of them, maybe thousands, and above them on the cliffs muzzle flashes from German guns as they fired down onto the beach.

It was clear to him that the town had split in two now, and while the Germans were gaining a foothold in the west the east was still held by the Highlanders. He realised that, if he was right, by crossing the bridge he was danger-ously close to the Germans. Lamb dodged between doorways, walked up one street and was met by a German. There was no clear perimeter. He ran left and again through a maze of small alleyways along the backs of the quayside houses. Then, dodging out again onto the quay, he ran down some steps until he was on the jetty by the boats, which had been here since the start of the war. He heard a voice calling from behind him: 'Come up. Come up here.' It was English, but with an accent. Lamb turned, thinking it might be a French officer addressing him, and then he saw a group of German soldiers led by an officer calling down to men on the other side of the bridge. 'Come up. Up here, Tommy. You're safe now.' As Lamb watched, men on his side of the bridge, French and British, began to lay down their weapons and climb up the pier.

The garrison was surrendering, and the night, though getting darker, was lit up. Flames from the burning town reached high into the night sky like darting fingers, and all the time the darkness was torn by the sound of small-arms fire. Every few minutes another explosion signalled another hit by one of the German guns, but the most prevalent sound that met Lamb's ears was that of men's voices – a constant hum that told him that what had once been organised brigades, regiments, companies and platoons was now little more than a rabble. An ugly rabble.

Moving south now towards the general's repositioned HQ, Lamb passed a cinema, its posters still in their now smashed glass frames. *Le Jour se leve*, with Jean Gabin, had been the last film playing when the cinema had been shuttered and padlocked. But the doors had been smashed open and a dozen drunken French soldiers had ripped out the red plush velvet seats and were sitting in them on the quayside, drinking stolen wine and brandy.

Lamb drew his revolver and walked past them without comment, on past the grand hotels and villas, until he found the station. Another half mile took him alongside a municipal park in which more soldiers had made camp. Then off to the right, up a smart tree-lined drive, he saw a building guarded by a line of British infantry. This was

301

a modest villa, built close to the local church. Lamb walked up. 'Is this General Fortune's HQ?'

The sergeant, a poker-faced Glaswegian, replied, 'Sorry, sir.'

'I need to see him. Lieutenant Lamb.'

'I'm sorry, sir. No one in or out without authority. That's our orders.'

'Sergeant, I need to see General Fortune. Now.'

He saw a face behind the sentries. Captain Thompson pushed through. 'It's Lamb, isn't it? You can let him through, Sergeant. I'll vouch for him.'

'Thank God. Is the general here?'

'Yes, but I'm afraid it's almost all up for us. Between you and me, I don't think we're going to get away.'

Lamb, knowing that he must not mention the colonel or the beach at Veules, said instead, 'Miss Dujolle, is she here?'

'Yes, she's in the basement with the MO and some medics. She's done well, Lamb. Good to have her with us. The general's in here.'

They found Fortune standing staring out of the window at the burning town.

He turned when they entered and Lamb saw instantly that his features were changed. The pressures of the last few days had etched themselves deeply into his face, which was sallow, almost corpse-like. He managed a smile. 'Lamb, how good to see you. What to all this though, eh? Well, perhaps there's still a chance, eh?'

'Perhaps, sir.'

Both knew that they were lying.

Fortune turned to his aide. 'Thompson, you have ordered that all stores and equipment be destroyed? Everything.'

'Yes, sir. Just as you said.'

'Only personal weapons to be carried. And the bagpipes, of course.'

Lamb said, 'I came to say goodbye, sir.'

'Think you'll get away?'

'I intend to try, sir. With my men. If we can.'

Fortune came across and grasped his hand firmly. 'Well, good luck then, Lieutenant. Let's hope you make it back. Who else is going to be left to command? Whoever gets back from this mess, we're going to need men like you.'

'Good luck to you, sir.'

Fortune shrugged. 'My luck, as you can see, has run out. Goodbye, Lamb.' He turned away, and as Lamb was leaving with Simpson, added, 'Oh, you'll find Miss Dujolle downstairs in the basement. Lovely girl. Brave too. Seen a lot.'

As Simpson had directed him, Lamb walked down the stone stairs to the basement. They were lined with band-aged soldiers, and the place reeked of blood, sweat and ether. From the dimly lit cellar rooms around him came moans punctuated by the occasional scream. Lamb walked past them, catching glimpses of men undergoing surgery. In a small room towards the end of the corridor he found her. She was standing at an operating table, with her head down, concentrating. A man lay on the table, half his face cut by shrapnel. A military surgeon, a captain, was probing the wound, removing shards of metal shrapnel and glass.

As Lamb entered Madeleine looked up, and instantly he caught her gaze and saw the sharp breath as she noticed him. He felt invigorated, transported from the scenes of horror around him. He smiled, and the doctor, who had also looked up, shot him a quizzical look. 'Yes? What is it?'

'I came for Miss Dujolle, sir. Rather urgent, I'm afraid.'

Madeleine looked at him with pleading, anxious eyes and shook her head. The doctor replied, 'Well, Lieutenant, this is rather urgent, as you can probably see. Can't it wait? Suture, please.'

Madeleine handed him one. Lamb nodded, 'Yes, I'm sorry,' then left and waited outside. After ten minutes she emerged, drying her hands. She looked exhausted, her face grey and drawn.

Lamb asked, 'Will he live?'

'Yes. But he's lost an eye and he'll never talk again. But he'll live.'

'I hear you've been a wonderful nurse'.

She looked at him. 'Oh Peter, if you'd only seen them. All so young.'

'Come on, we've got to go.'

'But I'm needed here.'

'Madeleine, come on. It's our only chance. The Germans will be here soon. We can get away.'

She hesitated, but only briefly, and then went with him up the stairs. In the hall he made her put on a heavy soldier's greatcoat and a tin hat, pushing up her hair beneath the brim.

'There, a British soldier if ever I've seen one.'

Outside, they pushed past the sentries and walked back into the town through the chaos, and Lamb was glad of her disguise. They began to walk up the same road he had come on, and then, realising that would take them towards the German sector, he changed tack and cut across behind the station to the east side.

There was a shout from behind them: 'Open fire,' and a crackle of shots rang out. He knew what it meant. The rearguard was engaging the enemy, who must now be perilously close to the south of St Valéry. There were more shots, then machine guns and grenades as the enemy responded. A British officer's voice rang out: 'Every man for himself!'

Lamb grabbed Madeleine and, keeping her close by his side, started to run up through the streets towards the eastern perimeter. They made for the church where he had encountered the Black Watch and were moving steadily towards the east cliffs when Lamb saw a flash from above and ahead of them. A stream of red and white tracer bullets crossed the night sky over their heads, and instinctively he pushed Madeleine down to the ground ahead of him. 'Jerry machine gun. They must have taken the churchyard. I just hope Maclachlan got away first. That means they've cut off Veules from St Valéry, on the coast at least.'

Another machine gun opened up, raking the beach behind them. Clearly the Germans were up there in some force. 'We'll have to strike inland and then come round to Veules that way.'

They edged round a wall, got to their feet and walked back into the town a little way before climbing up again on a road leading further inland. Soldiers, mostly French, were still streaming into the town, and Lamb told Madeleine to pull up the collar of her coat.

At the top of a hill they left the town and headed into open countryside. The outskirts were strewn with abandoned vehicles and Lamb was just contemplating trying to start one of the trucks when his eye caught something in a ditch up ahead. He climbed down into the ditch and with an effort managed to lift a motorcycle up and onto the road. He cast a brief look down at its dead owner, a British dispatch rider, and climbed back out. Righting the bike, he sat on it and tried the kick start. Nothing. Damn, he thought. He kicked again, and again no response. A third time, and amazingly the Royal Enfield growled into life.

Lamb smiled at Madeleine. 'Come on. Get on, grab hold of me and hold on for dear life.' She climbed aboard and he turned the bike, let out the throttle and they moved fast along the road. The countryside sped past them in the night and the wind pushed Lamb's goggle-less face back. It felt impossibly good. He shouted to Madeleine, 'We'll be there soon now. Hold on,' and cranked up the speed.

They drove through open farmland and to their left the

fog-hung sea stretched away from the cliff road. After two or so miles up ahead Lamb could make out the silhouettes of buildings. If he remembered correctly from the map, that would be Manneville, and once they were through there a left turn would take them back up to Veules.

He was driving without a headlight, but as they drew closer he could see signs of activity and then he heard a shot, followed by others. Rifles mostly, and pistols. Hoping that the noise of the engine would be drowned by the now constant gunfire, he carried on driving, and as he reached the first of the buildings, a farmhouse on the left of the road, he slewed the bike off the road and stopped. He pushed down the stand and dismounted, before helping Madeleine off. Then, pistol in his hand, he pushed her behind the cover of a farm wall and began to walk forward on his own. He could make out a silhouette up ahead, a man kneeling behind a wall, staring away from him. Lamb pointed the gun at his back and, seeing the helmet was British, called out, 'I've got you covered. Who are you?'

Without turning the man replied, 'Mullens. Major, Kent Yeomanry, attached RHA. Who are you?'

'Lieutenant Lamb, North Kents, sir. Thank God.'

The man turned and smiled at him, overjoyed to see a fellow officer from the same county. 'We've a bit of a fight on our hands, Lieutenant. Village is full of Jerries, but we've got to get through. We were told there were boats at Veules, and this is the only way.'

'Yes, we're headed there too, sir.'

'We?'

'I have someone with me, wounded. Back there, in cover. What's your plan, sir?'

'None. We've got them surrounded. I guess there's only a platoon in there. Perhaps a half company. I've about 150 men. There's only one problem.'

'Sir?'

'We only have revolvers.'

'I'm sure we'll manage it, sir.'

The major smiled. 'Shall we, then?'

Lamb nodded. 'After you, sir.'

The major yelled across the farmyard and Lamb saw a hand wave back: 'Sarnt-Major. On my word.'

Mullens paused for a moment, flipped open the chamber of his revolver to check the bullets and, closing it, shouted: 'Charge!' before bursting out from behind the wall. Lamb was up and with him, running as fast as he could across the wide farmyard, yelling some nameless word remembered from bayonet drill in Tonbridge. Rifle bullets sang in the air around them and hit the ground at their feet, but in seconds they closed on the Germans on the other side, firing as they went. Lamb saw a German go down in front of him, the bullet smashing into his shoulder, and another, shot in the face. The night was alive with screams, British battle cries and the shrieks of the wounded. It was all over in a matter of minutes. Lamb stood, his heart pumping and temples throbbing above a pile of corpses. One man, wounded in the thigh, had thrown down his gun and was holding his hands in the air. Lamb motioned him to his feet and checked him for grenades.

Mopping up was a short process. The fight had been at close quarters and the Yeomanry's handguns had been mostly fired point-blank. Still, there were a few prisoners. Mullens came over to Lamb, who had opened his revolver to reload but had found with alarm that he was out of ammunition. He made a note to himself to ask Mullens before they parted.

'Thank you, Lieutenant. Now where are we off to?'

'You need to head left out of here, but make sure it's the same road or you'll end up in Blosseville and miss the boat.'

'Thank you. I'm sure we'll muddle through.'

But Lamb wasn't so sure. One wrong turning and they'd be taken prisoner. He saw the motorbike standing where he'd left it and began to walk over to it. As he did so the colonel's orders came back to him. He turned back to the major. 'Come along, sir. Come with us. I know the way.'

They trudged along the road to Veules in the pitch black, hoping that they would not be silhouetted against the glowing sky. Luckily no one fired at them. Madeleine, who had said nothing all the time they had been in the village, stayed close to Lamb and kept up the pretence of being a wounded British soldier. After a while the farmland gave way to houses and Lamb realised this must be the colonel's village. There was no sign of the enemy, and the only men were a few of Maclachlan's Jocks, ferreting in the deserted houses for provisions. Up ahead Lamb could see the cliffs, and before them a high dune. As they neared he made out the first of the gullies. There were five of them, the colonel had said.

He turned to the major. 'Right, sir. You get your chaps down there to the beach. I'll wait up here with my man and direct any others. He stood at the top of the gully and as the gunners slid down to the sand he looked back towards St Valéry, hoping to see more men.

Madeleine stood beside him, shivering, despite the huge coat. She turned to him. 'Do you think others will come?'

'I don't know. I don't know how many the colonel told about this place. We'll go down ourselves soon. I just want to make sure we get everyone we can away.'

He had just finished speaking when he heard voices out in the night coming from the direction of the town. Lamb drew his revolver, then remembered that he was out of ammunition and had forgotten to scrounge any from the Yeomanry. He swore, but kept his pistol pointed in the direction of the noise. Gradually he made out a

308

group of men walking towards them through the darkness. British uniforms. 'Who are you?'

'Jimmy Dallmeyer, A Squadron, 1st Lothians. And five of my men. We've a wounded officer too. We're trying to get off. Someone, a colonel, mentioned a boat on the east beach. Are we going the right way?'

'You've found it. Down there. You'll find some gullies. That's the way.'

They walked in out of the night and Lamb looked at their tired faces, but when he saw the officer he gave a start. 'Good God! Brigadier Meadows. It's Lamb, sir. Lieutenant Lamb.'

The brigadier moved his head towards him, but Lamb saw to his horror that the man's eyes were entirely covered by a bandage. 'Lamb. Great heavens. There's a stroke of luck. There you are, Jimmy. I told you I was good luck. This is the fellow I was telling you about. 'Straordinary chap. Well done, Lamb. Where are we to go?'

'Not far, sir. Just a few more yards and you'll be on the beach.'

'Seen what they've done to me, Lamb? Bloody Boche. Can't see a damned thing. Blinded by a grenade. What the bastards couldn't do in '16 they've damn well managed now. Still, 'spose I was too old anyway. Not my war, d'you see? Your war now, you young chaps. I don't deserve to get back. What use am I? And like this?'

Lamb shook his head. 'You may be no use at all, Brigadier, but you did me a favour and now I'm doing you one. You're going home. Careful, sir. See you on board.'

Lamb watched as the Lothians helped Meadows down the gullies and through the dunes. There was a shout from below and a man in naval uniform came bounding up one of the groynes. 'Lieutenant Killam, HMS *Codrington*. We're here to get you off, but you should hurry. We've seen Jerry trucks heading this way from the east.'

Lamb thanked him and, with Madeleine in front, edged down the gully to the beach. Five orderly queues snaked through the dark across the sand towards the sea, each of them controlled by a naval officer, and Lamb watched as the men waited their turn to get into the little landing boats that would ferry them out to the waiting destroyers. There must have been eight or nine large ships of the line out there, he thought, plus a number of smaller boats, and his heart leapt at the thought that they might just succeed in getting off more than he had hoped.

The rain was heavier now and the fog and the oil cloud still hung over the Channel, and Lamb could only thank God that so far the German artillery was bombarding the town and had not turned its attention to the little evacuation from Veules. He looked around the beach for signs of his command. The colonel had done well, for the sand was a mass of khaki-clad men. Lamb's stomach felt hollow as he wondered for a moment whether his men were among them. Surely they could have not come so far, only to be beaten at the last? Then he saw them, unmistakable, lined up in the fourth queue. Bennett and Mays even looked as if they were smiling as they lit up. He walked across with Madeleine.

He tapped Bennett on the arm. 'Sarnt Bennett, you might need to dress that line.'

Bennett beamed at him. 'Mister Lamb, sir. Thank God. We'd just about given you up. And the lady too. Hello, Miss.'

The others turned round and, seeing Lamb, broke ranks to come and see him.

Lamb looked about. 'Any sign of the colonel, Bennett?'

'Well, he turned up here an hour ago, sir, with the best part of a battalion, 2nd Duke of Wellington's, almost 500 men. They're over there. Haven't seen him since.'

Lamb cursed. He had known that the old man wanted

his chance to clobber a few of the Boche, and it crossed his mind that the colonel himself might be captured. 'I'll hang back. You men get yourselves aboard. I'll catch you up. Bennett, you help Miss Dujolle.'

Madeleine shook her head. 'No. I'll stay with you.'

Bennett nodded. 'Me too, sir. I'm not leaving you here.'

Bennett stepped forward and with him, much to Lamb's surprise came Valentine.

'Corporal?'

'In for a penny, sir. I'd like to see it out, if you don't mind, sir.'

Lamb knew better than to argue with any of them. He searched the faces of his men. 'Sarnt Buck, you're in charge, until I get back, that is.'

Mays stepped forward. 'Sir, I know he's a colonel and all, but we don't want to lose you now. Not after what you've brought us through.'

Lamb looked at him. 'Thank you, Mays. That means a lot to me. But I think someone should make sure that the colonel gets away. I have a feeling he's rather more important than he might seem, and it looks as though that someone has to be me.'

Mays nodded, and Lamb and the others turned and began to walk away from the queue and back towards the dunes. The sky above St Valéry glowed orange with the flames from burning houses. Madeleine sat down on the sea grass and wrapped the coat around her while Bennett, Valentine and Lamb stood, looking across the high dunes, back towards the town.

An hour later Lamb was still peering into the darkness beyond the dunes. He turned and looked towards the beach. The orderly queues of British and French soldiers had gone now, replaced by a milling mass of Frenchmen, unsure of what to do or where to turn. As he watched, the Royal

Navy beach party landed their boat, and while two ratings guarded it with levelled sub-machine guns Lieutenant Killam climbed out and walked across to Lamb. 'I'm sorry, Lieutenant, but I'm told it's now or never. The Captain's very anxious to get away. They've already sunk four ships off the harbour. They're bound to turn on us soon.'

'But I'm waiting for someone. A colonel on the Staff.'

'Sorry, Lieutenant. My instructions are most specific. We wait for no one, not even the general. Commander Elkins's orders. We have a time to go, and the Jerries won't wait. If we don't go now we won't be going anywhere.'

'I see.'

He walked back to Madeleine and Bennett. She was sitting on a sand dune wrapped in the coat but without her tin hat on now. Lamb bent over her and, not caring any more what anyone thought or made of it, held her in his arms and kissed her as if he would never see her again. Which he believed might well be true. He looked into her eyes. 'You have to go now, my love. You mustn't stay.'

She shook her head and looked away. 'I won't leave without you. No.'

He turned to Valentine. 'Take care of her, Corporal. We'll join you soon, I'm sure. I've just got to try and find the colonel.'

Valentine shook his head. 'Sorry sir. I can't do that.'

Lamb stared at him. 'It's an order, Corporal.'

'Sorry, sir. I'm not leaving without you, Mister Lamb. Sorry, sir. That's the way it is. Either we both go or we both stay.'

Lamb turned to Bennett. 'Sarnt Bennett? What do I do? You heard him.'

'Yes, sir. And I'm not going neither.'

Lamb shook his head and turned to Killam. 'Lieutenant, would you help me, please? Will you take care of this young lady? She must get to England, at all costs.'

'It's most irregular, but yes, I'll do it. God knows there are stranger things going on on this beach. Goodbye, Lamb, and good luck. I hope you find your colonel.'

Lamb knew that Madeleine was too weak to fight him, and he knew too that she realised this was their only hope, that if there was some way of his reaching her he would find it. She looked at him for a last time before Killam ushered her into the boat. Lamb looked away as it cast off.

Bennett stood beside him. Valentine meanwhile, desperate for a piss, wandered off behind a nearby dune. Bennett spoke. 'Right, sir. What do we do now?'

'Now we wait for the colonel and hope that he turns up before the Germans. And then we try to find another boat.'

There was noise behind them – the sound of a gun being cocked. Lamb began to turn slowly. He did not want to be shot in the back. He had not expected the Germans to arrive so soon.

'Hands up please, gentlemen.' The voice he heard was not German, but English, and raising his hands in the air he turned quickly, and found himself looking into the eyes of Captain Campbell.

Campbell had changed. He was thinner and paler and his left arm was strapped across his chest. Most strikingly, the right side of his face was a mass of burnt flesh, on which someone had tried to place a dressing, with little success. But it was his eyes that most alarmed Lamb. They had a look of utter madness about them. He pointed the gun directly at Lamb's head and leered at him: 'My dear Lieutenant, how very slippery you are. Like an eel. How hard to catch! But here we are at last.' His voice was slurred. Lamb was sure he had been drinking, perhaps to numb the pain.

Lamb stared at him. 'I heard you were dead.'

'I believe there was a rumour. I did get a bit shot up, as you can see. We ran into some tanks near Fécamp.

Made a bit of a mess of my face.' He grimaced. 'Hurts a bit too. So, Mister Lamb, what are we going to do with you? You appear to be above the law. Or do you just have friends in high places? Either way, if the military process won't do what is necessary, then I will.' He straightened his arm as if he was about to shoot.

Lamb played for time: 'And what then, Campbell? What of you?'

'Oh, I've a plan all right. I've a little boat near here. Dinghy. Bought it off a Frog. She's in a cave round below the cliffs. I just have time to row out to the ships and then home, and no one's any the wiser.'

Bennett said, 'You bastard.'

'Tut tut, Sarnt Bennett. Speaking out of turn to an officer. You need a lesson in manners.' In a split second Campbell turned the gun on Bennett and pulled the trigger. The bullet hit him in the shin and, as he fell to the ground with a cry of pain Lamb ran at Campbell. But the captain backed off and turned the again gun on Lamb, with a few feet to spare.

'No, no, Lieutenant. You can't die a hero's death. You attacked me, a superior officer. Remember? You and Bennett. Do you know what that feels like? Do you know how frightening and insulting that is? Your problem is that you're not a real officer and you're most certainly not a gentleman. You part-time Johnnies think you can swan into the army, my army, but you can't. It's not like that. You have no code of honour, no idea of what's right. You're a fake, Lamb, not a proper officer. You won't win this war. You're a bad lot, and you need to be weeded out and culled.'

Lamb said nothing. He looked across at Bennett, who was writhing on the ground, clutching his wounded leg.

'What d'you think, Lamb? Would that be fair? Would that be . . .'

Campbell stopped suddenly and stood transfixed for a moment before grasping madly at his back. He spun round, and Lamb could see the hilt of a knife protruding from his shoulder as he sank to his knees on the wet sand.

A figure appeared from behind Campbell. Valentine said as he walked towards them, 'In the nick of time, sir, wouldn't you say?'

Lamb saw a movement to his left but was too late to shout a warning as Campbell raised his gun again and fired. Valentine clutched his left shoulder and crumpled to the sand, and in the same instant Lamb threw himself on Campbell, knocking the gun from his hand. Campbell screamed as Valentine's knife slipped deeper into his shoulder and Lamb punched hard into the wound. Lamb saw another more slender knife in the space between their faces, up and flashing in Campbell's hand, and felt it being pushed up against his neck. He raised his hand to Campbell's wrist and grasped it, but the point of the blade was on his throat now and it was all he could do to hold it away. He felt the tip prick the skin and a trickle of blood on his stubble.

Then, with a swift single action of massive strength, he turned the blade and pushed down hard. The knife slid deep into Campbell's neck and lodged itself in his carotid artery. The blood flowed freely, and Lamb looked into the captain's staring eyes until they glazed over.

Lamb stood up and wiped his hands on his trousers, then ran over to Valentine. The corporal was sitting up against a dune with his hand on his shoulder and Lamb could see that the fingers were covered in blood.

'You're hit. Let me see.'

'Not bad, sir. First time. Doesn't hurt as much as I thought it would.'

Lamb looked. The bullet seemed to have hit Valentine's

left shoulder and Lamb wondered if it had passed through his lung. He'd been lucky. 'I think you'll live.'

He looked across to where Bennett was lying and hurried over. 'How is it, Sarnt?'

'Bloody hurts, sir. He'd have shot you, that bastard.'

'Thank you, Sarnt. You did well.'

He ripped the leg of Bennett's trousers and exposed the wound. The bullet had passed through the muscle of the tibia and the exit wound was not a pretty sight. 'You need attention too. Come on. We'd better get you out to that ship if we can. We'll have to leave the colonel to the Jerries.'

He helped Bennett to his feet and, supporting him on his shoulder, walked back to Valentine, who had managed to get up and was staunching the wound. They looked down at Campbell's body, the blood crusting on the sand.

Lamb turned to Valentine. 'That's the second time you've saved my life, Corporal. I thought you bore me a grudge.'

'On the contrary, sir, I admire you.'

'What?'

'Well, sir. Life's so simple for you, so black and white. For men like me, sir, it's all about shades of grey. We need men like you, sir. What Captain Campbell said – that was nonsense. His army's washed up. This lot shows that. There's no mindless code of honour any more. Not the ridiculous sort he meant. Of course there's decency, but the army's different. We need new men. Men like you are going to win this war.'

Lamb shook his head. 'No, Valentine. On the contrary, men like you will win this war, and you'll win the future too. Come on, let's see if we can find Campbell's boat.'

There was a sudden explosion from behind them.

'Christ, we'd better get a move on.'

As they began to hobble towards the cliffs, hoping that

they would find the cave Campbell had mentioned, they were disturbed by a noise from one of the gullies on their left and surprised to see a British soldier sliding down the dunes onto the beach, driving before him at gunpoint a furious German officer.

The colonel smiled at them broadly. 'Lamb, you waited. Thank God. Had to come away with something else, you see. Sort of souvenir, if you like. Good for morale. Just to prove we can do it. Found this brute standing by a tank at the top of the cliffs. Answers to the name of Kessler.'

They found Campbell's boat, a small motor launch with an outboard, moored in a cave, and between them, with Kessler tied up in the prow, Lamb and the colonel managed to heave it into the water. They helped Valentine and Bennett in and made them as comfortable as they could before getting in themselves, and as they did so Lamb saw movement above the dunes: the lights of half a dozen vehicles. 'Christ, they're here. Come on.'

He tugged at the outboard motor, but she refused to start. Again. Come on, he thought. For me. Come on, you bugger. He pulled and the motor sprang into life, sending the little craft ploughing into the water and away from the beach. Behind him he could hear shouts and then an officer giving a command. Bullets struck the water around them. One of them hit the side of the boat, sending splinters into the air. More shots whistled past his ears. He laughed and then felt a sudden stabbing pain in his arm, close to where he'd been hit at the Dyle, and then his sleeve was drenched in blood. Carefully, he moved seats and took the rudder with his left hand.

They were making good speed and he could see the destroyer ahead of them. She had a head of steam up and was obviously preparing to move, and he prayed they would see them approaching. As they grew closer, a

German gun opened up from the cliffs. The shell flew straight but landed a little short of the *Codrington*, rocking their boat with the force of the explosion underwater. Then they were hard alongside.

Shouts came from high above them and Lamb stood up and helped Bennett to the side. A rating had climbed down the netting and grabbed at the sergeant's arm, hauling him up over the slippery ropes. Valentine was next, and then the colonel, pushing Kessler before him. Finally, Lamb managed to scramble up the net and climbed the railings onto the deck, half pulled over by two sailors.

He could feel the ship moving beneath him as another shot came in, closer. The destroyer began to move faster through the waters of the Channel, out to sea.

Lamb bent double and retched up sea water, then straightening up he scoured the deck for his company and Madeleine. It was packed with British and French soldiers, many of them wounded. A sea of faces stared back at him and then, in a far part of the deck, close to a bulwark, he saw a group of bedraggled men. He found Bennett, gave him his shoulder and together they crossed the deck, pushing through the crowd.

Corporal Mays saluted him with a smile. 'Hello, sir. Didn't expect to see you here.'

'To tell you the truth, Mays, I didn't expect to be here either. Well done, all of you. Good work.'

The colonel came pushing through the crowd and clapped Lamb on the back. 'Excellent stuff. According to the Captain we've got off a good 1,500 British and 900 Frogs. Not bad for a night's work.'

'Not bad at all, sir. Well done. Where's your souvenir?'

'In irons in the hold. Where he belongs. Well done, Lamb. Couldn't have done it without you. We're going to need men like you and these chaps here to rebuild this army.'

'But we've lost the Division, sir.'

318

'Not the whole Division. We've taken off almost a brigade here, and Stanley-Clarke's embarking Arkforce. Besides, you can't destroy a division. As far as I'm concerned it's a victory.'

Mays interrupted: 'Sorry, sir, but there's someone who needs to speak to you urgently.'

Lamb turned to see Madeleine, standing wrapped in a dark blue naval blanket. Beside her was Crawford, his right arm bandaged in a sling, his head encased above the eye-line with bandages. His face looked horribly sallow and Lamb could only guess what he had been through – but he was smiling: 'Lamb. What the devil took you so long? We've been waiting here for ages. Of course I've had the very best medical attention. Your girl here . . .'

'I thought I'd told you, once and for all . . .'

But then he saw Madeleine's face and he knew he could not lie any more. He looked at the men around them on the deck – men who had come through hell with him and who lived to fight again. As the destroyer drew ever closer to the English coast he knew, too, that he had accomplished at least in some small way what the colonel had asked of him: a retreat to victory. And for himself, most importantly of all, there would be a new beginning.

Historical Note

The campaign in France in 1940 was one of the bitterest ever fought by a British army. Outgunned and outnumbered by the Germans, the BEF did its best to hold off the enemy offensives, but ultimately, as is well known, was forced to retreat. The story of Dunkirk is the stuff of legend. That of St Valéry however is less well known.

The 51st Highland Division had landed at le Havre in January 1940 and then moved to Belgium where it was attached to the French on the Maginot Line. In May 1940 when Hitler invaded it held the area of the Saar. Then, on May 22nd it was ordered south west in trucks and trains and arrived on May 31st on the lower Somme where it was placed in a reserve line from the coast down to South East of Abbeville.

The divisional commander, Major General Victor Fortune, was fifty-six at the time and enormously respected. Fortune had commanded 1st Black Watch in the First World War and had earned a DSO. The problem for the Highlanders in this new war though was that this time Fortune was answerable to the French.

The 51st had orders to hold the German advance south until General Sir Alan Brooke was able to cross the channel to Le Havre with reinforcements. Of course these reinforcements did not arrive in time and the Highlanders were left isolated.

The Somme here was difficult terrain; a meandering river and a canal with bluffs rising above it, which was soon to be easily defended by the Germans.

For although the 51st was meant to be in defensive role, the French were determined to counter-attack the German bridgehead at Abbeville. Two such attacks were mounted and while the Scots did well, the French were beaten off forcing the Highlanders to retreat. In one day the Highland Division lost twenty officers and five hundred and forty-three other ranks.

On 5th June the Germans themselves counter-attacked in great force and despite resistance drove the Division back to the River Bresle. Communications were down and the battalions could only hold strong-points and were continually bombed and strafed. At one point the 4th Camerons were dive bombed near Martainville by Stukas and could only lie down in clover fields for cover. There, so exhausted were they, that they fell asleep, even though under attack.

By the end of that day a further twenty-three officers and five hundred other ranks had been killed or wounded or were missing.

The latter days of the French campaign were all about confusion in the high command of both allied armies and a lack of clear orders. Fortune's men could have escaped had they been given the right orders in time and this of course is what Lamb tries so desperately to enable them do.

The French by this stage were all for falling back towards Rouen, away from the sea, intent on defending Paris. Fortune was reluctant but felt obliged to obey them. In his own mind however, he now nurtured the idea of an evacuation from Le Havre, along the lines of Dunkirk.

The French of course would hear nothing of it and eventually, seeing that if he followed the French plan his Division would be taken prisoner, Fortune went over General Altmayer's head. On June 9th he ordered a fighting withdrawal to Le Havre. However, as he was still under French orders the actual movement could not be carried out before the 13th. And by then it was too late for the Highlanders.

By that time the Division had had no rest since May 30th. The 1st Black Watch for example had held the river bank on the Varenne at Martigny for five hours, under constant attack.

It is vital to realise that the 'Highland' Division was not only composed of Highlanders. Fortune's command also included seven regiments from the Royal Artillery and Royal Horse Artillery, four companies of Royal Engineers, the 2nd/7th Duke of Wellington's Regiment, Princess Louise's Kensington regiment, 7th Battalion the Royal Northumberland Fusiliers, pioneers from the Royal Scots Fusiliers and the Norfolk Regiment and sections of the RAOC and RASC.

It is thus quite feasible for Lamb, with his platoon of Black Jackals and the various 'odds and sods', to have come under the umbrella of the 51st at this stage in the break up of what was left of the BEF.

Fortune had also created Ark Force, under fifty-three year old Brigadier Arthur Stanley-Clarke, in an attempt to hold a line of evacuation around Le Havre. Included in its ranks were elements from the Border Regiment, the Sherwood Foresters and the fictitious Jackals' real sister Kentish regiment, the Buffs (Royal East Kents).

On June 10th however, Ark Force was cut off from the rest of the Division by the German advance and it became clear to Fortune that his only plan now was to evacuate from the small fishing port of St Valéry.

The Royal Navy came in to the little harbour on the 11th, providing nine destroyers offshore to take off the Division and tried time and again to get close enough to do so. But by this time the Germans had positioned their powerful 88mm cannon on the cliffs and several ships were lost.

In the end a number of the Highlanders did escape, as Lamb and his men do, further down coast at Veules les Roses, four miles east, where they were taken off by the destroyer *Restigouches*. In total though only one thousand three hundred and fifty British and nine hundred and thirty French soldiers got away in this way. Ark Force fared rather better, managing to have some four thousand men evacuated from Le Havre over the nights of June 11th and 12th.

Early on the 12th the Germans sent in envoys asking for Fortune's unconditional surrender. They were rejected and Fortune issued the order 'every man for himself'. The French had already surrendered but Fortune ordered their white flags to be cut down. But defeat was a foregone conclusion and finally at 10 a.m. on June 12th Fortune took the decision to surrender.

Around eight thousand men from 152 and 153 brigades along with ancillary troops were captured, along with Fortune himself and his staff.

The rank and file were marched off as slave labour to the Nazis's salt mines in Silesia. Many of them died either there or on the way. Exact figures for those who never returned are hard to find but probably run into thousands. Their officers were sent to Oflag VII-C in Laufennear Salzburg, where to stave off the boredom they famously composed the reel of 51st Division, still a favourite at Highland balls.

St Valéry was one of the greatest disasters ever experienced by the British Army. Far greater than the Charge of the Light Brigade or the First Afghan War. But it has been largely and perhaps deliberately forgotten.

A recent book by Saul David considers the possibility that Churchill might have been directly to blame for the loss of a division and certainly it is not beyond the bounds of possibility that the Prime Minister might have been behind such an idea. Churchill, who had served with Scots on the front line in the Great War, was well aware of the special relationship between the Scots and the French that had been nurtured in that conflict and might have reasoned that that if he 'gave the Scots away' the French would take this as a pledge of loyalty. He might have considered this necessary as some of the French commanders saw the 'miracle' of Dunkirk as a betrayal in which on Churchill's express orders, ninety percent of the troops evacuated had been British.

Writing later in his account of the war (*Their Finest Hour, Second World War*, vol ii) Churchill himself declared that his concern was that the 51st might be driven back to Le Havre and thus separated from the other (French) armies. It is a muddled passage. He blames the French: 'It was a case of gross mismanagement for this very danger was visible a full three days before.'

There can be no doubt that Churchill was determined to support France as long as possible.

Even after Dunkirk he planned a second front and on June 12th, long after the end of the Dunkirk evacuation and the very day on which the 51st surrendered, he eventually sent Alan Brooke with the 52nd Division to Cherbourg as the 2nd BEF. They stayed just four days before being returned home.

Why else too would Churchill's famous speech made on June 4th, the day after the end of the Dunkirk evacuations, contain the words 'We shall fight *in France*, [my italics] we shall fight on the seas and oceans, we shall fight with growing confidence and growing strength in the air, we shall defend our island, whatever the cost may be. We shall fight on the beaches, we shall fight on the landing grounds . . .'?

Churchill apparently believed that given a show of support, the French would continue the struggle from their colonies, giving Britain enough time before the USA eventually joined in the war.

Churchill might also have thought that the French would order a general retreat before they did so. But if this was the case, then he really was gambling with a Division.

The facts are clear enough. In the early hours of June 8th, the War Office was sent word from the front that unless the 51st Division was given orders to retreat from the River Bresle, it would be surrounded. The War Office sent no order and a vital day was lost before the French agreed to the British withdrawal. Had Churchill at least placed Fortune in command or at least under British orders rather than French, the retreat could have begun immediately and the British being motorized, would have arrived at the embarkation points much sooner than their French allies. This though was something Churchill could not countenance in the face of French fury over what had happened at Dunkirk and so once again the finger points at him.

As late as June 10th, the War Office was still telling the 51st that they could not actually evacuate without direct orders from the French. By then of course it was too late.

While Colonel 'R' is a fictitious character, it seems possible that certain inspired and forward-thinking officers of his sort would have operated outside the aegis of the War Office at a time when the Intelligence service was in some turmoil before the establishment of SOE by Churchill and Hugh Dalton in July 1940.

Certainly on occasion it was possible for the generals to exert influence over the Ministers. On the evening of June 14th, Alan Brooke, commander of the 2nd BEF then at Cherbourg, told Churchill in no uncertain terms in a half hour telephone conversation, that it was imperative to evacuate all remaining British forces from France, an idea which up till then the PM had not been willing to contemplate. Brooke recorded in his notes: 'Churchill told me . . . I had been sent to France to make the French feel that we were supporting them. I replied that it was impossible to make a corpse feel, and that the French Army was, to all intents and purposes, dead . . . He insisted that we should make them feel that we were supporting them, and I insisted that this . . . would only result in throwing away good troops to no avail.'

Surely, here is Churchill using the same argument he had with the 51st Division, even after their loss? This suggestion is strengthened by the fact that even though after their conversation Brooke believed he had been given permission to evacuate the 2nd BEF immediately, he was told the very next day by the War Office that it could not in fact be evacuated and should remain in France 'for political reasons.' It was only the following day that he was finally given the go ahead in another counter-counter order from the War Office.

What further proof is needed of Churchill's capability of using British troops as bargaining tools?

The situation also mirrors that before the Dunkirk evacuation when Lord Gort, commander of the BEF, having decided to evacuate, spoke to the CIGS General Ironside. Ironside was appalled by the idea and advised a withdrawal south to Amiens. Churchill, likewise dumbfounded, far from approving any Dunkirk plan vetoed it and told Ironside to order Gort down to Amiens. It was only on May 25th, when the politicians back in Britain had no alternative but to face the facts, that Churchill agreed to the evacuation from Dunkirk, a 'miracle' for which he would later take much of the credit.

It seemed to many that the 51st must be finished after St Valéry. It had after all ceased to exist. But as Colonel 'R' tells Lamb, you cannot kill a division.

So it was that the 9th Highland reserve Division then back in Britain was renumbered 51 and its brigades changed from 26, 27 and 28 to 152, 153 and 154. It also incorporated elements of the original 154 brigade which had escaped from St Valéry, notably men of the Argylls and 4th Black Watch.

With Fortune in captivity, the new 51st Highland Division came under the successive commands of Generals Cunningham, Ritchie and Stanley-Clarke. Ultimately though it was General Douglas Wimberley, a Highlander himself, who remade the 51st Division. Known to his soldiers as Tartan Tam, Wimberley had tartan and the new Divisional cipher, HD in red inside a red circle, put on the mens' shoulders and painted just about everywhere else so that the Division soon became known as the 'Household Decorators'. By the end of 1941 it was battle-ready and shipped off to Egypt.

Famously, at El Alamein in October 1942, the new 51st Division went forward into the attack with the bagpipes playing and under crossed searchlights which seemed to many like a Scottish saltire of white on blue. The battle was a chance for the Division to take revenge for St Valéry and this they did in full measure.

Two years later, in June '44, shortly after 'D' Day, elements of the 51st retook the Normandy port and five of the original Highlanders who had escaped capture there in 1940 played their pipes in the town square.

As senior British officer in captivity Victor Fortune

worked constantly to improve the conditions of his fellow POWs. He suffered a stroke in 1944 but refused repatriation and made KBE shortly after his liberation in 1945. He died in Scotland in 1949.

Colonel George Honeyman was captured at St Valéry. He was awarded the DSO in 1945 and died in Scotland in 1962.

The massacre by the SS Totenkopf Division of ninety-eight civilians and a small garrison of British troops on May 21st 1940 at Aubigny-en-artois is well recorded. The names of the dead are inscribed on a memorial in the village.

The holding action on the bridge at Essars is well known as having been carried off with much bravery by the Royal Irish Fusiliers and in particular by 2nd Lieutenant Mike Horsfall. To avoid any confusion and potential embarrassment concerning the entirely fictitious Captain Campbell, I have changed the names and the regiment to the invented 'Borderers'. That notwithstanding, Lamb's run-in with the Captain and his subsequent response are not dissimilar from recorded incidents which took place across northern France during the retreat when command structure and morale broke down. I hope that the reader will forgive this use of author's licence in order to paint an evocative picture of one of the most troubled moments in the history of the British Army, which nevertheless was distinguished by numerous episodes of extreme heroism, courage and self-sacrifice.